The Middle of Nowhere

Paula Duncan McDonald

For Jim

1921

There are places on earth where life has to work harder to survive, and only the hardy, the most adaptable and resilient, thrive. The northern edge of the Chihuahuan Desert west of the Pecos River was such a place. For countless seasons the land had a crust and in some places, tall grass grew. Crust and grass kept the peace between prolific winds and scarce water. Hardy plants and animals lived their lives and the Mescalero Apaches, whose footprint was light, did not damage the crust or the grass.

A time came when people who didn't know about the crust, and who thought the grass perpetual, said the Apaches must leave. By 1886, the United States government had cleared the land of all but a few renegades and free land was offered to other people who would settle there. Ephraim and Kate Chapman married that year and took the offer. They began their lives together making a ranch in Reeves County, Texas.

It sometimes happens that a land of dangers and hardships wrests the hearts of the people who lay claim to the land. The people who live there think they own the land but victory over privation and hardship binds them to that which they have conquered. So it was for Ephraim and Kate. They met the arid land of heat and cold and great high sky on its own terms. The land allowed them to stay. They had seven children there and four still lived. Their daughter Skitchy was the youngest.

....

Skitchy was not quite pretty but not plain either. Her tall graceful figure, wide warm smile, easy charm, and the way she looked at people straight in the eye were usually the first things people noticed about her. Her face was triangular, somewhat squared off at the chin, with a straight nose and sparkling hazel eyes. Her sister Belle told her wearing her straight brown hair cut short gave her a slightly tomboyish look, but Skitchy had no patience for fiddling with her hair. Uncomfortable in clothes she considered fancy, she dressed plainly. Even so, at fifteen she was beginning to attract the attention of young men.

Quite aware of that, Kate Chapman didn't want to let her daughter go to barn dances until Skitchy was at least sixteen. However, she knew she was going to lose the argument over that issue when Buddy taught his young sister to dance.

Buddy, a handsome man in his early twenties, tall like his father, strong, smart and inquisitive, full of life and laughter, was popular with most everyone, not least with the young ladies of Reeves County. Skitchy had adored him for as long as she could remember. Thrilled when he paid special attention to her, she could hardly contain her delight when he taught her to dance.

Ephraim Chapman had ordered a Victrola and records from a catalog when Minnie and Belle, his oldest daughters, were girls. Both girls had gone away to school before there was a high school in the county. They learned to dance there and taught Buddy, who even as a boy had been an enthusiastic dance partner. Ephraim danced with his daughters as well. Sometimes even a reluctant Kate, more inclined to work first, then play if she had time, took off her apron and joined in.

Ephraim especially loved watching Skitchy and Buddy dance together, tapping his foot to the music with a well-worn boot. "Can't have too much fun," he told their mother when she thought they should be about their chores. "Chores will always be there. Can't always count on the fun. Best take it when it's there."

"Skitch," Buddy said, laughing, "no man's going to ask you to dance more than once if you step on his toes." As she struggled to learn the steps and move with the music, he encouraged her. "Mark my words," he told his young sister, "being a good dancer will take you a long way. Men like it when you make them look good on the dance floor. Not to mention that you're more fun to be with." When he had said, "Honey, you're dancing mighty well. Lots of fun to dance with you," she had beamed and redoubled her efforts.

....

Buddy took Skitchy to her first barn dance. She wore a dress Mama had made for her in her favorite shade of green. Her sister Belle had fixed her hair for the occasion, waving it with her fingers as much as Skitchy would allow.

Skitchy felt jittery and self-conscious at first when she walked into the Daniels' barn with Buddy. But when he grinned at her with such warmth and guided her with such firm ease, the jitters fell away. He danced the first dance with her, making sure they covered the whole sawdust floor so that everyone could see her dancing.

"Smile at me once in a while when I'm your partner," he whispered to her. "And at anyone else you want to say hello to or might want to dance with." When she stumbled on a tricky step she felt his hand firm on her back, guiding her back to the music. "Don't pay that any mind," he said softly. "Everybody does that once in a while. Best way to handle it is laugh it off," and he laughed lightly and spun her around gaily.

"Buddy," she said when the dance was over, "thank you with all my heart. I'm surely the luckiest girl I know to have you for a brother."

He had grinned broadly at her. "Just doing the best I can for my little sister. What else is a brother for?"

....

It was at that dance in the Daniels' barn that Belle Chapman met Pinkney Campbell.

Belle was just over five feet tall, several inches shorter than the much younger Skitchy. She had delicate features, with a narrow nose and small well-formed mouth set in the same almost square jaw as her sister. Her brown hair was lighter than Skitchy's and she wore it in the latest bobbed style. The harsh West Texas wind and sun had barely begun to etch her face.

Playing the trumpet with Tom Floyd's band, Pink watched her from the platform where the band played. Annabelle the belle, as her family sometimes teasingly called her, stood out in a pretty lavender taffeta dress and close fitting laced boots with shapely heels. She danced gracefully and gaily with different partners. She was about Pink's age and one of the most attractive unmarried women in the county.

He introduced himself during a break. "Excuse me, ma'am, my name's Pinkney Campbell. People call me Pink. What might your name be?"

Belle looked up at him with a smile. "Belle Chapman," she said. Then in a direct manner that startled him a little, she added, "Don't think I've seen you at any of the dances before."

"I've only been here a short while. I work for George Norton and live out at his place. I play with the band."

"I noticed you'd joined Tom's band," Belle said lightly. "It's unusual to hear a trumpet in a band around here. Adds a nice sound, Mr. Campbell. You play very well."

Pink wished he had more time to spend with her but he knew the band's break would be over soon. "Miss Chapman, I'm sorry I can't ask you to dance. May I call on you?"

Pink Campbell was slender but muscular. A handsome man with sandy hair and clear blue eyes, his features were well proportioned, not unlike the pictures of men in the ads in magazines of the day. He thought himself short, however, and tried to make up for that by dressing nattily and moving with something approaching a swagger. Belle had been taken with his good looks and easy manner, and liked that he spoke without the twang that saturated the West Texas voices she heard every day.

The Methodist preacher who came from Odessa once a month would be holding services in Pecos the following Sunday and Belle suggested, "Let's meet after church. We can eat together at the potluck, if you'd like that." Gathering for a potluck meal after church was a popular social event and Pink was delighted by Belle's invitation.

"Yes, ma'am. I'd like that very much."

....

At the dance, Skitchy had noticed Pink on the platform that served as a makeshift bandstand. She liked his casual sandy hair and blue eyes and the energetic style of his trumpet playing. She listened eagerly when Belle told her, "I met that new man living out at the Norton's. We're going to eat together at the potluck on Sunday."

"Oh, Belle, sure enough? He's so good looking! What's his name?"

Belle smiled when she said, "Pink Campbell. Isn't that a funny name? It's really Pinkney but he calls himself Pink. I've never known anyone with a color for a name but he seems quite nice. Maybe I'll wear my pink dress in honor of his name." Then when she saw that Skitchy had taken her seriously she squeezed her sister's hand lightly. "Law, I was teasing, Skitch. I wouldn't do something as silly as that."

On Sunday morning as they dressed for church, Skitchy thought Belle seemed very casual as she put on the yellow print cotton dress and straw hat she most often wore to church. "Aren't you excited?" Skitchy asked, her own voice excited. When Belle said nothing but just glanced at her,

Skitchy said nothing more. She knew not to press her sister when she saw that look.

She thought Belle might be thinking of Sam. The young man she had planned to marry had been killed in the war, the first time he was in battle. Skitchy had heard Belle crying by herself many times but she rarely spoke about him. One day not long after Minnie, the oldest sister, had married and left the ranch, Belle had asked Skitchy, "Is there anything you want to say about Sam? Or anything you want to ask me?"

"I don't think so. Not right now anyway."

Belle said very quietly, "Then we'll not speak of him again." And they hadn't. But Skitchy thought she saw sadness still lingering underneath her sister's grace sometimes, like this morning. Belle hadn't married or even encouraged any of the young men who had been interested in her.

....

It was a cloudless morning, already fiercely hot by the time the church service began. Men carried their coats and put them on only as they entered the school building that served as the Methodist church when the preacher came to Pecos. Women fanned themselves as they sat in the chairs set up for the service. People visited with each other while they waited for Maud Dillingham to start playing the small organ. Pink made it his business to seat himself two rows behind the Chapman family, not too close but close enough for them to hear that he not only had a fine voice, but knew the hymns well. He sang robustly even in the heat. He wanted them to know he was a church-going man.

After the service while the older women set out casseroles, pots of beans and chili, platters of fried chicken, slices of watermelon and Pecos cantaloupe, peach cobblers, pecan pies, and applesauce cakes, Belle found Pink. "Good afternoon, Mr. Campbell. It's blistering hot today. Wouldn't you like to take off your coat? We're very informal at the potlucks." Pink appreciated how gracefully she made him feel comfortable. Smiling at him as he hung his jacket on the back of a chair, she said, "I'll leave my hat on this other chair to save our places. Please come and meet my family before we sit down to eat."

Pink liked all the Chapmans as soon as Belle introduced him, first to her father and mother, then to her brother Buddy and sister Skitchy. They all had a relaxed manner about them. If they were curious about him, it was not apparent.

Skitchy's curiosity may not have been apparent, but she was afraid the spark she felt between herself and Pink might be. She was careful not to be too forward since it was Belle he was having the meal with. But she watched Pink as closely as she could without calling too much attention to her attention, and listened to everything he said that she could hear.

Pink felt the spark, too, he would tell her long after that day. He'd always been drawn to petite women who made him feel taller. But that day his eyes had followed the tall girl in the simple dark blue skirt and white cotton blouse he'd just met as she walked away with her family. As he turned to go with Belle to their places at the table on the other side of the room, he felt awkward and confused.

....

Pink was freed from his awkward and confused feelings by what happened two weeks later between Belle and Jackson

Tieger. Jackson had been one of Belle's dance partners the evening Pink met her at the barn dance and had been with her at other social events from time to time. He had watched her at the potluck as she and Pink ate together. Jackson always watched her. He watched for any sign that her grief for Sam Mueller was subsiding enough for her to open her heart to another man. He wanted to be that man. But he had seen that any man who tried too hard or pressed her too much was quickly dropped. He took care not to make that mistake.

A slender man, Jackson was taller than Pink, not as tall as the Chapman men. He had a broad forehead, square chin and prominent cheek bones which seemed all the more prominent beneath deep-set brown eyes. At twenty-nine his dark brown hair was already receding and thinning. Jackson was not handsome but there was something about him -- a presence -- that often arrested peoples' attention.

In the middle of a morning already growing hot, Belle was coming out of the Pecos post office, carrying a large package, as Jackson was going in. Belle slipped on the stone steps. Jackson caught her as she fell, picked up the package which had slipped out of her arms and stood holding it. When she had looked up at him, in that unguarded moment he saw warmth in her usually cool hazel eyes.

"Thank you, Jackson. I can't believe how often you seem to be in the right place at the right time."

"Would you like to have coffee or something with me?"

Belle sensed something more than a casual invitation and hesitated. But then the moment when he had caught her as she was falling, when she had felt that hard place inside her melt just a little, that moment glimmered again. She said softly, "Thank you. I'd like to."

As they walked over to the Pecos Hotel Jackson's heart was pounding. Much to her surprise, so was Belle's. They ordered coffee in the hotel dining room, the only people there this time of day. Jackson didn't often find himself at a loss for words, but on this occasion he hadn't been able to think of much to say except for what he'd wanted to say to her for years.

"Belle, I care for you very much. There's nothing that would make me happier than to always be in the right place at the right time for you. Would you consider us seeing each other seriously?"

Belle, searching, did not drop her eyes from his. Finally she took a deep breath and answered, "If we start to see each other seriously, will you agree that either of us can just say if it isn't right? That'll be the end of it?"

"It'll be however you say, Belle. You have my promise on that."

....

Skitchy rushed up to her best friend, Brin O'Brien, at the high school the first day after Belle told the family about herself and Jackson Tieger. "Come with me," Skitchy said breathlessly, taking Brin's hand and leading her away from the other girls.

"Brin! You'll never guess what! You know that man I told you about? Pink Campbell? The one I met at our church potluck? Well, Belle isn't going to be seeing him after all. She and Jackson Tieger have gotten serious all of a sudden. So it won't be a problem if we were to get interested in each other."

"You mean you and Pink Campbell?"

"Uh-huh."

"Sure enough, Skitchy? Oh, he's so good looking."

14

"You bet!"

"Will your folks let you see him? He's a lot older."

"Law, Brin, you sound like Mama! I don't see why in the world everybody makes such a fuss about how old somebody is. Besides, he hasn't even asked to see me yet. But I think he will. I saw how he looked at me when we first met." The girls giggled. "Besides, what harm can it do if I talk to him at dances and after church and we get to know each other?"

....

Three months later, Skitchy and her mother worked together one afternoon in the kitchen. Kate Chapman was peeling potatoes at the sink. A small woman with an upright back even as she worked, her brown hair was heavily streaked with gray and pulled back into a bun pinned at the neck. She had the same straight nose and almost square chin as her daughter. Her mouth was narrow, the lips thin, and her once fair complexion had been dried and lined by years in the arid heat and cold of West Texas. Only calm hazel eyes that sometimes still held a twinkle didn't look older than her fifty-two years.

Skitchy, cutting the potatoes into strips for frying, said in the calmest voice she could muster, "You were sixteen when you married Daddy. He was ten years older than you. I'm almost sixteen and Pink just turned twenty-seven. Isn't that pretty much the same?" Skitchy was determined to go with Pink on the picnic Belle and Jackson had planned. Still, she took care to make her voice soft, knowing Mama wouldn't stand for being pushed. "You've gotten to know him some from visiting after church. I thought you liked him."

"Well, he's a pleasant enough young man. And he has a fine voice."

Skitchy couldn't see her mother's face but thought her voice was softening a little. Church was important to Mama. They might not even be having this talk if Skitchy hadn't met Pink at church and she took it as a good sign that Mama remembered Pink's singing. She didn't mention that she and Pink had also seen each other at barn dances. "And Belle and Jackson will be at the picnic," she said, knowing that would help.

Hands still busy and without turning, her mother finally said quietly, "Well, I guess you can go if it's all right with your daddy."

Skitchy tried to catch the sound that came up into her throat, not wanting to sound too excited. "Oh, Mama, thank you. It means a lot to me."

"I know it does, sugar." Her mother spoke so softly Skitchy could barely hear her.

Skitchy found her father on the porch repairing a broken bridle. Ephraim Chapman was a tall man, almost gaunt, with a full head of silver hair and sharp features which still had a trace of the handsome man he'd once been. Years in the sun and wind had worn deep creases in his face. They had failed to conquer a sparkle in his eye or a ready easy smile beneath the full mustache he had kept from his youth.

It was usually easier for Skitchy to work things around with Daddy, but he spoke plainly and seriously as she sat near him on the porch steps. "Pinkney Campbell hasn't been around these parts very long. Don't know a lot about him, but he doesn't seem to have made much of himself for a man his age. Isn't making a go of farming cotton in ranch country. Don't think he will. Not enough rain most years. Best you don't get involved with him."

Skitchy didn't take up that argument. Instead she said, "Daddy, haven't you always said not to judge someone until you've walked a mile in his shoes? I'm just wanting to get to know Pink better." She didn't mention the way her body fluttered when she was near Pink. Or the thrilling that had come up into her throat when he had kissed her at the last dance, outside the Daniels' barn during one of the band breaks. She took her father's quiet thoughtfulness as a good sign, and waited. When he looked at her she looked back and said in a straightforward voice, "Please, Daddy?"

Daddy said yes.

....

Pink felt nervous when he and Jackson arrived at the Chapman ranch in Jackson's Model-T to pick up Skitchy and Belle for the picnic. This was the first time he'd been to the Chapman ranch and the prospect of being with Skitchy's parents in their home felt quite different to him from times they'd visited after church. He felt more nervous as Jackson turned off the main graveled road and Pink got out of the car to open the gate to the ranch and close it after Jackson drove through. He felt still more nervous as they drove up the scraped road in a cloud of dust and stopped at the edge of the swept yard, bare of any plants, surrounding the prosperous looking frame house. He was very glad to see Skitchy when she came out to greet them.

"Hi, Pink. Hi, Jackson," she called out gaily. "Come on in the house. Belle's not quite ready but she won't be a minute."

She took them across the yard and into the house, through the front room to the kitchen. Ephraim Chapman sat at the big well-worn oak table in the middle of the room, sipping ice tea as he read the newspaper. His back was straight yet relaxed, his collar unbuttoned and shirt sleeves rolled up.

Kate Chapman, her muslin dress obscured by an apron faded from many washings, was stuffing a chicken at the drain board next to the sink. She smiled at them over her shoulder but did not stop her work. "I expect Belle will be down in a minute. Would you boys like some ice tea while you're waiting?"

Ephraim stood and shook hands, first with Jackson, then with Pink. Pink had thought he couldn't feel any more nervous, but he did as he felt the older man's eyes looking him over.

"Might as well sit down and have some tea. Likely to be more than a minute waiting for Belle," Ephraim said with an affectionate chuckle as he sat down himself.

"Now, Eph," Kate said reprovingly.

Jackson smiled broadly and said, "Well, sir, I've always thought Belle was worth waiting for."

Pink heard the warmth in Jackson's voice, felt the ease he seemed to have with the Chapmans. He thought of his own family. How rare it had been to feel warmth, to laugh freely. He had sensed that his own deep inner feelings were unwelcome in his family and had learned to keep them to himself. He felt stiff and clumsy sitting there in the Chapman's kitchen and said little as Jackson and the Chapmans chatted. He felt relieved when Belle finally came into the kitchen. Pink and Jackson both stood as she came in.

"Well, don't sit back down," Belle said, her voice bright. "Let's not waste a minute of this beautiful day."

Pink crossed the room to Kate Chapman, still feeling stiff but finding his voice. "Thank you, ma'am, for the tea." Shaking hands with Ephraim, he said "Sir," with a nod.

Skitchy and Belle were already on their way to the car. Pink was glad to hurry after them.

Outside, Skitchy called out to her brother in the corral. "So long, Buddy. Don't be too hard on that horse!" She turned to Pink and explained, "Buddy would've come up to the house to say hello but he's breaking a new bronco. He's had his hands full with this one."

Buddy waved and Skitchy said, "He's quiet when he's working a horse. Doesn't want to spook it." Pink waved back.

....

McMinn Springs was an oasis in arid West Texas. Unexpected in the dry sandy soil sparse with plants, a natural spring bubbled up from a rocky outcropping and cool fresh water collected in a rocky pond before it flowed into a creek that had carried life for as long as anyone could remember. Tall cottonwoods had rooted themselves there, the only big trees for miles around. McMinn Springs saw less wind than most other parts of West Texas, sparing it all but the worst dust storms. Today the air was clear, the sky blue and high, laced with a few wispy clouds.

A perfect day for a picnic! Belle thought, as she and Jackson picked a spot, spread out an old quilt under the trees. "Let's go for a walk before it gets any hotter," Belle said to Jackson. Then to Skitchy and Pink, "You don't mind, do you, if we go off by ourselves for a bit?"

Skitchy grinned at her sister. "Have fun." She stretched out on the quilt with her hands behind her head, looking up through the trees at the lace clouds and the high high sky. This was her favorite place in the world and she was thrilled to be here with Pink Campbell, alone with him for the first time.

Skitchy usually paid little mind to what she wore, but she wanted to make sure she looked nice today and had asked Belle to help her. She wore a dark brown muslin skirt, with dark stockings and sturdy laced shoes, and a soft rose colored blouse. She had borrowed a close fitting hat with light and dark rose colored stripes from Belle, who encouraged her to wear it to set off her complexion. And, Skitchy suspected, cover her straight brown hair.

Sitting there under the cottonwood trees, Pink watched Skitchy relaxing on the quilt. "A penny for your thoughts," he said.

"Oh, I was thinking how much I like this place. The spring here in the middle of nowhere. The pond. The water's always cool. And the trees. I like being this close to the mountains. I'm not sure if it's true but they say big sheep with big curved horns live in the mountains and can go any place they want, no matter how steep. They can jump across wide places without losing their footing. I'd surely like to see those sheep."

"Then I hope you will one day."

Skitchy was curious by nature and she'd never been more curious than she was about Pink. They'd talked together before, but at the dances or after church there were always lots of people around and she hadn't felt she could ask him about himself as she wanted to. Today she could. Shifting slightly, she turned her head toward him. "Why did you come to West Texas?"

Usually uncomfortable when people asked that question, Pink found that when Skitchy asked he wanted to tell her. "You knew George and Emily Norton?"

"Uh-huh, but not well."

"My uncle Charley told me about George not long after I came home from the war. They were friends from the old days when they were army buddies in the Spanish-American War. George never really seemed to get over that awful flu that went around after the big war. My uncle said George was looking for someone to help him with his cotton farm till he could get back on his feet. He and a couple of other farmers were trying some new things with irrigation and new fertilizers and he wanted to keep that going, too." Pink paused, looking to be sure Skitchy was really interested. He liked this young woman and didn't want to bore her. She seemed to be listening intently so he went on, "I figured if George and the others were right, it could make all the difference in the world for farming, even here where drought's such a big problem. So I decided to try my luck cotton farming. That's why I came."

Pink said nothing about how hard it had been to adjust to life on the farm in Iowa after the war. He was proud of having been a wagoner in the army, driving trucks and ambulances, one of only two men in his outfit who knew how to drive. He'd never been outside of Iowa before shipping out to France and all he had seen and done had changed him. He hadn't joined in, even when his buddies ribbed him, when they drank or played poker or went to whore houses, and he hadn't been more than friendly with the French girls who liked American soldiers. Still, when he came home he'd felt pinched by the strict Presbyterian ways of his family, especially those of his mother.

Skitchy could hear the sadness in Pink's voice as he said quietly, "George didn't get better, though, and he gave up on the new ideas." As he stopped speaking and dropped his eyes, Skitchy dropped her eyes also, sensing his emotion, not wanting to embarrass him. When she looked at Pink again he was looking at her with a kind of tenderness behind the eyes that she'd never seen before in a man. Afterward she would think that was when she had begun to love him.

Skitchy already had a good idea about the rest of Pink's story. Still, she listened as before when he began to speak again. "After George died, Emily told me she didn't want to stay here. She was going to move back to her family in Louisiana but she offered to let me stay and work the land. I keep a share of what I make and send her the rest." Skitchy knew it was hardscrabble farming in years with scarce rain and Pink was having a hard time of it. Neither of them spoke of that.

When Belle and Jackson came back, Belle and Skitchy laid out fried chicken, potato salad and pickles and poured ice tea from a thermos. Talking with each other easily as they ate, they decided to wait a while to cut the watermelon Jackson had brought.

"I have my camera in the car," Jackson said. "How about some pictures?"

"You bet!" Skitchy replied enthusiastically. "Wouldn't you like pictures, Belle? Pink?"

Jackson took Skitchy's picture sitting on rocks near the creek, her long slender legs stretched out in front of her. She was not smiling, excited but not wanting that to show too much. After Jackson took her picture Skitchy asked, "Will you please take one just of Pink for me? I'd like to have one very much."

"You bet. How about on the same rocks where I took your picture?"

Skitchy grinned. "Oh, that would be wonderful!" She thought Pink looked incredibly handsome in his straw hat, jacket and tie. She planned to put his picture in a box where she kept private things that meant a great deal to her.

Pink stepped up quickly. He was glad Skitchy wanted a picture of him. He knew people, especially women, liked his clear blue eyes and thought him good looking, and that was apparent in the jaunty angle of his hat and the jaunty posture of his hand on his slouched hip. He was used to being noticed even though it often made him uncomfortable. He was especially glad Skitchy had noticed him because he liked her very much indeed. She was young but he felt at ease with her. And with himself when he was around her.

Jackson took Belle's picture, too. She was delighted to have her picture taken in her new dress even though she didn't want her delight to show too much, to seem too vain. Her mother had ordered white lawn fabric from Dallas to make the straight-topped low-waisted dress to look like a picture Belle found in a magazine, using a pattern she cut from newspaper. Belle wore a wide brimmed straw hat she had trimmed herself with ribbons.

Jackson had frowned a little at first when Belle told him she wanted to ask her sister and Pink to join them on the picnic. Belle explained, "Mama and Daddy will only let her see him, just the two of them, if they're with somebody they know. Please, Jackson. You'll see. They'll want to be by themselves some of the time. We'll have our time."

There wasn't much Belle wanted that Jackson would say no to, so he had said, "You bet, darling. I'm sure it will be fun."

"Thank you," she said, squeezing his hand, smiling up at the dark haired man whose deep-set brown eyes always seemed to smile at her.

When the picture taking was finished and they had eaten the watermelon, Jackson brought out coffee. He had one thermos laced with brandy for Belle and himself, another with just coffee for Skitchy, who wanted to drink brandy but didn't, and Pink who didn't touch any kind of alcohol. They lingered for almost another hour enjoying the coffee and the light breeze that had come up.

As the sun dropped low enough in the western sky to cast its rays where they sat under the trees, Jackson said, "Well, as much as I hate to say it, I think it's time for us to get these ladies home, Pink." They talked and laughed as they slowly gathered things up, all of them still buoyant with the delight of the day.

As they drove back to the ranch, Skitchy was full of ideas. She said gaily, "Buddy's riding in the rodeo in McAllister next week. I want to go. There's a dance afterward. I think it'd be lots of fun if we all went together."

"Well, I'd love to join you for the rodeo but I'm playing with the band for the dance," Pink said. Hating to see Skitchy's face fall, he'd also felt the old pull of having been taught from boyhood that dancing was somehow wrong. He'd come to terms with that during the war. After all, he played music for people to dance to. Still, he'd never felt completely comfortable dancing himself. Pushing down his discomfort, he said hastily, "How about if we go to the rodeo and let me see if I can work out something with Tom. Have a set or two off so we can dance some."

Jackson asked, "Belle, would you like to go?"

"Sounds like fun."

Skitchy began to think about being at dances where Pink played with the band and she didn't dance much. She said a little more petulantly than she wanted to sound, "Well, dancing some is better than not dancing at all. And of course the rodeo will be fun." She was still busy being annoyed when Jackson turned off the main gravel road and on to the narrow dirt ranch road.

Pink got out to open the gate, Jackson drove the car through, and Pink closed it after them. By the time he got back into the car, Skitchy had begun to feel uneasy, her annoyance forgotten. As they passed the storehouse and the old windmill, she felt even more strongly that something was wrong. Belle felt it, too, and frowned as she looked over her shoulder at her sister.

Jackson saw the look and asked, "What is it, honey?"

"I don't know," Belle replied, her frown deeper. It was too quiet. No one around the house or either of the bunkhouses or the storehouse, the big corral or the small corral, not even any of the Mexican hands at work off in the distance. No one in sight anywhere.

"Something feels funny. Not right," Skitchy said warily. Then she saw a motionless dark shape in the corral. Was it a horse? She couldn't be sure but she was sure of the dread that had come into her stomach.

Jackson stopped the car close to the house. As the dust began to settle, Ephraim Chapman came out, the screen door slamming behind him. Face drawn, his shoulders slumped and his step was slow and heavy. Skitchy saw his rifle standing by the front door.

Scrambling out of the car Belle barely breathed, "Daddy, what's wrong? What's happened?"

"Daddy?" Skitchy whispered.

"Buddy," Ephraim choked out his son's name.

As Skitchy got closer to him she could see the pain in his eyes, pain deeper than she'd ever seen in anyone's eyes. She didn't run to him as she wanted to.

"Buddy," Ephraim began again.

Skitchy saw her mother come to the screen door, then turn away, melting back into the gloom inside the house. She noticed Mama was not wearing her apron and her mother didn't take off her apron for no reason. Belle started to walk quickly toward the house, Skitchy close behind her.

"In the front room," Ephraim said thickly.

The shades were drawn but even in the dim light they saw Buddy's dust covered body lying on the long table. He still wore his boots and his shirt was open. His head was turned at an angle unnatural to someone living.

Skitchy stood as if paralyzed for a moment, finally moved unsteadily to her brother's body. A deep sob rose up from the depths of her.

Belle laid her hand softly on Buddy's leg. Jackson hesitated for a moment, then stepped behind her, gently put his hand on her shoulder. He could feel her body trembling. As she reached her hand toward his, he was afraid he'd made a mistake, that she would push his hand away. But she put her own hand on his and even in this moment of shock and awfulness his heart leapt, joy mixing with sorrow. She was allowing herself to be comforted. She was allowing *him* to comfort her.

Ephraim and Kate, hands clasped tightly, stood at the head of the table. Ephraim was motionless, frozen, except for his eyes full of pain looking down at his son. Kate was also still, but Pink could feel her steady presence even as her eyes brimmed with grief.

Pink stayed near the door, not sure what he should do, wishing there was something he could do. He'd seen agony like this during the war but this was different. And he felt keenly that he was a stranger here.

"There was a rattlesnake in the corral. It spooked the bronco and he threw Buddy. His neck broke when he hit the ground. He'd already passed away when Eph got to him." Kate Chapman's voice was the voice of the midwife and nurse who had spoken terrible news on other occasions.

No one moved or said anything else as long minutes passed. After a while Pink heard someone on the porch. Hank Schmidt, the head ranch hand, knocked softly and took off his well-worn and sweat-stained hat as he stepped inside. He had sent someone to Pecos to get the doctor and to send a telegram to Minnie, Belle and Skitchy's older sister. "Doc Hartman's here, Eph." He nodded to Kate, "Ma'am, I'm so sorry."

Skitchy turned from Buddy's body, convulsed with another deep sob. Pink moved toward her just enough to let her know he was there. She came to where he was standing. "He's getting cold already," she whispered. "Oh, I can't believe this. . . . Buddy . . . Buddy." She sobbed again and Pink put his arm around her.

"Would you like to go outside?" he asked softly.

She nodded mutely. Outside they walked over to the corral, Pink's arm still around her shoulders. He could feel her body shaking. The snake was gone. Ranch hands had taken the horse's carcass away. She saw buzzards circling in the distance. Skitchy knew her father had shot the horse. She looked intently at the pool of blood someone had partly covered with dirt, trying to take in what had happened.

Pink stood close beside her. She still shivered and he asked, "Are you cold? Shall we go back inside? Or I could get my coat out of the car for you."

She shook her head. "Let's go in the kitchen."

There was a pot of coffee on the stove and he heated that up. They sat at one end of the big kitchen table drinking the coffee. Long minutes passed.

"You know, it was Buddy who gave me my name," Skitchy said, her voice laden with sadness.

Pink looked at her, encouraging her to go on if she wanted to.

"I was pretty little. Had a bad rash. My skin itched like crazy and I couldn't stop scratching. Buddy was so funny and sweet. Started fooling around. Pretending he itched, scratching himself. He was jumping all around laughing. Called us itchy skin people. I couldn't say the words right. Said skitchy people. So then I started calling myself Skitchy. That's been my name ever since." She seemed to be looking into a distance Pink couldn't see. After a minute or so, she shook her head. Her eyes came back into the kitchen.

"I'll tell you the name my parents gave me if you promise never to call me that."

"I promise."

"Lucy" she said, almost chuckling in a way Pink thought sounded like her father. "Lucy Melinda. It's a perfectly lovely name. It just never felt like my name. Skitchy always seemed to be my right name and it was a present from Buddy." Her voice choked on a deep sob.

Jackson came in to the kitchen quietly, alone. "Some neighbor ladies are here to help Kate see to Buddy's body. Telegram came from Minnie and Bob. They're coming tomorrow. I think it's time for us to go, Pink."

Pink walked with Jackson out to his car. He wondered how the night could be so clear, so beautiful, the sky so high and wide and paved with stars, when something so hideous had happened that day.

....

The funeral was in Pecos. Kate and Ephraim had decided to have the graveside service mid-morning so people wouldn't have to stand in the merciless sun in the hottest part of the day. A slight breeze had come up. They'd put a notice in the newspaper and when Skitchy saw so many people there, she thought, Law, half the county must be here.

The crowd of mourners faded from her awareness, however, when she came near the grave. The full weight of what they'd come there to do felt overwhelming to her. I don't think I can stand this, she thought. She was usually able to push things away she didn't want to think about, but she couldn't push this away. And she couldn't walk away from it. She told herself she had to stand it somehow. Cry some more later. If I start crying now, it feels like I'll never be able to stop.

She tried to listen to what the preacher said about Buddy passing into eternal rest in the arms of the Lord. She found no comfort in that idea and as she stood there thinking about her brother, she decided she didn't believe in eternal rest in heaven. Or hell for that matter. I don't have to believe all that, she told herself. Buddy himself had taught her that. Just keep it to yourself, he had said, if you decide not to believe everything you hear in church so you don't aggravate Mama. She felt a warm surge of gratitude and love for her brother. She desperately wanted the coffin to somehow open and for Buddy to sit up and it would all have been a ghastly nightmare. But she didn't wake from the ghastly nightmare and the preacher droned on.

Pink also found it hard to listen to the preacher. All around him was bare dry earth and tombstones. Some newer granite stones stood straight and undamaged, many older weather-worn ones were leaning or crumbling. No grass, no trees, scrubby weeds were the only green he saw and they were caked with dust. A huge ant hill swarmed with ants close to Buddy's open grave. A few graves had spots of color but he saw that the flowers were fake and muted with dust. Pink felt oppressed by the harsh surroundings. Could they not spare some precious water for what seemed to him to be sacred ground? He looked away, unable to look at Buddy's coffin or any of the people who had come to bury him here. He struggled to pray but his own voice was as dry as the dry ground. When the time came to sing a hymn, he couldn't sing.

The services were almost over when Pink saw three small tombstones on three small graves. Tombstones with Chapman names. Surprised he hadn't noticed them before, he saw that William Albert Chapman had lived for a day. Harrison Taylor Chapman had lived for five years. Andrew George Chapman had lived for eight months. No wonder, he thought, the family had doted on Buddy, the only son who lived past childhood. Pink felt tears well up from deep within him. He didn't try to stop them.

Ephraim Chapman didn't try to stop his tears either. He would have liked to be like other West Texas men who kept their grief private. He couldn't. He'd borne much during his lifetime and learned that he could only endure what he must by letting the tears come when they would, yielding to forces that were beyond him. He liked to think of himself as like a tree he'd seen in a picture in one of his books when he was in school in Falls County, long before he had any thought of coming west to build a life in the hard pull land where he now stood. He still held in his memory the lines of the tree in the picture, bending in the wind. A tree might look weak when it bent in a high wind, yet such a tree might survive. He was not proud of bending but he knew he could endure the loss of this last son no other way.

Kate stood beside him, her hand fast in his. He could feel her grief, as deep as his own. As it had always been in their life together, she steadied him as much as he steadied her. Once, when she'd been a young midwife and the mother of three small children had not lived to give birth to a fourth, she'd told him, "Eph, people depend on me to be strong. Take care of things. I need to keep my grief apart from what I need to be doing as best I can. I can almost always do that. The Good Lord helps me." He was grateful for her strength.

Kate was grateful for the man standing by her side and for the living daughters, themselves grief stricken, standing near her. They hold the promise of life going on, she thought. That will help me stay strong. Nevertheless, grief filled her heart, penetrated into the marrow of her bones, as it had when she'd lost each child. Each one lost had taken something vital from her, but the searing loss of this one by whose grave she stood was the worst of hard losses. She prayed for the strength to bear it, as she must. She looked up at the tall man beside her, in whose hand she had put her own long ago. I can bear it, she told herself, if I just keep standing by his side.

....

When Pink arrived at the ranch road after the funeral, two youngsters Pink didn't know were at the gate, opening and closing it for visitors. Cars and wagons were parked all along the side of the road and the yard was full. A few horses were tethered to the corral fence. The front room of the Chapman ranch house was already crowded and people spilled over onto the porch and into the kitchen. Women were putting out dishes of food on the big oak table for today, filling the ice box and drain board with enough food for the family for the next few days.

Skitchy stood with Minnie and Belle by the front door, greeting people as they arrived, receiving condolences and sometimes weeping embraces. All three sisters wore high-necked ankle-length dresses with long sleeves. Skitchy's was dark gray. Minnie and Belle both wore black like their mother, Belle's dress adorned with a small lace collar fastened with a cameo brooch. Pink thought Skitchy looked graceful and dignified, standing so tall and straight beside her smaller sisters. She seemed so composed to him, he was amazed at her strength.

"I'm so glad you're here, Pink," she said tearfully. "If you don't mind waiting, we can eat together in a while."

Pink nodded as he squeezed her hand and moved along in the line of mourners to the settee where Kate Chapman sat, her husband standing behind her in the dark suit he had worn at the cemetery. "Mrs. Chapman, Mr. Chapman, I don't have words to say how sorry I am."

"Thank you, Pink." He wanted to say more, but their attention turned to someone standing behind him and Pink moved away.

....

Later, pacing on the front porch of the Norton farm house, Pink was glad to have some time to himself to think things through. He had not changed the clothes he wore to the funeral, only taken off his coat and tie. It felt good to run his hands through his short pomaded hair. He looked out over the field of cotton, over the flat land beyond that stretched to infinite horizon in one direction, to the distant blue mountains in the other. The sky above him seemed higher and wider than he could ever have imagined at home in Iowa. Did he want to stay in this vast empty dry place? This place he'd already learned was anything but an easy place to live in? And he needed to think about the difference in his and

Skitchy's ages, about the same difference as between Belle and Skitchy. He had known that, of course, from the beginning, but not in the way he knew it now. Three dead brothers, four now, had testified to how young Skitchy really was. A schoolgirl.

"I must not fool around with her," he said aloud, startled to hear his own words. He stopped pacing. Staring out again across the cotton fields beginning to fade into dark shapes as the sun was quickly disappearing against the flat horizon, he felt restless. He lit a cigarette, took several deep drags. "Be careful, Campbell. You better be sure."

....

Two weeks later Pink sat on his porch visiting with Tom Floyd. Tom was lanky and slow in his movements. His angled face had a hard-bitten look, as if he already felt beaten down by the world at thirty. There was an air about the way he wore worn blue jeans, a clean but unironed shirt, boots, and a straw cowboy hat, that seemed to say he didn't care what people thought of him. Pink had started playing the trumpet in Tom's band at dances because he enjoyed making music and making some extra money. He had also liked getting off the farm for some fun, which had included opportunities to meet young women from around the area. Tom had become the best friend he had. They sat and talked, smoking cigarettes. Tom drank the second of two beers he had brought with him, Pink sipped cold coffee.

"She's young, Tom, but I like her a lot. Better than I've ever liked any girl. You think I'm crazy?"

"Don't know, but, dang! Sure wouldn't walk away from 'better than I've ever liked any girl' without giving it a chance. Eph Chapman could be tough, though. Won't be easy to win him over when it comes to one of his daughters. Skitchy in particular. The man dotes on her."

Pink respected and admired Ephraim Chapman. He respected him for having been one of the first men to acquire open land west of the Pecos River. His ranch was now prosperous after years of staggering work, through ordinary and extraordinary droughts, and raids in the early years by bands of renegade Apaches. Pink most admired Ephraim's straightforward easy manner that won people over easily.

"I like him. He's a good man. And Skitchy says she's a lot like her father. She likes me. Maybe her father can get to like me, too."

1922

Skitchy and Brin O'Brien talked and giggled as they left O'Brien's Mercantile Store in Pecos where Brin worked for her father on Saturdays. Both of them carried sacks of groceries and supplies Skitchy and her father would take home to the ranch. They hurried along the boardwalk toward the livery stable where Ephraim Chapman had left the wagon for the morning.

"Can't be late. Daddy will have a fit."

"Well, tell me while we walk really fast. I want to hear everything, Skitch." Brin, pretty with light brown hair curled around her round pink cheeks, could hardly contain her excitement. She was eager to hear all the latest news about her best friend and Pink Campbell.

"Well, we've been seeing each other. At dances and we've eaten together at all the church potlucks. I was able to work it around so Mama and Daddy let me go with him on a picnic with Belle and Jackson. We had some time to ourselves."

"My mama and daddy are a lot more strict than your folks, Skitchy. They don't let me see boys alone. Don't think they'd let me see a man that much older at all. You're so lucky."

Skitchy suddenly felt so much older than her friend. How could she tell Brin about the thrill that came up into her throat when Pink kissed her during band breaks in the dark outside the barn? How could she tell her about last Saturday night when Pink touched her breast through her blouse and she hadn't wanted him to stop? She had wanted him to take off her blouse, but of course she couldn't tell him that. And anyway, someone might have seen them and Pink had to go back to the band in a few minutes.

"Well, maybe I am lucky," Skitchy said. She decided to change the subject. "Mama said I could order a new dress from the Sears Roebuck catalog. Can't make up my mind. They have a pretty bright green one. Surely do like the color, but I don't know if maybe a print would be better with spring coming. What do you think?"

"Law, Skitchy Chapman, since when have you paid any mind about what you wear?"

"Well, I want Pink to think I look nice."

"Margie and Lizzy say you've changed a whole lot and I think maybe they're right. Pretty soon maybe you won't even want to go around with us girls anymore."

"Oh, Brin, it isn't like that." But Skitchy knew there was some truth in what Brin said. She only wanted to be with Pink. He was all she could think of.

....

"Belle honey, what do you think about Skitchy and Pink Campbell?"

Belle was with her mother in the kitchen. Her father and Jackson had gone out to the small corral to see the new foal. She put on one of her mother's aprons and stood at the stove browning flour for gravy. Heat from the wood stove added to an already hot day and she wiped her brow with a corner of the apron. "Well, I think they may be getting pretty serious."

"I think so, too. But I wonder if it's a good thing."

Surprised, Belle looked at her mother over her shoulder but couldn't read her face. "Thought you liked Pink."

"Well, I do. Seems like a good man. He's a lot older than Skitchy but maybe he can steady her a bit. But she may get tired of that. She has so much spark. He doesn't have much that I can see."

"I don't know, Mama. I don't know him real well, but I think maybe he has a quiet strength inside that doesn't show much."

A moment passed before Kate went on. "Think he can make a go of this cotton farming?"

"I don't know anything about cotton farming but I think he'll do the best he can." Belle was quiet for a moment. "Are you worried for Skitchy, Mama?"

"Guess I am, a bit. Maybe we should've sent her to the sisters' boarding school in Odessa where you and Minnie went. I was glad when the county high school opened and she could stay at home to go to school. Seems like maybe she's gotten grown up ideas faster than you girls did, though. Maybe too fast."

As the men came onto the back stoop, stamping the dust off their boots, mother and daughter heard them still talking about the foal. Getting lemonade from the icebox Kate said,

"I want Skitchy to be happy and content. Like you are, honey."

....

Even at McMinn Springs late in October, heat rose from the shimmering land. There would be no new tinges of green beyond the springs until rain came to wake up slumbering plant life. Skitchy and Pink sat cross-legged on an old quilt under an old cottonwood. They had finished their roast beef and biscuit sandwiches, carrot salad, and pecan cookies, took turns sipping iced tea from the top of the thermos.

Pink took out his pocket knife. Humming softly, he began to carve their initials into the thick corky bark of the cottonwood. Skitchy felt her heart beat faster as she watched, still faster as she decided to say what she wanted to. Never mind what Mama and Belle said about her maybe being too forward.

"Sugar, I love you so much! I know girls aren't supposed to be the ones who bring it up but I've been thinking about us maybe getting married when I finish school."

"Sweetheart, I've been thinking about it, too."

Skitchy grew even more excited when she heard him say that. Her heart was beating faster even before Pink drew her toward him. He leaned over to kiss her, a long kiss that brought up the thrilling flutter in her throat. She felt confused after some time passed, however, and he'd said nothing more. She was sure she could hear Pink's heart beating as fast as her own, but his silence didn't seem to be saying the same thing as his kiss. He went back to carving their initials.

After a time he asked, "What do you think your folks would say?"

Skitchy felt her body stiffen a little, but she wanted to sound confident. "I know they want me to be happy."

"Well, I want you to be happy, too. And I'm about the happiest man around when I'm with you. But what if your folks think we're getting serious too soon?"

She wondered if he might be talking about himself thinking they were getting serious too soon, as much as about Mama and Daddy. She was still thinking about that when he finished the initials and carved a heart around them.

"There!" he said, standing away from the tree. "Now anyone can see that SC and PC love each other!" He threw his arms around her, kissed her.

Skitchy thought, he said he'd been thinking about us getting married. He carved our initials for anyone to see. I think he's just being careful about Mama and Daddy. She considered herself engaged from that day on.

....

But as Tom Floyd had predicted, it wasn't easy for Pink to win over Ephraim Chapman when it came to marrying his daughter. Or Kate Chapman either. Ephraim and Kate talked about Skitchy and Pink one evening as they sat on the porch of the ranch house. The wind had died down and the dust it carried had settled.

"She's so young, Eph. Younger than I was at her age."

"She hasn't had anything like the responsibilities you did at her age. You'd already been taking care of your little brothers for two years before your pa married Ada."

"I like Pink. But you said yourself he's old enough he should have something more to offer than trying to farm cotton. On a place he doesn't even own."

Eph responded to the displeasure in her voice with an affectionate chuckle. Kate didn't often speak with irritation about anybody.

"Well, he plays the trumpet, too. Can raise a fuss with young women."

"Law, Eph, don't joke. It's our girl he's raised a fuss with." She put her head back against the back of the rocking chair, closed her eyes. A few deep breaths later she looked at him. "Let's ask her to wait until she's eighteen before she makes up her mind. She thinks she's in love with him but I think it might be just a passing fancy. She's got a good head on her shoulders. Give it a while, she may cool down."

"I need to ponder on that."

Eph rose, stretched his lanky frame. He walked out to the corral. His favorite mare walked over to the edge of the enclosure, whinnied and tossed her head, nosed his hand. He rubbed her nose affectionately. After a few minutes, he turned, walked slowly back to the porch.

"Kate, you know as well as I do that Skitchy's as strong-minded as she is passionate. I expect she'll wait until she graduates. Doubt she'll wait much longer. Mark my words, we may make things worse if she thinks we're trying to wrangle her out of being in love with Pinkney Campbell. And we don't want them to eat supper before saying grace."

"Law, Eph," she sighed. "Never thought to be having a talk like this about our baby girl so soon."

....

Kate had invited neighbors to the ranch the following Sunday for scripture reading, prayer and hymn singing, something she often did when no preacher came to Pecos for church services.

"Mama, can I ask Pink to come on Sunday?" Skitchy asked.

Kate looked up from her sewing machine. Well, she thought, it's good for them to be reading scripture and praying together. And best they spend time here instead of off by themselves. "That'd be fine," she said.

When Skitchy came back into the room a little later she was surprised when her mother said, without looking up or stopping her foot on the sewing machine treadle, "Do you think Pink would lead the singing? He has such a nice voice."

"I'm sure he would, Mama. I'll ask him. He does have a nice voice, doesn't he?" This was so much more than Skitchy had expected, she had trouble keeping the excitement out of her voice. It's going to be fine with Mama, she thought happily.

....

On Sunday morning Pink came a little early to help set things up in the front room. He saw everyone was dressed informally, not like they did for services in Pecos. He took off his coat and tie, rolled the tie up and put it in his coat pocket. It was the first time he'd been in that room since that awful day when Buddy Chapman lost his life and he felt an unspeakable sadness. But then Skitchy came in from the kitchen and he felt his spirit begin to lift. She was dressed in a denim skirt, leather boots and soft leather vest, her hair pulled back and tied with a ribbon. She looks so nice, he thought, and her manner was gay and light. He joined her in doing the small tasks of preparation. Later, the hymns seemed to touch that place in him where he felt things so strongly, where the heart-ghosts were. As he sang, he sang out the sadness and joy mingled within him.

After the gathering he was helping to put things away as the neighbors left when Kate approached him.

"I was very touched by your singing," she said, almost shyly.

"Thank you, ma'am," he said, somewhat flustered and not knowing what else to say.

"Would you like to stay for the noon meal with the family?"

"Yes, ma'am, I'd like that very much," he responded enthusiastically before she turned and went to the kitchen.

The meal was as much talk and laughter as pot roast, mashed potatoes and gravy, cornbread and greens. They all exclaimed with delight when Kate took a warm peach cobbler from the oven. Belle brought a pitcher of cream from the icebox. Skitchy poured coffee. Pink enjoyed himself enormously and was struck once again by how different the Chapman family was from his own. Sunday dinners at home in Iowa had been mostly dour preludes to Bible study in the afternoon. He thought more than once during the meal how much he didn't want to do anything to hurt or anger these people.

After they finished the meal, Kate, Belle, and Jackson got up more or less in unison, began to clean up the table and stack dishes on the drain board by the sink. Skitchy brought a big canning jar filled with dried pinto beans. Ephraim began to shuffle a deck of cards.

"We're going to play poker. Losers do the dishes," Skitchy explained to Pink's puzzled face. "Here," she said as she pushed the jar of beans toward him. "Help me count these out. A hundred for each of us."

Pink was dumbfounded. Not only was there not going to be Bible study, they were going to play cards! Poker! His thoughts raced, pulling him one way, then another. He'd watched poker games in the army but had never quite shaken his mother's stern warning against card playing, which could lead to gambling. Presbyterians didn't gamble. Maybe it isn't gambling if it's only in fun, he thought, no money at stake. He didn't want to seem righteous or disrespectful when the Chapmans were including him in their family game. He decided to play.

He lost badly. And had the most fun he'd had in a very long time. When his beans were gone, ending the game, Skitchy and her father had the biggest piles in front of them. Belle had the smallest pile.

"Well, Pink," Eph said genially, "you and Belle have fun." He and the others hung around the kitchen, talking and laughing, playfully ribbing the dishwashing losers, pointedly doing nothing to help.

When it was time to leave Pink said warmly, "Mrs. Chapman, thank you for the wonderful meal. That cobbler was the best I ever tasted! I enjoyed the whole day so much! Thank you for including me."

Skitchy walked him out to his car. "See," she said happily. "It's going to be fine with Mama and Daddy. Don't worry." He squeezed her hand, but didn't kiss her goodbye, in case anyone might see them. He didn't want to put any strain on the welcome he'd been given that day.

1923

"Stop the car, please," Skitchy said, her voice light but serious. "I want to talk about something."

Pink heard the slight quiver in her voice as he pulled over. He was taking Skitchy home from a barn dance on a night in late March and they were bundled up against the cold that made even the hardy mesquites and greasewoods shiver. A close to full moon was bright enough for him to make out the expression on her face. She seemed calm but when he took her hand, he felt her trembling.

"What is it, honey?" he asked.

She had the jitters but also felt a strong resolve. It was unmistakable in her voice as she took a deep breath and began slowly, "Been thinking a lot about us, Pink. About getting married. About when we might get married." Her words started to come faster. "I'm sure Mama would like Brother Samuel to marry us. Probably Daddy would, too. But

Brother Samuel wants to have talks with couples before he marries them. He made Belle and Jackson wait for months. Then when he was finished talking it was another two months before he came to Pecos for weddings. Why don't we just go ahead and get married?"

Pink, taken by surprise, frowned a little. Skitchy hardly caught her breath before her words rushed on.

"Oh, Pink, I love you so much. I don't want to wait for months."

He felt torn. He measured his words as carefully as he could. "Honey, I want us to get married, too. But I don't think we should just run off and get married without even telling your folks."

"Law, I didn't mean to run off without telling them. I just meant we'd tell them we've decided to get married. We don't want to wait like Belle and Jackson did for Brother Samuel. We want to get married at the courthouse in Pecos as soon as I finish school."

"I love you, honey, but I don't want us to start off with trouble between us and your folks. Let me have a talk with your father. Let's see what he says. Then we can decide."

That sounded reasonable to Skitchy. But she didn't want to be reasonable. She wanted to be married. Pink was already coming to know that determined look.

"But we can get married as soon as I finish school?"

Her passionate enthusiasm was what he loved most about her. He felt caught up in it. It's astonishing to be loved like that, he thought. Only a fool would turn away from that. Feeling the weight of his words, he said, "If that's what you want, honey. Yes."

....

It had been cloudy all morning. The sky seemed too dark for the middle of the day when the little caravan of cars drove up to the courthouse. Skitchy wore a new blue dress and a dark blue velvet cloche trimmed with rose-colored velvet roses, a gift from Belle. She thought Pink looked wonderful in his dark suit, the same one he had worn for Buddy's funeral but brightened for today with a colorful tie. The ceremony was short. Skitchy spoke her vows in a clear firm voice and listened eagerly to Pink's promises to her. Then they were man and wife! She looked down at the narrow gold band on her finger. Looked at the reality of it. Married! She and Pink were married!

A few minutes later they were hurrying to the car as the dark sky lowered. Thunder rolled from the clouds, lightning flashed. The sky opened and hard rain began just as they drove up to the Pecos Hotel.

In the hotel dining room a table was already set for them. "So beautiful!" Skitchy exclaimed. "Thank you, Belle! Thank you, Jackson!"

Jackson scanned everything and was quite satisfied with all the arrangements. "Would you like to sit here, next to Skitchy?" he asked Kate. "And Eph, next to Kate?" The older couple settled themselves, stiffly Jackson thought, while he helped Belle with her chair. Pink helped his bride into hers and sat down beside her.

Pink saw that the older man he admired so much sat stiffly all during the meal. Ephraim Chapman didn't often wear a suit. Pink couldn't be sure if his now father-in-law felt stiff in the suit or would have seemed stiff, no matter what he was wearing that day. Kate seemed more relaxed but also more quiet than usual. She was dressed for the occasion in a rose cotton dress, her hair pulled back into a bun as she always wore it. Pink was so happy to have Skitchy as his bride, yet another part of him wished they had waited a little longer, as the Chapmans had wanted. Waited to be married by the preacher. He could have urged that. But he hadn't. And Skitchy was happy.

"Thank you, Jackson, for arranging this meal for us," Pink said. "It means a lot to both of us that you're all here."

"You bet!" Skitchy beamed. "This is the happiest day of my life!"

From time to time during the meal Skitchy felt impatient, imagining how it would be when she and Pink were upstairs, alone. Her body felt eagerly alive and she wanted to be all the way married. She was quite ready when it came time to hug everyone goodbye. Her excitement mounted as she climbed the oak staircase, hand in hand with Pink, to their room.

Skitchy unpacked the new night gown she had saved since Christmas in the hope of its becoming her wedding night gown. It was the softest white cotton with a little lace trim around the neck and cuffs, fastened with pearly buttons. She hoped Pink would like it. Think she looked beautiful in it. Then she laughed softly when she thought she would probably not be wearing it very long after she got into bed. She imagined herself joyfully picking it up off the floor the next morning.

"What's so funny, honey?"

"Oh nothing, sugar. Just thinking something funny about nightgowns."

Pink watched her, amazed at his good fortune, married now to this delightful girl!

When Pink turned out the light, Skitchy turned toward him and returned his kiss passionately. "I love you, Pink. I'm so happy." She felt a brief moment of disappointment when he didn't take off her nightgown, but she quickly pushed that away, not willing to have anything spoil their first night together. He was sweetly gentle with her. Their yearning for each other routed inexperience. Neither of them heard the howling wind or the rain when it began again, driving against the window.

....

As they drove to the cotton farm the next day the sky was high and cloudless. Yesterday's rain had drained away from the hard packed rutted road.

"I'm a married woman now," Skitchy said, her voice rippling with light-hearted laughter. "This married woman would like to know how to drive. Will you teach me, Mr. Campbell?"

"Sure, Mrs. Campbell. But I'll have to teach you how to take care of the car, too. If you're going to drive a Model-T you need to know how to keep it running. You have to make repairs and change flat tires. A Model-T has a lot of flat tires on gravel and dirt roads."

"I'd love to learn! I'm very handy you know. Right now? Can I start right now? With the driving part? It could be a wedding present."

Pink pulled over. "Well, it's about the funniest wedding present I ever heard of. But why not?"

Skitchy, excited, got out of the car quickly. She came around to the driver's side, slipped behind the wheel. She learned faster than most men, Pink noted, and it wasn't long before they were off.

"This is easy! Even more fun than I imagined. I want to drive all the way home!" Driving along with a fine cloud of brown dust trailing behind, Skitchy said gaily, as much to herself as to Pink, "I'm the luckiest happiest girl in the world."

....

The farm house was small and old, much of the paint peeling. It was surrounded by cotton fields except for a small scraped yard. As she brought the car screeching to an abrupt stop in front of the house, laughing, he watched her a little nervously. She'd been there before of course and had already brought her things there, but today was different. It was to be her home now.

She walked up the steps and onto the porch of the house, feeling as if it was all happening in slow motion. Pink opened the door for her and she walked into the front room. Turning to him, she put her arms around his neck, kissed him.

"I want so much for you to be happy here," he said softly. "I know the house is not much."

"Law, this is so much nicer than what Mama and Daddy had when they were first married. Did you know the storehouse was their first house? Just that one room with a dirt floor. They lived there for more than two years before Daddy built the ranch house. Minnie was born there."

"Well, you have a wood floor!"

"And a husband I'm crazy about!" she said, bubbling in her happiness. She kissed him again. "Now I'd like to go to our bedroom. I love saying that – *our bedroom*!"

Pink hadn't moved into the bedroom when Emily Norton left. He'd stayed in the screened-in back porch where he had slept and kept his things when he worked for the Nortons. To get the bedroom ready for Skitchy and himself, he'd cleaned the iron bed, made it up with the sheets and pillow cases

Minnie had embroidered as a wedding present, and the quilt Skitchy's friends had made for her. He oiled the oak chest of drawers and tall clothes cabinet, bought a small mirror and hung it over the chest of drawers. He hoped Skitchy would like the room even with its faded wallpaper.

She was actually a little disappointed but was annoyed with herself for feeling that way. She could see how hard he'd tried to make it nice. She turned things around in her mind. "Pink, you've done so much. Thank you, sugar!"

Lying in bed later, Pink felt happy and was a little amazed by her warm animal pleasure. He said, "I'm so glad our lovemaking's good for you. I've heard sometimes women have a hard time at first."

"I've heard that, too. Maybe it depends on the couple. How much they love each other. Anyway, I'm just fine, and I want us to make love every day!"

"Well, that'd be fun. But I'll need to be up first thing in the mornings and sometimes I'm pretty tired at the end of a hard day." He wished he hadn't said that even before he felt Skitchy's body sag, heard the disappointment in her voice.

"Can't first thing in the morning wait at least a few days?"

Trying to make his voice lighter than he felt, he said, "Well, honey, you married a farmer. A hardscrabble one at that. But we can give ourselves an extra hour tomorrow morning before I get to work."

The rooster woke her before sunup. Skitchy lay close beside the still sleeping Pink. Okay, Skitch, she thought, you can't work this around. You married a farmer. Best get used to being a farmer's wife. She was brightly awake and cheerful by the time Pink woke. After they made love and he'd gone to fix bacon, biscuits and coffee for their breakfast, Skitchy pulled on her dungaree overalls and boots. She presented herself in the kitchen.

"Well, put me to work."

1924

It was a hot day, haze hanging in the air. Pink's heart was singing, he felt so proud as he and Skitchy left the bank in Pecos. They'd brought in a good crop and had just deposited enough money to see them through to the next season. They wouldn't have to borrow from the bank as he had in the past.

"Let's go over to the hotel," he said. "Get something cold to drink to celebrate!"

Skitchy was proud of the work she'd done in the fields and at picking time, working alongside Pink. Proud her work had contributed to the money they'd made. But she didn't feel proud about the crop, as Pink did. Awful lot of work, she thought, and not that much to show for it. Good we won't have to borrow from the bank. Glad about that. But Law, is that the best we can hope for? It pained her to think her father might have been right about cotton farming.

"Something cold sounds great!" she said with as much enthusiasm as she could muster. She didn't know what else to say when her thoughts and feelings were so different from Pink's.

"Next year," Pink said as they drank their lemonade, "we might be able to afford to hire two or three Mexicans to help with the picking. It won't be so hard. Get the crop in earlier, too, that way, and we might get a little better price."

Skitchy looked down at her red rough hands. Being a cotton farmer's wife is different, she thought, than I'd imagined. Well, Skitch, this is what you said you wanted. Best you don't pay any mind to the rest of it.

Making her voice as bright as she could, she said, "Sounds good, sugar. I hope we can do that."

....

Josiah Tieger, Jackson's grandfather, had owned a small hotel in McAllister for years. But when his wife died in the crushing epidemic of flu that began just before the end of the big war and three years of the worst drought in years crippled businesses all over town, he'd lost heart. He'd begun to neglect the hotel. And himself. As he became more erratic and cranky, his family came to see him less and less often.

Except Jackson. Jackson knew Josiah not as a cranky old man, but as the grandfather who encouraged him to do something besides be a rancher or farmer if that's what he wanted. Who taught him to play checkers and dominoes. Who gave Jackson his old Model-T Ford and was always glad to see the young man whenever Jackson drove the thirty miles over the dirt road to McAllister. The two of them would talk and play checkers or dominoes after they ate fried chicken or chicken-fried steak and mashed potatoes and gravy. Josiah always tucked a dollar for gas in Jackson's pocket when it was time for him to say good-bye.

Jackson had been distressed when he saw his grandfather sinking. He didn't know what to do about it except keep coming to see him. But after a time, Josiah no longer talked much or ate much of the fried chicken Jackson brought. Sometimes even their domino game didn't hold his attention. The hotel, built of local stone, was sturdy, but it didn't take long for the dry wind to peel paint from the wood porch, doors and windows. The last of the hotel guests eventually peeled away as well. Finally Josiah had boarded up the front door and windows and lived in a small room next to the kitchen.

One Sunday when Jackson went to see the old man he found his grandfather slumped over the kitchen table, cold coffee spilled on the floor. A scrawled note had been left on the office desk. "I want Jackson to have this place if he wants it. Maybe he can make something of it. Any money in the safe he can have that to help him get started. Josiah Tieger."

There was nothing besides the scrawled note to make anybody wonder if Josiah Tieger had taken his own life. But Jackson would always wonder. It gave him some comfort anyway to think maybe his grandfather had somehow been able, by his own strength of will, to leave a life he no longer wanted to live. One final vigorous act of a once vigorous man.

....

"There was some money in the safe," Jackson told Belle. "With what we've saved, I think we could make a go of it.

We wouldn't have to pay rent. I'd do most of the work to fix it up. How would you feel about living in McAllister?"

"I know how much you've always wanted to be in business for yourself, Jackson. This seems like a wonderful chance for you. For us. Would we not be paying rent because we'd live in the hotel?"

"Grandpa built private quarters off the lobby for himself and Grandma. He stopped living there after she passed away. Rooms need a lot of work but I recollect when they used to be really nice. I'm thinking to get those fixed up for us first. Tackle the rest after that. We'd have to live in not so nice for a while. Wouldn't be like our house here in Pecos. It would be ours though."

"And I can help. I'm not handy with tools but I know how to order supplies. Keep track of things. I used to help Daddy and Buddy with the books for the ranch. I can fetch things and help with clean up. I'll do whatever I can."

Jackson beamed at her. "Can't believe I'm still finding out wonderful surprises about you!" He gathered her in his arms and whispered, "My darling, darling Belle!"

So that afternoon Jackson and Belle decided to move from Pecos to the smaller town of McAllister and go into the hotel business. Jackson quit his job at the Bank of Pecos and on a Sunday early in July, one of the hottest days they'd had all summer, they moved their things into the small room off the kitchen where they would live while Jackson worked on their private quarters.

....

"Got a letter from Belle today," Skitchy told Pink as she put bacon and onions into the beans boiling on the stove.

"They finished the part of the hotel where they're going to live. Ready to start on the rest as soon as they're all moved in. It's gone faster than Jackson had been thinking."

Pink dropped his boots onto the floor and stretched his legs, wriggling his toes. "That's good. They must be happy."

"Sugar, do you think we could ever do anything like that?"

"Anything like what? Fix up an old hotel?"

"Well, no, not fix up an old hotel. They couldn't be doing that if Jackson's grandfather hadn't left him the hotel. I don't know. I mean something that we'd do for ourselves. Something that would be our own."

Pink laughed lightly. "I thought you liked cotton farming."

She turned her face away, not wanting him to see her frown. When she thought the frown was gone she stirred the beans and sat down at the table. "Please don't tease, Pink. I know you don't want to always be a cotton farmer either. In particular not on somebody else's land. I just wonder if we might think about what else we might do someday."

"We don't have enough money to even think about that, Skitchy."

"Well, I was thinking it'd be good if we thought about what we might want to do. I think it would be easier to keep working hard and saving if we had something to save for."

That was the way Ephraim Chapman thought and talked and Pink was pretty sure Skitchy was saying something she'd heard her father say. He sighed deeply. "Maybe, but I'm way too tired to think about that right now."

Skitchy thought about the future almost all the time. She didn't understand why Pink rarely seemed to. She felt annoyed. Well, maybe angry, if she told herself the truth, with no buts about it. Even more angry that he didn't want to even talk about it. She tried to push away those thoughts. After all, they were both working as hard as they could. How could she ask for more than that. She was quiet as they ate their supper of beans and bacon and cornbread. And quiet for a long time afterward.

Pink wanted to say something more to her but he couldn't make his thoughts straight and words wouldn't come. When they were ready for bed, he said as he climbed in beside her, "This old bed sure feels good to a tired man. Good night, honey." He knew he'd disappointed her by not talking about their future. He didn't want to also disappoint her if his hardness wouldn't come.

It wasn't long before Skitchy could tell from his breathing that he'd fallen asleep. She told herself that maybe he was just tired. Made herself swallow the tears that wouldn't listen.

....

Pink was headed north on the old packed dirt farm road that he often took as a shortcut to get home when he saw distant dark clouds rolling toward him and lowering. "Oh-oh," he said aloud, "that doesn't look good. Might be a blue norther!" He stepped on the gas.

Even after all this time living in West Texas, it still surprised him how fast these clouds could move. The rain began before he'd gone another two miles. He stopped the car, rolled down the window curtains. Soon the Model-T was being pelted by a mixture of rain and hail. He drove slowly, leaning forward, peering through the windshield, wishing he could see better.

"Oh, boy!" Pink groaned when he felt the car veer, felt the wheels slip into muddy loam and come to a halt. He got out of the car, pulling his cap down and his sweater around him. "Sure is cold!" His heart sank when he saw the right wheel spokes were buried almost up to the hub. "Well, best to wait in the car." He knew anyone coming by would stop to help.

....

Skitchy sat at the kitchen table, cranky. "You said you'd be back by two. Where in the world are you?" she said aloud to the absent Pink. She took the pot of beans and bacon off the stove, sat the pot down hard on the top of the oven. She put on her heavy jacket and went out to the front porch.

Thunder rumbled as she pulled the door closed against the wind. Looking north she saw the dark rolling clouds. Lightning flashed, flashed again. All around her cotton plants shivered. Soon hail clattered on the metal roof. She peered down the road but could see nothing. Not cranky now, she whispered, "Where in the world are you?"

....

Pink looked at his watch again. It had been two hours since the car got stuck. He'd promised Skitchy to be back long before now. The hail had stopped but rain was pouring down harder than ever. "This country! Ten inches of rain a year and we get all of it in one day!" He sat in the car for another half hour. Still talking to himself, he said, "Okay, Campbell. Better start walking."

....

Pink should've been home hours ago. Skitchy fixed a plate of beans for herself, ate only a few bites. Drank a cup of coffee. She went back out to the porch and stood for a while, willing the Model-T to come into view. Finally, shivering, she went back in the house, pulled the old rocking chair up to the window, wishing that rocking could sooth her as it had when she was a little girl.

....

At first Pink thought he heard a train ahead. But he was nowhere near the rail line. He hadn't even come to Refugio Creek yet. Trudging along the road in the heavy downpour, soaked and cold to the bone, he lifted his eyes now and then to see if he could tell where he was. He was puzzled by the roar. He thought he saw the old bridge over the dry creek bed that would tell him he only had about half a mile to go to the Marshall place. Then it disappeared. Was he hearing things? Seeing things?

He trudged on. Then stopping, he was suddenly alert. He wasn't hearing things. He was close to Refugio Creek. The roar was coming from there. He hurried now, up the slight rise of the bank where the bridge should've been. He'd never seen water in the creek bed but now a rushing torrent of water engorged it from side to side. The torrent swept along rocks and boulders, dead trees, brush, mud, the crumpled skeleton of the old bridge.

Suddenly he felt the wall of the creek collapsing under him. He tried to catch hold of a small mesquite tree but the thorns ripped his hands. He slipped down into the torrent and the force of the swift swollen current grabbed him. He couldn't hold on and felt himself being pulled under. Gasping for breath, he was rolled over and over, pummeled by gravel and debris, careening off boulders and trees.

"Oh, my God!" he cried out before he blacked out.

....

"Pink!" Skitchy screamed. Something was terribly wrong. Terribly wrong the way something had been terribly wrong the day Buddy was thrown by the bronco. She wanted to do something but didn't know what to do. She was alone. Two miles to the nearest neighbor and it was pouring rain as hard as she'd ever seen. And what if no one was there?

She was about to start out anyway when she thought she heard a car outside. She raced to the door. It was a Model-T. But it wasn't their Model-T.

"Belle!"

Belle heard the quaking fright in her sister's voice. "Skitchy! What's wrong?" Belle hurried up the steps, Jackson right behind her. "Honey, what is it?"

"Pink," Skitchy gasped. "He hasn't come home. I feel like the day Buddy . . . I'm so scared . . . I don't know where he is. I'm so worried. Don't know what to do . . . What should I do? Pink! Oh, Pink! Law . . ." Sobs choked her.

Belle glanced at Jackson. He pulled the rocking chair close to the stove. Belle guided her sister into it, kneeling beside her, holding her hands. Jackson stood looking down at the two women, concern written on his face. Skitchy heard him put the coffee pot on the stove. She looked up, suddenly puzzled.

"What are you two doing here? How did you . . ."

"We were on our way home from Pecos when the storm hit," Belle said. "Could see it was a blue norther. You were close so we came here to wait it out."

Seeing Skitchy calmed a little, Jackson spoke urgently. "Skitchy, any idea where Pink might be? Where did he go?"

"He took some tools he borrowed back to Ike Tottle. Planned to stop by Tom Floyd's after that. He said he'd be back by one or two."

"Then maybe he's just waiting it out at Ike's or Tom's."

"Maybe. But I don't think so. We had a little fight . . ." She dropped her eyes, embarrassed. Then, fear stronger than embarrassment, she swallowed hard and went on, "He would've made sure he was back by the time he said. I was mad at first when he didn't come home. Then when I had that awful feeling . . . I'm so scared something's happened to him." She began to shiver.

Belle put her sweater around her sister's shoulders. "Jackson, I think we should listen to Skitchy. If something's happened I could never forgive myself if we didn't try to find him."

Jackson asked, "Skitchy, coming back from Ike's or Tom's, would he come on the main road? Or take the short cut?"

"I think the short cut. Unless the rain had already started. Don't think he would've gone on the old dirt road in heavy rain."

"We came on the main road. Didn't see him. Maybe we just missed him. But if he was on the old road he might have gotten stuck out there in the middle of nowhere. I'm going to see if I can find him."

"We're going with you," Belle said. "Best we're all together and you might need help if he's stuck."

....

Pink came to, caught in the limbs of a greasewood not yet swept away from its precarious place on the wall of the creek. Groaning, he worked his way along the little tree toward the bank. Feeling the small thorns grabbing at him. Praying without words. The rain had almost stopped but the swollen torrent still tore at him. "Hold on, hold on," he whispered urgently. To the little tree. To himself. His foot slipped. He clutched the wet branches, willing himself to ignore the pain in his torn hands. "Hold on." His foot slipped again. This time his boot caught in a branch he could push against. "Hold on. Hold on." He thought he could make it. He pushed hard. His legs failed him. He rested, breathing hard.

"This time." It was a prayer. He pushed again, using all the strength he had left. And he was out! Afraid to rest, he pulled himself away from the creek bank before he let himself collapse on the frigid soaked ground.

....

Pink stirred. Skitchy got up from the chair next to the bed and leaned over him. He looked drawn, his skin was pale. Worried, she smoothed his sandy hair, damp with sweat.

"Pink." No response. "Pink, sugar."

He was badly bruised and scraped. Doc Hartman had said nothing was broken and he didn't think there were internal injuries. He had told them, "He's in greatest danger from exposure to the cold. He may have been lying wet on the cold ground for a long time. It's very important to keep him warm."

Skitchy went to the kitchen where Kate Chapman was heating bricks to wrap and put under Pink's feet, and flannel blankets they were changing every twenty minutes. Skitchy saw her mother working there, brushing sweat away from her forehead. Saw the pallet where she took scraps of sleep. Saw the plate of beans Skitchy had put on the table for her, only half eaten. It's always been like this, Skitchy thought. Mama's always there when someone needs her. Mama, so always there I don't see it. See *her*.

"Mama?"

Kate looked up, again brushing sweat away from her forehead.

Filled with love and appreciation for her mother, Skitchy said warmly, "Thank you for being here, Mama. Thank you for all you're doing for Pink. For both of us."

"Glad I can help, sugar." Kate believed the good Lord had put her on earth to serve others. Serving others satisfied something deep within her and had seemed the most natural thing in the world to her for as long as she could remember. Particular joy came from serving the ones she held closest to her heart. The depth of feeling in Skitchy's voice touched her mother's heart where she stored such things, and she returned Skitchy's warm smile. They looked at each other for a long moment both would remember and hold dear. Then what needed to be done called Kate's attention. She put the warmed blanket in Skitchy's hands.

"He moved a little when I spoke to him," Skitchy said. "Didn't look like he heard me, though."

"He's had a lot of laudanum, sugar. Keep talking to him. He can probably hear you and that'll do him good."

....

"Skitchy?"

Startled from half-sleep, she leapt from the chair.

"Pink! Pink sugar!" She sat carefully on the bed beside him. She'd told herself not to cry but disobedient tears burst from their well. He tried to reach for her. She put her cheek against his, afraid to get too close and hurt him. He turned his head to kiss her cheek. His lips found hers, softly.

"Lay with me, honey."

When they woke, late-day sunlight slanted through the window.

"I'm hungry," Pink said, more alert than he'd been before.

"I'll get you some soup. Mama fixed beef soup and left it for you."

"I thought I remembered your mama being here."

"She's been helping so much to take care of you. She's about the best nurse in the county."

After she fed him the soup, Pink lay back on the pillows. "I don't know what happened after I got out of the creek. How did I get home?"

"Jackson and Belle came here." Pink looked surprised. "They'd been in Pecos. Came to get out of the storm on their way back to McAllister. We all went to see if we could find you. When we found the car on the old road, Jackson figured you must've started walking. Then we saw the Refugio bridge down. So much water in the creek. We were afraid . . ." Her voice choked on a sob and trailed off.

He held out his hand to her. She took it, squeezed it tight. "I was scared, too," he said softly. "More scared than I've ever been in my life."

"We all got the car out of the mud, then I drove to the ranch to get Daddy. He brought horses."

"You drove? By yourself?"

"Uh-huh. The rain had almost stopped. I was sure I could do it. I told Jackson I could do it. And I did. Jackson went to get Ike Tottle. You know Ike always comes with his dogs when somebody's lost."

"I thought I remembered dogs."

"By the time we all got back the water had gone down enough for Ike and the dogs to search the creek. Daddy rode on one side of the creek, Jackson on the other. Looking for you. Word got around, I guess. Tom Floyd and Billy Dan Simpson and Robbie Hitchens came to help cover more ground. But the dogs found you. When they started barking, that's how Daddy found you."

"I'm grateful," Pink sighed. "I'm so grateful to everybody. And grateful to God."

"Grateful isn't nearly a big enough word." A sob caught in her throat. "My brother Harrison drowned in the creek when he was little, Pink. They say hardly anybody has ever been caught in Refugio Creek and lived. Sometimes they don't ever find people. They wash down the creek to the river and down the river to the Gulf." She grew very still and very quiet as she sat looking at him.

You've been silly, she told herself. Making so much of not liking cotton farming. Not enough planning for the future. Not enough lovemaking. He's alive and that's what matters. That makes up for an awful lot of things. She lit a cigarette for him and put it to his mouth. Then lit one for herself.

"You're smoking."

"Uh-huh."

1925

Late in the afternoon, work finished for the day, Belle and Jackson sat sipping ice tea in the shade on the hotel porch. Belle was grateful for a light breeze after a hot, still day. She put a cigarette into her silver and bone holder and he lit it for her. She smiled at him, then grew quiet as she sat smoking the cigarette.

After a few minutes Jackson said, "What is it, honey?"

"Oh, I was thinking about Skitchy and Pink. Got a letter from her yesterday. The widow woman who owns the farm passed away and her family in Louisiana wants to sell the land. Some oil wildcatters want to buy it. You know that well came in at Big Lake. Guess somebody thinks there might be oil up there around those farms, too."

"Do they know what they're going to do?"

"No, not really. They can't afford to buy the land even if they wanted to. But it sounds to me like they've had enough of cotton farming. Skitchy has anyway." She sat quietly again, deep in thought. When she looked up, she saw that he was waiting for her. She took a long draw on her cigarette, drank the last of her tea. "I was thinking maybe we could ask them to come here. They could work for us. Lot of work still to be done to get the hotel ready to open and it would give them a chance to save up some. They're hard workers, both of them. Skitchy's often said Pink's good at fixing things. Might surprise you how handy Skitchy is. I was thinking maybe they could live in that room off the kitchen we lived in at first as part of their pay. When a room upstairs is ready, they could move up there. What do you think?" She put out her cigarette. Her eyes followed Jackson as he stood up, stretched. Paced back and forth on the porch.

"Do you think Pink would take help from us? He's so dadgum proud."

"I think he might if we put it that they'd be a big help to us." She put another cigarette in her holder and as he came to her to light it she added, "And it seems to me it surely would be a big help to us. We could open the hotel sooner."

There had been talk around McAllister about drilling for oil nearby. If that happened, which Jackson believed it would, there would be lots of business for the hotel from the oil men and maybe some of the field workers, too. He'd been thinking about opening the hotel even if they weren't completely ready. With help from Pink and Skitchy they might be able to open sooner than he'd hoped.

Jackson stopped pacing, looked at his wife. Softly, but with enthusiasm, he said, "That's just what we should do! Sweetheart, I'm going to fix us a bourbon and soda!"

....

Skitchy had the jitters as she and Pink drove into McAllister. She'd been in the town before. Quite a few times in fact. But she'd never given a thought to what it might be like to live there. She noticed for what seemed the first time how much smaller it was than Pecos, the dirt main street narrower, downtown only two blocks long. She could see a church up ahead and a patch of green that she supposed must be the small park Belle had mentioned in her letters. She could see houses beyond the downtown and on side streets. The hotel was near the train station, a sturdy stone building with its bleached sign badly in need of paint.

"Well, here we are, sugar," she said. She glanced at Pink but was unable to read anything about what he might be feeling. "Oh, there's Belle!"

Belle had been sitting by the lobby window, sewing as she watched for them. Worried when they were so late arriving, she came outside quickly when she saw their Model-T pull up in front of the hotel.

"Come on in. It's much cooler inside and I've got some lemonade made. Jackson's gone to the post office. He'll help you unload the car when he gets back. Come on in now. Make yourselves at home."

It was indeed cooler in the lobby, out of the heat and with a ceiling fan stirring the air. Looking around, Skitchy noticed the oak counter and stairs, pressed tin ceiling, patched walls ready for painting, a pot bellied stove against the back wall, a settee and chairs, some of them covered with old sheets. It was nicer than she'd expected. Jackson and Belle had obviously already done a great deal of work.

"Feels good to finally be here. We had two flat tires!"

"That's aggravating," Belle said, her voice sympathetic. "Well, you can get a good rest now. We want you to take as much time as you need to get settled. Come and let me show you your room." She pointed out Jackson's office as they passed it, and took them through the kitchen. "Use the kitchen anytime."

The small room off the kitchen was the same room where Belle and Jackson had lived until they finished work on their new quarters. Belle had made new curtains and insisted on painting it Skitchy's favorite shade of green to make it as nice as possible for her sister. "Here you are! Hope you'll be comfortable. Please be sure to let me know if there's anything you need."

Skitchy heard the pride and also the warmth in Belle's voice. She hadn't realized how much she'd missed her sister. Dear Belle. Proud, loving, lovable Belle. "Everything looks just wonderful." She turned and hugged her sister. "I can't say a big enough thank you."

"Yes, thank you," Pink added, suddenly aware that he'd said nothing in the swirl of arrival and greeting and affection between the sisters. "We both really appreciate everything, Belle."

....

Later, alone in their new room amidst suitcases and boxes, Skitchy and Pink looked at each other for a long silent moment before they moved toward each other. Pink took her in his arms and after a time said, "I told you when we were first married I hoped you'd be happy in our home together. I still wish for that, even here."

She tightened her arms around his waist. "I hope you'll be happy, too. I know coming here hasn't been easy for you."

When he began to release his arms, Skitchy could tell that his mood had shifted. "Can you believe we had all this stuff in the car?" he said, looking at the boxes and laughing. She could hear fatigue in his voice.

"I'm worn out," she said, wanting to make it easier for him. "Let's wait to start unpacking until tomorrow. Just get out what we need for tonight. All right, sugar?"

"Sounds good to me. I'm tired, too. It was a pretty big day."

"You bet!" Skitchy said. "Much bigger than any in a good long while!"

....

Two days later they were working upstairs with Jackson, patching holes in the walls, repairing the floor and windows, painting the first room at the top of the stairs. Belle worked downstairs where it was cooler, making curtains for the windows.

As they worked, Jackson told them, "Twice someone has come in wanting a room even though anyone could see we weren't open yet. One man paid fifty cents to have a bath and sleep on the floor of the lobby with his bedroll. So I'm tickled to be getting this room finished. If someone's willing to put up with the rest of the mess I surely don't want to turn away a paying customer.

"Makes sense," Pink agreed. "It all makes so much sense. How you've figured out the work, Jackson."

Obviously in a light hearted mood, Jackson went on, "Took all this time to get as much done downstairs as we have. I can hardly believe how fast the work is going on this room, with all three of us. I want to do those two rooms at the back next, the ones that look out at the garden. Connect them with a door. Thought you two could move in there as soon as they're ready. Then figure out what to do with that room downstairs where you are now." Laughing, he said, "You two will be the first to occupy the bridal suite. Or the senatorial suite. Or the anything-the-person-who-rents-it-wants-to-call-it suite. For now we'll call it the Campbell suite!"

That night Pink said, "It was fun working with Jackson today. I've always thought he was so serious. I didn't realize he had a sense of humor."

Surprised, Skitchy looked up. "Course he does. He has a very serious side and he's very hard working. But he surely likes to have fun, too. I think he's a wonderful man."

Pink was a little startled and wondered why he winced when Skitchy said that.

....

"Merry Christmas, everybody!" Belle smiled happily as she plugged in the lights on the Christmas tree in the hotel lobby to applause from everyone gathered around. Jackson thought she looked beautiful in a bright blue silk dress with a pleated skirt and tiny buttons down the front, her bobbed hair waved in the new style.

When Jackson had said, "I'm going to have a big cedar brought down from the mountains for the grand opening," Belle had gasped, hardly able to believe they could have such a thing.

"On the ranch we had all-thorn bushes for Christmas trees. Stuck a cranberry on each thorn. Don't mind telling you stuck our fingers, too." She laughed lightly, remembering. "We popped corn, strung it on thread. Draped the strings around and tied colored ribbons or yarn on." As they stood arm in arm when they had finished decorating the cedar, admiring the blue, red, and green lights, shiny colored balls, and silvery tinsel, tears came into her eyes. "Jackson, this is the most beautiful Christmas tree I've ever seen in all my life!"

There was also a big pressed glass bowl of red apples on a table covered with green felt topped with a lace tablecloth, along with platters of cookies. Folding card tables had been set up with cards, dominoes, checkers, and jigsaw puzzles for the enjoyment of their guests, many of them friends invited for the evening. The festive mood was just what Jackson had wanted to create. He watched from the side of the room with great satisfaction. "There are people from town who'll want to see what we've done," he'd said. "We'll have the first paying guests staying in the hotel." Just as he'd planned, all ten guest rooms were full.

After most of the guests had gone home or to their rooms, a few friends stayed on. The men took off their coats and ties and Jackson brought out bourbon and brandy as everyone sat around the Christmas tree. The country was still engaged in what Jackson derided as the "noble experiment" of Prohibition. But as he explained to Belle, "You can get most any kind of alcohol you want if you pay cash for it and don't thumb your nose at the sheriff." The mellow mood lasted well into the evening.

When everything was put away and they were alone, just before Jackson unplugged the Christmas tree lights, he took Belle in his arms. They danced in the happy silence of the lobby.

....

When Jackson had served drinks for those who stayed late, he'd known Pink would decline the alcohol but offered it, out of courtesy, along with coffee.

"Thanks, Jackson," Pink had said, taking one of the coffee cups.

When he came to Skitchy with the tray of drinks and cups of coffee, Jackson said, "I think anybody who's worked as hard as you have to make the grand opening happen should have anything she wants to drink."

"Why, that's cordial of you, sir!" She had drunk one bourbon and soda and part of another, laughing and flushed with pleasure, even though the taste was much stronger and not as pleasant as she'd imagined it would be. She had soon felt tipsy, much to her annoyance.

"I'm just going to lie down for a little while," she told Pink. "Then I'll be back." But she hadn't come back. Pink found her sleeping soundly on their bed, still wearing her new dark green taffeta and net dress, matching stockings and new pumps.

Alcohol was one of many things forbidden in the strict Presbyterian home in which Pink had grown up. Dancing and card playing for fun were no longer forbidden as he saw it, but alcohol was different. When Skitchy had asked him why he didn't drink, he had replied, "I don't think it's right."

Pink wished Skitchy wouldn't drink either. He'd been taken by surprise when Jackson had offered her bourbon. He'd said nothing. She was glad and said nothing more about it either. But after that, she drank whenever she wanted to.

1926

"Honey, I want to make a dining room between the lobby and the kitchen. Good business to serve meals," Jackson told Belle. "I'd like to hire Reba Borden to do the cooking. She's that black woman who used to work for Horace Lee Johnson before he sold his café. They say her biscuits and pies are the best in town."

"I think that's a wonderful idea, Jackson."

"She has a young boy. Hutch. She takes him with her when she works. Would you mind if he was around? Be with her in the kitchen most of the time. She says he knows how to help her in the kitchen."

"That sounds fine."

"I'd like to hire her now then. She's looking for work and might not be later on, when the dining room's ready. She can cook for us in the meantime."

Belle smiled. "A cook! Well, we've come up in the world, haven't we? Law, I recollect Mama cooked three meals a day on a wood stove. For a half dozen ranch hands, for a long while, besides our family. Before Daddy built the new bunkhouse and cookhouse. Did you ever dream, Jackson, that everything would work out so well for us here?"

"Well, honey, to tell you the truth, I dreamed about it. Didn't know it'd actually happen, though. Everything just seems to have fallen into place. I'm so grateful to my grandfather."

"I'm grateful to your grandfather, too, for giving us a start. But honey, this is your doing, all that's happened since we came here. I'm so proud of you!"

"I'm proud of us both. Couldn't have done it without you. That sounds so corny, but I really mean it. Thank you for all you've done, my darling sweetheart."

Belle took out her bone and silver cigarette holder. When she didn't find a cigarette in her apron pocket, Jackson took the holder from her. He put a cigarette from the pack in his shirt pocket into the holder and handed it back to her, lit it.

"One day I want you to have a gold holder. Or any kind of beautiful holder you want."

"That's so sweet, honey. But you probably don't know Daddy bought this holder for me in Fort Worth, for my eighteenth birthday. I wanted a holder so much. But everybody teased me about it. Said I was vain for wanting to smoke with a holder, things like that. Except Daddy. They all shut up when he gave me this one. It means so much to me, I don't know if I could ever use a different one."

"Well, how about if you don't have to use a different one? You can have two. Use whichever one strikes you at the moment."

"That'd be the height of luxury," she said laughing. "Like having a cook!"

....

"Pink," Jackson said one cloudy morning as the two men worked to enlarge the chicken coop behind the hotel. "I want to make a dining room between the kitchen and the lobby. Be much obliged if you and Skitchy would stay on. Help me with that."

Pink stopped his hammer in mid-air and looked up, surprised. "Really? I thought we were getting close to done here."

"I can hire someone else if you want to move on. Never mean to take your work for granted. But you've come to be like my right hand around here. And I know Belle and Skitchy love being around each other. Be hard when you leave."

"I've thought about that, too," Pink said. "Leaving being hard, I mean."

"What are your plans?"

"We don't really have any plans. Just talked about some things. I wanted to go to college before the war. I thought I might be a veterinarian. Growing up on a farm it was always the animals I was interested in and liked taking care of. I talked to Doc Vroman in Pecos, thinking maybe he could use an assistant but he said he couldn't." Pink couldn't believe he was talking to Jackson about these things. He hadn't even talked to Skitchy about these things. But the words had tumbled out and it felt good.

"I'd never have guessed that," Jackson said. "But then the last thing in the world I wanted to do was be a rancher like my father so I don't think along those lines. About animals, I mean."

"What would you have done if your grandfather hadn't left you the hotel?"

"I'm not sure. I always dreamed of being in business for myself. But hard to imagine I could ever have done it without my grandfather's help. He left me some money besides the hotel. That was a really big help getting started. Don't know if you know about that."

"No, I didn't."

"And maybe even more important, he always encouraged me to do what I really wanted to. I don't know if I could've done that on my own, either. My father discouraged me pretty much. Said I was a dreamer. What would I actually have done if I'd just had myself to rely on? I don't know. I liked my job at the bank. Most likely I'd have just stayed there."

Pink grew quiet, suddenly feeling overwhelmed with the unfairness of Jackson's good fortune contrasted with his own lot in life. "Not all of us have been as lucky as you, Jackson." He hated hearing the biting tone in his voice but couldn't help it.

Puzzled, Jackson looked at Pink. "That's true, of course. Lots of things in life seem unfair. I'm very grateful for my good fortune. Think the best way I can show it, say thank you to my grandfather, is to use what he gave me well. I think he'd be proud of what I'm doing."

"I'm sure he would. Everything you do seems to turn out well."

The way Pink said the words made them sound like criticism to Jackson and he felt himself withdraw. After a moment, he said, "Have I offended you in some way, Pink? Surely didn't mean to."

Pink's voice softened a little but still had an edge to it. "No, Jackson, no offense. Not at all. I think maybe I just need to think over some things about what I want to do."

Jackson had no idea what had happened to turn Pink so irritable. He thought the best thing to do was to leave the man to himself. "I need to tend to some things," he said, keeping his tone as even as he could. "Can you finish up here?"

....

The next morning Pink knocked on the door of Jackson's office. "Can I talk to you for a minute?"

"Of course. Come on in." Jackson felt a bit wary but this morning Pink sounded more like the Pink Jackson was used to. "Have a seat."

"I came to apologize, Jackson. Don't know what got into me yesterday. I really appreciated our talk. I'm impressed with what you've done here and I feel awful to think I may have damaged what Skitchy and I have here with you and Belle."

"No damage. Not as far as I'm concerned." Jackson held out his hand. "Let's just not pay it any mind."

Shaking Jackson's hand, Pink felt relieved that his sour words yesterday had not angered Jackson. "Skitchy and I would like to stay and help with the rest of the work if that's still all right."

"You bet."

Jackson sat at his desk after Pink left the office, hoping he'd done the right thing. Probably best to not pay it any mind, he thought, as he'd said. But he resolved to be more careful about showing Pink his cards.

....

The dining room opened for Thanksgiving. Jackson had hired Martita Morales in early October to do the hotel laundry and help with housekeeping. He taught her how he wanted customers to be served in the dining room. A sign on the boardwalk outside the hotel advertised Thanksgiving dinner, and he put an ad in the *Enterprise.* Reba Borden's reputation as a cook was pretty well known in McAllister. The tables were full.

The Tiegers and Campbells ate Thanksgiving dinner after all the guests had left, amid much toasting to the success of the new venture.

"And a particular toast," the host beamed, "to you, Skitchy and Pink. Obliged to you both for how hard you've worked to make this all happen by Thanksgiving. It couldn't have happened without you." He and Belle and Skitchy drank their brandy and Pink his coffee.

....

As Belle and Jackson got ready for bed, Belle was thoughtful. "Jackson, there's something I want to talk to you about. If you're not too worn out."

"Not too worn out if you have something on your mind, honey. What is it?"

"What would you think about having Skitchy and Pink stay on? Skitchy told me they haven't saved quite enough to get started somewhere else. Seems like Pink's been a big help with work around the place. At the front desk, too, and doing things for guests when you're busy."

Jackson hesitated. He hadn't told Belle about what had happened when he'd asked Pink to stay on to help with the work on the dining room. Nothing like that had happened since. In fact, everything seemed to be going very smoothly and Pink was working harder than ever.

"I am going to need the help. Things have gone much better and much faster than I figured. It's been a godsend to have him. Skitchy, too. I'd have needed to hire another Mexican girl to help Martita if Skitchy wasn't here. And I can see you and Skitchy love being together. I'll talk to Pink."

....

"Jackson asked me today if we'd stay on," Pink said as he got undressed. "He says he still needs help and I can see he does. It'd be good for us to save up more before we move on. I think we should do it, much as I hate to."

Skitchy was already in bed, wishing Pink would hurry up so she could snuggle close to him and warm herself. "I'm so cold, sugar. Come get in bed. Then let's talk." When he had climbed in beside her and they were lying close together, she said, "Staying on seems like a good idea to me, too, sugar. Why do you say you hate to?"

"Well, I was glad to have the work when we had to move from the farm. But I'm not crazy about working for Jackson, to tell you the truth."

"Why? Thought you liked him."

"I don't like working for him. I feel beholden. I'd rather get my own job, know that no one's doing us a favor."

"I don't see that Jackson's doing us a favor. You just said yourself you can see he needs help around the place. He'd probably just hire someone else."

"You're saying pretty much the same things I've said to myself. Living here we can save more than we could any place else where we'd have to pay regular rent. And I don't have anything else in mind yet anyway. I think we should stay."

"Fine with me." Skitchy scowled there in the dark, confused by the things Pink said, wondering at how little she seemed to understand him sometimes.

....

Everyone gathered by the registration counter to watch the telephone being installed, then went behind the counter to admire it sitting grandly on the desk, touch it.

"Imagine being able to just pick up the telephone and talk to someone all the way across town!" Skitchy exclaimed. "What's the world coming to!"

"I don't think it'll be too long before most everybody has a telephone," Jackson said. "It *is* what the world's coming to."

Later he told Belle, "The telephone's a wonderful thing for us, honey. So glad McAllister finally got service. It's not just a convenience. Some people will call ahead. Make sure we have a room. Much easier for me to order things. I think it's going to be great for business."

"Law, Jackson, it's wonderful! I'm so proud!"

....

Jackson took a rare picture of Kate and Ephraim Chapman in their Sunday clothes, standing arm in arm in front of the windmill and cistern near their ranch house.

Later, when she looked at the picture, Skitchy noticed both her parents looked worn and tired. She wondered that she'd not noticed that before.

Minnie and Bob had come two days before and planned to stay until tomorrow. Skitchy and Pink and Belle and Jackson had driven to the Chapman ranch from McAllister. They planned to stay for the noon meal and dishes poker before driving home again in time for Jackson to be at the hotel desk by the end of the day. It didn't happen often now that they were all together and Skitchy thought the day felt special. Jackson took another picture of all of them gathered on the front porch before they went in to enjoy the meal of fried chicken, mashed potatoes and gravy, peas, and Minnie's bread pudding, a favorite of everyone in the family.

The day took an unexpected turn, however, when the meal was over. Ephraim announced, "No poker today. Let's just get these dishes done. Go out on the porch and sit a while in the shade. It's a nice afternoon since the wind died down."

Everyone knew he must have something on his mind and pitched in with the dishes and general clean up. Skitchy thought his voice had sounded solemn. She wanted to know what Belle thought but Belle was talking with Minnie as they went outside.

"No easy way to say this so I'll just say it straight out," Ephraim said when everyone was settled on the porch. "We're pondering on selling the ranch." His facial expression and tone of voice were serious but not solemn now, Skitchy noticed.

She looked at her mother but Mama's eyes were on her husband. Skitchy could read nothing in her unchanged body posture and facial expression. She thought that probably meant this was going hard with Mama. She was used to her mother's taciturn manner when something was difficult for her.

"Daddy!" Belle gasped. "Why?" She knew how they felt about this place. They'd settled here when the land was almost all open range. They'd fought off ordinary and severe droughts, dust storms, and two raids by renegade Apaches. Four children had been lost here and were buried in this county. Belle thought her parents were like the mesquites. The tough little trees put down roots deep enough to reach ground water, sometimes seventy-five feet, people said. Any rancher or farmer who'd ever tried to wrest them from the land knew how tenaciously each one clung to its place.

Jackson's face turned serious but he said nothing. Minnie and Bob did not look surprised and said nothing.

Skitchy had seen things on visits since her marriage she hadn't noticed when she still lived on the ranch. For several years her father had hired more ranch hands than in earlier years. His step had become steadily slower. She'd seen that something else wasn't the same as when Buddy was alive, working alongside his father, learning all he'd need to know when it was his job to run the ranch. Some of Daddy's zest for life had gone out of him.

Ephraim stood and stretched his tall lanky body, walked to the edge of the porch and back again. "An oil company wants to buy the ranch."

Everybody knew about the first well in Howard County, two years later a big strike at Big Lake, followed shortly by a gusher at Santa Rita. None of those strikes was that close to the Chapman ranch, but that didn't seem to dampen excitement about oil all around the area.

"They're offering a fair price for the land and shares in the company. If they find oil, we'd come out way ahead." Ephraim paused. When nobody said anything he added, "And you know we're not getting any younger. Time for us to get along."

They all knew that Ephraim and Kate had already talked it over, had already decided together, or if Eph decided, Kate would stand firmly by his side. Otherwise Eph wouldn't have brought it up. That was their way.

1927

Tom Floyd's band was playing near McAllister and he stopped by the hotel to visit with Pink. Jackson met him as Tom came in to the lobby.

"Pink's working out back," Jackson said. "I'll let him know you're here." Jackson's voice was cordial, as was his habit, even though he didn't think all that much of Tom. "Like some ice tea?"

"You bet. Something cold would surely taste fine on such a hot day," Tom responded.

"I'll ask Pink to bring it out. So long, Tom."

After Tom and Pink settled on the hotel porch, Tom noticed Pink's slight frown.

"Anything wrong, buddy?"

"I get sick of Jackson sometimes. Or maybe I'm just sick of myself. He bought the drugstore a few doors down when the owner died. He's putting in a soda fountain now to bring in more customers. I've no doubt that's just what it'll do. Just like how well everything's going with the hotel. Everything he touches seems to turn to gold and I feel like I'm marching in place. I hate it that I'm still working for him. I'd like to get clean out of this town!"

"Dang! Wondered about you and Skitchy staying here so long. Had no idea you felt like this, though."

Pink stood up abruptly. He looked down the street at dust eddying in little swirls. His eyes met Tom's briefly before he looked away again. "I don't know, Tom. I felt alive during the war. I was scared sometimes, sure, but I felt like a man. It seemed like I was part of something that really mattered. It just wasn't the same when I came home. I thought it was because I needed to get off my folks' farm." He laughed sourly, "And my mother drove me crazy." He sat back down. "I thought it'd be different striking out on my own down here, but cotton farming was rough when you couldn't count on enough rain when you needed it. Things picked up when I met Skitchy, but since we came to McAllister I feel as dry and lifeless as this dang country around here."

"What about Skitchy? How does she feel?"

"She's very happy here. She's made friends and she loves being with Belle. I haven't told her how much I hate it, just talked about moving on when we can. But I don't know what I'd do. And the more time goes by, I don't know if I can ask her to give up everything she loves here for something I'm not even sure about myself. I feel trapped, Tom."

"Well, you bet women complicate things," Tom mused, half laughing, half serious. He pulled a pack of cigarettes out of his pocket, offering one to Pink. "Alma won't marry me unless I quit going all over with the band. I love that woman but I sure can't see myself settled down in the middle of nowhere with a wife and kids. Going no place."

"What're you saying, Tom? Are you thinking about maybe going someplace else?"

"You bet." Tom had said more than he meant to, but now that it was out, his face hardened and he went on in a terse voice, "First chance I get. I'm dadgum sick of West Texas!" He took a long draw on his cigarette.

"I'm sick of it, too." Pink looked as if he'd startled himself saying that, as he in fact had.

"Looks like we both have a lot to figure out."

....

"Pink, I'm real late this month. I feel sick to my stomach almost every morning. I wonder if maybe I'm going to have a baby, sugar."

"Really? After all this time?"

"I'm not sure. But I think maybe. I talked to Emily. She's my best friend in McAllister and I can talk to her about things like that. And she has four kids so she knows how it is. She thinks maybe I'm pregnant. I think I should find out for sure. I'd need two dollars for the midwife."

"I think you should find out."

Later, when he was alone, Pink felt joy and dismay. Joy that maybe he and Skitchy were going to have a family after all, an idea he'd just about let go of after four years married. Dismay that if he had a family to take care of, he might be stuck in McAllister for a long time. Working for Jackson.

....

Skitchy came bursting into the hotel lobby late the next afternoon. She took Pink's hand, pulled him from behind the counter and hurried upstairs. "Well, you're going to be a daddy," Skitchy said, grinning, as soon as they came into the room and closed the door.

Not sure what to do, he put his arms around her carefully and kissed her. "Can I hug you? Do I need to be careful?"

"No, silly, not that careful. Law, Pink! Isn't this just about the biggest surprise in the world?"

"It is surely that."

....

As Skitchy had burst in the front door of the hotel, Hutch Borden had burst in the back door, sobbing. There was no sweetness in the sweet big eyes that usually lit up his dark face. The young boy's clothes were torn and his face and hair were bloodied, his right eye was hugely swollen. One of his shoes was missing.

"Hutch!" Reba knelt beside him, wiping his face with her apron. "Honey, what's happened?"

"Some white boys chased me after school. I couldn't run fast enough. They caught me in the field I go across to get home. Two of them held me. The others started hitting me with sticks. Calling me names. One boy had a baseball bat. They said I shouldn't be going to school. Oh, Mama, it hurt so bad." He began sobbing again.

Reba's thin face was stone and her voice calm. Her mind and heart were racing. "Anything hurt inside you? Not feel right?" She ran her hands over his arms and legs. "Anything hurt when I touch it?"

"It's mostly my eye that hurts." Through his sobs he said, "Mama, they said they'd keep after me if I keep going to school. But I want to go to school. I like learning things. I like going to school.

"I'll talk to you about that in a bit. Right now we need to take care of your eye. Get you cleaned up. Later on we'll go see if we can find your shoe."

Later, Reba sat beside the pallet she'd made up for him in the kitchen so she could keep a close eye on him. As she changed the cold cloth on his eye, she said, "Hutch, honey, some white people don't think it's all right for black people to go to school. As long as you were going to the black school it was all right with most people. But when the black school burned down and the white teacher wanted to change things and said black children could go to school with the white children, there was bound to be trouble."

"Can't I go to school anymore?"

"I have a good job here with Mr. and Mrs. Tieger. We don't want to make any trouble. Not for them and not for us. I was afraid for you to go to the white school even when they said you could but I swallowed being afraid so you could learn something. We had to try. But nothing's changed, honey. You make trouble by going to school, they're going to hurt you. Try to fight back, they're going to hurt you more. Maybe kill you. It's not fair but it's never been fair for black people. My daddy was a buffalo soldier in the United States Army after he was a free man. His black regiment kept this part of Texas safe for white people when the Apaches didn't want them settling here. But his children, your Uncle Moses and me, still couldn't go to school. For sure not with white children. Nothing's changed."

Hutch was quiet as Reba changed the cold cloth on his eye again. After a time he looked at her with tears in his open eye and deep sadness in his voice. "Surely would like to go to school but I don't want to make trouble."

"If anyone asks you what happened to your eye, or anything about what happened, you say you tripped and fell."

"Mama, you and Preacher always say it's wrong to tell a lie."

"Isn't telling a lie, honey, when you tell white people a story they'd rather hear than the truth, if that's what it takes to stay safe."

"Even Mr. Tieger and Mrs. Tieger and Mr. Campbell and Mrs. Campbell?"

"Even them, honey. You can never be sure what any white person will do if they think a black person is too uppity. Even if it'd be all right with one or two of them, best tell them all the same story. Just to be safe."

Reba sighed as Hutch grew quiet and fell asleep finally. To the sleeping child she said very softly, "Law, a hard kind of school today, honey."

....

"Hutch says he tripped and fell," Belle said to Jackson. "His eye looks terrible. He rolled his sleeves down when he saw me looking at the welts on his arms. The whole story doesn't make much sense to me." Belle was scowling as she waited for Jackson to gather his thoughts.

"I'm surely sorry about what happened to Hutch. But I don't think we should get involved."

"He's just a little boy. I'd hate to think someone hurt him like that on purpose. Does look that way to me, though."

"Think Reba beat him?"

"Law no, I don't think that for a minute. I don't think Reba would ever do that. I think they're afraid to say who did it. He hasn't gone to school the last two days. Said he isn't going to go any more. Surely didn't want to talk to me about it. He could hardly wait to get out of the kitchen and go work in the garden even when it was obvious it hurt him to move. Reba doesn't say anything."

A shadow passed over Jackson's face. His voice was dark as he said, "Ever since the little black school burned down out there and they said any black children that wanted to could go to the white school, I've been expecting trouble. Lots of people think the races shouldn't mix like that. They're bound to make it hard on the ones that do try to mix. Belle, Reba works for us. They could even make it hard on us if we try to do anything about this. I have to ask you to trust me about this. We should stay out of it."

....

Skitchy sat in Jackson's office with Jackson and Belle, the door closed. "The swelling's gone down now," Skitchy said. "But Reba told me this morning she's afraid Hutch is going to be blind in that eye. Just makes me sick, this whole thing."

Jackson said, his voice even. "Unfortunately there isn't much we can do about it."

"I think Reba knows who did it. She wouldn't tell me, but I'm pretty sure she knows. Can't the sheriff do something?"

"Skitchy, this is a sorry business. Most white people won't tolerate it if they think blacks or Mexicans over-step their place. They'll stop it any way they can. When I used to come to McAllister to visit with my grandfather, there was a café down the street. People could also get food and take it out. I used to pick up fried chicken there sometimes. Bring it right here to this hotel. The man who owned the café started letting black people come in the front door to pick up food instead of going around to the back, even eat there in the café. They warned him. He didn't stop and they burned the place down. I recollect walking down there with my grandfather to see it after the fire. It's where the boot maker's shop and shoe repair is now."

Belle gasped. "I didn't know any of that."

"Neither did I," Skitchy echoed.

"Never wanted to frighten you. Almost all of this kind of thing happens where most of us don't see it. If Reba wasn't working for us, we probably wouldn't know anything about what happened to Hutch. I don't know anything about what happened to the black people who went to the café or tried to eat there. But mark my words, what happened to the café owner was meant to be a big message for everyone doing business in town. Surely was for my grandfather. He warned me when we were standing there looking at the burned out café. I haven't forgotten his warning. It's why I don't want to try to do anything about Hutch. Not about what happened to him or what's going to happen about school for him."

Skitchy sat quietly. Part of her wanted to take a stand for Hutch. She liked him and she liked Reba. She didn't like the unfairness of it all or remaining silent while the unfairness was allowed to stand. But another part of her heard how much could be at stake for Jackson and Belle. And for her and Pink for that matter, since they worked for Jackson. And no ifs, ands or buts about it, for Reba and Hutch.

Finally she said with resignation, "I see what you mean when you say this is a sorry business, Jackson. I'm glad you're the one who has to decide. I hate having to decide about hard things."

1928

Skitchy moved the blanket to look at the sleeping sweetness of her newborn daughter. She was still deeply tired but tried to smile at Pink. He stood beside the bed, gazing down at his rosy baby girl and pale wife.

It had been a difficult birth but memories of the long hours of pain, the danger and fear, had already begun to fade. Kate Chapman smiled at her daughter as she straightened the covers.

Skitchy smiled back as best she could through deep fatigue. She was grateful that her mother was there. Grateful that she'd been there, rubbing her back, encouraging her, knowing what needed doing at every turn and doing it, welcoming the first cry of new life, lovingly laying the newborn child in her arms. "Thank you, Mama," the new mother whispered.

"You need sleep now, sugar."

The last doctor in McAllister had died in the flu epidemic ten years before. Kate Chapman had been midwife to many women in the county and Skitchy would have wanted her mother to midwife the birth of her child even if a doctor had been in town. Kate took the baby, nodded at Pink as she passed. He, along with everyone else, credited her with saving the life of both mother and baby. "Thank you, Kate," he said softly.

He kissed Skitchy on the forehead. "Get some sleep now, honey."

Skitchy wanted to sleep, but thoughts tumbled in her head. She thought she might not have children. Her friends Emily and Brin both told her she could keep from getting pregnant if she got up right away after making love and douched, with vinegar in the douche water. Skitchy had never done that. She wanted children. And besides, she loved lovemaking and loved to lie close to Pink afterward until they both fell asleep. Belle and Jackson didn't have children either and Belle was happy. So as the years had passed, Skitchy figured she could be happy, too, even without children. But now Constance Alice Campbell had arrived after all. As Skitchy felt relief and happiness seep through her weary body, she turned over and let sleep overtake her.

....

"Pink, I want to go with you when you take Mama home," Skitchy said.

"Well, that's fine, honey, if your mama thinks it's all right for you to go."

"I already talked to her. She says it's time I got out some."

When they sold their ranch the Chapmans had bought a small hotel in Kermit. Skitchy liked the town. Some buildings looked a lot like the ones in McAllister or Pecos but the new ones, built since oil was found in the area, and the many cars on the main street, gave the town a look and feel that was different. Bustling, Skitchy thought. And she hadn't seen her father in what seemed like ages. She looked forward eagerly to a visit to Kermit.

....

Ephraim Chapman came out to meet them. He put his arms around his daughter and held her close for a long time.

"Surely good to see you, sugar."

"Oh, Daddy, I'm so glad to see you." Skitchy thought how wonderful it had always felt when her father held her like that, no less now that she was a grown woman with a child of her own.

Turning to the baby in Kate's arms, Eph beamed, "Just as pretty as her mother."

"Oh, Daddy."

"Pink, a fine family you have here! Come on inside now out of this hot sun. Some ice tea waiting for you."

Skitchy rested for a while in the back room but it was hot and no breeze came through the open window. She felt restless and soon joined the others. As she came into the room, she heard her father talking to Pink.

"The place is busy all the time. Lots of people come over to Kermit from Wink. It's only six miles, and you can't find a place to stay over there. A Mexican woman comes in to help with the laundry and cleaning but I haven't been able to find anyone to help run the place. Oil's the only thing on just about everybody's mind."

Ephraim stopped talking when he saw Skitchy. "Come on in, sugar. That's enough talk about the hotel for now. Let's go out to the kitchen. Reckon your mama will just about have the noon meal ready."

After they had eaten Skitchy went into the back room again to nurse the baby. She fell asleep and didn't wake when her mother came to take the baby and put her down. Hot and sweaty when she woke, Skitchy was surprised and annoyed to see by the light in the room that she'd slept a long time. She felt cranky as she joined everyone on the shady front porch of the hotel.

She thought Pink's voice sounded strained as he spoke, "Honey, I'm so glad you're up. We need to be getting started for home soon. It's pretty late."

Skitchy frowned. "Wish you'd waked me up sooner. I've hardly had any time to visit. Can't we stay a little longer?"

Kate quickly stood up as she said, "It was me who didn't want to wake you up, sugar. Thought you needed a good rest. I've packed supper for you to take with you."

In the car Skitchy and Pink were both quiet, the baby asleep on Skitchy's lap. Skitchy could feel something heavy in the quiet. After a time she asked, "Something the matter?"

Pink wanted to wait for a better time to tell her about his talk with Ephraim. However, when he hesitated, Skitchy asked, her voice insistent, "What were you and Daddy talking about?"

"He wanted to know if we'd move up to Kermit and help them run the hotel." He hadn't meant to be quite so blunt and regretted it immediately when he heard Skitchy's quiet gasp. Then he thought he'd better get it all out, so he went on, "I thanked him for the offer but I told him I just couldn't do it. Told him I'd had a taste of the hotel business working for Jackson and it isn't for me."

Skitchy sat staring ahead, saying nothing. When she spoke Pink was pretty sure she was frowning even though he couldn't see her face as he drove.

"I just can't believe you'd decide something like that and not even talk to me about it. Law, Pink, that's a big decision. It's my life, too. And the baby's now, too. How could you shut the door, just like that? Without even talking to me."

The agitation in her voice had escalated as she spoke and Pink felt himself cringing. When he didn't speak Skitchy went on, her voice stinging needles to him, "And it's not like you have some other great prospects. Not that I know of."

Pink tried to get hold of himself. After all she wasn't saying anything he hadn't said to himself. But he knew he couldn't do this thing her father had proposed. He pulled the car over to the side of the road.

"Please, honey, slow down a minute," he pleaded. "Please listen to me."

"All right. I'm listening."

There was no missing the sharp edge in her voice. Pink said as evenly as he could, "Honey, honestly I was afraid you'd want to move up there and I just can't do it."

His voice sounded weary and sad and Skitchy's coldness melted just a little. But then she thought about what a future in Kermit might hold. My folks are getting older and Pink and I might own the hotel someday. A business of our own . . . and a new life in a bustling town now . . .

"Why can't you do it?"

This was going the worst way Pink had imagined it might go. He'd wanted to be able to really tell her how he felt and have her understand, and this already had all the makings of a fight instead. He spoke as calmly as he could, not feeling calm. "I don't want to fight with you, honey. I really don't.

Can't we please just go on home now and talk about this when we've both settled down some?"

"Doesn't sound like there is much to talk about. You said you already told Daddy no."

"Well I did," Pink said, deciding he might as well say it all now. "Honey, please listen. I care so much how it is for you but I hate everything about the hotel business. I'm not like Jackson. I don't want to be like Jackson. I'd rather be flat broke than have to be in the hotel business."

Skitchy's voice softened a little. "I had no idea you felt like that. Felt so strongly about it."

That was enough for Pink to think maybe he wouldn't have to also say how much he hated West Texas and didn't want to be any more tied to the place than he already was. Wouldn't have to say how he didn't think he could live under the same roof with her father, the man whose respect and good will he so wanted but couldn't seem to earn.

The baby began to stir and Skitchy looked down at her. The last thing in the world she wanted at that moment was to have to attend to the baby. She wanted to be sympathetic for what she could hear and feel in Pink's plea, but she felt a bleak emptiness at the dimming of the bright future she could see for them in Kermit. She had stored her disappointment and resentment that Pink didn't seem concerned about their future in the vault of her most personal inner thoughts when he'd nearly drowned in Refugio Creek, and nothing else mattered except that he'd lived. But that was a long time gone. Other things did matter now. Not being able to see anything she could do about those things weighed heavy in her heart.

"Let's go on home now before Connie wakes up," she said, resignation thick in her voice.

Pink started the car and pulled back onto the road. Maybe it was going to be all right that he'd said no to Ephraim Chapman's offer.

....

"Emily told me Amelia Earhart is in Pecos!" Skitchy's voice was excited as she burst into the kitchen.

Pink stopped the coffee grinder. "I didn't hear. Who's in Pecos?"

"Amelia Earhart!"

"Who's Amelia . . . what was it, Hart?"

"Law, Pink, Amelia Earhart's just about the most famous woman in the country! She's a flyer. Just crossed the Atlantic Ocean in an airplane. First woman to ever do that. I think she's wonderful! I want to go to Pecos to see her and hear her."

"What in the world is someone like that doing in Pecos?"

"Emily says she's flying across the country. She had to stop for gas. But then there was something wrong with her plane. She's staying in Pecos while it gets fixed. And let those thunderstorms pass they say are coming."

"Well, honey, I can hear how excited you are but we can't just drop everything and run off to Pecos. We both have things we need to do here."

"You don't have to go if you don't want to. I can drive. Take Connie with me. Emily wants to go and take her two girls. They can help look after Connie. Maybe I can even visit with Brin while I'm in Pecos. Haven't seen her for ages. I'll stay up late when I get back and get everything done."

"Skitch," Pink said, his tone serious, "I don't think you should be staying up late when you're just getting started again with your work around the hotel. And how would you nurse the baby if you're driving? Emily and her girls can't do that for you."

Skitchy's face darkened. Pink knew that look and hated it. He tried to soften his voice as he said, "Maybe we can work something out for tomorrow or the next day. How long will this woman be in Pecos?"

"I don't know. Guess it depends on how long it takes to fix her plane. And what happens with the thunderstorms. I don't want to miss seeing her but guess I can wait till tomorrow. And she's not 'this woman' even if you don't know who she is." Skitchy's voice dropped and she said quietly, "And by the way, I'm not going to keep nursing the baby. Hardly anybody still nurses babies. I'd rather give Connie formula like my friends do."

"What does your mama say about that?"

"I haven't talked to Mama about it. Not going to. She thinks women should nurse babies because they always have. But times have changed. And it's up to me how I feed my baby. You know what's the best thing about Amelia Earhart? She's showing women that they can have a say about things. Decide what they want to do and not do."

The thunderstorms blew over. Amelia Earhart's plane got fixed and she took off early the following morning. A bitterly disappointed Skitchy told herself that she would never again let herself be talked out of something she wanted to do as much as she'd wanted to see and hear a woman who flew her own airplane.

1929

Jackson stood looking out the window of the lobby, sipping a second cup of coffee he'd taken with him after breakfast on the way to his office. It was March, the beginning of the windy season, and dust was no surprise. But that morning there was so much dust blowing that the buildings across the street were barely visible.

It was dusty in West Texas much of the time and people usually paid it little mind. Dust stirred up by wheels and feet on the dirt streets of small towns like McAllister was easily picked up by eddies and gusts. Low-growing mesquite and greasewood trees, all-thorn bushes, purple sage and a few other hardy plants scattered across the floor of the desert's edge weren't enough to prevent the sandy soil from blowing around. Strong winds, especially from the north, regularly produced dust storms but they were regarded mostly as something to put up with and clean up after. Some of the old-timers even joked that dust storms were a good thing because they made everybody set more store by the clear blue days that had once been common.

Belle came to stand beside Jackson at the window. "Don't recollect ever seeing dust as thick as this," she said, wrinkling her nose into a sneeze.

"I don't either. Don't see any people out."

Skitchy came in with Connie, dressed to go out. "What's going on?"

"The dust is really bad. I wouldn't take the baby out in it."

Skitchy came to the window. "Shoot! I was going to have coffee with Emily."

"Well, go ahead if you want to. I'll take care of Connie."

"Oh, would you, Belle? Thanks."

Skitchy gave the baby to her sister and bundled herself up, wrapping a scarf across her face. "So long," she said gaily.

A minute or two later she came back, coughing. "You were right! Feels like being sandpapered out there. I could hardly breathe. Only got as far as the drug store before I turned around. I wish Emily had a telephone. Guess she'll just have to figure out I'm not coming."

The dust had settled to a haze by nightfall. After everyone talked about how dense it had been, it was more or less forgotten. It would only be remembered later as the beginning of something none of them would ever forget.

....

It was a wonderfully cool October afternoon and all the windows were open to welcome the first day cool enough to promise a break from the long summer heat and the persistent dust storms. Connie, rosy and robust, sat in her high chair.

She seemed partly puzzled and partly delighted with all the fuss going on around her. Reba had made a chocolate birthday cake for her and the grown-ups offered her bites of it as they sat around the table after the noon meal.

"Well, sweetie, hope you like your new dolly."

"My friend Emily gave you this book. Lets look at all the pictures at bedtime."

Connie yawned and everyone laughed. While Skitchy put the little girl down for her nap, Reba brought coffee from the kitchen and began clearing the table. Belle poured coffee. Jackson passed around a box of cigarettes.

"Marvelous cake, Reba. Whole meal was just wonderful, no ifs ands or buts about that. Thank you. Please be sure Hutch gets a piece of cake."

Reba beamed, as she usually did when Jackson praised her. "Loved making it for her, Mr. Jackson. She's just the sweetest little girl."

"She is," Belle said. "Hard to believe she's a year old already, isn't it? It'll be so much fun to see what her next year will bring."

....

Later that day Jackson took the receipts from the hotel and drug store to the bank as he always did on Thursday afternoons. Belle, working in the garden taking out summer's remains, the last green that would be around the hotel for a while, was surprised to see him coming to the back entrance. He usually came in through the lobby to greet anyone he might see there. Then she saw the strained expression on his face.

"What is it, Jackson? Something wrong?"

"Everyone was talking at the bank about the stock market taking a big tumble today. Really big tumble. It's been rocky for a while but today was tough. They say there was so much selling the ticker tape couldn't keep up. Nobody knows what's happening. Looks pretty bad."

Belle didn't know what to say. He didn't look or sound like himself.

"Let's go inside," she said finally, as calmly as she could.

Jackson closed the office door. "I don't know what to do, Belle. Some people are selling even when they don't know what price they're getting. My friend Jim Thornton told me he sold almost all his stock. Can't see doing that in a panic but he might be right. It's so hard to know." He dropped his head into his hands.

Belle had never seen him like this. She sat quietly, waiting.

Finally Jackson straightened his shoulders, but when he spoke it was without the confidence Belle was used to hearing in his voice. "I think the best thing is to sit tight. See what happens tomorrow."

....

Tomorrow things had settled down. The market bounced back somewhat and most everyone in town who owned stocks breathed a sigh of relief. Jackson's sigh of relief, however, was a wary one.

On Monday everything deteriorated. "Ticker tape couldn't keep up again today," Jackson told Belle, his voice dry. "So much selling, it's like trying to stop a hemorrhage. People are scared. I don't know, maybe I should sell. But we'd lose so much. Prices are so low. We'd probably lose more than half the value of our stocks."

On Tuesday he told her, "There's even more panic selling. Jim says his brother doesn't think there's any chance the market will recover."

"You mean Hank Thornton, president of the bank?"

"Uh-huh," he said, his voice sounding miserable. "I should've sold when Jim did." His head hung very low. "Just couldn't believe the bottom would really drop out."

Jackson spent most of Wednesday in his office with the door closed. He calculated their losses, trying to figure out where they stood. When Belle looked in late in the afternoon he gestured to her to come in. His usually even manner and voice were saturated with strain.

"Honey, it's really bad. We've lost almost everything we had in the market."

"Are we going to be all right?"

"I think so. May be rough for a while but I think we can make it."

....

The next Monday the bank didn't open for business. Rumors flew around town and out to the surrounding ranches and farms, and a crowd gathered in front of the bank. People pounded on the doors and windows, demanding their money. The doors were locked. The shades were drawn. Whether there was anyone inside or not, no one responded.

Jackson didn't join the crowd pounding on the bank's doors. He put up a Closed sign on the drug store for the day. As soon as he got back to the hotel, he telephoned Hank Thornton, the bank president, to try to find out what was going on. There was no answer. No answer at the bank. No answer at Hank Thornton's house. He called Jim Thornton, his good friend and Hank Thornton's brother.

When he hung up the phone Jackson turned to Belle, his face contorted and drained of color, his voice choked. "The bank's failed. Everything's gone." His face hardened. "Hank Thornton shot himself."

Impassively, Jackson went to his office, sat down at his desk. Belle could see him through the window of the closed door, staring silently at nothing Belle could see with an almost icy calm. She thought Jackson had as much grit as her father but this was going hard with him. Best to leave him with his own thoughts, at least for a while.

Awfulness jumbled her own thoughts and her feelings of fear and loss threatened to stampede within her. Jackson had said they could make it after the stock market crashed but could they still? Their money was deposited in the bank. Was that all lost too? She knew Sally Thornton, Hank Thornton's wife -- no, widow -- pretty well. Should she call her? Go there? What could she say or do at a time like this? A taste like ashes in her mouth, she was not sure she could even speak. Pacing back and forth in the lobby helped only a little to ease the cramp in her belly.

After some time, she heard the creak of Jackson's desk chair as he stood up but he didn't come out of the office. She wanted to comfort him and be comforted herself, but tried to calm herself. She decided it was best to let him come to her when he was ready. When he finally emerged Belle could smell bourbon on his breath. Jackson kept a bottle in the office, sometimes offering a drink to visitors who came there to see him, but she had never known him to drink alone. Certainly not this early in the day.

"Belle, there's some cash in the safe. And what I keep for petty cash at the drug store and here. That's all the money we have. I don't know what we're going to do."

....

Skitchy and Pink held each other close under extra quilts against the sudden cold of the October night. And the sudden cold of knowing that everything they'd saved had been in the Bank of McAllister and was now gone.

"Skitch, I don't know what we're going to do."

She could feel his body trembling. She didn't know what to say so she said nothing for a long while. Finally she began to think about times her father had come up on adversity. The persistent optimism about tomorrow that she believed she'd inherited from her father began to make its way through the despair.

"We'll work it out somehow, sugar. Always some way to figure things out." Those were her father's words she heard coming from her own lips. As she spoke them, however, they became her own. She said again in a stronger voice, "We can do whatever we have to."

Pink hugged her more tightly. "You're wonderful, honey," he said. "You make me feel like we really can come through this. Maybe we can figure out some way to make it, even if we do have to begin all over again."

After Pink had rolled over and fallen asleep, Skitchy was awake for a long time.

1930

In January Jackson let Martita Morales go and cut Reba's hours. Then in March he let Reba go.

Pink told Skitchy, "I don't see any way he can keep paying us much longer either. There aren't many hotel guests. People aren't coming in for meals. He already cut the hours he keeps the drugstore open and he told me he's going to close the soda fountain. We'll be lucky if he can keep letting us work for food and a place to live."

This is it, Skitchy thought, when in early May she saw Jackson's pinched face and heard his pinched voice as he asked them to come into his office.

Jackson felt sickened, seeing the strained look on Skitchy's face, the impassive stoniness on Pink's. I've got to do this, Jackson told himself, swallowing his pride with great effort. No other way.

"Best I can do is trade you room and board for your work. Food is short but I don't think any of us will starve. I'm so sorry," Jackson said, doing what he could to remain stalwart but feeling betrayed by the bleakness he could hear in his voice.

After they went upstairs, Skitchy said to Pink, "Law, I'm just so thankful I can help Belle with the laundry and cooking and you still have some work at the store."

She thought back to the afternoon when Martita had said to her as they put clean laundry away in the linen cupboard, "Mrs. Skitchy, I don't know how Jorge and I can keep going. Jorge says there's not much business at the store. Mr. Wilson tries so hard. Cuts prices on many things. Gives credit to families who have hungry children. But the people don't come in like they used to. Jorge works not even half as much as he did before. He thinks Mr. Wilson will have to let him go pretty soon. And I think maybe Mr. Tieger will have to let me go, too." Martita's dark eyes filled with tears, the beauty of her dusky young face distorted by fear.

"Martita, I'm so sorry. What will you do?"

"I think we have to go back to Mexico. When Mr. Wilson told Jorge he must work only half the hours he'd been working, we moved to our older brother's house. We cannot stay there much longer. Pedro's house is very small. He doesn't have enough food for his own family. His wife is pregnant again. It's very bad for them. I think Pedro despairs."

Skitchy liked Martita and felt sorry for her and her brothers. But she'd also thought that afternoon that their bad luck might turn out to be good luck for her and Pink. "Pink," she'd said that night as they got ready for bed, "Martita says she thinks her brother's going to be let go at the mercantile store. What would you think about talking to Mr. Wilson. See if he can use you once in a while after Martita's brother is gone." Most of Mr. Wilson's money had been deposited in the First Bank of Pecos and it had not failed. Wilson's Mercantile Store was still in business. "I figure the first person to come in asking for work will probably be the one to get some if there is any."

Pink had asked the tall, silver-haired Mr. Wilson for work and did get work from time to time. Usually he unpacked and shelved goods in the grocery department, sometimes waited on customers when Mr. Wilson needed to be away from the store.

"Honey," he'd said to Skitchy, "you said you thought we could make it and it looks like maybe we can. I'm thinking Jackson and Belle will probably let us keep living here if we keep working and help out with food. We can now, with my work at Wilson's."

So when Jackson proposed exactly that, Pink said with no hesitation. "Jackson, we know you've done everything you could. Skitchy and I both appreciate how hard you've tried to make everything work. We're just grateful we can stay on."

....

Jackson rose from his desk when he saw the two elderly women come in to the hotel and approach the counter. They were both plainly dressed in long dark muslin skirts and white blouses. Each of them wore an old fashioned hat primly perched on hair pulled back into a bun. The taller woman, whom Jackson judged to be the elder of the two, tilted her head down, looking at him over wire rimmed glasses.

"My name is Etta Cox McCabe," she said in a firm voice as she extended her hand. "This is my sister, Rita Cox Colquitt."

The smaller woman nodded, her pale blue eyes smiling. She had a lively look about her, Jackson thought, and he liked the firm grip with which she shook his hand.

"What can I do for you, Mrs. McCabe, Mrs. Colquitt?"

"We want to know if you rent rooms to people who want to live at the hotel," Mrs. McCabe said, her voice a little more tentative. "And provide meals."

"That can be arranged," Jackson said, thinking quickly on his feet. He'd never thought of the hotel as a boarding house but full time guests paying full time rent sounded quite appealing. He felt confident Belle could and would make room for two paying guests at the dining room table. "How many rooms would you like?"

"Just one. My sister and I'll share a room. How much would that cost?"

"Fifty cents is the usual charge for one room for one night. Of course you ladies would be sharing a bed." Hastily calculating in his head, he said, "Living here all the time, I can offer you a monthly rate. Thirty dollars, including meals for both of you. I'm sure you know times are hard. The food will be plain. Same food my wife and I'll have."

The younger sister spoke for the first time in a very soft, very clear voice, "We surely do know times are hard, Mr. Tieger. We're widows. Times have been hard for us, too." She ignored her sister's scowl, knowing very well that Etta didn't want her to tell everything, but determined to start off on what she considered the right foot. "Our big old house in San Saba Springs was too much for us. We need to cut back on expenses generally."

Still scowling, Etta McCabe grunted a little stiffly. "One room with good plain meals will be just fine. Thirty dollars will be just fine."

Later Jackson would tell Belle, "Mrs. McCabe seems kind of stiff. Think maybe this was a hard thing for her to do. She might relax some after we get to know each other. Mrs. Colquitt seems more friendly. I think you'll like her. Having them pay room and board will surely make things a little easier for us."

"Glad for that," Belle said without hesitation. "We could use a little easier."

....

"Martha Hoffman came in to the store today," Pink told everyone sitting around the table after a supper of eggs scrambled with pieces of bologna, beans and cornbread. "She said the state doesn't have enough money to pay her or any of the teachers so she was paid in scrip this month. She wanted to know if the store would let her pay for some things she needed with the scrip."

Belle was puzzled. "Scrip? I don't understand. What is it?"

"She showed it to me," Pink said. "It looked official, like it came from the government. It said that 'at some time in the future this coupon will be redeemed by the State of Texas at face value.'"

"What did you say?" Skitchy wanted to know.

"I told her I'd have to ask Mr. Wilson. What do you think, Jackson? Would you take this scrip if someone wanted to pay for something with it here or at the drugstore?"

"I'd like to talk to some people at the bank in Pecos. See what they think about it. But I don't think so. Some time in the future sounds pretty vague to me. Who knows when the state will be able to redeem the coupons? Or if they ever will? I'm already having a rough time of it buying things to stock the drug store. I think it might be a lot worse if customers were paying with this scrip instead of cash."

"What about the school? The children?" Belle wondered worriedly. "Will Miss Hoffman keep teaching if she isn't paid?"

Pink said, "She told me she wants to keep teaching. She said they told her she'd be paid in scrip every other month. Get her regular pay the other months. But she's afraid she won't be able to make it with her regular pay just every other month so she hopes someone will take the scrip. I told her I'd talk to Mr. Wilson in the morning."

"Law, what are things coming to!" Belle exclaimed. Most everyone around the table murmured agreement.

Jackson stood up abruptly and started walking around the room, his face impassive. "I'm just as worried about what things are coming to if we don't get some rain pretty soon."

"How long has it been?" Belle asked. "Seems like a year."

"More than a year," Jackson said. "There's jittery talk all around town about crops failing. People with shallow wells don't have any water. Shorty Fallon tried to make a joke at the barber shop the other day about his well drying up and the bank drying up and feeling like he was drying up, and nobody laughed."

Nobody said anything. Everyone got up from the table and started clearing the dishes with the grave calm of those who defend themselves in adversity by standing together for strength. After putting on thick skins and composed faces.

....

At the mercantile store the next day Mr. Wilson told Pink, "I'm going to bet on Texas. I think the State of Texas will keep its promises and I'll get paid later on. Tell Miss Hoffman I'll take the scrip coupons for the sake of the children. They need their teacher to keep teaching."

"I think he's a fine man," Skitchy said when Pink told her what Mr. Wilson had said. "Glad you're working for him."

However, two months later Mr. Wilson told Pink, "I'm not going to be able to keep taking scrip the way I have. As soon as word got around that I'd take the scrip coupons quite a few people came in to the store with them. It's become a big problem for me. I still have to pay for everything I buy for the store with real money. Nobody wants to pay with real money if they have any scrip. From now on, I'll only take scrip from the teacher. And only when it's first issued by the state. It's for the children, so they can keep going to school. You tell people that if they want to know why I'll just take scrip from Miss Hoffman."

Jackson told Belle when they were alone, "I'm glad I didn't start accepting scrip. It was hard to say no when Mr. Wilson was taking it. Put a lot of pressure on me to take it, too. Even harder, though, when you do something and then later it feels to people like you're taking something away from them. Best not to have started in the first place."

Belle didn't disagree but she was glad Mr. Wilson would still take the scrip from Martha Hoffman. She valued education highly and didn't like to think about what might have happened to the school children if their teacher wasn't in the classroom. The school children didn't know about the

State of Texas needing to pay teachers and other state employees with what amounted to an IOU with no due date.

1931

"Just got a letter from Mama and Daddy," Belle told Jackson as she walked into his office. Jackson looked up, knowing it was important if Belle came in when he was working. "They're going to sell the hotel in Kermit and move to Big Lake. They're planning to move into Minnie and Bob's little rent house." She saw a shadow move across Jackson's face. "You don't look surprised."

Somber, he said, "Well no, guess I'm not. The hotel business isn't easy even when times are good. To tell you the truth, I always thought it might be harder than your folks figured to go from running cattle to running a hotel. Not to mention moving from the ranch into an oil boomtown. Just hope they don't lose too much on the hotel."

Belle was thoughtful. "I wonder if maybe they thought Skitchy and Pink would help them with the hotel. Mama said something about that once."

"I wondered about that, too. Pink has a good head on his shoulders and knows something about the business from working here. Seems like that could've been a good thing for all of them."

"I thought so, too. I thought maybe Skitchy and Pink would even take over the hotel after a bit. They were arguing about something right after they came back from taking Mama home after Connie was born. Something Skitchy wanted to do but Pink didn't. She never mentioned anything but I could see she was pretty upset about whatever it was. Wonder if it could've been about this?"

"Honey, I know how much you care about your family. But sometimes it's best not to try to figure everything thing out. Nothing you can do about this anyway."

"You're right. I know you're right." Belle sighed and left the office. She sat for a long time by herself in the kitchen over a cup of coffee that got cold before she'd drunk half of it.

....

Skitchy sighed deeply as she plunked herself down on a chair near Belle in the lobby. "Emily told me today that her sister Betty and her husband are going to lose their farm. They took out a loan a couple of years back. Now they can't make the payments. Haven't had a good crop since this awful old drought started. The dust storms have made it worse. Even if there'd been rain, Ralph doesn't think they could've sold their cotton for enough to make the payments. Prices have just been too low. They tried to talk to the bank in Pecos to get more time. Answer was no. A nice no, Betty told

Emily, but no is still no. Law, things just seem to get worse and worse, Belle," Skitchy groaned.

"What are they going to do?" Belle asked, sympathy in her voice.

"Emily doesn't know. She's very worried for her sister. Ralph wants to get out of West Texas. Start over somewhere else. Betty's afraid this is a tough time to be trying to start over. They might go to Ralph's family in San Angelo but things are tough for them, too, Emily says. Emily thinks Betty and Ralph are both so down they can't think straight."

Belle saw Skitchy's face darken. "What are you thinking, honey?"

"That could've been us, Belle. Pink and me. We were just barely making it cotton farming. I don't see how we could've kept going with the drought. And the awful old dust. And the depression. I can never thank you and Jackson enough for giving us the chance to come here."

Belle put down the sock she was mending and looked directly at her sister. "Honey," she said, her voice firm and clear, "we're still Chapmans even if we're both married. You'll always have a place to live and something to eat as long as I have a place to live and something to eat. I know it would be the same if things were the other way around."

"You bet," Skitchy said softly, grateful for the truth of it.

....

It was the middle of December. Lightning scribbled in the sky. Rain blustered against the windows in the early afternoon but it lasted less than two minutes, barely dampening down the dust on the hard-packed ruts of the streets. It brought no relief from the merciless drought.

Jackson kept the pot bellied stove in the lobby going during cold snaps and most everyone had gathered there. Skitchy played with Connie on an old quilt spread on the floor. Belle worked a crossword puzzle nearby. Jackson puttered behind the reception desk. The elderly sisters, Etta McCabe and Rita Colquitt, played cards at a folding card table near the stove.

"Lucky Pink could get some work today," Etta McCabe said, peering at Skitchy over the wire-framed glasses that sat on her beaked nose.

Skitchy thought Mrs. McCabe looked like the witch in one of Connie's picture books when she looked at anyone like that. But she would never say such a thing out loud and kept the laugh to herself. "You bet. Always glad when he can get work," she said.

Pink was often paid with groceries, and if there was food like stale bread or apples still good enough for applesauce, anything that couldn't be sold but could still be used, Pink asked for it. Mr. Wilson always gave it. The little community at the hotel was always grateful for any extra food. When he came home late that afternoon, Pink was carrying not only a box of food but had a small Christmas tree tucked under his arm! Jackson took the box as Pink set the tree down. Skitchy took his coat and cap and hung them on a peg near the pot-bellied stove.

"Mr. Wilson didn't bring in many trees this year. No big ones, but he sent this one so Connie would have a Christmas tree. He said he thought the little girl with the sweet smile deserved a nice Christmas."

Connie's eyes grew wide. Even at three, she understood from the teary pleasure of the grown-ups that this was a special thing.

Etta McCabe and Rita Colquitt helped Connie cover the table by the lobby window with green felt and a lace tablecloth. The little tree was placed on it with much ceremony. Jackson strung lights on it while Belle opened the box in which ornaments had been stored since the grand opening of the hotel had been celebrated with a grand tree. She let Connie pick out the ornaments she wanted, counting out fifteen as the right number for the small tree. Everyone gathered around when Jackson plugged in the lights, smiled and wished each other Merry Christmas. No one spoke of all that had happened since there had been a big tree in the lobby.

....

Skitchy felt worn out in body and spirit as she and Pink climbed the stairs the day after Christmas. "Glad to call it a day," she said wearily. "More than ready to call it a year, too. I surely hope 1932 will be better."

"Honey, I want to talk to you about that," Pink said as they went into their room and closed the door.

Hearing the somber tone of his voice, Skitchy was curious about what he had on his mind. She sat down on the bed. "Is that why you asked Belle if Connie could spend the night with them?"

"Yes. I've been wanting to have a chance to talk, just the two of us. It's so cold. Let's get into bed and talk."

Pink lay facing Skitchy. His voice was serious when he started to speak in low tones. "Tom Floyd is going to Wink to see if he can get a job in the oil fields. He says if a man can get hired the work is steady. The pay is pretty good. I'd like to go with him. See if I can get a regular job."

Skitchy didn't like the sudden tension she felt in her stomach. "What about Connie and me?" she said, not sure what the tension was trying to say.

"There isn't any place for workers' families to live, the town has grown so fast. The oil workers live in tents outside of town. But I figure Belle and Jackson would let you stay here. It'd be hard for a while but maybe we could get ahead some."

Skitchy felt her stomach tighten even more. She knew Wink was just a few miles from Kermit, where her parents had bought the hotel when both towns had swollen in the oil boom. "You didn't mention anything like that when Daddy wanted us to move to Kermit, help them with the hotel. We could all be living there now. Getting ahead some." She could hear the edge in her voice and supposed Pink could, too.

Pink could hear it but tried to ignore it. "This is different, Skitch. Your folks wanted us to work at the hotel. You know I didn't want to be in the hotel business. I wouldn't want to work in the oil fields either, if I had a choice. But the depression has changed everything." He didn't want to say that going to Wink would also be a chance for him to get out of being beholden to Jackson. Get out of the hotel business. If he could get some money ahead as he hoped, maybe even get out of McAllister. Maybe even get out of West Texas. He couldn't bring himself to tell her all that.

Skitchy had a sense that there was more than Pink was saying. But she herself didn't want to say all she was thinking. She didn't trust Tom and his big ideas. She wanted Pink to get ahead but this just didn't sound right to her. She decided she'd ask Jackson what he thought first thing in the morning. Maybe I don't really know, she thought, and I don't want to try to talk Pink out of something if it would help us get ahead. "Let's sleep on it, honey," she said. "Both of us do better when we give things a little time."

....

Skitchy knocked on the door of Jackson's office the next morning. "Can I come in?" she said softly. "Sorry to interrupt what you're doing, Jackson, but I surely do need to talk to you."

"Come in, Skitchy. Have a seat," Jackson said, smiling. "What's on your mind?"

"I recollect hearing you talking with Daddy and Bob about the oil boom around Kermit and Wink but I wasn't able to follow what you all said. Now Pink's thinking about going with Tom Floyd to try to find work in the Wink oil fields. I feel scared that may not be such a good idea. Will you please tell me what you were saying about the boom and the depression? What you think about that?"

"Well, I said a lot of things, Skitchy. But more important, it's not my business to tell you or Pink what you should do."

"Oh, please, Jackson. Pink listens to Tom. They're good friends, but I don't think Tom knows what he's talking about half the time. It's like him to rush off after what he thinks is a good idea. But what if he's a bubble off plumb about this? I don't want Pink to just go with him without knowing more about what he might be getting into. But I don't know anything about it either. You know about things like this. I trust you, Jackson. This could be important for Pink and me and I don't know anyone else I can talk to about it."

Jackson hesitated for a moment. He didn't think much of Tom Floyd or Tom's judgment about things. He was beginning to have more doubts about Pink, too. Not thinking enough for himself, he thought. Too easily swayed by other people. Jackson felt reluctant to say anything that might seem critical of her husband to Skitchy, however. But he also didn't want to encourage her about something he thought foolish. He needed to give himself time to sort this out. "I'll get us some coffee. Then we'll talk," he said and left the office.

Skitchy felt jittery about what she might learn, but happy Jackson had agreed to talk with her. She was glad when he came back with the coffee.

"So, is how the depression may affect the oil boom what you want to talk about?"

"I think so. I guess so. What I'm trying to figure out is whether or not it's a good idea for Pink to go to Wink and look for work in the oil fields. I don't know if he really can find a job. If he can, he might make enough money for us to be able to live on our own, at least after a bit. But if he can't get hired full time at a good wage, that's a different story. If it doesn't work out he won't have his work with Mr. Wilson anymore. Maybe not with you either. Then where would we be? We have Connie to think about now, too."

"I can see you've got a lot on your mind," Jackson began. "I'll tell you what I've read or heard, Skitchy. But I can't tell you and Pink what I think you should do. You have to make up your own minds about that. Agreed?"

"You bet," she said firmly.

"Well, to begin with, oil prices have been falling ever since the stock market crashed."

"I didn't know that," Skitchy said.

Jackson could hear the worry in her voice. He'd decided the best thing was to try to keep this as businesslike as he could. He took care not to let his caring concern for her and for Connie creep in. "Big problem when prices keep falling. Prices can get so low it costs more to get the oil out of the ground and ship it to where it needs to go than they can sell it for. If things get that bad, my guess is they'll stop drilling."

"That doesn't sound very good."

"I don't know for sure but I don't think it takes many people to keep the wells pumping that are already pumping. Probably jobs like Tom's talking about are in drilling."

"But there might not still be drilling jobs. If things go sideways."

Jackson said nothing, letting Skitchy be with her own thoughts.

"How long do you think there might still be drilling jobs?"

"I have no idea."

"Thank you, Jackson. Thank you for talking with me like this. It means a lot to me."

He breathed a sigh of relief. He thought their talk had gone well and felt he could relax with her a little. "If our business talk is finished, how about a brotherly hug?" he said warmly. He was surprised to see tears in her eyes.

....

That night when Skitchy and Pink went to their room she said, "Sugar, I've been thinking a lot about what you said about Wink. I don't think you should go. We're doing all right here. Why give up everything here and take a chance on something like that?"

Pink heard the conviction in her voice. He felt some of the energy drain from him even as he tried to gather his thoughts. "Tom says there are good jobs. Why do you think it would be taking a chance?" His voice sounded a little louder and a little more argumentative than he meant it to be or wanted it to be.

She told him of her conversation with Jackson as calmly as she could.

"Jackson says?" he said sourly. "Jackson who knows everything."

Her voice, too, was louder than she wanted it to be. "It wasn't like that at all, Pink. He just answered my questions." She added quickly, softening the edge in her voice, "And I'd miss you something awful. I don't want you to leave Connie and me. Please don't go, sugar."

Pink felt himself crumpling. Knowing he would not go to Wink with Tom. Knowing that Skitchy and not he had recognized the need to know more than he knew before making such an important decision. Knowing that Jackson once again was the man who knew what needed to be known. He sat on the edge of the bed, bewildered that he could've felt such eagerness to do something that now seemed foolish.

Skitchy had expected an argument, maybe even a fight. But not this. She, too, felt bewildered.

1932

Jackson stamped his feet on the hotel porch to shake off as much dust as he could before he came into the lobby. Seeing Belle, Pink and Etta McCabe in the lobby, he called out, "Look at this!" and laid out the new issue of the *McAllister Pioneer* on the reception counter. "The *Pioneer* reprinted this picture from the Amarillo paper. No wonder! I've never seen anything like it in my life!"

Belle gasped. The picture of a huge deep gray cloud darkening the sky took up half the front page. The headline read: BLACK BLIZZARD HITS AMARILLO.

"What is it?" Etta McCabe asked in her high-pitched voice, her sharp features frowning at the picture.

His voice excited and strained, Jackson said, "Have a seat and I'll read the article out loud."

"Skitchy's in the kitchen," Pink said. "Let me get her. She'll want to hear it, too."

Jackson started to read as soon as everybody was settled:

"A huge black cloud, estimated to be ten thousand feet high, rolled around Amarillo this morning, on sixty mile per hour winds, according to the Weather Bureau. An official said it was not a rain cloud or a cloud filled with ice pellets or a twister or a regular sandstorm and the way it moved was not like anything anyone recognized. The Bureau recorded it in their logs as 'most spectacular.'

From Amarillo the huge cloud moved north 75 miles where it passed over the small town of Dalhart, briefly blotting out the sun before it dumped what seemed to be something like dense dust. Dark colored dust covered streets, blew its way inside buildings, stung eyes, noses and throats, cut people's skin, and made them cough up coal-colored phlegm.

This paper will print more details when more is known about this most spectacular phenomenon."

There had been thick dust this spring, much heavier and more dense than usual, in McAllister, too, but nothing like what they were reading about in Amarillo and Dalhart. Etta McCabe went to tell her sister because their cousin lived in Dalhart. Soon everyone in the little community at the hotel gasped in disbelief or stared silently at the picture of the black cloud as the newspaper was passed around.

The community now included Belle and Jackson, Skitchy, Pink and Connie, Etta McCabe and Rita Colquitt, Reba Borden and Hutch, and Alma Floyd.

Reba and Hutch were living there because Skitchy had persuaded Belle to give them a place to live in trade for their work. After Jackson had let her go, Reba found bits of work here and there. Then even that had dried up in the withering depression that was parching the people as much as the withering drought was parching the land. She'd been evicted because she couldn't pay the rent on the two room dirt floored house on the edge of town where she and Hutch lived.

Skitchy knew how much Belle had missed Reba but had pleaded her case without bringing that up. "Reba knows how to make do with so little. You know how she is. And she's a much better cook than either one of us. Hutch'll do whatever he can. And you saw how Connie clapped her hands and ran to Reba when she came that time with the rag doll she made."

However, when Belle had spoken of this to Jackson, she'd been surprised when a shadow crossed his face and he said, "I was glad to have Reba working for us. I feel wary, though, about white people and colored people living together."

"I hardly know what to say," Belle said tentatively. "Surely be easier to have her doing the cooking, and other work like she always did. She and Hutch have no place to live since Reba can't find work. We aren't really using that little room off the kitchen now. I thought of it as trading their work for a place to live. Didn't think of it as having them live with us. But I suppose they would be."

Jackson was thoughtful for a time. Finally he'd taken a deep breath and said, "Well, the hotel has a big roof. I guess we can make room for all of us."

So Reba and Hutch had moved into the little room off the kitchen, grateful to trade their work for a place to live and something to eat.

Alma Floyd was living there because Tom had gone to Wink to see if he could find work in the oil fields. Tom had asked Pink, "Do you think Jackson would let Alma stay at the hotel? Just until I see if I can get hired? Then I'd need to find a place in Wink or Kermit. I'd send her money for food and rent as soon as I can."

"Well, I think he might and I'll put in a good word for you. I'm sure Skitchy will, too. She and Alma have gotten to be good friends."

Despite feeling the pressure of so many people depending on him, Jackson had agreed to let Alma stay. He thought well of Alma and she was Skitchy's friend. Those factors outweighed what he thought about Tom.

So Alma had stayed in McAllister when Tom went to try his luck in the Wink oil fields, despite her embarrassment at feeling like she was living on other people's charity. Once perky and pretty, with curly light brown hair and sparkling blue eyes, Alma was now thin and looked drawn. She helped out where she could at the hotel and once in a while at the drug store when Jackson needed to have supplies unpacked and put away. Like everyone else living at the hotel, she put what money she could in a jar on a kitchen shelf. Food and other necessities were bought with these pooled resources to supplement eggs from the chickens raised in back of the hotel, vegetables and melons from Belle's garden now worked mostly by Hutch, and milk from a goat Jackson had taken as payment from a hotel guest.

....

Skitchy found Alma sewing one afternoon by the lobby window where the light was best, compensating for needing glasses she couldn't afford. "What is that you're making?" Skitchy asked.

"I call it a split skirt. Everybody seems to think women should always wear skirts." Alma laughed with a sharp tone in the laugh. "But every woman who rides a horse knows what it's like to have to ride sidesaddle in a skirt. So I thought maybe I could figure out how to make something that would look like a skirt but would be split like pants so you can ride astride. I started it a long time ago. Tom always made fun of it. Said it was a silly idea. I put it away when I got tired of hearing him talk like that but I decided last week to see if I could finish it."

"I think it's a great idea! Growing up on the ranch I wore my brother's old pants or rode sidesaddle. Wish I'd had something like this. What did you call it?"

"Split skirt. Just made up the name. Tom thought that was silly, too."

"Well, I think it's clever. Will you let me see it when you're finished?"

"You bet. May take me some time, though. Belle asked me if I'd do some patching on the hotel's quilts. I just work on the split skirt when I have spare time." Alma grew thoughtful. After a time she said, "You know, Skitchy, it would sure enough help me out if I could use you for a model once in a while. If I could pin the split skirt together while it's on you, it would save me lots of time."

"But I'm taller than you. Does that matter?"

"I can make allowance for that."

"You bet then."

....

"I'd like to take Connie to the new Sunday school next Sunday," Pink said to Skitchy as they left the church and walked down Front Street toward Main Street. The preacher had announced a new program being started for children as young as Connie. Pink's wish to have Connie take part in it didn't surprise Skitchy.

"Not so sure it's a good idea to start kids that young," she said. "I believed everything I heard in church when I was little. Didn't even think about it. Kids believe what grownups tell them. I don't think it's good to teach kids all those things when they're too little to ask questions or think about it."

"You heard the preacher say they'd just be listening to Bible stories and coloring pictures that illustrate them. If children aren't taught young they may never value religion at all."

"It's not like she isn't being taught, Pink. You teach her by going to church. Singing in the choir. Praying with her when she goes to bed. I think we all teach her as a matter of fact. Belle told me Connie asked her how come you don't drink. You think it's wrong but her mother and aunt and uncle and other grown-ups don't think it's wrong. I don't think she'll be taught to understand differences like that in Sunday school."

"Well, maybe she'd get better answers at Sunday school than she does from Belle. You and your sister go to church but it seems like it's mostly for fellowship. Your mother seems to be the only one in your family who really takes her faith and the Bible seriously."

"Your answers," Skitchy shot back, "are not necessarily the only answers to things. Everyone in my family's honest and trustworthy. Always ready to help someone in need. I think that's way more important than believing everything the Bible says. Even Mama would say that if you asked her."

Pink fell silent as they were coming close to the corner of Main Street. He didn't want to be arguing with Skitchy where they might see other people or be seen. He stopped, took Skitchy's hands in his, looked at her earnestly. "Please, Skitchy. Faith matters a lot to me. I want it to matter to my daughter, too. Having Connie go to Sunday school is very important to me."

"All right," Skitchy said softly. "I'll agree to it because it's so important to you." But she resolved to make sure

Connie also learned that she didn't necessarily have to believe everything she'd be taught in Sunday school.

1933

Hutch, hot and sweaty from working in the garden, came into the kitchen and whispered to his mother as she rolled out biscuit dough. Reba looked at Belle, pouring a cup of coffee at the stove, took a deep breath before she spoke.

"Hobo man out back asking for food, Mrs. Belle. Can I please fix him a plate of food?"

Belle went to the door and looked at the man standing near the chicken coop, some distance from the back door. He was very thin, dirty and unshaven, his clothes ragged, his worn hat full of holes. Fear came up into her throat.

"They come more often lately," Reba said. "Can't find work and they're hungry. This man says he'd do some work around here if we have any, in exchange for food."

"No," Belle said, shuddering. "He should move on." Reba said nothing and Belle grew thoughtful. "Reba, you say these men come pretty often?"

"Yes, ma'am. They're hungry. Only way they can get food is to steal it or ask for it. I figure they're good men if they ask."

Belle looked directly at Reba. "Have you been giving them food?"

"Yes, ma'am." Reba said, eyes down as she cut the dough into rounds and put them on a baking pan. "I give them beans or leftover gravy and biscuits if we have any. Hutch and me, we take less then."

Belle grew thoughtful again. "You can fix him a plate, Reba. Hutch, take it out to him please. But tell him he must not come back again."

"He won't come back again, Mrs. Belle," Reba said. "They never do. They're just moving through."

"How do you know that?"

"Preacher Isaiah at my church says they come in on the train. Catch a ride in an empty box car. Find a meal if they can. Then most of the time they catch the next train out. Sometimes Preacher lets them sleep overnight in the church. Black or white or brown, they talk to him. He says they're mostly good men who can't find work. They're hurting bad in their souls and just trying to keep from starving."

Belle stood at the door and watched the man eat the beans and give the plate back to Hutch. She didn't know he saw her until he tipped his hat to her and walked away. "Reba," she said, "you can give them food. You don't have to take less, you and Hutch. We can spare a little to keep someone from starving."

Later, when Belle told Jackson about the hobo, she added, "Law, it's been so hard for us I clean forgot about other people out there."

"It's very bad out there, Belle. I haven't talked much about how bad it really is. Maybe it's best you know, though, since it came into our own back yard today." She seemed to be listening intently, her face earnest. Maybe I've been trying to protect her too much, he thought, and went on. "Looks like the stock market has finally bottomed out but things aren't getting any better. Businesses have been hit hard because people aren't buying things. Unemployment is up to 25% and there are no new jobs. No big surprise, is it, that not many people are buying things?"

"Well, I knew we haven't been buying things the way we used to. Haven't even thought about buying a new dress in ages. Nobody has a new dress in McAllister that I know of."

"Farmers around here can't get much for what they grow. Lots of people are hungry because they don't have any money to buy food. Sorry ugly circle just keeps going round and round. Some of the businessmen in town are just barely hanging on. Mark my words, some of them are going to lose everything. I see the signs. I think a lot of people don't want you to see, but they're having a pretty tough time even holding their heads up." Jackson put his face in his hands and when he looked up Belle saw tears in his eyes, rare in the years they had been together. "There have been times I haven't been sure we could make it, honey."

Belle sat quietly for a moment, head down and hands folded in her lap. When she looked up, Jackson saw tears in her eyes as well. "I've learned so much from you, Jackson, about so many things. Most of my life I just thought mostly about myself and the people I felt close to. Now I want to know about what's going on in the world. I need to know. I don't want to be just a silly ignorant woman who leaves it to you to shoulder everything." She stood up and came to stand in front of him. "I'm so grateful we have a place to live. And enough food. And people around us who care about us. And you don't have to shoulder everything alone, Jackson. If we make it through, we make it through together. If we don't, we go down together. That was the deal."

"Hmm, the deal," Jackson said softly. "Well, I tell you, I think I got about the best deal a man could possibly get."

....

Skitchy woke in the middle of the night when she heard Connie crying fitfully. As she went into the other room, Skitchy could hear the five year old's raspy breathing. A touch told her Connie was feverish. Skitchy closed the door and turned on the light, picked up her daughter and sat down in the rocking chair. She held the child close, trying to sooth her. Suddenly, Skitchy felt her daughter's body grow extremely hot. Connie began to shake. Her face took on a bluish color and her mouth foamed. Scared and not knowing what to do, Skitchy put Connie down on the bed and raced downstairs.

"Reba. Reba." She pounded on Reba's door.

A sleepy Reba in a tattered nightgown opened the door. "Mrs. Skitchy?"

"Reba, I'm so sorry to wake you. Connie's very sick. I don't know what to do. I recollect you told me you know how to nurse people. Can you help me? Can you please come upstairs with me?"

As Skitchy told Reba breathlessly what had happened, Reba stopped halfway up the stairs. "I'm going to the kitchen, Mrs. Skitchy. Bring Connie down there, as fast as you can." The urgency in the black woman's voice frightened Skitchy but she could also hear that Reba seemed to know what was wrong and what to do. Skitchy took the rest of the stairs two at a time.

By the time Skitchy got to the kitchen carrying Connie, Hutch was filling the sink with water and adding a small amount of ice to the water. "Put her in the water," Reba said calmly. "Keep holding her, so she doesn't slip or get scared. Quick now. Just leave her pajamas on. Need to get her fever down." On a cloth Reba poured a small amount of a liquid from a bottle she'd taken from her old black satchel opened on the kitchen table. She squeezed the liquid drop by drop into Connie's mouth.

Belle, awakened by the commotion, appeared at the kitchen door in her robe. "Law, what is it?" Her face blanched when she saw her niece. "Connie!"

"She's very sick, Belle," Skitchy said over her shoulder.

"Can I do anything?"

"Yes, ma'am," Reba said. "Bring some towels. Then get some dry clothes for her."

By the time Belle came back with the clothes, Pink following her, Connie's body was calm and cooler. Reba was cradling the little girl in her arms, squeezing more drops into her mouth, telling Skitchy, "Happens like this sometimes when a little child's fever shoots up like that. I think she'll be all right now. Someone needs to watch her just in case it happens again."

"I'll sit with her tonight," Pink said, his voice tender. He took Connie in his arms and carried her upstairs.

"I can't believe Jackson slept through all this," Skitchy said.

"Jackson could sleep through just about anything," Belle laughed softly as she fixed some coffee. "I'll tell him about it in the morning."

Hutch cleaned up the kitchen while the women sat around the table drinking coffee, quiet but not ready to go back to bed.

Still pale and obviously drained, Skitchy said, "Reba, I can never thank you enough."

"Neither can I," Belle added.

"No need to," Reba said softly. "I love that little girl, too."

....

Christmas was lean that year in McAllister. Nevertheless, Connie's brush with death had reminded everyone that life still went on, even in the midst of depression, drought, and dust. Like plants sleeping in parched soil until precious water wakes them, the groggy spirits of the people waked as Connie started to run around and play again. Sprouts of awakened aliveness could be seen around the hotel by the middle of December.

"I think it'd be fun," Skitchy told Belle, "if we put all our names in a box. Everybody draw a name and give that person a gift on Christmas Eve. The gifts wouldn't have to cost much. What do you think?"

"Sounds like a great idea to me."

"Oh, let's do it, Belle! And I think it's only right for Reba and Hutch to be part of it. That's very important to me."

"I agree!" Belle said enthusiastically. The sisters went together to Jackson's office to make their case.

Skitchy began, "Jackson, Belle and I both understand why you've been so careful to keep some separation between Reba and Hutch and the rest of us. But we both think they should be part of the exchange of Christmas gifts."

Belle added quickly, "We might have lost Connie if it hadn't been for Reba. And it wouldn't be right to leave Hutch out."

This was just the kind of thing Jackson had feared when he'd said Reba and Hutch could live at the hotel in exchange for their work. But he couldn't argue with the affectionate logic of the two women standing there, shoulder to shoulder. "That'll be fine," he said, trying to keep his tone light but knowing a day could come when they might have to deal with having ventured into territory where boundary signs between white people and black people had become blurry, maybe even too faded to read. "Reba has surely earned a place here."

After they left Jackson's office, both smiling, Belle said to Skitchy, "You tell her."

"I will and don't worry, I'll work it around, about the gifts and about taking part. She'll be fine, you'll see."

Skitchy put Connie, Etta McCabe, and Rita Colquitt in charge of finding a box and decorating it. Names were drawn with much light-hearted fun the next Sunday afternoon. Soon a good deal of whispering could be heard around the hotel. Doors were often closed that were usually open and much laughter gave hints of innumerable conspiracies.

Mr. Wilson brought no Christmas trees, large or small, to the mercantile store that year, but he did bring in cut cedar boughs and gave a large one to Pink. The table by the lobby window was covered by Connie, assisted by Auntabelle, with somewhat worn green felt and a lace tablecloth. They laid the cedar bough, tied with bows made from Connie's red hair ribbons, on the table with three shiny red apples. Etta McCabe and Rita Colquitt went shopping at Wilson's to buy what they needed to make cookies, a rare treat, to array on a pressed glass plate to be placed next to the cedar bough and apples.

....

"Can I please go first?" Connie said in happy impatience when the gift giving began on Christmas Eve. Hutch's blind eye was covered with a patch but the other grew wide when Connie handed him a package wrapped in newspaper and tied with one of her green hair ribbons. "You have to give the ribbon back, though," Connie said, and everyone chuckled. As he took off the wrapping and stared at a book, Connie said, "I know you like to read. Thought you'd like to have a book of your very own, so I'm giving you one of mine. I hope you'll like it."

Connie received a new rag doll Reba made from sewing scraps. There was also a small dress for the doll like one of Connie's, and tiny pajamas, so she could change the clothes. "I just love her!" Connie said joyfully, and kissed Reba on the cheek.

Skitchy, amazed and delighted, laughed when she saw that Alma had given her the split skirt she made. "Pretty sneaky, pretending to have me be a model for you."

Alma smiled through tears as she said softly, "Your encouragement to finish making it meant so much to me, Skitchy. More than you can ever imagine. That and liking the name I made up for it. I wanted you to have it from that day you found me working on it."

Skitchy had taken Pink's boots to the boot maker for new soles and heels, trading two pairs of Connie's outgrown shoes for the work. She'd cleaned the boots herself and put in new laces. "Thanks, honey," Pink said. "Fixing the holes with cardboard hasn't been working too well." He laughed awkwardly, which Skitchy knew covered the embarrassment and annoyance of a man who liked to dress well and didn't have enough money for new boots or even to have the old ones repaired.

Rita Colquitt gave Jackson a pint of brandy. Etta McCabe gave her sister a cameo brooch that had belonged to their mother and opened a sack from Pink holding two oranges, her favorite of all fruits and a rare treat. The brandy and oranges would be shared the next day as Christmas treats, welcomed by everyone even as they would protest about personal gifts turning into gifts for everyone.

Hutch read a story about a scarecrow coming to life on dark nights and after adventures, taking up his job in the garden again when the sun comes up. He presented the page on which it was written, which he had decorated using Connie's crayons, to Alma.

Belle's delight at receiving a bright red lipstick and another of bright pink from Jackson was apparent to all. It didn't matter to her at all that she'd be the first woman in Reeves County wearing the bright new colors when few women wore any makeup. In fact, Skitchy was sure as she watched her sister apply the bright color to her lips later that day, that Belle liked being the first one to have anything new. She'd always been like that with her dresses and hats and shoes. Why not lipstick? And it had been a long while since Belle or anyone else had anything new.

The last gift was for Reba, clearly not used to receiving gifts. Belle had a small gold cross on a gold chain that Reba had admired, and there it was, resting on a square of satin in its little box. Reba looked at the cross in disbelief. "Law, I've never had such a thing in my life!"

Jackson said, his voice filled with warmth, "Reba, you're a fine woman. We're very fortunate to have you here with us."

Belle added, "May you wear it with pleasure and pride, with our thanks for all you've done."

Reba did, never seen after that night without it around her neck.

1934

The dust storms had been worse than ever during April and May, followed by one of the hottest driest summers anyone could remember. Dust seemed to hang in the air. So when Skitchy looked out the window one early September morning when she got up and saw that it was clear and calm, her first thought was McMinn Springs.

"It would just tickle me if we could go on a picnic at McMinn Springs," she said brightly to Pink as soon as he was awake. "Connie'll be starting school soon. Today might be the only chance we get. It's been ages since we were there. I think it'd pick up our spirits. Everybody's been so grouchy."

Pink, sitting on the edge of the bed, stretching himself awake, felt his own grouchiness lift a little in response to Skitchy's enthusiasm. "Well, I was supposed to work at the drug store today but I can probably work something out with

Jackson. We're short on gas but a picnic sounds like fun. We could sure use a little fun. Let's go."

Connie helped Reba fill a sack with bologna and cornbread sandwiches, deviled eggs, pickles, a thermos of ice tea and an apple Mr. Wilson had sent home as a special treat for Connie. All the Campbells felt light-hearted and Pink sang, Skitchy and Connie singing along, as they drove, a cloud of dust rolling behind them.

But when they got to McMinn Springs they were taken aback. The pool had almost disappeared.

"What happened to the water?" a dismayed Skitchy cried.

Pink said, "I read something in the paper about farmers taking water from the springs for irrigation but I never dreamed it'd be like this!"

Tears welled up in Skitchy's eyes as she stood looking at the rocky pool bed. "It isn't just the pool. It's this whole long old drought. And the dust that just doesn't stop. And the depression. Law, it's awful." Pink put one arm around her and took Connie's hand with the other as she stood beside her parents, quiet, watching. Skitchy dropped her head on Pink's shoulder with a deep sigh.

They turned away finally and spread a quilt under the trees. The cottonwoods had rooted themselves near water, preparing for drought long ago. Their leaves were dusty but still green, the only green they could see.

"At least the trees are still here," Skitchy said.

....

When the Campbells got home Belle's door was open. Skitchy saw her sister pacing in the front room of her quarters, muttering something Skitchy couldn't hear. Skitchy knocked softly on the open door. "Something the matter, Belle?"

Belle stopped pacing and looked at the calm voice speaking to her. Her own voice shrill, she said, "Another old hobo came around this afternoon. Stole one of the chickens. Hutch saw him. Yelled and ran after him but couldn't stop him. He got one of my good laying hens."

"Sorry to hear that," Skitchy said gently. She wanted to say something more, seeing how fussed her sister was, but wasn't sure what that should be. Hoping it wouldn't sound lame, she said, "You must be aggravated."

Belle hardly seemed to hear. "We give them food when they ask. Did that old tramp think he's the only one having a hard time? Makes it all right to just take what belongs to other people?"

"Maybe he didn't think to ask, honey," Skitchy said gently. "Maybe he didn't think at all. Do you recollect when Daddy used to tell us about seeing people go loco when they were up against more than they could handle? Like when families on the pioneer trail lost their wagons in a river crossing? Times like that? Maybe this is a time like that for that old hobo."

Belle frowned and looked at her sister with that look Skitchy had long known meant Belle wasn't thinking straight. She'll be herself after a while, Skitchy thought. "I'm going to help Connie get settled," she said. "I'll be upstairs if you want to talk later." She passed Jackson on his way downstairs as she went up and from his manner when they exchanged hellos she wondered if he, too, had gotten that look.

....

145

By late afternoon Belle had calmed down. She'd been by herself in her quarters and was about to go to the kitchen to get some coffee when Jackson brought her a bourbon and soda. She looked up gratefully as she took the drink. "Thank you, honey. Sorry for getting so riled up. Snapping at you. Snapped at Skitchy, too. I don't know what got into me. It was just a chicken. Don't know why it bothered me so much. Somehow it felt like that old hobo took something much more than a chicken."

"You've given away food to hobos lots of times," he said gently. "But you gave it. Feels different when someone steals it. Doesn't matter if it's a chicken or a tidy sum, if it catches you just right it can throw and hog tie you."

"You understand, Jackson," she said gratefully.

"It was like that for me when we lost what we had in the stock market when it crashed and then the bank failed. I felt like everything was gone. Clean forgot we still had the hotel and the drug store. Still had each other." His voice broke and it took a minute for him to get hold of himself and finish what he wanted to say to her. "You can't just let yourself stay hog tied. You can choose to not pay it so much mind or let it keep you hobbled."

Belle was listening intently now. She knew he was talking about himself as much as about her. She also knew that no one had talked with her like this since her father had stopped so many years ago, when his words seemed to fall on deaf ears. "I don't quite know what to say right this minute, Jackson. But I hear you. Just need to think about it for myself for a bit."

"I love being around when you think about things, honey." He smiled broadly at her and kissed her on the cheek. "I think you're so smart, Belle. A lot smarter than you maybe think you are."

Belle looked after him as he left to go back to his office. Surely smart when I decided to marry you, Jackson Tieger, she thought.

....

Skitchy saw the elderly sisters go past her door, both with their hats on and carrying their purses. Connie was spending the night with Belle and Jackson. Skitchy had been wanting to talk with Alma and with no one upstairs to overhear or interrupt, she decided to go to Alma's room.

"Alma," Skitchy said nervously, closing the door, "can I talk with you about something personal? Something you can't repeat to anyone. Even Tom. Tom in particular."

Combing her hair and arranging it this way and that as she looked at herself in the small mirror on top of the oak dresser, Alma said, "Well, Tom's not around. Anyhow, I know how to keep a muzzle on. Friends should be able to talk to each other and not have to worry about anything."

Skitchy hesitated. Something told her maybe Alma was not the right person for her to be talking to, but she'd already started so she pushed her hesitation aside and settled herself in a chair. In halting words she began, "It's about Pink. Our lovemaking." Long pause. "Sometimes we start to make love but then he loses interest or something. We can't . . . that is, we don't . . . finish . . . He can't finish. He won't talk with me about it."

Alma turned toward Skitchy, looking sympathetically at her friend. "Oh, Skitch, that just happens to men sometimes," Alma said lightly. "Sensitive thing for them. Probably why Pink doesn't want to talk about it. Tom won't talk about it either. Nothing to worry about." She returned her attention to the mirror and her hair.

Disappointed by the lightness of Alma's manner and words but determined now that she'd started the conversation, Skitchy went on. "But it's gotten a lot worse lately. I feel awful when it happens. I'm just left hanging there, all excited, and . . . then nothing. I can tell Pink feels bad when that happens." She dropped her eyes in embarrassment. "I tried to tell him I don't necessarily need him to be hard. He could use his fingers. He doesn't want to. Or seem to be able to. Or something. I don't know, when he won't say anything."

Alma, hearing the tone of Skitchy's voice, turned toward her again. "When it first happened with Tom I talked to my mama about it. She told me the best thing to do is not complain or make him feel any worse. That's worked out pretty well for Tom and me."

Skitchy had hoped for much more from their talk but she didn't think it was going any further. "Well, thank you, Alma. I appreciate being able to talk about it." But she felt no less frustrated than she had before the talk.

....

"Sugar, you look so nice for your first day of school," Skitchy said to her daughter as Connie stood in the lobby to have her picture taken by Uncle Jackson.

"I like my new dress and shoes. Thank you so much, Mama." Skitchy had made the dress from flour sacks, which now came printed with colorful prints to stimulate sales. Mother and daughter had spent more than half an hour at the mercantile store going through all the sacks to pick out two matching ones with pink flowers on a light green background that Connie liked and thought pretty. Belle had helped her pick out just the right shade of pink ribbons to tie at the ends of her long brown braids.

Skitchy and Connie had also spent quite some time trying on shoes at the Shoe Exchange Mr. Wilson had set up in a section of the hardware department that hadn't been seeing much business. Families could bring in kids' shoes they'd outgrown and trade them for shoes outgrown by someone else. Skitchy had suggested the Exchange after she'd traded Connie's shoes to the boot maker last Christmas and other times with some of her friends in town who had older or younger children. But often the sizes didn't work and she had gotten the idea that if a lot of families participated, it would work much better. And it had.

Skitchy also made sure Mr. Wilson was credited with making the Shoe Exchange happen, providing space at his store and publicizing it with posters and notices in the newspaper. Mr. Wilson became a hero to many of the mothers in town and the surrounding ranches and farms. Pink became one of the few men in town who could count on work, whenever Mr. Wilson had any work.

As Connie was about to set off, Skitchy said, "Sugar, you have your handkerchief?"

"Yes, ma'am. Right here in my pocket," and she patted the deep pocket Skitchy had sewn on the dress just for this purpose.

"Be sure to hold it over your nose and mouth if you're outside and the dust is blowing. That stuff is bad for you to breathe."

"I will, Mama."

Belle hugged her niece. "These are for you, honey," and she gave Connie a little sack containing a set of jacks. "I thought you might like to have them if you're indoors for recess when the dust is blowing."

Eyes wide, Connie put the jacks in the pocket with her handkerchief. "I love to play with jacks just about anytime! Thank you, Auntabelle!"

Skitchy said cheerfully, "I'll want to hear all about school when you get home." She kissed her daughter and watched her walk down the street until she turned the corner and was out of sight. Then the mother turned and sat down hard in a chair near the door, her face drawn.

Everyone except Connie knew Skitchy was worried about the little girl breathing the awful dark dust that so often hung in the air even long after a duster had blown through. The ones who'd been there to see Connie off melted away silently, except for Belle. She brought her sister a cup of coffee before she, too, left Skitchy to her private thoughts.

They'd all heard stories about Lubbock, Amarillo, and places further away, north of Texas, stories about livestock suffocating, of people, especially children, dying from dust pneumonia. Skitchy knew it wasn't as bad as that in McAllister, but still she was fearful for Connie. She wanted Connie to go to school, to be able to play outside. But what if the dust here didn't have to be that bad to hurt her child? Everyone knew now that the huge dark clouds roaring high into the air were the earth itself, plowed bare of its hardy native grasses and dried by drought, the earth itself heaved into the air by fierce winds. It was different from the more or less nuisance dust people in West Texas were used to, and it overflowed the plains as storms brought dense dark dust even to McAllister. The dust had become as depressing as the depression and almost inseparable from it in many people's minds.

Just day before yesterday Pink and Hutch had shoveled away mounds of the awful stuff which had drifted against the back wall of the hotel, carefully uncovering what was left of Belle's garden. Pink picked a few cantaloupes and some vegetables, put them into a basket and hauled it into the kitchen.

"The lettuce was ruined but the melons and most of the squash and peas are all right. This storm was another bad one," he sighed.

Belle's sigh echoed Pink's. "How about the chickens and the goat?"

"The goat seems to be all right. Lost two hens but I think the others are fine. I'll need to make some repairs to the coop but there isn't enough wood and I'll need some more nails. I'll see if Ike Tottle has any old stuff I can use. Or maybe I can find something at the store."

"Trade the melons if you need to." Belle sighed again. "Law, I hate this awful old dust."

....

It was the first weekend after Thanksgiving. Skitchy stood nervously with Pink and Mr. Wilson in front of the mercantile store to open the Christmas Exchange by plugging in the lights of the small Christmas tree. Skitchy wore the blue dress she'd worn at her wedding, her hair newly cut short in a straight bob. Pink wore a jacket and wool pants even though the seat of the wool pants was shiny from wear. A large poster advertising the Exchange stood on an easel beside them and the *McAllister Pioneer* had informed everyone in the area that they could bring Christmas baked goods, jams and other canned goods, clothing, and miscellaneous articles to the store and exchange them for other things. Everyone was invited to the opening of the Exchange.

"Merry Christmas!" Mr. Wilson beamed, resplendent in a gray suit that wasn't new but wasn't shiny in the seat of the pants, Skitchy noticed. "Now come on in. Pink will help you find things and explain how the Exchange works if you don't know. Come right on in!"

As people began to move into the store, Belle and Jackson came up to Skitchy, still standing by the Christmas tree. Belle hugged her sister.

"You've done a wonderful thing here, Skitch, you and Pink."

"Just made so much sense to me to expand the Shoe Exchange. Help people trade with each other. Make a happier Christmas for a lot of folks. Surprised no one else had thought of it."

"Well, you thought of it!" Jackson said enthusiastically. "Great idea! And you and Pink made it happen."

"Don't know why it was so hard to convince Pink he should bring it up to Mr. Wilson. He got shy or something, I guess. Anyway, when he finally did, he told Mr. Wilson it was my idea. He really wanted Mr. Wilson to know that. But I never expected Mr. Wilson would include me in the opening ceremony!"

....

The holidays over, Skitchy sat down in the lobby to have a cup of coffee with Belle. Belle put a cigarette into her silver and bone holder and held the package out to her sister.

"Smoke?"

"No thanks." Skitchy sipped her coffee and then after a time said, "Well, guess I'll take that cigarette after all." She looked strained and sounded strained.

"What's the matter, honey?"

"Pink told me this morning the Christmas Exchange was a big success. Folks loved it. Store did quite a bit more business during the holidays than Mr. Wilson thought it would besides. He's thinking about keeping it going. It's a lot of work but some women from the churches have offered to help out as long as Mr. Wilson is willing to keep setting aside the space for it."

"Sounds like a good thing. But you sound annoyed or something."

"It is a good thing. I'm annoyed . . . well I don't know if I'm annoyed exactly. I just wonder how come a group of women have to talk to Mr. Wilson about keeping the Exchange going. Why Pink doesn't think of things like that. And it would've been fine with me for him to take credit for thinking of it. I want him to get ahead with Mr. Wilson. Pink almost seems to put himself down."

Belle's voice was softer than her sister's as she said, "I don't know if you know how much Jackson's daddy wanted him to be a rancher. Even when he knew Jackson hated ranching. Jackson always wanted to have a business. He might even have made a mess of ranching. Maybe Pink isn't good at business the way Jackson wouldn't be good at ranching."

"I sure don't know what Pink is good at then." Skitchy heard her own voice sounding like an echo of her father's, warning her so many years ago that Pink didn't seem to have much direction in life. That she shouldn't get involved with him. She didn't so much wish she'd listened to her father as wish that Pink would prove him, and her, wrong.

....

Pink took a cup of coffee with him to the empty lobby to drink while he read the *Pioneer*. After a while he realized he wasn't reading. In fact, he was just looking at the newspaper without seeing what he was looking at. He put the paper down. He felt sure Skitchy was disappointed in him. He was surely disappointed in himself. Disappointed with his life. He had to do something or he felt he might be stuck in this dark hole of disappointment forever.

As he glanced down at the newspaper this time he saw the picture of the McAllister High School Panthers quarterback, throwing arm back to pass the football. Memories flooded him of his own playing days as quarterback for his high school team back home in Iowa. He had been a pretty good player even though he was not tall or powerfully built. Those had been good days. Suddenly an idea came to him. It was a small idea but maybe big enough to help him get unstuck.

He'd watched the Panthers lose another football game on Friday. Buck Jamison, the quarterback, had thrown some passes that were off the mark and called some plays that didn't move the ball the way Pink thought they should have. Ike Tottle, sitting beside Pink and griping as he always did when the team lost, told him that Johnny Corrigan, the team's coach, had been a center in his playing days. "Just doesn't know how to coach the backs. I'm not the only one thinks that. A lot of the boosters do. Dadgum it, heard Johnny say it himself."

So the next Monday afternoon Pink watched the team practice from the empty stands. After practice ended, Pink went down to the field as Coach Corrigan was putting away a few last things.

"Pink, what brings you down here?"

Johnny Corrigan was a big man, older than Pink. Pink felt small standing next to him. After a momentary hesitation Pink hoped wasn't noticed, he said, "I used to play a fair game, Coach, and I wondered how you'd feel about me maybe working with the Jamison kid. I was a pretty good quarterback and I can see a few things that might improve his passing."

"That'd be great, Pink. But I don't know how much longer we're going to be able to play. The boosters want the team to keep playing, but this dang dust is bad for the boys to breathe. Some of the parents are jittery."

"Well, if I can help I'm willing to do it for as much of the season as you're playing."

So Pink started working with the Panthers' quarterback, and later the receivers, every afternoon the team was practicing, if he wasn't working at the store. He did help to improve the team's passing game, and that was no small matter in a town crazy about high school football. His success with the team and his visibility on the sidelines at games gave Pink himself a big boost in the eyes of Mr. Wilson. Also in the eyes of Ike Tottle and the other team boosters, and others who dropped by Wilson's Mercantile Store fairly often to talk football. And do a little shopping while they were there.

....

"I wish you'd come to the game tomorrow, honey," Pink said as he and Skitchy went upstairs after supper. "The Panthers are playing for the League championship. And it may be the last game the team plays until this dust settles down."

"I'm not interested in football, Pink. You know I never have been. Crazy as that may seem to everybody else in town. Glad you're having fun but Law, you spend an awful lot of time and energy on it."

Pink felt a thud in his stomach. I wish she could see what I'm trying to do, he thought. It's fun but it's also something I've been able to do in this town to show people a little of what I can do. And Mr. Wilson said just the other day that what I'm doing with the team is bringing in customers to the store, wanting to talk a little football. I'm trying to get ahead besides having a little fun. I don't know why it makes me feel so sad that she doesn't seem to see that.

Skitchy felt his wordless sadness. She felt annoyed that he didn't talk to her about the sadness. I should still try to encourage him, she thought. "I know it's been hard for you, Pink," she said. "Has been for all of us. Sorry I've been so cranky. Good luck tomorrow. I hope the team wins the championship. Do the whole town good." She wished she felt less grudging, but at least she got the words out.

The Panthers did win the championship and as Pink got ready for bed his enthusiasm was plain to see and hear. "The boys played a great game! It looked for a while there like they'd take us but Jamison and the whole team hung in there and got it done! I'm so proud of them."

"Congratulations! You've done a great job with the team, Pink."

Skitchy felt his hardness brush against her as he settled in bed beside her. Guess I should touch him or at least kiss him, she thought sourly. But why should I have to make love just because he's hard? Plenty of times I wanted to and he didn't. She turned over, half hoping he would put his arm around her and draw her to him.

After a long minute she said, "Good night, Pink."

"Good night, honey."

1935

Severe drought was now in its fourth year on the high plains and high desert. The land and the people were parched. High wind season was March, April, and May and the first day of March brought an immense dark oily sand storm from the north to McAllister. Along with blasting wind, strings of static electricity crackled, sparking from barbed wire fences, singeing plants. A second storm came the next day. Another the day after. People walked around as if in shock, unable to believe this could be happening again, until coughs, raw throats, itching eyes, cracking skin, and irritable souls made it indisputable.

Jackson was determined to keep life as normal as possible, so he and Pink and Hutch silently stuffed windows and doors with strips of rag to keep out as much dust as they could. Reba got out buckets and rags and cleaned up what they couldn't keep out. For the first five days.

"No more, Reba," Jackson said on the sixth straight day of unrelenting blowing dust. Resignation was as thick in his voice as the drifts that made McAllister look like a town unwittingly built on low shifting sand dunes. "Take care of the kitchen so we're not eating this stuff. Do the best you can to keep one guest room clean in case someone comes in for a night. Everything else, wait till it's over."

Every day the winds died down late in the day but before the dust could settle, another morning brought another storm. Some were worse than others but there was no day without blowing dust for twenty-seven days. Everybody's nerves were on edge.

"Law, isn't it ever going to stop?" Skitchy lamented as she looked out the lobby window.

....

The wind died down early in the afternoon on the Saturday before Palm Sunday. Then the next morning, Palm Sunday, McAllister woke to clear skies, clean air, no wind. It felt like Easter a week early.

Reba got out rags and buckets again to clean up the accumulated dust. Connie wanted to help and soon others joined in. It had been a long time since cleaning seemed like anything but a thankless, useless job. It seemed to raise everyone's spirits to triumph over the dust that day.

When they finished, Skitchy called out gaily, "Let's have a picnic."

"A picnic!" Connie immediately echoed, clapping her hands in delight.

Belle knew the little spring that had sustained the small square of the park for years had dwindled to a trickle. She doubted the park would seem very welcoming after a month of dust storms. "It'll be so dirty at the park," she said, but when she saw Connie's face fall with disappointment, she felt badly.

"Well, we could have a picnic right here," Skitchy said brightly.

Belle quickly joined in with her sister's enthusiasm. "Spread quilts out right here on the floor!"

"This is going to be a very funny picnic," Connie laughed joyfully.

They all took sponge baths and dressed in fresh clean clothes. Belle brushed cornmeal through her hair and Connie's. As she was braiding Connie's hair, Connie asked wistfully, "Auntabelle, do you think we'll ever be able to wash our hair again?"

"No drought lasts forever, Connie dear. It *will* rain again. When it's rained enough the cistern will get filled up. We'll have plenty of nice soft rain water for washing our hair and lots of other things." She took a box of ribbons from the dresser drawer and held it out for Connie to choose which color she wanted to wear.

"Blue, I think. Do you think blue would look pretty, Auntabelle?"

"Blue would look very pretty. Just right to go with the blue flowers in your dress." She tied the blue ribbons on Connie's long brown braids. Smiling at the young girl, she said, "You look just lovely!" Connie looked at herself in the mirror, turning so she could see herself, the blue ribbons in particular, and grinned. Holding hands, Belle and Connie went down to join the others who were going to church.

Before she left, Belle told Reba, "I've been saving those two hens that haven't laid eggs in months for Easter but let's have them today. Go ahead and fry them up." Turning to

Hutch, she said, "See if you can dig out any greens from the garden that are still good. If there aren't any we'll have canned."

"Yes, ma'am," he said, already on his way.

After they got home from church Connie put on the small apron that Skitchy had made for her, just like her own. Connie joyfully helped make applesauce oatmeal cookies with raisins, a rare treat. Belle used the last of the potatoes in the pantry to make her special potato salad that everybody loved. Alma made deviled eggs and spread peanut butter lavishly on Reba's hot biscuits. When everything was ready, everyone helped carry the food with much ceremony to the quilts spread out in the middle of the lobby. Skitchy grinned at Reba when she saw her carrying the platter of fried chicken. She was wearing the muslin apron printed with yellow flowers her cousin in Lubbock had made for her one Christmas, and which Reba wore only on special occasions. Reba grinned back.

Later, everyone played cards, a lighthearted game of Hearts. Everyone except Reba and Hutch, cleaning up in the kitchen, and Etta McCabe, who was unraveling one of her old sweaters. "All out of yarn," the old woman explained, winding the thread into a big ball, "but I figured out a way to get some." When the card game ended, Connie fell asleep on the settee and Skitchy let her sleep there. Jackson brought out brandy and put it in the coffee for anyone who wanted it.

Jackson stood by the lobby window, drinking his brandied coffee, smoking a cigarette. Looking out at the clear afternoon light, he noticed birds flying low down the street, all in the same direction. Quite a few birds. Then he saw rabbits, jackrabbits and cottontails, streaming down the street in the same direction. "What the devil?" he exclaimed, sounding perplexed, bringing Belle to the window beside him.

"What is it, honey?"

"I have no idea," he said, and stepped out onto the porch. He looked to the northeast, the direction from which the birds and rabbits had come. His stomach suddenly knotted as he saw an ominous dark line on the horizon moving toward them. "Oh, no," he whispered hoarsely, and rushed back inside.

"Close all the windows!" he shouted to Skitchy, closest to the door. "Hurry!" He yelled loud enough to be heard in the kitchen, its door open, "Hutch, make sure the goat's inside the shed! Get the chickens in the coop if you can! Make sure the door is locked tight when you come in! Belle, make sure all the other doors are locked downstairs! Pink, close the windows and doors upstairs!"

Connie woke up, rubbing her eyes. "What's going on? What's the matter?"

....

The storm had started early that morning, far to the north, in North Dakota. As a cold front collided with warm currents, violent wind came up suddenly. It screamed over the naked plains, picking up a tremendous load of heavy black sand. The temperature plunged thirty degrees in front of the leading edge of the huge rolling monster as it moved southward at more than sixty-five miles an hour. The thing was alive with static electricity. It was wider and higher than any duster before, blocking the sun, making the sky so black that people couldn't see their own hands. A few Weather Bureau offices telegraphed ahead to warn of the storm's approach, but it was a Sunday and word spread slowly. The biggest worst duster ever moved so fast that few people had any warning before things suddenly went black.

McAllister was on the fringe of the storm. It reached there late in the day when the wind had died down to about thirty miles an hour. Black Sunday, as it was called later, would not be nearly as black in McAllister as it was in the Texas panhandle and farther north. With dark humor, the people of Reeves County would call it their Dark Gray Sunday. Still, the swollen cloud carried a tremendous load of dark oily dirt laced with static electricity.

"Why is it getting so dark all of a sudden?" Connie wanted to know.

"It's the dust, sugar," Belle explained. "Kind of like clouds on a dark rainy day, except the clouds are made of dust." Wind began to howl around the corners of the hotel and oily sand rattled windows upstairs and down. Lightning flashed, sometimes very close to them. Again and again and again.

"I don't like it," the seven year old child said. "It's scary." There wasn't a grown up in the hotel who didn't feel the same way. No one wanted to be alone and everyone huddled around the pot-bellied stove in the lobby, including Reba and Hutch.

"Best you stay in here with the rest of us," Jackson had told them.

We need to do something, Skitchy thought. Not just huddle here. We'll all get loco. "Let's play some more Hearts," she said, trying to keep her voice light.

Belle thought that sounded like a good idea but didn't have the heart for it. Rita Colquitt said, "Just don't think I can, Skitchy. I feel like I can hardly move." Skitchy sat down on one of the quilts still on the floor, shuffled the cards and started playing Rummy with Connie.

"Can I watch?" Alma asked, already sitting down.

Pink quickly joined them, both parents talking and trying to keep Connie's mind on the card game.

A strong gust shuddered the lobby window hard, spraying it with heavy sand. Jackson feared the glass might break. He couldn't think of what to do if that happened. Not usually much of a praying man, he prayed that everything would hold.

"Make some fresh coffee, Mr. Jackson?" Reba asked.

"You bet. Thank you, Reba. Coffee would be good." They would drink three pots before the wind died down as night fell, the dust dying down with it.

No one seemed ready to go to bed until Jackson finally let the fire in the pot-bellied stove burn itself out. It felt to Skitchy as if she and all the others were moving in slow motion as they went to their rooms.

....

The next morning Jackson checked over the hotel, then went to see how the town had fared. He came in to the kitchen two hours later where Belle and Skitchy were helping Reba once again clean up the dust that had sifted through the back door and windows. "Everything looks all right here as far as I can see. Thank goodness for stone! Grandpa knew how to build something to last. The paint is pretty much gone on the doors and windows, but they were already in bad shape." A hint of resignation crept into his voice. "News in town is pretty good. George Hannon and Andy Frederickson lost some livestock. I'd guess we'll hear that some other ranchers did, too. There's wind damage all around town. Stuff that got dumped or piled up in drifts was too heavy a load for some of the old roofs. Part of the fire station caved in. Looks like Barney Wright may've lost his boot shop. Lot of cars won't start."

"And that's the good news?" Skitchy said dispiritedly.

"Well, the news from Amarillo is a whole lot worse. Nobody knows yet how many people didn't make it there. Lots of livestock suffocated. The Weather Bureau says somebody in an airplane thought the duster was two miles high and two hundred miles wide."

"Well, I think it's plenty bad enough here." Skitchy went on, her voice strained and choking back tears, "Maybe the worst thing is having a beautiful Sunday make us think all those awful old dusters were over. Now we know they aren't. Maybe they won't ever be. After yesterday, it looks like they're even getting worse."

....

Some people in McAllister collapsed in despair, but most did the best they could to cope in the wake of the Black Sunday storm. Church attendance went up. So did business at the bawdyhouse on the edge of town. Business in bootleg whiskey was brisk as Sherriff Conger looked the other way. The twin Hicks brothers who owned the livery stable and Barney Wright, who made boots and repaired shoes and had lost his shop, had all had enough and made plans to move away with their families. Men went about making repairs to houses, businesses, schools, and cars if they could do the work themselves. Women got out their rags and buckets and cleaned up the dust in their homes as they always had.

Pink went down to the high school and joined the players, parents, and boosters who shoveled the heavy dirt off the Panthers' playing field. Afterward he tossed a ball around with some of the players.

Jackson told Belle, "The Pecos radio transmitter is finally broadcasting and I'll figure out some way to pay for a radio. Can't count on birds and rabbits for news. We need to know what's happening."

Belle, who'd been working crossword puzzles for hours on end, brightened. "I'd be tickled to have a radio."

Skitchy looked up from her letter writing. "I'd like to listen, too. If you don't mind, Jackson."

Alma, mending and patching the hotel's old quilts, also looked interested, although she said nothing.

Jackson chuckled, "Looks like I'd best keep it out here in the lobby."

Connie crawled cozily into bed each night for a week with Auntabelle and listened to stories with happy endings until she was sleepy.

When Reba wasn't busy in the kitchen or with her bucket and rags, she sat quietly at the kitchen table, sometimes with her eyes closed, and no one disturbed her.

Hutch watched Jackson and Pink to see how men conducted themselves.

....

Tom Floyd came back to McAllister in May looking older and thinner than when he left for the Wink oil fields. He told Alma in a strained voice, "Oil prices had already gone down from a buck thirty to ten cents a barrel when I got there. They weren't drilling any new wells. I was lucky to get some work on pump jacks but even that fell off after a while. Prices went down some more. I heard rumors saying to four cents. They cut my hours way back. That's when I wrote you I couldn't send much money. They let me go two days ago. Dang oil business. Dang depression."

Alma's face was strained. When she spoke her voice was strained, too. "What are we going to do now?"

"I hope we can stay here for a while. I need to ponder on everything."

Later Jackson told Belle, "I can understand how Tom hoped he'd find steady work up there. But I think it was mostly wishful thinking. No matter how much oil is still in the ground in the Wink fields, market's dried up. Your folks are lucky they didn't take much oil stock as payment for the ranch like some folks did."

Kate and Ephraim Chapman had made nothing on the oil stock they had from the sale of their ranch. Two drilling attempts on the land had come up dry and plummeting prices had done the rest. Fortunately they'd put some of the money from the sale of the ranch in the bank in Pecos, which was still in business. They'd been able to live on that even when they lost what they'd deposited in the failed bank in Kermit. The Chapmans had moved into a small house in Big Lake owned by Minnie and Bob. Skitchy and Belle both knew their parents were weary. Weary from the loss of so much of what they'd worked so hard for. Weary from so much moving around after most of a lifetime lived on the ranch.

Belle shivered, thinking about her parents, but turned her attention to the Floyds. "What are we going to do about Alma and Tom, Jackson? I know they're Pink's friends and Skitchy has gotten to be good friends with Alma. But probably everybody in West Texas would like to live here for nothing." Jackson frowned. Belle went on, "Can't see putting them out on the street. But Law, even if it doesn't cost us anything to let them keep the room, how are we going to feed them? Lots of empty stomachs. Not many paying customers."

Still frowning Jackson said, "Let's give it a little while. Maybe I can figure something out." He felt much as Belle did about the Floyds but didn't like to think of himself as letting people down who were counting on him.

A little while came and went. Alma and Tom seemed to avoid everyone else as much as they could. They ate very little at meals. Tom tried to sell his guitar but no one was willing to spend the little money they had to buy a luxury like that. He went to every business in town. No one had any work. He had better luck when he borrowed a horse from Ike Tottle and rode out to the ranches and farms around McAllister. He got some work mending fences for a rancher who paid him with a side of beef.

Many ranchers slaughtered cattle they could no longer afford to feed and Tom happened by at the right place at just the right time. The beef was welcomed with great delight at the hotel, a luxury they had not enjoyed for quite a while. They ate roast beef for the noon meal on Sunday, along with Reba's biscuits and gravy, and swiss chard from the garden. Reba made a beef and macaroni casserole the next day. Then beans flavored with beef fat and a little meat, followed by a richly flavored beef soup. All these meals were eaten with gusto. Reba cut the rest of the meat into chunks to be canned.

....

One evening not long after that, Tom sat with Pink on the hotel porch. He took a long draw on his cigarette. "I'm thinking about maybe trying to get to California, Pink.

Alma's sister in San Diego says a man can pick up something sometimes if he's not too picky. We can stay with her until we can get a place of our own."

Pink was stunned. "California! Are you crazy, Tom? How would you even get there?"

"Well, buddy, I was wondering if you'd let me have your car. You're not driving it. When I get work, I'll send you some money for it. Alma's sister says she can loan us enough money for food and gas to get there."

Pink lit another cigarette, offering Tom one. "I have to think about that, Tom."

....

Talking with Skitchy later, Pink was careful to choose his words when he brought up his conversation with Tom. "Skitch, he's my best friend. He's helped me out plenty of times. I'm thinking to let him have the car."

Skitchy was dismayed. "Do I have anything to say about it? I think it's as much my business as yours."

Pink paced from one side of their room to the other, trying to keep his voice down. "Tom'll be good for it if he can, and if he can't, I can't see how we lose much. It's an old car and we don't have money for gas. Lord knows when we will. There's no way to sell it here if we wanted to. Why not take a chance on Tom?"

Skitchy felt it was all wrong but she couldn't come up with a good argument against what Pink was saying. She was pretty sure Pink had already made up his mind and she was as angry about that as about the car itself. "What I think doesn't matter then?" was the only thing she could think of to say. Her voice was shrill, which annoyed her.

Pink shot back angrily, "Well, what do you think? Have your say."

When Skitchy didn't say anything for a minute that felt like ten to Pink he turned abruptly and stalked out of the room, slamming the door on his way out. Skitchy said out loud to the departed Pink, "So much for keeping our voices down."

....

When Pink came back Skitchy was already in bed. "Are you asleep?" he whispered.

"No."

He undressed without speaking and crawled in beside her, moving close to her. "I'm sorry, honey. I don't know why I got so mad. I do want to know what you think."

Skitchy felt her heart unfreezing and she could feel Pink's hardness pressing against her. She didn't touch his hardness, though. Not yet. "I know we can't afford gas right now. But having the car means a lot to me. I miss being able to drive. I'd like to go see Mama and Daddy. Oh, Pink, it just feels awful to think about not having the car." She was a little annoyed with herself when the tears started to come, wanting to speak calmly and seem reasonable.

Pink put his arms around her. "What you want does matter, honey. We'll keep the car." They made love that night, an infrequent happening between them now.

....

Skitchy knocked softly on the door of the Tieger's private quarters. She didn't like to disturb her sister or Jackson in their quarters but she couldn't find Connie. The young girl had gone outside to play but wasn't on the porch or in the back yard of the hotel, the two places she usually played. When Belle opened the door, Skitchy asked, "Belle, is Connie with you?"

"She's in the kitchen, playing checkers with Hutch."

"Playing checkers with Hutch?"

Hearing the surprise in her sister's voice, Belle said, "She asked me if he could teach her to play and I told her it was all right. Was that a mistake?"

"No, I'm just surprised. I thought Jackson didn't want her to spend too much time in the kitchen with Reba and Hutch. I know he wants them to do their work, not spend their time looking out for Connie. Can't imagine he'd want Hutch to be playing games with her."

"Oh, he's said things like that, but not lately. I told him Reba and Hutch don't have something to do every minute. And Connie always asks first. I think it's good for her to learn how to mix with black people and still respect our differences."

"Not sure she sees any differences, Belle, to tell you the truth."

"Well, playing checkers, you may be right. You should look in on them. They're so serious. You'd think they were playing for big stakes. They're surely cute."

Skitchy went into the kitchen and there were Connie and Hutch, just as Belle had said, hunched over the checkers board at one end of the kitchen table. Neither of them even seemed aware that she'd come into the kitchen.

"Good morning, Mrs. Skitchy," Reba said cheerily. "Help you with something? Hutch, say good morning to Mrs. Campbell."

Hutch was now as tall as his mother, his shoulders wide even though he was still thin, and the beginnings of a beard announced approaching manhood. He looked up from the checkers game, startled. "Good morning, Mrs. Campbell. Sorry. Didn't hear you come in. I was so engrossed in our game."

Skitchy was surprised to hear Hutch use a word like engrossed, that he'd even know the word, but she said nothing. "That's all right, Hutch. Connie, finish your game. Then come upstairs."

"Yes, ma'am."

As Skitchy was going up the stairs a few minutes later, she heard her daughter hoot loudly in delight. When Connie came into the room, grinning broadly, Skitchy said, "Sounds like you won the game."

"First time I ever beat him!" she said triumphantly.

....

Later in the day, Skitchy saw Hutch working in the garden from her upstairs window and went down to the kitchen, wanting to speak to Reba alone. She found Reba sitting at the kitchen table shelling peas. "Don't get up," she said to Reba. "I'll get myself some coffee." She took the cup to the table. "Mind if I sit with you?'

"Law, Mrs. Skitchy, you can sit with me any time you want to."

"I'd like to talk to you about Hutch, if that's all right."

Skitchy thought she saw Reba's shoulders stiffen and a shadow passed over her face, fading just as quickly.

"I'm just curious about something, Reba."

"Yes, ma'am." Reba's eyes were on the peas.

"This morning when Connie and Hutch were playing checkers, Hutch said something. Used a big word. Actually a word not a lot of grown ups I know would use. I know he's a bright boy but he doesn't go to school. I'm curious how he'd know a word like that."

"Well, he reads a lot," Reba said, still sounding somewhat guarded.

"I didn't know that. What does he read?"

"Connie let him read her books. He's read all the ones she has quite a few times. But the big words he probably gets from the newspapers."

"The newspapers? What newspapers?"

"Mr. Jackson stacks up the papers there when he's finished with them," and Reba gestured with her head toward newspapers neatly stacked in the corner. Skitchy was surprised she'd never noticed them before. "Hutch covers some of the little plants in the garden with them when the sun's hot. I use them to clean the windows. Put on the floor after I mop. Things like that." Reba darted a look at Skitchy, then added, "Hutch reads them first."

Skitchy's jaw dropped in amazement. "I always thought it was a shame he couldn't go to school. I never dreamed he'd be so determined to learn anyway. You must be very proud of him, Reba."

Her guard softened now, Reba said softly and Skitchy thought maybe proudly, "There's more, Mrs. Skitchy, if you sure enough want to know."

"Uh-huh. I'd like to know."

"Has to be a secret, though. Could be trouble if people knew."

"You bet. I recollect all too well the trouble that cost him his eye."

"Hutch doesn't just read. He writes, too. Writes stories. Some he makes up. Some he writes about things that happen as if he was writing stories for the newspaper. Miss Hoffman likes them. She says she thinks he might even be able to be paid for them some day if he keeps on writing."

"Miss Hoffman, the schoolteacher?"

"Yes, ma'am." Reba had already said more than she meant to and perhaps ought to, but she had come to trust this white woman whose daughter was up to her neck in something her mother knew nothing about. That bothered Reba. She decided to tell everything. "Connie takes Hutch's stories to Miss Hoffman at the school. Miss Hoffman reads them. Sometimes she writes things on them she thinks would make them better. Connie brings them home again afterward. Miss Hoffman would like to send him books but she's afraid someone might see them. The stories are easy to mix in with Connie's papers. Nobody pays any mind."

"How long has this been going on?"

"Well, it just kind of happened little by little. Miss Hoffman always felt bad when Hutch had to stop going to school. She was the one who wanted the black children to be able to go to her school when the black school was burned. She was very upset after they changed their minds about that. Told me one time she was sorry in particular about Hutch because he's so bright. She wanted to help him. Could never figure out a way until Connie started to school."

Skitchy was listening intently but said nothing so Reba went on. "It was Miss Hoffman's idea for him to read the newspapers. Writing stories was his idea. Connie's idea to take them to Miss Hoffman. Mrs. Skitchy, I know I should've told you when I found out myself. I was afraid. I knew they might make trouble for Miss Hoffman. For sure make trouble for Hutch. But I didn't think they would for Connie, and I wanted him to get some education so much. Hope you're not mad."

"No, I'm not mad, Reba. I do wish you'd told me about it, but I'm glad for Hutch to get some education. And you're right about keeping it our secret. I'd like Hutch to know, though, that I'm glad for him. And Connie should know that I'm in on the secret. I'll talk to her."

"Yes, ma'am."

As Skitchy left the kitchen, she murmured, "Oh, Belle, you have no idea how much Connie is mixing with black people. And doesn't see differences."

....

When Franklin Roosevelt had been elected President in 1932 with 88% of Texas' vote, the government had started programs to help the country cope with unemployment, and promised many others. So far West Texas had only promises. One promised program had been construction of new roads and repair of existing ones. People had grumbled for a while when no road work came to West Texas counties. Then gradually the complaints faded into the vast reservoir of dashed hopes and disappointments that no one talked about any more.

When word first got around that there were going to be jobs working on Reeves County roads after all this time, Tom Floyd was among those who doubted it. "Sounds too much like what I heard about the talk of work in the Wink oil fields. Found out different when I went up there."

But everyone who lived upstairs in the hotel heard Alma screaming at him in their room that night, "I know you're still down about not going to California. But you've got to do something. You've got to at least try. Got to go see, Tom. You've just got to."

So Tom did go see. He was in a jovial mood when he told everyone at supper that evening, "Fifty-seven men showed up to apply. Only five jobs. I was dadgum lucky! Job starts in a week. Going to be hard work. Pay isn't great. But no one's complaining." A few people even had a feeling of cautious new hope.

....

There were also changes for Pink at the mercantile store. In the summer, Mr. Wilson's wife had a stroke and passed away without warning. Mr. Wilson looked to Pink to manage things for a while.

"He's going to pay a regular salary until he comes back to work. I can still bring home groceries like I've been doing," Pink told Skitchy.

Skitchy threw her arms around his neck. "Oh, sugar! Sad about his wife. I don't wish sorrow on anyone. But what a wonderful thing for us!"

"I feel the same way," Pink sighed. "It's been a long time since I caught a break."

But the two of them didn't feel the same way about what to do with the money Pink earned. Skitchy discovered many things she wanted that she hadn't been able to think about wanting for a long while, now that there was some extra money.

"I don't think of it as extra money," Pink said as evenly as he could when he disagreed with Skitchy about anything. "I think we should save as much as we can. Mr. Wilson will come back to work, and when he does, my job will go back to the way it was." Pink didn't want to tell Skitchy how impotent he'd felt about not being able to take care of his family the way he wanted to and thought he should, that he was afraid of feeling that way again.

"We've been pinched for so long, Pink," Skitchy said, complaint in her voice. "Why can't we enjoy a little of the extra? Still save most of it?"

So they argued about spending money at all, let alone on what. When Skitchy bought new cotton fabric instead of using flour sacks to make a dress for Connie, Pink said, "That's a silly extravagance. Flour sacks don't cost anything. We need to save all we can."

Skitchy shot back, "We've done without for a long time now. How can you not want our daughter to have something nice once in a while?"

Pink fumed when Skitchy bought a loaf of bread as a special treat. "Reba makes the best biscuits and cornbread in town. What are you buying bread for?"

"Goodness, Pink, this is a small thing. What are you making such a fuss about?"

When Connie heard her parents arguing like this she said, "Auntabelle, I think maybe it was better when Daddy didn't make any money."

Auntabelle didn't disagree.

1936

Ephraim Chapman had pneumonia early in March. He was up and around after awhile, but Minnie wrote in the middle of April that he just didn't seem like his old self. She thought a visit from Belle and Skitchy might cheer him up. "Mama could use some cheering up, too," she added in her letter. "Imagine money is tight for you as it is for us. But if you can find a way I think it would do them both good."

Skitchy told Belle, "Bet you Daddy isn't doing nearly as well as he says in his letters. And Mama doesn't say anything. She must be worried. I think we should go for a visit if we can figure a way."

Belle agreed and the sisters started figuring. Skitchy wanted to drive, but Pink didn't like that idea.

"The car hasn't been driven much. I'm afraid it might not make it there and back. I hate to think of you maybe stuck out there on the road in the middle of nowhere."

Skitchy argued, "I know how to fix it, Pink. Fixed it lots of times."

"But that was always pretty close to home, Skitchy," Jackson said. "Big Lake is more than two hundred miles. How about if I drive you?"

He told Belle privately, "I traded for some cigarettes when Ed Hausenfluck was afraid he might lose his store. Put them away. I figured they might come in useful sometime and we could always use cigarettes. I can trade some and come up with enough gas for the trip. Please don't say anything to anyone about the cigarettes, though. I want to save them for times like this."

So it was decided that Jackson would drive them to Big Lake and come back and get them in two weeks. Alma and Reba would look after Connie while Pink was busy at the mercantile store and working with the Panthers.

....

Kate and Ephraim had been staying with Minnie and Bob since Ephraim got sick. The house was crowded after Belle and Skitchy arrived. Minnie made up a pallet for her sisters on the floor in the little used front room, pushing furniture out of the way to make room for their suitcases which were left open on the floor. Making do like this was the way it had always been in the family. Skitchy found it comforting.

When Skitchy saw her father, she was alarmed. He was pale and had lost a good deal of weight. But even more, there was a look in his eye she didn't like. "As if he's looking somewhere out into space or something," Skitchy said to Belle. "Worries me to see him doing so poorly," she wrote to Pink just after their arrival.

The three sisters had long talks among themselves and with their mother, and even though they talked about many things, the conversation seemed to always come back to Daddy and their concern for him.

Skitchy longed for long talks with her father also, just the two of them, like the old days before she was married. But he tired easily now and the talks were short. "My mind wanders," he told her. She was careful not to say anything about her life, and in particular about her marriage, that might worry him. Sometimes she fed him scrambled eggs, coaxing him to eat. Sometimes she read to him while he rested. Sometimes they just sat together, not talking at all.

....

Skitchy woke early one morning feeling sick to her stomach. She got up as quietly as she could and just made it to the bathroom before throwing up.

Kate heard her and came into the bathroom. "Are you all right, honey?"

Skitchy shook her head and sat down on the floor, leaning her head back against the wall.

Kate's gaze passed over her daughter thoughtfully. After a while she asked gently, "Honey, are you pregnant?"

Skitchy had missed a period but that had happened before, and Pink's melting hardness had meant less and less love making, so it never occurred to her that she might be pregnant, especially so many years after Connie's birth. She was dumbfounded by her mother's question. "I don't think so, Mama." But then her thoughts whirled round, hastily calculating about how long it had been since she and Pink last made love, recalling how she'd felt in the early weeks of her pregnancy with Connie. "Well, I don't know. Maybe. "

By the time Skitchy and Belle went home, Skitchy knew she was going to have another baby. She'd talked with Mama and Minnie about seeing the new doctor recently come to McAllister, about having the baby at his hospital.

"Honey, it's up to you, of course," Kate had said, "but if it were me, I'd have the doctor this time. And I know you understand I need to take care of Eph. You wouldn't be able to count on my being there when your time comes."

Minnie had urged, "Skitchy, you had such a hard time before. You're older now. Best you not take any chances."

Skitchy hated thinking about not having her mother with her as midwife but deep down she thought it best too. She just didn't know how Pink was going to take it. How he was going to take spending the money. How he was going to take having a baby at all after all this time.

....

"You just can't be pregnant." Pink looked stunned and stepped back a step.

Skitchy didn't close the distance. Oddly, her attention went to his hair, receding and thinning. He'll be forty when the baby's born, she thought. Pretty old to be daddy to a new baby. Then she shook her head and quickly turned her attention back to the baby. "I can hardly believe it myself. Last thing in the world I ever expected."

"It couldn't be at a worse time. I don't see how we're going to make it with another mouth to feed."

"I've thought all those things, too. And there's something else. Mama needs to be taking care of Daddy. She thinks I should have the baby in the hospital anyway, after the trouble I had when Connie was born."

"How much will that cost?"

"I don't know. I thought I'd wait a while to see the doctor but sooner or later I need to. Guess I'll find out then. Maybe we can work something out with him. I don't know what else to do."

She felt some painful cramping and had some spotting a month later. She knew she should see the doctor, even if it was sooner than she planned. "I like Dr. MacLeod," she told Pink when she came home from the recently opened McAllister Clinic and Hospital. "He knows how tough times are for everybody. Says he'd never turn away someone who needed his care. We can pay him whenever we can."

"Well, that's good news, but Lord only knows when that'll be. That could be a debt we have for a long time."

Skitchy felt trapped by circumstances she could do nothing about. She was pretty sure Pink felt the same way but he didn't speak of that and neither did she.

"You're okay? Everything is okay?" Pink asked.

"Uh-huh."

"That's good," he said. Skitchy thought she heard resignation in his voice.

"Uh-huh." She knew she heard it in her own voice.

....

Two weeks later Pink sat on the bed in their room at the end of the day, wordlessly pulling off his boots. Skitchy saw his shoulders were slumped. She sat down on the bed beside him, feeling slumped herself. Wish I knew how to comfort him, she thought. Wish we could find a way to comfort each other. A sob started its way up from her sad heart but she stopped it at her throat. She was still thinking about what she might say when Pink spoke.

His voice despondent, he said, "Mr. Wilson told me today he'll be coming back to work next week. He'll have to cut my hours."

She usually hated it when they talked about anything having to do with money but at this moment she welcomed it. She wished she'd listened to Pink about saving more of the money he'd made during the time Mr. Wilson had been away from the store. Maybe she would have felt that way anyway, she thought, but with the baby coming . . . .

"I feel so foolish," she said, "for spending money I didn't need to. Even more for fighting with you about it. I'm so sorry, sugar." After a minute or two she said very quietly, "I know the baby couldn't be coming at a worse time." Then she surprised herself by saying what she hadn't let herself think even in the most private of moments. "I wish this baby wasn't coming at all."

"I've been praying about it. I can't believe I could feel this way about a new life. About our child. Maybe it's just going to take some time to get used to." Pink reached for her hand and held it tightly. They sat together, hand in hand, for a long time before they went to bed.

....

The government had done nothing but talk about the dust storms that continued to plague beleaguered people in a wide swath from southern Nebraska to the Texas panhandle, now dubbed the Dust Bowl. But after an Oklahoma dust cloud blew all the way to Washington, Congress voted for a national conservation agency, and the President talked to the nation about his plans. Meanwhile the storms continued unabated. The worst ones continued to reach McAllister with a fringe of wind, static electricity, and oily dark dirt. Another monster storm dumped its awfulness in late spring. It was nowhere near as big a load as on Black Sunday but big enough to cause some damage in town, suffocate several head of livestock on ranches and farms, and further depress everyone's spirits. Discouraged people in West Texas paid little mind to the far away words of far away talkers. Even the President of the United States.

Skitchy felt like she herself was suffocating in the dusty hot wind. "Law, Belle, I'm already worried sick about Connie breathing this awful old dust," she groaned. "Can't see it's ever going to be different. I just hate to think about bringing another child into it."

Belle was well aware of the stories about children dying from dust pneumonia. Worried herself, she reached for her sister's hand and squeezed it. Doing the best she could to offer some encouragement, she said, "Mama and Daddy made it through tough times, Skitch. We will, too."

....

Skitchy sat alone in the lobby on a hot dry afternoon three weeks later, trying to read the newspaper. She felt a flutter in her belly and put a worried hand where she had felt the flutter, recalling the cramping from before. Flutter again. She gasped. "It's the baby. The baby moved!" She pressed lightly where she'd felt the movement, recognizing her child, alive within her own body. The stubborn resistance she'd been unable to shake off seemed to melt, all at once. Just as suddenly, in its place was love and acceptance of the new life moving within her. She left her hand there. After a time she spoke very softly through soft tears, "Well, little baby, it's been hard to make a place for you. I'm sorry about that. You are welcome."

That night when they were in bed she told Pink, somewhat tentatively, what had happened that morning. He put his hand gently on her rounding belly, kissed her softly.

"I'm glad for it. We'll make it somehow."

Yes, it had just taken some time, Skitchy thought.

....

Margaret Jane Campbell was born in early December. The birth was long, as Connie's had been, but eased by chloroform. Mother and baby were doing well. Dr. MacLeod let them come home from the hospital after five days with Skitchy's promise to rest in bed for two weeks.

A wide-eyed Connie, standing very close to Belle, touched her baby sister's arm carefully. "She's so soft."

"And beautiful, isn't she?" Belle said to Connie, her voice quiet and affectionate. Then looking at the tiny pink baby girl, she said, "So small! I clean forgot how tiny newborns are."

Belle loved Connie as if she were her own child, but at that moment she was keenly aware the eight year old girl beside her was not hers and as she looked at Skitchy's second child, a wave of sadness welled up from deep within her. She'd never spoken to anyone, even Jackson, about the emptiness she felt at times, not having children of her own. She'd certainly never speak of it at a time like this. She must not allow her sad emptiness to alloy the joy she felt for her sister. She shook herself, lifted her head, resolved never to speak of it at all. She kissed Skitchy on the cheek, took Connie's hand and walked with her downstairs.

....

One morning, not quite a week after mother and baby came home from the hospital, Reba took Skitchy's breakfast up to her. Reba found a shivering Skitchy, complaining of feeling cold and asking for another quilt. Her skin was hot when Reba touched her, her forehead clammy. Pink had gone to the mercantile store early that morning, so Reba went to Belle, mending a blouse in her room.

"Mrs. Skitchy is sick, Mrs. Belle. She has a fever. A big fever. I think she's awful sick."

Belle called Pink at the store. "Pink, Skitchy has a fever. I think I should call the doctor."

"Please do whatever you think best, Belle. I'll be home as soon as I can close up here."

By the time the doctor arrived, Skitchy was delirious. After he examined her he went downstairs where he found Pink and Belle waiting in the lobby.

"I'll do the best I can for her but she's very sick. I must tell you honestly that she may not live."

Reba, listening from the kitchen, stepped into the lobby. "Excuse me. Mrs. Belle, Mr. Pink, can I please speak with you? In the kitchen?" In the kitchen she said softly, "I've been midwife and nurse to my people for a long while. I think I might be able to help Mrs. Skitchy. I'm afraid she might pass to the Lord if she doesn't get what she needs real soon."

Dr. MacLeod's medical practice had been in Wink before coming to McAllister, mostly treating men injured in the oil fields. When the dwindling population of Wink oil workers no longer required the services of five doctors he'd come to McAllister, which hadn't had a doctor for many years. He was uncomfortably aware of his inexperience with obstetrics and gynecology. When Belle told him what Reba had said, Dr. MacLeod showed the character that was to earn him the respect of the people of McAllister for a long lifetime.

"Reba, Mrs. Tieger tells me you're an experienced midwife. Let's sit down and have a cup of coffee in your kitchen. I would like you to tell me what you think about Mrs. Campbell."

They emerged from the kitchen half an hour later, unlikely partners. Reba told Belle some things they'd need, got the well-worn satchel filled with bottles and packets of herbs she kept in her room. Then she and the doctor went up to Skitchy's room together.

Skitchy lived.

....

Early in the morning two days after Christmas, Skitchy and Pink were wakened by Rita Colquitt's shrieks.

Pink knocked sharply on the sisters' door. When there was no answer, he went in cautiously, not wanting to startle or frighten. He found the elderly woman sitting upright in the bed, staring at the cold and stiffening body beside her, not seeming to comprehend what she was seeing.

"Mrs. Colquitt, will you let me help you out of bed?" Pink asked gently.

She looked up and took his hand. "Yes, dear. Thank you."

He stopped briefly to tell Skitchy, "I think Mrs. McCabe passed away in her sleep. I'm taking Mrs. Colquitt down to Belle."

Everyone was shocked, except Dr. MacLeod, who knew Etta McCabe had a weak heart. She hadn't told even her sister.

"The bed was so empty last night," Rita Colquitt told Belle, Jackson, and Pink the next morning at breakfast, pushing away the plate of scrambled eggs, biscuits and gravy she'd hardly touched. "Sister and I always slept in the same bed when we were girls. Then we married within a month of each other. Both of our husbands passed away from the flu in '18. I had no children. Sister lost her boy when he was small. After a little while, it seemed like the most natural thing in the world for us to live together again. When we came here to live, guess I thought we'd always be together. Like we were when we were girls."

Late that afternoon she sat in a chair in the lobby, wearing a still-beautiful even if old fashioned blue silk dress with a lace collar, her hair curled and pinned away from her fine-featured face. As Jackson passed by he thought he heard her humming.

"Mrs. Colquitt, can I get you anything?"

She looked up at him and smiled a small smile. Her voice thin, she said "Some bourbon, Jackson, if you don't mind. I think it would do me good."

Astonished, since he'd never seen either her or her sister drink, Jackson asked, "With soda, Mrs. Colquitt, or without?"

"Without, thank you. Just a little ice."

When Jackson brought the bourbon, she said, "I think I've lived here long enough for you to call me Rita. Yes, I'd like you to call me Rita. Sister never thought people should call us by our first names because we were so much older than everybody else." She sipped her bourbon. "She didn't think we should drink alcohol either." Then to her absent sister she said quietly, as if explaining herself, "I'm on my own now, Sister. I want to just do as I please."

Etta McCabe was buried in the McAllister cemetery two days before the turn of the new year. After having been so gravely ill, Skitchy's first venture out was to the funeral. Sitting on a chair Pink brought for her, she clasped his hand firmly. Both of them felt sad for the life that had ended, but grateful for the life that had not ended and for another that was just beginning.

1937

In a corner of the lobby, six week old Margaret slept in a bed made up in a dresser drawer, covered with a small quilt that had once been Connie's, freshly patched with remnants of printed flour sacks, thanks to Alma Floyd. The baby wore a sweater Etta McCabe had begun knitting with the last of the yarn unraveled from her own old sweater, and which Rita Colquitt had finished.

No one at the hotel had known that Rita Colquitt knitted, since it had always been her sister's knitting needles they watched flying and heard clicking in a steady rhythm even when she was talking. Rita explained, "Sister was so much better at it than I was. I thought it best to wind the yarn for her. But I'm glad to be knitting again. I like knitting."

Skitchy, writing a letter to her mother at the table nearby, had not been up and around long since the harrowing fear for her life had everyone in its grip. She still tired easily. Reba took care of the baby most of the time. Connie looked often to Belle for mothering and spent most nights with her aunt and uncle.

Skitchy wrote in the letter: "I'm just so lucky to have so many folks around to help take care of my little girls. Pink's been lucky, too. Still has some work at the mercantile store even now that Mr. Wilson's back at the store full time. He has been able to get some other work for a day or two once in a while on the road crew with Tom Floyd. That's because veterans are being given preference for government work, when it comes up."

....

Sally Thornton, widow of the McAllister Bank president who'd shot himself when the bank failed, came in to the drug store one morning when Belle was there alone. Sally was a little older than Belle, but looked much older. She wore her light brown hair pulled back in a bun, her brown eyes had lost their luster and the color had gone from her cheeks. No longer enjoying the position of prestige in town she'd once had, instead her presence seemed to remind people of all they'd lost and many in town kept a cool distance. The slender woman had an air of loneliness about her. She and Belle were still friendly, and she'd come to show Belle a quilt she'd made from printed sugar sacks.

"Belle, I wonder if you might be needing quilts at the hotel. If you do, could I trade this quilt for some things I need?"

Sally was a creative quilter and this quilt was as lovely as it was unusual. "This is beautiful," Belle said. She'd told Jackson only a few days before that many of their quilts were in bad shape and wouldn't take much more mending and patching before they just fell apart. "Think maybe we can work something out, Sally. I'll talk to Jackson."

Sally, obviously relieved, added, "I have others and could make more if you could use more."

....

A week before, another conversation about quilts had taken place at the hotel. Alma had been mending and patching old quilts for Belle and Jackson for some time. One day as she'd put one aside she thought just too far gone, Skitchy picked it up, looked at it thoughtfully. "You know, Alma, it's too bad these things wear out so much in the middle and around the edges. Parts are still good. I wonder if you couldn't make something out of the good parts."

Alma glanced up, surprised. "Like what?"

"Oh, I don't know. Maybe a jacket for Connie. She's growing so fast. She surely could use something for cold days."

The two women talked about it for a while and decided to try making a vest together, easier to make than a jacket and requiring less goods. After experimenting with how to cut an old quilt and sew something new from it, they indeed produced a vest. They'd just finished it when Belle came in from the drug store with Sally Thornton's quilt to show to Jackson.

Belle was quite taken with the vest. "I love it! I wish you'd make one for me."

Skitchy's surprised eyes met Alma's surprised eyes. This was Belle, lover of beautiful clothes, wanting them to make a vest for her out of cast-off quilts.

"You bet," Skitchy said enthusiastically, energized by this unexpected turn of events. "We'll start on it today."

Skitchy and Alma sorted through the old quilts and chose two with Belle's favorite colors. They didn't have enough buttons that matched so they used different ones they thought looked nice with the colors and patterns of the quilt pieces. The buttons added to the charm of the unique garment.

Belle was delighted with the vest when she tried it on and turned to look at herself in the mirror. The blend of faded colors looked beautiful and the fabric, soft from many washings, was very comfortable to wear. "I'm going to wear it to church next Sunday," she said enthusiastically. She did, and it seemed as if every woman and girl who saw it wanted one.

So it happened that the hotel got Sally Thornton's new quilts and Skitchy and Alma got the old ones. Mr. Wilson let them put their vests on sale at the mercantile store, paying him a small amount of each sale. The first three sold or traded immediately. "Looks like you ladies have made something special here," he told them. "I'll take more."

The next ones sold or traded, too, even in these hard times. After they had used all the hotel's old quilts they started to buy others from people in town. When word got around that Skitchy and Alma would pay a little cash money for old worn out quilts they soon had a stack of quilts to work with.

As demand for vests continued, Skitchy said to Alma one morning, "What would you think of asking Sally Thornton to help with the cutting and sewing?"

"We could sure enough use the help."

Pleased to have work, Sally not only contributed a third pair of hands but showed them how to work more easily and quickly with the quilt pieces. She also suggested adding embroidery to strengthen spots Alma and Skitchy had thought too worn, making more of the old quilts usable and adding to the beauty and charm of the finished vests.

It sometimes happens that when a ready seed falls into just the right spot, even in rocky terrain and thin soil, scanty moisture can surprise the seed into new life, however unlikely that sprout may seem. Skitchy would not be able to say when she first began to think that the work the three women were doing had actually sprouted into a small business but her conviction grew that this was so. So did her optimism and excitement. When she finally spoke of it one afternoon, Alma and Sally were surprised but quickly responded to Skitchy's enthusiasm with their own. Soon they began to talk about what to call their enterprise.

"How about using our initials?" Alma suggested. "S for Skitchy, A for Alma, S for Sally. SAS."

"I like that," Sally said. "We could embroider SAS into each vest."

"That gives me another idea," Skitchy said, grinning with imaginative delight as they worked. "We're surely three sassy women. Making a business out of not much but our own sassiness in the middle of a depression. Why not call ourselves what we are: sassy. Sassy Quilters!"

Sally and Alma looked at each other and burst out laughing. Sassy Quilters was born.

....

Seeing the pile of old quilts stacked in the corner going down and the jar once full of buttons nearing empty, Skitchy said to Alma and Sally one afternoon, "I'm thinking we shouldn't depend on people hearing about us and bringing their cast offs to us. How about using some of the money we're making to buy gas? I could drive out to ranches and farms. Maybe even to other towns. I'm good at visiting with people and working things around. I bet people have old quilts we could get if I were to come looking for them. If someone has enough old ones they might even trade for one of Sally's new ones and we wouldn't have to pay cash so often. Maybe people would trade for their old buttons, too, or maybe sell them. Say a couple dozen for a penny. You two are much better than I am at making the vests. I'd still help with them as much as I can. But we need materials."

"Think you could do that?" an astonished Alma asked.

"I think so, but Law, I don't know. Only one way to find out."

Alma and Sally put down their work and were listening with rapt attention. Skitchy saw the excitement growing on their faces. "My old friend Brin and her husband James Lee have been running O'Brien's Mercantile Store in Pecos since her father can't any more. Bet they'd put our vests in their store. Then we'd have them in stores in two towns. If people want to buy more vests than we can make with the quilts and buttons we have, let's get some more quilts and buttons. Make more vests and make more money! Never mind the dadgum depression!"

....

Skitchy felt jittery when she started out on her first trip. She'd asked Belle to help her choose what to wear and fix her hair, wanting to make a good impression on the people she'd call on. She'd thought about what she would say. Excited and eager, still she felt jittery when she got into the Model-T and drove out of McAllister.

She felt even more jittery as she pulled into the Jefferson's farmyard. The family lived a few miles from town but she'd picked that as her first stop because she knew Melinda Jefferson from high school days. Skitchy was grateful to hear that her voice was steady when the curious Melinda came out of the house to meet her. Words came naturally and the jitters melted. She left the Jefferson farm with two old quilts and some buttons.

She drove past the Daniels' farm where she'd gone to her first barn dance. That happy memory deteriorated into anguish when she saw the crumbling hulks that had once been the house and barn. The Daniels had lost their farm and disappeared from Reeves County. Now their farm, too, was disappearing into the dusty earth. She shuddered and pushed all that away. She had things to do.

Her second call yielded no quilts and two dozen buttons, the third five old quilts. She started for home then, both excited and tired from the new experience. Enormously pleased with the result, her heart soared as she drove along in the Model-T. Maybe this is how Amelia Earhart feels, soaring in her airplane, she thought.

The experience of soaring would become familiar as she made more trips. Even when she had to stop to make repairs on the old car or change a tire, her heart soared with the confidence that she could do what she needed to. Was actually doing it. Doing all of it!

....

Pink had made it clear he wasn't crazy about what she was doing. "I don't know about spending good money on old worn out quilts and buttons, not to mention gas. And I don't like you driving all over the place by yourself, Skitchy, talking to strangers."

"Law, I don't think I need to be afraid of folks around here, Pink. My family's lived in Reeves County a long while. I know who folks are even if I don't know them personally. It's not like I'm talking to strangers. And Sassy Quilters is making some money over our expenses."

So Skitchy continued to make her trips, to gather the things Sassy Quilters needed. Brin and James Lee Cooper did sell Sassy Quilters vests in O'Brien's Mercantile Store in Pecos and sales went as well there as they had in McAllister at Wilson's. Before long Pink had stopped talking about how he wished she wouldn't go on these trips looking for old quilts. Once or twice Skitchy thought about what she'd do if he flatly put his foot down. She was glad she didn't have to finish that thought.

....

Skitchy planned one more stop looking for old quilts and buttons before driving on to Pecos for a short visit with Brin before she went home. She pulled through the gate of the Martin ranch in the early afternoon. Wade Martin had been one of her brother's best friends and she thought briefly about the girlhood crush she'd had on him when he visited at the Chapman ranch or she saw him ride with Buddy at rodeos. Smiling to herself at the faded memory, she hoped she'd see him even though she knew he'd probably be out on the range this time of day. She hardly knew Nettie, his wife, but looked forward to visiting with her and hopefully bringing home some quilts after what had proved to be a lean day.

She saw him working in the corral, repairing rails. He stopped what he was doing when she drove into the raked yard. Walking toward her she saw a tall sun toasted and sweaty man, muscled arms exposed by rolled up shirt sleeves. A pushed back straw cowboy hat that had once been white showed close set eyes, somewhat flat nose, prominent cheek bones and a wide mouth in a square jaw, craggy features attractive even if not handsome.

"Skitchy! What brings you around here?"

She explained what she wanted and Wade said, "Nettie's gone into Pecos. Expect her back before too long. How about some ice tea?"

"You bet. I've been on the road for a while and it's blistering hot. But guess I don't need to tell you that," she laughed, noting his sweaty body. She could tell he was looking her over, too, as they walked toward the house. She felt flushed.

"How long has it been since we've seen each other, Skitchy?"

"Not since Buddy's funeral, I guess. Good to see you, Wade."

She sat down in the shade of the broad front porch. When he went inside, she looked around. The Martin ranch was larger than the Chapman ranch, she remembered Buddy telling her, so it surprised her to see that the ranch house was smaller, one story, and in need of paint. Guess there's not much painting of houses, she thought, in this awful old depression. The barn, bunkhouse and cookhouse all looked to be in good repair. The whole place had an orderly look about it. She felt a momentary pang of missing the ranch where she'd grown up.

He brought the tea and sat down on the step near her. He rolled a cigarette and offered it to her.

"Thank you," she said. He lit it for her, then rolled one for himself.

"Don't mean to keep you from your work, Wade. Please don't feel you have to keep me company. I don't mind waiting for Nettie."

"I'd enjoy visiting for a bit. Don't get much company. And I'm curious about what you're wanting old quilts for."

She told him about the vests and about Sassy Quilters. He seemed so interested she went to the car to get the vest she carried with her to show people what she was talking about. She'd learned that women were more likely to let her have their old quilts when they saw the vest. Sometimes they even talked about buying one. However, this was the first time a man had been this interested.

"The vest's good looking, Skitchy. Really different from anything I've seen. Great what you sassy women are doing!" he said, grinning.

She grinned back, delighted by his enthusiasm. "Thank you, Wade. Feels good to have that kind of encouragement."

"Well, what else would you get? It's a spunky thing. Deserves to be encouraged."

"Oh, you might be surprised. Not everybody thinks that."

He thought there might be something underneath what she said but thought it best not to pursue it, since she didn't say anything more. "Well, I wish Sassy Quilters all the best."

"And what about you, Wade?" she asked. "I'd love to catch up with you, too."

A shadow passed over his face and was gone as quickly as it came. She saw it, though. Wonder what that's about, she thought. Well, don't pay it any mind. He'll talk about it if he wants to.

"The ranch keeps me very busy," he said. "My father passed the year after I got home from Southwestern. My mother the year after that."

"Sorry to hear that."

"That's kind of you. It's been some years now. I brought it up meaning to say the ranch fell to me sooner than I was really ready. I was still learning when I had to start running it. Got married soon after that. I didn't keep in touch as much as I'd have liked. Always meant to visit with your folks after Bud passed. They were very good to me. I always felt at home at your ranch."

"My folks thought the world of you, Wade. We all did." She suddenly felt flushed again and dropped her eyes. "May I have another cigarette?" she asked to cover her fluster.

She saw the way he looked at her as he lit the cigarette for her. He's married, Skitch, she told herself. So are you. Don't be silly. You didn't see anything.

Another half hour passed as they continued to talk easily with each other, Wade in no hurry to get back to the corral, Skitchy having decided to skip the visit to Brin.

Finally she said, "Well, I think I'd better call on Nettie another time. I want to get home before dark."

"You're welcome any time," he said, and meant it.

She saw him in the car mirror, watching her as she drove away.

He stood looking after her even when she was out of sight. "Well, well, well. Surely never expected that when I got up this morning."

....

Sally Thornton spent most of her time at the hotel now.

Skitchy had been watching Sally come there every morning with her back straighter, her eyes brighter. She cut her hair and wore it curled close to her face, wore brighter colors even though the clothes were old. No longer keeping her eyes mostly on her work, saying little, now she laughed and talked as much as Skitchy and Alma did.

So Skitchy wasn't surprised when Sally said one afternoon when they were alone, "I'm so lonely living by myself. Feel like I'm rattling around in that big sad empty house. I have some money left from what my mother left me and with what I'm making from Sassy Quilters I can afford to pay a little rent. Do you think Belle and Jackson would let me live here?"

Skitchy liked Sally and welcomed the friendship they had developed. "I think so. Mrs. Colquitt has lived here for quite a while. As nearly as I can tell, having that rent every month has helped Jackson keep things going. I could talk to him and Belle first if you'd like me to."

"Be obliged if you would, Skitchy," Sally said warmly. "I'd like to know I'd be welcome."

....

When Sally moved her things to the hotel three weeks later, including furniture from the parlor of her house to replace worn chairs and a settee in the lobby, everyone was surprised to see Dr. MacLeod arrive with her. The tall lean man was there all afternoon, carrying Sally's trunk upstairs with Jackson, helping her unpack boxes upstairs in her new room.

When Belle asked, "Would you like to stay for supper?" he accepted enthusiastically.

Good looking and with an easy grace, Dr. MacLeod had a way of putting other people at ease. His deep blue eyes looked directly at the person he was talking to and he listened attentively when someone spoke to him. Much to Sally's delight, everyone at the table quickly dropped the formality they'd adopted for conversation with the doctor and seemed comfortable calling him John when he invited them to.

"Where are you from, John?" Jackson asked. "What brought you to McAllister?"

"I grew up on my family's ranch in Williamson County. When I decided I wanted to be a doctor, it seemed natural to start at Southwestern since it was right there in the county. Then my father thought I should see something more of the world and I wanted that myself so I went to medical school in New York. That was a good experience but I never really felt at home there. When I was ready to begin practicing I wanted to come home to Texas. Hadn't thought about West Texas, to tell you the truth. But the pay in Wink was very good for a brand new doctor so I took the job."

"And what did you think when you got there?" Skitchy wanted to know, her own enthusiasm for the bustling oil boom towns still vivid in her memory.

"Well, the town and oil fields were interesting and exciting in a way. But I'll tell you, on the train coming west I wondered about mile after mile after mile of dry flatland with almost nothing green in sight. So different from where I grew up. Was afraid I might've made a mistake and was coming to the middle of nowhere." The table grew quiet and he added quickly what he'd been planning to say anyway. "West Texas people put that to rest pretty fast. And that's been even more the case since I came to McAllister." Smiling broadly he said, "I'm very happy here. I expect I'll live here the rest of my life."

"We're all surely glad to hear that," Belle said warmly. "You can be sure McAllister is glad to have you."

After supper, when they gathered around the radio to listen to the news as the little community at the hotel did almost every evening, John MacLeod joined them. When news of Japan's invasion of China came on, Skitchy noticed a shadow cross his face but he said nothing.

"He's concerned about what's going on in the world, isn't he?" Skitchy remarked to Sally the next day.

"He's afraid there may be another big war."

"Sure enough? Because of China invading Japan?"

"It's the other way around. Japan invaded China. John's worried about what's happening in Europe, but Japan makes him uneasy, too."

Skitchy felt embarrassed by her ignorance and didn't continue the conversation. She promised herself to pay more attention in the future to what was happening in the world outside West Texas.

....

As John MacLeod kept coming to the hotel, Skitchy could see that the isolated widow and the doctor had truly found each other. Other people noticed as well and before long there was much talk in McAllister about the couple.

"I don't pay any mind to the talk," Sally told Skitchy and Alma, but there was an edge in her voice. "If he doesn't care that I'm more than ten years older than he is, why should they? And yes, we have a meal together in his rooms above the clinic when he needs to be easy to find. If he thinks someone might need his medical attention. So what?"

Skitchy thought that might be true as far as it went, but she could feel the crackle of energy between her friend and the doctor. She imagined they were not enjoying each other's company in his rooms only for a meal.

Whether that was true or not, what Skitchy imagined fueled her longing. She knew Pink felt discouraged as the depression pressed on, the county road work at an end and his hours at the mercantile store short. She'd tried to encourage and comfort him but he still seemed withdrawn. They'd made love only a few times since Margaret was born, and twice last month he'd turned away from her intimate approaches.

As Skitchy imagined Sally and a vigorously exciting lover together she went upstairs early more than once, alone, and wept bitter hot tears.

....

Etta McCabe and Rita Colquitt had discovered soap operas not long after Jackson bought the radio. Rita could still be found in the lobby every weekday morning listening to her stories, as she called them. She waited to hear the program she expected but instead there was a news bulletin.

"Law, Sister," Rita said to her sister as if she were there beside her, "I'd better go find Skitchy. She'll want to hear about this."

A teary Skitchy soon found Belle working in the garden and told her, "I just can't believe it! Amelia Earhart's plane's gone down over the Pacific Ocean. They can't find her. How could she be lost? She's the greatest woman flyer ever." She had never forgotten that she'd missed the chance to see the famous flyer when her plane was being repaired and fueled in Pecos.

"I'm really sorry, honey. I know she meant a lot to you."

"I believed in Sassy Quilters because of her, Belle. She made me think women could do something, even in a depression. I did something with Sassy Quilters and I'm proud of myself." More proud, she thought, than I've ever been of myself. Or even thought I could be.

"What you've done with Sassy Quilters is just wonderful. You and Sally and Alma have all done a great job. You most of all! I'm so proud of you! If Amelia Earhart helped you find that in yourself, then I say good for Amelia Earhart, too."

Skitchy hugged her sister for a long minute, grateful for Belle's understanding.

....

Skitchy thought about the Martin ranch more than once as she planned her trips to look for quilts. She felt nervous when she thought of calling there again even though she told herself there was no reason to. Finally one day she decided she was just being silly. Wade had said he thought Nettie had some old quilts and Sassy Quilters needed them. There was no reason not to go there. No reason at all.

It was a dry calm morning, a snap in the air of cool weather to come, when she let herself through the gate of the Martin ranch. She saw no one around as she drove up to the house. She waited for a minute, taking a couple of deep breaths, then knocked on the door.

"Skitchy! Good to see you!" Wade was barefoot, wearing only blue jeans, shaving lather on his face, towel in hand, when he opened the door. "Come on in." As he wiped the soapy lather from his face, she wondered why in the world stubble on the man's face made her tremble.

"Afraid you've missed Nettie again," he said. "She left some quilts for you, though. In case you came back. She goes into Pecos quite a bit to visit her mother and help her. Sarah's been pretty sick for a while now. Nettie does the cleaning and laundry and cooks her meals. Would you like some coffee? Go on in the kitchen and help yourself. I'll just finish shaving. Get some clothes on."

She wanted to say, Oh, I wish you wouldn't, but bit her tongue. Law, Skitch, what's the matter with you? Just get the quilts and go, she thought. She poured two cups of coffee and sat down nervously at the kitchen table.

"Well now," he said as he came into the kitchen, "that's a welcome sight." She wasn't sure if he was talking about the coffee she'd poured for him or her sitting there at his kitchen table.

"It was good of Nettie to leave some quilts," she said, hoping her nervousness didn't show. "We never talked about what I can pay. I need to see how much good there is left in them. Sometimes if there are enough quilts we can use I can trade a new one for the old ones."

"I'm sure whatever you think is fair will be fine." He made no move to go and get them and Skitchy felt flustered about what to say next, so she said nothing.

"Glad I was still here and not already gone out to the range." Wade offered. "There's not as much work to be done now, after the government burned so many of my cattle. But I'm still usually out by this time."

"What?" Skitchy said, puzzled. "I don't know what you mean. The government burned your cattle?"

"Government program bought cattle, calves mostly. Killed and burned them. Trying to keep prices up on the ones that were left. That part seemed to work fairly well. Sure is hard, though, to stand there and watch cattle I bred put down.

And I hated to see good food go up in smoke when there are so many hungry folks around. At least some of the hands I've had to let go managed to carry off a calf or two before they were burned. While I had coffee with the government agent," he said, half-grinning.

Skitchy thought of the side of beef Tom Floyd had taken as pay for working for a rancher near McAllister. How welcome the meat had been at the hotel. "I can't imagine it," she said. "Burning cattle, I mean."

"Well, seems like a sorry state of affairs to me. But I guess the government knows more than I do about how to deal with this dang depression."

She looked up, saw him looking at her. "Would you like to stay for a while, Skitchy? I'd be glad of your company. Maybe you could ride out to the range with me. I need to check some fences. Look at a well and windmill. Maybe fix a thing or two. Then we could have a bite to eat. There's a nice spot not far from the well."

"I haven't ridden for ages," she said wistfully, remembering how much she used to love to ride. "I could put on some old blue jeans I've got in the car. I have them with me for when I need to make repairs or change a tire. Could I borrow a hat?"

"You bet," he said grinning. "I'll make a lunch for us while you change. I have a horse in mind I think you might like. Come out when you're ready and take a look."

There was just a moment when she hesitated. Just a glimmer that she was about to make a momentous choice it would be best to think about. But she didn't think. Instead words came from a part of her a long way from her head.

"Sounds like fun!"

....

207

They ate the lunch of peanut butter and banana sandwiches in the shade of the overhanging bank of a dry creek where a cluster of mesquites grew taller than usual. They sat on a worn blanket he had in his saddlebag. He drew water from the well, wonderfully cool and refreshing in the midday warmth.

"I'm interested to hear more about your ranch, Wade," Skitchy said as they finished eating. "Besides the cattle burning. I've heard ranchers are having a hard time of it on account of the drought as much as the depression. Is it like that for you?"

Wade was surprised at his reaction to Skitchy's question. Nettie never wanted to hear about ranch difficulties. He avoided letting discouragement show around the hands who worked for him. Even with other ranchers, he was cautious. Too many conversations had left the tomorrow person he naturally was uncertain about tomorrow. Skitchy's interest couldn't have had a more different effect on him. It felt like a welcome antidote to the toxicity of keeping all that within himself and he felt his spirit lifting. Trust that, he told himself.

"I'd like to talk to you about the ranch, Skitch. It weighs on my mind and it means a lot to me that you're interested. But today I'd just like to enjoy your company. Today took such a wonderful and welcome turn when you knocked on my door."

He rolled two cigarettes, lit them and handed one to her. It was a beautiful clear afternoon, the sky blue and so high above them, the kind of day West Texans had prized but sometimes taken for granted before blowing dust made them rare. A soft breeze had come up, rippling the grass. The horses grazed nearby. Skitchy felt happier than she could remember feeling for a long time.

When she put out her cigarette, she lay back on the blanket, hands clasped behind her head. "I feel kind of drowsy," she said lazily.

Good gracious, he thought. Wonder if she has any idea how wonderful, how wonderfully desirable, she looks. Don't want to mess this up with her. But I surely don't want to let the chance pass either. Might not come like this again.

He watched her, saw her eyes close. Moving closer, he propped himself on his elbow and bending over her, kissed her gently.

Eyes still closed, she smiled, "Well, that doesn't encourage a nap."

"Wasn't meant to."

She opened her eyes, looked into his. Wide awake now, Skitchy felt her body leap up. Wanting him. Longing for him. She put her arms around his neck and pulled his mouth toward hers. This time his kiss was not gentle but insistent and hungry.

"Wade."

"Do you want me to stop?"

"No. But everything's going so fast."

"We can ride back if that's what you want," he said, his voice serious. "But if it is, we need to go now."

"I don't want to ride back. Just need to take things a little slower. No, I don't want to go slower either. Sounds like I don't know what I want, doesn't it?" She was quiet for a minute. He waited for her. Then in a firm clear voice she said, "I know this, Wade: I've never wanted anything in my life more than I want you. Want you now."

He slipped his arm under her head and kissed her again, letting the reins on wanting her drop away. She felt herself spinning, spinning, unleashed passion flashing shooting stars that fell, finally, on the dry open range.

....

Alma and Tom Floyd finished loading the old truck Tom bought with money saved from his road work and Alma's work with Sassy Quilters. A small crowd had gathered to see them off.

"Oh, Alma, I'm going to miss you so much," Skitchy said, tears in her eyes as she hugged her friend. She could feel Alma shaking a little.

"I'll miss you, too. I'll write as soon as I can when we get to California. Please write me every chance you get."

Skitchy kissed Alma's cheek and stepped back. Pink shook his friend's hand firmly. "I wish you the best, Tom. You take care now." And the Floyds were off in a cloud of dust and waves from the crowd, already beginning to disperse.

Skitchy moved slowly into the hotel lobby, still stunned that this had actually happened.

"Can't believe they're gone," she whispered softly to Sally.

"Anyone want some coffee?" Belle asked. "Reba has a fresh pot made."

There was a nervousness in the air, everyone wanting to talk about the Floyd's departure but no one quite knowing what it was that wanted saying.

Tom had talked about going to California off and on for months, but no one had paid it much mind, except for Pink. Then one evening as they all sat around the radio listening to the ever darker news from Europe, Tom had announced, "I'm going out to California. Get one of those jobs making airplanes Alma's sister keeps writing to her about. President keeps saying we aren't going to get into war in Europe. But those outfits in San Diego are making bombers for somebody. Don't much care who, if I can get in on the work."

Pink had thought those same thoughts but couldn't bring himself to just tell his wife he was going. Hoped she would come with him, but was going. Tom could. Tom had. And now he and Alma were on their way.

....

Even while Alma had been getting ready to leave for her new life in California, Skitchy and Sally had begun to talk about what was to become of Sassy Quilters. Sally had mused, "It's going to be harder with just the two of us. I know one or two quilters I think we could get to help with the cutting and sewing if we pay them for piece work."

Now, the day after Alma's departure, Skitchy said, "I've been thinking about what you said, Sally. About maybe needing to hire someone to help with making the vests. Also been thinking about having to go farther and farther away to find quilts. I've just about got all the ones from people around close. Selling the vests has been getting harder, too. Most of the women and girls in the county who want vests have them. I think we were getting to a crossroads even without Alma leaving."

"There's something else, Skitchy." Sally sighed, took a deep breath. "John wants to marry me."

Skitchy looked at Sally. "And . . .?"

"And I want to marry him," Sally said softly, smiling shyly as she dropped her eyes to her lap. After a long pause she went on, "He'd never ask me to give up Sassy Quilters. But I know he'd like me to help him at the clinic when I move there. Oh, Skitchy, I've been going crazy thinking about what to do. Even more after Alma told us she was leaving."

Skitchy heard the catch in Sally's voice. She reached over and took her friend's hand. "I'm so proud of what we've been able to do."

Sally nodded. Neither of the women spoke for a while.

With a catch now in her own voice, Skitchy said, "Daddy used to say sometimes things just line up and make a decision for you. I have a few call back visits I need to make. Then let's finish as many vests as we can with what we have to work with. Get them sold. We've had a great time with Sassy Quilters. We'll always have that."

Sally nodded again. The two friends hugged and Sally went to meet John MacLeod just coming up the steps of the porch of the hotel.

....

Coming downstairs to an empty lobby late that afternoon, Skitchy felt Sassy Quilters coming to an end as a heaviness in her heart coming up into her throat. It stuck there. She turned on the radio, moved around restlessly as she listened to the news from Europe. Europe seemed far far away and only added to the heaviness she felt. She turned off the radio, sat down in a chair looking out to the street, smoked a cigarette.

She thought of Wade Martin as she sat there. He also seemed far far away from her life in McAllister. Yet something had wakened in her that day on the range with him. Whatever that something was, the bright memory of it began to ease the heaviness. Not at all sure what to think about that and unable to imagine the direction her life might take now, she went into Jackson's office. Took a bottle of bourbon out of the cupboard. She didn't think he'd mind her helping herself. She poured a drink and took it out to the lobby. Sipped the bourbon slowly.

....

The telegram from Minnie said Ephraim Chapman's health had taken a turn for the worse. The doctor didn't think their father would live much longer.

"Let's leave tomorrow," Belle said. "Jackson'll drive us. He told Pink he doesn't need to stay here to look after things. Be all right for a few days, even if someone comes wanting a room. Daddy's more important."

"I'll ask Reba to take care of Margaret. I'm sure she will. I'd like to take Connie with us to say good-bye to her grandfather. Pink doesn't think that's such a good idea. Thinks she's too young. But I think nine's old enough. What do you think?"

"I think it is, too," Belle agreed. "She'll understand. Might even feel left out if she can't be there. It's not for me to say, but I think it's important for her to go."

"All right then. I'm going to take her."

When they arrived, Minnie said, "Daddy's in bed in the back bedroom. It's the room with the most light. You know how he always liked that."

Belle and Skitchy went in. Kate sat quietly by his bed, his hand in hers. She rose when she heard her daughters enter the room, motioned to them to step into the hall. "He's very tired. Think it'd be best if you go in one at a time, just stay for a short while." Her voice was soft yet strong.

Skitchy was not surprised. Her mother was always strong, even in the most difficult of times. "Of course, Mama, whatever you think best. What does the doctor say?"

"Well, let's talk about that in a little while. Eph's been so anxious for you to get here. He even made me promise to wake him if he was asleep."

Belle went in first, came out quickly, tears in her eyes. She just shook her head and went into Jackson's arms. As they walked out to the porch where the others were waiting, Skitchy went into the sick room.

"Daddy?" she said softly.

Ephraim opened his eyes. He smiled at his youngest daughter, and held out his thin hand to her, obviously with effort. She squeezed it for a moment, brushed his still thick silver hair back, kissed his forehead. Then she sat beside him where he patted the bed to show her what he wanted.

"Oh, Daddy, I love you so much." But no tears. Not yet. Plenty of time for that. Right now she just wanted to be with him.

In a weak voice Ephraim asked, "How's my girl?" They looked deeply at each other. Skitchy stroked his hand, wishing she could actually tell him how she was but knowing she couldn't do that now. And wouldn't be able to ever again. When he fell asleep, she quietly left the room and joined the others on the porch to hear her mother say what Skitchy already knew. He was dying.

When Pink went into the room his heart filled with tears. Some of the tears were for the dying man. Some of them for what might have been between them, but now never would be. Ephraim coughed as he tried to speak, finally patting Pink's hand. Pink got control of himself and stepped out of the room. Outside, he passed Belle and Connie sitting on the porch without speaking and walked alone down the dusty street.

"Where's Daddy going, Auntabelle?"

"I don't think he's going anywhere, honey. Some folks just need to be alone at a time like this."

"I'm glad I'm not alone. I'm glad I can be with you."

Belle hugged her young niece. "And I'm glad I can be with you, honey. Let's go get some lemonade, shall we?"

....

That night, Skitchy was the last before her mother to say good-bye. She said only "Daddy" as she stroked his forehead and kissed him. Ephraim opened his eyes when he heard her voice. She thought he wanted to say something to her but he never did. She would always wonder what it was, or if she had imagined it. He didn't wake up the next morning.

When Skitchy found her mother lying on the bed beside his body in the morning, she burst into tears. Kate rose and they held each other, weeping. Finally Kate said, "I want to be with him for a little while longer. Then we'll get him ready. Will you tell the others, please?" Skitchy nodded. She wanted to be with him herself but she left the room. He didn't belong to her.

....

Ephraim and Kate Chapman had planned to be buried in the Pecos cemetery where their sons lay. However, that was before the depression and unpredictable dust storms changed the plans of many people about many things.

"Seems foolish to go all that way," Kate said to the assembled family. "Spend that much money when Eph could be buried here in Big Lake. It's a sorrow that we won't be buried in Pecos but I know he'd want us to use good sense. I can live with it if all of you promise to see to it that I'll lay alongside him when my time comes."

"Of course, Mama," Minnie said firmly. Everyone else nodded as Kate looked around.

"Well, it's settled then."

....

Most people thought of the big sky country around Big Lake as flatland. But to someone used to the unrelenting flatness west of the Pecos River, here subtly rolling hills relieved the eye a little without limiting the sky's bigness. The mesquites and greasewoods were a little larger and shrubby plants more plentiful. Pink was surprised to find the Big Lake cemetery also different from the cemetery in Pecos.

He'd braced himself as he remembered Buddy's funeral, so bleak as it had seemed to him. But as they approached the cemetery for Ephraim's burial, he saw green grass that seemed an oasis in the dryness surrounding it. A few families had planted trees, even some evergreens, near the graves of loved ones. Must water them, he thought, for they looked fresh and green even if not large. He saw few weeds. There were crumbling headstones but not many. He was glad Ephraim Chapman would lie here.

There was no great crowd of mourners at Ephraim's gravesite as there would've been in Pecos. Nevertheless the voices at prayer sounded warm and deep to Pink and he was glad for it. He sang the hymns from his heart for the man he'd so admired and respected.

Later Kate Chapman said to him, "Thank you, Pink, for your singing today. It comforted me."

"Me, too," Skitchy said warmly. "And Daddy always liked your voice so much. From the first time he heard you sing in church."

"I didn't know that."

"Well, he didn't always tell other folks things like that. But I recollect him saying it more than once."

Pink was surprised when tears came into his eyes.

....

"I'd like to visit Brin tomorrow," Skitchy told everyone at supper a few days after they got home from Big Lake. "Ran out of time when I was looking for quilts around Pecos the last time. Never did get to see her. I'd like to spend the afternoon if you'll look after the girls, Belle."

"You bet. Tell Brin hello. Haven't seen her for ages."

Skitchy felt a little twinge about the lie. But she wanted to see Wade. She imagined the warmth of his presence easing the loss of her father. She imagined his interest in Sassy Quilters making it easier to finish what she needed to do to see that through. But don't kid yourself, Skitch, she thought. You just plain want to see him again, too. With or without anything else.

She knew Nettie might be with her mother in Pecos or if she was at home, she figured she could work it around. Say she'd dropped by to thank Nettie for the quilts, go on to Pecos and actually visit Brin. At the very least, maybe she and

Wade could figure out some way to see each other if they had a chance to talk.

....

She hadn't planned on Wade's not being at the ranch. Her heart fell when she didn't see him around. Saw his horse in the corral, unsaddled. No answer when she knocked on the ranch house door. A ranch hand splitting mesquite into fence rails some distance from the house stopped his work and walked toward her.

"Ma'am, can I help you?" the darkly tanned sweaty man asked as he tipped his hat to her.

"I'm looking for Mr. or Mrs. Martin."

"Mrs. Martin's not at home. Boss went into town for supplies. He'll be back before long, I expect," the man said. "Sure you'd be welcome to wait. Or I can tell him something if you want."

"Thank you," she said, hoping her nervousness didn't show. "I'll wait for a bit."

She sat down in the shade of the broad porch to try to pull herself together. Should've figured somebody besides Wade might be around, she thought. That was stupid, Skitch. She pushed that thought away when she heard a truck coming toward the house and saw that it was Wade's truck. He was alone.

He could see someone on the porch as he drove along the road but couldn't see who it was at first, sitting there in the shade. His heart leapt when he saw Skitchy come into the sunlight, down the steps to meet him. He got out of the truck quickly, hurried to her but didn't touch her. Best be careful, he thought. Don't want to rouse curiosity. He called out to the hand splitting wood, "Tommy, when you finish up there, get this truck unloaded. When Marvin comes in from the range, he can help you store everything." The man touched the brim of his hat and resumed his work.

"Come on in the house," Wade said warmly. As they walked up the steps he said, "Surely sorry about your father," his voice somber. "I heard about it in town. He was a fine man."

"Thank you, Wade. It comforts me to know how much you care. But it makes me so sad to talk about him or even think about him. Let's not talk about him today. I want to be happy this afternoon."

"Whatever you say, Skitch. How long can you stay?"

"All afternoon." She dropped her eyes shyly. "If you have the afternoon free."

"I can make it free, sugar, and there's nothing I'd rather do!" He was eager for her but not wanting to push too fast, he kissed her lightly. "Some ice tea?"

She wasn't sure if he was just being courteously considerate but she thought so. That he was as eager to make love as she was. A little surprised at her own boldness, she said, "No thanks. I want something else."

He grinned and kissed her not so lightly, started to unbutton her blouse. She stopped him. "I want something in particular, Wade. Can we go wherever we're going to make love?"

"You bet," he said, curious. He took her to the back bedroom where the shades were drawn against the afternoon sun.

"Please stand right there," she said. Moving a few feet away, she stood facing him. "I want us to take off our clothes for each other. I've never actually looked at a man naked and

I'd like to. I want to really see you. See all of you. Will you do that with me?"

Grinning, he was already unbuttoning his shirt.

As her eyes roamed slowly over his body, she knew he was also enjoying her nakedness.

She'd seen the scars, a long waxy gash high on his left arm and a shorter blaze on his chest, the day she first saw him wearing no shirt. She'd been curious then but had said nothing. Now her eyes settled on the scars, tracing them intently.

"Do you want to know about the scars?"

She nodded. "I meant it when I said I wanted to see all of you. I want to know everything about you."

He wanted her to know him and standing there naked before her, looked at her as directly as she was looking at him. "My father took me with him to the saloon in Pecos on my sixteenth birthday. Said it was time I learned more about living in a man's world. After we'd been there for a bit he got into an argument with Jabe Alexander. Both drunk as hoot owls. Pretty soon they drew knives and went at it."

"Law!" Skitchy gasped.

"Nobody else was doing anything except putting down bets on who'd win the fight. I tried to break it up. Got cut pretty bad. Daddy didn't even see that I was hurt, so I got his gun. Yelled at them to back off."

"Weren't you scared?"

"You bet. But I was a fair shot even as a youngster. Some of the drunks even started betting on me. I was able to joke with Jabe and Daddy a little. Try to calm them down. Said they both knew better than to bring a knife to a gunfight, even if it was a kid who had a gun. I don't know what I thought I was fixing to do if they didn't break it up but I never had to figure that out. Jabe went and sat down and it was all over.

By then Daddy could see I was cut. Somebody took us to Doc Hartman's. Got stitched up and then we went home."

"Law, Wade. What happened after that?"

"Not much that was out in the open. Mama pitched a fit. She was so mad at Daddy for having gotten me into a mess like that. Daddy never talked about it again. But I learned some things about living in a man's world that I didn't much care for. That's helped me make some different choices than I might have made otherwise."

She looked deeply into the warmth of his smiling eyes, her own smiling back. He opened his arms to her.

"Whenever you're ready. If you like what you see. I surely like what I see."

Laughing joyously, she ran into his open arms, returned his impassioned kiss before gratefully slipping with him between the clean cool sheets.

They savored each other. Skitchy traced his scars with her fingers and lips. Each of them sensitive to the lightest touch given and received, they took their time until they could hold nothing back. She lay limp and happy in his arms afterward, drinking in the fragrance of him released by the warmth of their bodies, until he went to get a bourbon for them.

"You're one marvelous woman, Skitchy." He slipped in beside her and put his arm around her. She moved as close to him as she could get, reveling in their delight in each other.

When they'd finished their drinks, Skitchy said, "I'd love to ride and really stretch that mare's legs! Can we do that?" Then she hesitated, thinking of the unexpected encounter with the mesquite splitting Tommy. "Would that be a problem with the hands?"

"Nope. I know where they are. More than likely they'd keep their mouths shut but it'd still be best to ride away from where they're working. I'll saddle the horses whenever you're ready."

"I wore something to ride in." She showed him the split skirt Alma Floyd had given her. "It's better looking than old blue jeans and I can ride astride as hard as I want to. My friend made it for me. Do you like it?"

"You bet. Never seen anything like it but it suits you. You look wonderful, sugar." Grinning mischievously, he added, "With clothes or without."

She wondered why she felt shy when he said that when she was fully dressed. She hadn't felt shy standing naked in front of him. A little flustered she reached up to kiss him. "Ready to ride if you are!"

As they raced the horses across the flat rangeland, Skitchy whooped and laughed. Wade whooped and laughed with her.

"So glad you're having fun," he said as he took the old blanket out of his saddlebag, spread it on the ground for them to sit on when they stopped to rest the horses.

"Oh, I am!" She laughed gaily, then grew quiet as she looked around. "Where we were riding last time the grass was brown but high. Why is the ground almost bare here?"

His face darkened and his voice grew quietly serious. "Cattle graze it close. What's left withers. Can't replenish itself when there isn't enough rain. We haven't had enough rain in a long while. I don't have enough well water to irrigate the land. I fumed about the government burning my cattle but I'd be lying if I said I wasn't worried about how long I can keep feeding the stock I have left. Don't know what's worse, the depression or the drought. I can't afford to buy much feed. What little grass is left will all be cropped before too long if we don't get a good long soft rain soon."

"Surely sorry, Wade. Law, I hate these awful hard times." She reached to take his hand.

He felt less alone in his worry about his ranch as he heard the concern in her voice. Felt it from her hand. Saw it in her eyes. It felt good just to sit there with her.

After a time when neither of them spoke, he noticed she was looking toward the far mountains, blue in the afternoon light. "What are you thinking about, Skitch?"

"Do you know about sheep in the mountains? With big curved horns? They can jump from place to place, even steep places, and never fall? Is it true there are sheep like that in the mountains? Daddy and Buddy used to talk about them but I was never sure if they were teasing me."

"You bet there are. Bighorns. That's what they're called. Rams have the big horns. Females have short horns with just a little curve to them. They're sure-footed and nimble. Even the young ones. I used to go with my father when he hunted in the mountains when I was a boy. We saw them lots of times. He never got one though. They're very quick."

"I don't want to hunt them or kill any. I just want to see them. Would you take me, Wade? I've wanted to see those sheep for as long as I can recollect."

"Well, it'd be fun and I'd love to. Have to figure out a way we could do it without attracting attention to ourselves. Let me see if I can figure something out."

"Oh, that would be so wonderful!" She was quiet for a minute. The tone of her voice became more serious when she asked, "Are you worried about us attracting attention, Wade? I think about that sometimes. I have no doubts or regrets about us but I do think about what would happen if people knew. I feel so happy when we're together. It feels so right to be with you. I'd just hate it if anything went sideways."

"I can't recollect ever being as happy as I am when I'm with you."

"But I wonder about what's going to happen. You're married. I'm married."

"I haven't wanted to burden you with talk about Nettie and me. But you said before you want to know everything. I'll tell you everything if you really want to know."

"I do want to know."

He took a deep breath. "Hasn't been much for Nettie and me for a long while, Skitch. I thought we'd always be together when we married. Didn't believe in divorce. But it's been pretty bad. Even before you came along, I'd begun to think that if two people have really tried but can't live together, maybe they don't have to stay together. Stay married as if that still meant something." He paused. "I didn't know if I could let myself be with another woman the way things stood. Then that day you came looking for quilts I knew I could. And I would, if you wanted me as much as I wanted you. And I thought you did."

"How did you know? How much I wanted you?"

"Hard to put into words. You never felt like a stranger to me, Skitchy. It was as if I'd always known you. It was more than just wanting to make love to you." He laughed joyfully. "But I did want to make love to you that first day."

"I think I did, too, even though I couldn't let myself really think that then. Scared me a little. Maybe that's why I waited so long to come back."

He grinned at her. "I'm so glad you came back." He kissed her softly.

They made love again when they got back to the ranch house. Skitchy waited as long as she could before she said, "Well, I'd best be getting back. It was wonderful, Wade."

"I thought so, too."

Smiling as she drove away from the ranch, she thought, I've got a lot to think about.

1938

Wade was working on the enclosed back porch of his ranch house, repairing a torn piece of screen, when he heard the first drops on the metal roof. The sky had been darkening since he got up that morning. He'd paid it little mind. Clouds massed and were gone just as quickly, even when they teased with a drop or two of rain. He'd given up longing for rain.

He finished what he was doing and went to close the front door. When he saw the clouds were still there and in fact were lowering, he stepped out onto the front porch. He smelled that iron smell of rain coming he'd not smelled for a very long time. Splattering drops gathered into steady soft rain as he watched. The hair on his arms stood up as he dared to let himself think the interminable thirst that had cracked the earth, and at times his heart, might be over. This might be a real rain.

He went to the kitchen, fixed a fresh pot of coffee. He poured a cup and took it out to the porch. It was still raining. He sat down, drank the coffee slowly. It was still raining. He heard horses in the corral whinny and somewhere in the distance a calf bawled. Animal joy began to rise up from deep within himself to meet the animating rain. He hurried out of his boots and socks. There was already a little mud in puddles in the yard and he let out loud whoops as he wriggled his toes in it, danced in it, wanting the whole raining world to hear his joy. Later there would be things to do but now he held up his face and arms to the rain. Let rain pour off him. Let rain drench him.

....

In McAllister many people came out onto the streets. Rain at last! A few watched from windows, weeping relief. It rained most of the day. People made sure there were no leaks in the water cisterns collecting the runoff from roofs. Buckets and jars appeared all over town. Ministers at the town's churches began planning services of thanksgiving. Connie and Belle began planning to wash their hair.

Skitchy was as glad for the rain as everyone else, but hoped no one would notice that she was unusually quiet at a time when most everyone else talked and talked and talked about the rain. Preoccupied with her own thoughts about Wade, she wanted nothing so much as to go to him. To share with him what rain would mean to him, to his ranch, to his life. But she couldn't do that. She had to meet with Connie's teacher and there were things to attend to for Sally's wedding in a few days. These things were important to her, too, she reminded herself. Still she longed to be with Wade and it took all the grit she could find within herself to turn her feet toward the schoolhouse.

....

Skitchy felt nervous as she walked up the steps and shook rainwater from her jacket before hanging it on a peg by the schoolhouse door. She'd been puzzled when Connie brought home a note from Miss Hoffman, asking Skitchy to come for a meeting after school. The teacher had never done that before and Connie had said she had no idea what Miss Hoffman wanted to talk about.

Martha Hoffman was a plain woman. As petite as Belle, she wore her long blonde hair braided and wound about her head. A dark gray muslin dress made her fair skin look even more pale. But when she looked up from her desk, a light seemed to shine from her soft blue eyes and her smile made Skitchy feel warmly welcome. "Mrs. Campbell, good afternoon," the teacher said as she rose quickly and closed the door.

"Good afternoon, Miss Hoffman," Skitchy said, curious now as well as puzzled.

"Please sit down. Thank you so much for coming. I'm sure you must be wondering why I asked you to come, so first let me tell you this isn't about Connie. She's doing just fine in school. I asked you to come here because I have some wonderful news I want to ask you to pass on to Hutch Borden." She smiled broadly once again. Skitchy was more curious than ever. Martha Hoffman went on eagerly, "*Eagle* magazine had a contest for young writers. I sent in one of Hutch's stories and it won first place! They're going to pay him five dollars and his story will be published in the magazine. They say they will consider others stories he writes for publication. Will you tell him, please?"

Skitchy didn't know anyone who'd written anything published so the whole world could read it. Now she did. And it was Hutch! And he'd won prize money besides! Reba's Hutch who lived in McAllister, Texas! Astounded, she stared at Miss Hoffman.

"Mrs. Campbell? Is that all right? Asking you to tell him? I know there are people who won't like a black boy writing at all, and now he's won prize money to top off how much they won't like it. It's a hard story about a black boy growing up in Jim Crow country. I had him change the setting from West Texas to just somewhere in the south, without saying where it was, and sent the story in under a made-up name. But there are things in the story someone around here may recognize and there aren't many black boys who could have written it. They could make trouble for anyone involved with this. I knew I was taking a risk when I helped Hutch but I never meant to make trouble for anyone else."

"Oh, sorry, Miss Hoffman. I was just surprised, that's all. I'll tell him. Law, this is wonderful!"

In a somewhat hushed voice, Miss Hoffman said, "I didn't want to send this news in a note with Connie. I thought it'd be better if she didn't know anything about Hutch's story being published, or take a chance that anyone else might see the note. Probably be best if no one around here knows about this even though I'd like Hutch to have the recognition. But he's the one to decide about that. And his mother. Will you please tell them that, also?"

"You bet. I'll tell them everything you've said. This is quite a remarkable thing, isn't it?"

"It is! Hutch is very talented. This could be the beginning of who knows what for him."

"Wonderful what you've done for him, Miss Hoffman. I think McAllister's lucky to have you."

....

Skitchy caught her breath when she saw Wade coming up the steps of the hotel. Alone in the lobby, she felt herself flush. Her stomach knotted.

"What are you doing here?" she whispered breathlessly as soon as he was in the door.

"Here for the wedding," he said, grinning. "What do you suppose I'm doing here?"

She felt flustered and couldn't think straight. "For the wedding?"

"I'm the best man," he said, still grinning.

"Are you teasing me?"

"Nope. Came a little early," he grinned at her again, "to see if there's anything I could do to help."

He made no move to touch her but she felt as if he'd put his arm around her waist. She stepped back quickly, feeling jittery. "Law, Wade, you gave me such a fright!" she said, still whispering.

"If you're afraid of someone seeing us and thinking anything, it'd probably be better if you didn't whisper and act funny." He grinned again, then made his face serious. "John and I've been friends a long while. Played polo together on the Georgetown team when we were students at Southwestern. We lost touch with each other when he went east to medical school and I came back home to breed better cattle. When he came to West Texas and started at the clinic in Wink he looked me up. Now I visit with him when I'm in McAllister. He visits at the ranch when he can."

"I didn't know any of that. I've never heard of polo. What is it?"

"It's a game played on horseback. You hit a ball with sticks. Idea is to drive the ball through the other team's goal on a field something like a football field. Our small fast West Texas horses with their endurance gave us an advantage. John and I grew up on ranches and were both good riders. We had lots of fun."

John MacLeod walked into the lobby, smiling broadly. "Wade! Good to see you." The two men shook hands warmly. "Skitchy, do you know Wade Martin?"

"I do," Skitchy said carefully. "He was a friend of my brother."

"Sorry Nettie couldn't make it, John," Wade said, making sure Skitchy heard. "She's with her mother in Pecos almost all the time now. Sarah's very sick."

"Sorry to hear it, Wade. I surely appreciate your being here." Then John turned to Skitchy.

"Sally asked if you'd come up and help her with something. Anything you need me to do down here?"

Wade said quickly, "I'd be glad to help." Then grinning at Skitchy while John's head was turned away he said, "That's what I came early for."

Upstairs Skitchy repaired a small tear in Sally's dress, the seam pulled as she'd put it over her head. As she stitched, Skitchy said casually, "Sally, have you ever heard John talk about playing polo?"

"Oh, you bet. He's very proud of it. Quite something when a Texas team beat teams from the east. Once even one from England. That's how he met Wade Martin, his best man today. They were on the same polo team. Why do you ask about polo?"

"Just curious. Wade was actually a friend of my brother. He mentioned something about polo but I couldn't tell if he was teasing."

"If Wade feels anything like John does about polo, I suggest you don't get them started talking about it. Mark my words, you might hear way more than you ever wanted to know about polo," Sally said, laughing as the two women went downstairs together.

Standing beside Sally as she said her marriage vows, Skitchy was very aware of Wade standing on the other side of John MacLeod. She felt uncomfortable with Pink and Wade in the same room and was glad when the short ceremony was over.

After everyone had enjoyed coffee and the cake Reba had made, John and Wade went upstairs and brought down Sally's trunk. Wade said jovially, "I'm going to help John move Sally's trunk. How about the matron of honor and best man seeing the newlyweds home?"

Before a flustered Skitchy could find her voice Sally said, "What a wonderful idea! That feels so much more festive than if we just go home by ourselves!"

....

Wade drove his truck slowly, Sally's trunk in the back, Skitchy in the seat beside him but not sitting too close. Sally and John walked hand in hand the two blocks down Main Street, turned at Austin Street and walked another block. The two men carried the trunk upstairs to the rooms above the clinic. They had coffee laced with brandy that Jackson had sent in a thermos and talked for a while. When good nights were said and hugs exchanged, Skitchy and Wade went back to his truck.

It was dark now. Wade drove out of town. He turned down a farm road and pulled the truck over to the side of the road. "This is my friend Shorty Fallon's farm. No one else uses this road." He drew her close and kissed her. She shivered with the pleasure of touching him, of his hands touching her wanting body.

Reluctantly she said, "I need to get back before long."

"Please come to the ranch as soon as you can," he said, his voice urgent. "I don't think Nettie's mother will live much longer. Then Nettie will probably come back to the ranch."

Skitchy moved back from him just a little, trying to see his face in the dim light of the stars and a half moon. "Wade, I'd like you to tell me everything about how it's been between you and Nettie. From the very beginning."

"All right," he said quietly, his voice serious. "Nettie grew up in Pecos. But I hardly knew her until she spent the summer before my last year at Southwestern with her grandparents in Georgetown. When she introduced me to her grandparents, she told them my father owned a big ranch and I'd have it one day. I tried to explain that our ranch was a good one but that a big ranch in West Texas wasn't the same thing as a big ranch around Georgetown. Where you don't get much rain there's not as much grass so every head of cattle needs more land. Best to measure a ranch in how many cattle you can graze, not in acres. None of them seemed to understand what I was talking about." He paused, then took a deep breath and went on.

"I think, looking back at it, that the ranch looked very attractive to Nettie when her folks didn't have much. I doubt she thought about how much work it is or what it would be like to live there. John was always wary about her. Said he thought she'd had her sights set on me from the start. But I couldn't see it." He stopped, closed his eyes.

She let him be with his thoughts. When she could feel that he seemed ready to speak again she said, "Go on, Wade. Please."

The gentleness in her voice encouraged him. It felt good to him to let the words so long pressed down speak out. "When we got married she changed so much. She hated ranch life. She was critical of everything. Including me. Especially me. I tried so hard to please her but nothing I did was ever right. I just kept getting more and more down until I could hardly stand it. When she found out she was going to have our baby, things got a little better for a while. She was sick a lot, but not so fussy all the time. Then the baby was born too soon and didn't live." His voice choked.

Skitchy could feel his heart's heaviness. She longed to comfort him but couldn't think of how to do that so she waited for him. She was glad when he seemed ready to speak again.

He shook himself. "Sure you want to listen to all this?" he asked.

"Uh-huh," she said, wanting to keep her voice warm.

"All right then. The birth almost cost Nettie her life, too. Doctor told her she shouldn't have any more children. She told me that meant no more lovemaking. May surprise you, but that wasn't as big a thing for me as you might think. Nettie never much liked anything physical between us. Before we were married, she'd acted like she could hardly wait for us to make love. But after we were married, she'd more or less just lay there. I never liked feeling like she was just putting up with it."

Law, Skitchy thought, no wonder we fell into each other's arms. But she said nothing and kept listening.

"Things got worse again after the baby. I tried to get her to tell me what I could do to make things better, but she wouldn't have a reasonable conversation with me. I was always trying to guess what she wanted. What she needed. No matter what I did, it was the wrong thing. Just like it'd been before. I started to feel even more down than I had before."

Even as he spoke of those dark awful days, the oppressive weight began to lift from his heart a little. He turned toward Skitchy, saw her eyes shining even in the dimness. "Maybe you can begin to understand why it's felt so good to talk with you, sugar. Laugh again."

"Can't imagine you not being able to laugh. The way I recollect you laughing with Buddy and the rest of us. The way I know you now. That's like saying you weren't able to breathe."

"Sometimes I felt like I couldn't breathe." He took a deep breath before he said, "Well, I'm almost finished. I'd like to get the telling over with. When her mother got sick, Nettie started spending a lot of time with Sarah in Pecos. That was a big relief to me. But I started to dread thinking about a lifetime with her. When I decided to talk to her about getting a divorce, she threw a fit. Threatened to kill herself if I tried to divorce her. Said she'd rather go to hell that way than by being divorced."

Skitchy sat, stunned. "I don't know what to say, Wade. I can't imagine how you've lived with this."

"You asked me before what I want. I want to be free of her. It's important to me for you to hang on to knowing that came before wanting to be with you. I don't want you to feel responsible for any of what happens. That responsibility is mine. And Nettie's."

She moved closer to him. She wanted to comfort him even more than she had before, but still didn't know how to do that. When his arms reached for her, she met his kiss, grateful for it.

....

"Coach Corrigan asked me if I'd start working with the new quarterback," Pink said. Skitchy looked up from the laundry she was folding. "There hasn't been so much dust since it rained. Everyone wants the Panthers to start playing again. The team hasn't been playing for so long, Coach figures they'll need a lot of work. He wants to get a real early start. I'm going to work with all the backs on Monday, Wednesday, and Friday afternoons, starting next month."

"I'm sure you'll have fun."

"Mr. Wilson is arranging the schedule at the store to make sure I'm free those days. He thinks what's good for the team is good for the town and good for business. Lots of people like to talk football as much as they like to watch it. He thinks they'll like to talk it at the store, like they used to, with training starting. More people are already coming in, by the way, since we started selling penny cups of coffee with refills. That was a great idea, Skitch."

"People like to drink coffee and talk."

"I told Mr. Wilson that was your idea. You know what he said? He said you'd make a very good businessman."

"That's nice," she said and went back to folding laundry. "Good luck with the backs."

....

Sally MacLeod came up the steps of the hotel early one Monday afternoon as Pink was heading out for the Panthers football field. "Hi, Pink," she said gaily.

"Nice to see you, Sally."

Skitchy and Sally hugged and went to the kitchen. Skitchy heated up some coffee and they took their cups back to the lobby. No one else was there and Sally looked as if she had something on her mind. Skitchy settled back on the settee.

"So good to see you, Sally."

"Can't stay long but I wanted to drop by. Say hello. I want to talk to you about something, too. John and Wade have been talking about riding together for ages. Now they've decided to go riding in the mountains. The mountains got even more rain than we did here in McAllister. They think it'll be really nice up there. Wade has a friend in San Saba Springs who's going to let them use his horses. They're going on Friday, and I'm going with them. John and I thought you and Pink might like to come."

"I don't think Pink would be able to, Sally. He's working with the football team again. Friday's a practice day. He doesn't like riding much anyway."

Disappointment was clear on Sally's face. Skitchy dropped her eyes to her coffee cup, not wanting to show or say too much too soon.

Soon Sally brightened. "Nettie Martin isn't going either. Would you come, Skitch, even if Pink can't?"

Skitchy's heart started to beat faster. Wade had managed to arrange a trip in the mountains so she could see the Bighorns as he'd said he would. It was hard not to betray her excitement.

"I'd love to go. I'll talk to Pink. Maybe he'll come. But I'll come even if he can't. I've lived around here all my life. Never been in the mountains. I'd love to go."

....

"Go on, honey," Pink said. "I remember how much you've always wanted to see those sheep. Here's your chance. Go. And have fun."

Pink's voice was warm and Skitchy felt a tinge of guilt that dissipated almost as quickly as it had come. She wished things had been different between her and Pink. But they weren't different. She was still a young woman and had a young woman's needs and desires. And Wade Martin was meeting those needs and desires.

"I surely would like to ride up into the mountains. See those sheep! I think I'll go."

....

Skitchy got out her split skirt, cleaned her boots. She brushed her hat and made sure the cords that kept it secure weren't frayed in case it was windy in the mountains. She was trying to decide between a blue shirt and a brown one when Belle knocked on the door.

"Can I come in?"

"You bet. What do you think? Blue or brown?"

"Blue. You seem excited about this trip, Skitch."

"I am." Skitchy tried to make her voice a little more matter-of-fact. "I've been wanting to go to the mountains since I was a little girl. See the Bighorns. I know they aren't always where you can see them, but I hope I'll see them."

"I hope you will, too. Too bad Pink can't go."

"Uh-huh." Skitchy hoped her voice didn't sound hollow. "I want him to do what he wants with the football team, though, and he wants me to go on the trip."

"Mmm, I know he does. Do you think he would if he knew everything?"

Skitchy felt herself flush. "What do you mean?" she asked, suddenly jittery.

"I think maybe you know what I mean, Skitch. It's obvious you haven't been happy with Pink for a long time. Been written all over you for anyone with the eyes to see and the ears to hear. And been written all over you lately that something's changed. Is that something Wade Martin?"

Skitchy gasped, stunned. She'd been so careful. She'd tried so hard to be careful. How could Belle know about Wade?

"You don't have to tell me anything, Skitchy. But I love you and I think maybe you need to be able to talk to someone you trust who loves you." Belle paused, searching her sister's face. "Do you want to talk?"

Relief flooded through Skitchy's body as tension released she didn't even know was there. Tears welled in her eyes. "Oh, Belle, I've wanted to tell you. Didn't think I could. Or that I should." She sat down on the bed. Belle sat down beside her and took her hand.

"Well, I don't know about should, but about could, you can."

"I have been seeing Wade, Belle. I think I love him."

"Wade's a very attractive man. He hasn't been happy in his marriage either. I'm not surprised you two would be attracted to each other."

"How do you know he isn't happy in his marriage?"

"Honey, we live in a small town in a small county. Not much goes on that doesn't get around. Nettie Martin's been in Pecos with her mother. Talking around about a lot of things. My old friends in Pecos say Nettie thinks Wade's involved with someone. I figured it might be you. You two have been with each other the last while. Now there's this trip with him and the MacLeods. And honey, you've been glowing lately. Noticed it especially at Sally's wedding."

"I clean forget sometimes you lived in Pecos before you and Jackson came to McAllister. Do you think anyone else knows?"

"I haven't heard a word about you from anybody, but it might not come to my ears. I've always thought a lot of Wade. Don't think he's the kind of man who'd be careless or brag. I don't know anyone who thinks all that much of Nettie. But she is married to him, so naturally people talk."

Skitchy sat quietly, trying to think. She'd known that sooner or later she'd have to think about what was going to happen for her and Wade, but she'd always pushed such thoughts away. Right now she didn't want to think past Friday.

"I'd like to talk about it but I need some time to think." As Belle started to leave the room, Skitchy said softly, "We will talk, Belle. Thank you."

....

Rita Colquitt looked up as Skitchy walked through the lobby. "Oh, look. Sister," Rita said to the ghost sister sitting in the chair across from her. "Here's Skitchy. We've been wanting to talk to her about the Bighorns, haven't we?"

"Good morning, Rita."

"Good morning, Skitchy. Hear you're going into the mountains to see the Bighorns."

"I surely hope I'll see them. Been wanting to for a long while."

"Belle told me that. Sister and I used to see them when we were young girls. We lived in San Saba Springs. Sometimes our father took us up into the high places where they usually are. I loved seeing them. Always thought they were so beautiful. So sure-footed with their special hooves. Not many of them left now. That's what I wanted to talk to you about. I hope you won't hunt them or let anybody you go with hunt them.

"I'm not going to hunt them, Rita. I just want to see them."

"Well, then, I hope you will. It's grand to be able to do something you've wanted to do for a long while."

Something in the elderly woman's voice, a note of sadness or maybe loneliness, touched Skitchy. She decided to stay for a while and sat down. "I think so, too, Rita. I hope you've had things like that in your life."

"Oh, I have, dear. And I've also had things I wanted to do that I never got to do. Those leave a little hole in you. Sometimes a big hole. You don't want too many of those."

Skitchy could clearly hear the sadness now. "Would it be nice for you to talk about anything? Don't want to pry but I'm a pretty good listener. If you'd like to talk about anything."

Rita seemed to go inside herself. When she focused again on Skitchy's sympathetic face, she leaned forward and spoke very softly. "Never told anyone about the biggest hole in me. I think I'd like to now." She seemed lost in her memory for a moment, then a tear made its way down her cheek. "I loved a man once. It was after I was married. Didn't know what it was like to really love someone until I met Josiah. I wanted to be with him more than anything in the world. But I didn't get to. He wanted to be with me, too. But he said marriage vows are sacred. He wouldn't take me from my husband. I wanted to leave my husband and go to him. Josiah was afraid I'd regret it later on."

Skitchy could feel the hair standing up on her neck and arms. This story was much too close to the one she was living. Much too close. She said awkwardly, "That must've been very hard for you."

"My husband passed in the awful time when the flu took so many folks. When I heard Josiah's wife had passed, too, I thought maybe we could at least have our last years together. I knew he'd built this hotel so I came here. But Josiah didn't seem to still feel the same way I did."

Stunned, Skitchy interrupted, "Here? Do you mean this hotel?"

"Uh-huh. Josiah Tieger, Jackson's grandfather, was my Josiah. Much more happened in his life than happened in mine. Maybe he just changed. Anyway, I never meant to trouble him so I just went back to live with Sister. She never knew anything about Josiah. But when we needed to cut back on expenses, I suggested we come to live in McAllister. Rent a room here. Thought maybe living in the hotel Josiah built would fill up some of the hole in me."

"Has it?"

"No. But it gives me a little comfort."

Skitchy bent in front of Rita's chair, took the older woman's hands in hers. "Thank you so much for telling me about you and Josiah. I wish I could do something to help fill the hole."

"You have, dear. You listened." Over Skitchy's shoulder she said, "Sister, do you understand now?"

....

241

Skitchy felt her heart beating fast as Wade and John saddled the horses. It had rained all morning yesterday and John was concerned about slippery rocky terrain in the mountains. He had insisted they put off the trip if it was raining today and Skitchy had felt beside herself with not wanting the trip to be put off. But this morning had dawned clear and dry with little wind. Eager now to get started into the mountains, she swung easily into the saddle.

The climb was steep in places, the riding easy through more level grassy areas daubed with dark green, yellow green, and gray green. Near the end of a rocky outcropping they tethered the horses and walked out to look out over the land below.

Filled with delight, Skitchy exclaimed, "I can see McMinn Springs! Look! You can see the cottonwoods. They're so green! I'd no idea I'd be able to see so far! I think maybe I can see our home place. It's so far, though, I'm not sure. I was thinking so much about looking up to see the Bighorns I never thought about what it'd be like looking down." She stood silently then for a long time, looking out. Looking. Looking.

They rode during the late morning, ate their lunch of bologna sandwiches and pickles beside a creek, rode on in the afternoon. They saw deer and many small animals and different kinds of birds. They did not see Bighorns. When the angle of afternoon light told Wade they had to start back if they were to be in McAllister before nightfall, he slowed their pace and let Sally and John ride ahead. She thought maybe he'd say something about Nettie. About Nettie and him, but he didn't.

"I'm sorry about not seeing the Bighorns, Skitchy."

"Well, I'm sorry about the Bighorns, too. But thank you, Wade, for bringing me here. It's been a gift I'll never forget.

Maybe I'll see Bighorns one day. But whether I do or not, I'll treasure this day. Thank you with all my heart."

1939

Skitchy tried to be patient, holding Margaret's shoes while the little girl struggled to pull on her socks. She did her best to smile when Margaret held up first one foot and then the other to show her mother and aunt what she'd done, announcing proudly, "Do it by self!"

"Good for you, sugar," Skitchy said. "Now shoes." Skitchy put the shoes on and tied them. "Connie's waiting for you downstairs in the lobby. Mind you hold her hand."

Skitchy's smile faded as the child bounced out of the room, eager to go to the drug store. Margaret loved ice cream and Uncle Jackson would give her an ice cream cone from the soda fountain, newly reopened on Fridays if the Panthers were playing football in McAllister, and every Saturday.

"Are you all right, honey?" Belle looked at her sister, concern clear in her voice.

"I am," Skitchy said with a deep sigh. "But sometimes I wish so much that things were different. I hate feeling like I'm sneaking around with Wade." She thought fleetingly of Rita Colquitt and the sad hole she carried within herself that Josiah Tieger might have filled. "But Wade's changed my life. I want to be with him as much as I can. I feel so happy when I'm with him. Do you think I'm crazy, Belle?"

"No, not crazy. I'm just sorry this is what you have to do to find a little happiness. And somebody may get hurt sooner or later. Perhaps hurt badly. Maybe you. But I think you know that."

"I try not to think about it. Can't always push it away, though. Wade wants a divorce but Nettie won't agree to it. She doesn't believe in divorce. You know her mother passed but Nettie still spends most of the time at the house in Pecos. She hates living on the ranch. At least she's not around much. He's glad about that. But he's still not free. Nettie doesn't have any other family and Wade doesn't think she'd ever take up with another man. Sounds to me like she tries to make him feel responsible for her."

"And what about you and Pink?"

"I've been thinking a lot about Pink. Thinking a lot about myself, too, Belle. That day I was in the mountains I looked down at where I live. Thought to myself I've been living in the middle of nowhere and didn't even know it. I feel like I'm in the middle of nowhere in my marriage for sure."

Belle searched her sister's face, her eyes full of sympathy. "I'd no idea it was as bad as that."

"It is, Belle. I'd leave Pink if I could figure a way to take care of myself and the girls. I don't think I can go on living the way I was before Wade. I don't know what's going to happen for Wade and me but I don't think I can stay with Pink, no matter what happens with Wade."

....

"Skitchy," Sally said as they finished their coffee, "where did you get those pants that were like a skirt? What you were wearing when we went riding in the mountains."

"Alma gave it to me. She made it. She called it a split skirt."

"Split skirt? That sounds like Alma," Sally said with a chuckle. "But seriously, I've never seen anything like it. It was very attractive and you looked so comfortable riding in it. I've never liked riding sidesaddle. I'd go riding with John more often if I had a skirt like that. Will you lend it to me? Let me see if I can figure out how Alma made it, so I could make one for myself?"

"You bet." Skitchy went quiet and an unusual expression, not of excitement exactly but something like it, passed over her face.

"What are you thinking, Skitchy?"

"Oh, just recollecting when Alma and I made Sassy Quilters' first vest. We never dreamed how many we'd make and be able to sell. I hated it when it got so hard to find old quilts but nothing like that would happen if you and I were making split skirts. Kind of fun to think about what might happen if enough women liked them . . ."

"Mmm . . . I see. Well, let me see if I can make one. I'll be sure to keep the pattern if it turns out." The friends grinned at each other.

....

Pink asked Skitchy to go upstairs with him. "I need to talk to you about something." His voice sounded solemn.

Her stomach knotted. With every step up the oak staircase she told herself to wait. Told herself she didn't know yet what the something was. Wait. Wait. Wait.

"Sit down, honey, please," he said as he closed the door behind them.

She didn't think his voice sounded terrible. He pulled the chair over to the bed and sat down opposite her, taking her hands in his. She hoped he couldn't feel her trembling. Then she realized his hands were trembling, too.

"I heard something at the store today. They say the government's going to make a state park in the mountains around Fort Davis. They're going to build a lodge in the park where people can stay overnight. The whole thing's part of a program to create jobs and have something nice for people to show for it. And they say veterans will have preference for the jobs." He stopped to give her a chance to say something.

"Law, Pink, that'd surely be something." She felt what she said sounded empty, maybe even silly, but she didn't know what to say. When she'd collected herself she said, "You're a veteran. Do you think you can get one of those jobs?"

"I'm pretty sure I can."

"How long would the work last?"

He pulled his chair a little closer and squeezed her hands more tightly. "Men doing the work would have to live in the mountains in tents while the work is going on. It'll take about a year to build the lodge and everything else. I can make enough to pay what we still owe Dr. MacLeod and lots more besides. We'd be able to do whatever we want to."

"A year?" Skitchy's mind was racing, thoughts tumbling faster than she could sort them out. "And what happens to your job at Wilson's? Mr. Wilson will surely find someone else if you're gone that long."

"Maybe you, Skitchy. Why not? I've been thinking about that, too. Mr. Wilson said himself you're a good businessman. Businesswoman? Sounds funny, I don't know what to call it. But I think you could do it."

"I think I could, too, and I'd like that. Should I go talk to him? Would it be better if you talked to him?"

"I think we should wait until we know for sure I have the Fort Davis job. Then I think it would be good for you to go in yourself. Tell him I told you what he said about you and just ask him, straight out, if you can fill in for me while I'm gone."

Skitchy hadn't been thinking of what she'd be doing as filling in for Pink. The thought rankled her. For her, it would be working for herself. Making money herself. A sense of some independence she hadn't known since Sassy Quilters. Pink just seemed to be wanting her to keep his job at the store waiting for him, to step aside with no concern for herself when he came back.

"What's wrong, honey?" Pink asked, seeing her scowl. "I thought you'd be tickled about this."

Her thoughts had raced on past rankling annoyance but she didn't want to tell Pink those thoughts. Not yet. Even if she was only filling in for him at Wilson's, there were suddenly possibilities she hadn't expected to have. She could find out how it would be to actually live without Pink. For herself and for the girls. Make up her mind once and for all about leaving him. If she divorced him, he'd be able to pay something for the support of Connie and Margaret.

Skitchy's silence puzzled Pink. He didn't know what was wrong and he didn't know what to say.

Skitchy saw his puzzled look. "I am tickled," she said finally. "Maybe a little scared, too. A year's a long time."

"I know a year's a long time, honey. I'll talk to the girls and try to explain everything to them. Margaret's so little, it may be hard for her to understand. I think Connie will be all right about it once she understands. And they both have so many people they love and who love them around them all the time, I really think it'll be fine. I may have chances to come home sometimes. But even if I don't, I just think this is too good an opportunity to pass up."

"You bet," she said quickly. "I do, too."

Skitchy started to work at Wilson's Mercantile Store the week Pink left for Fort Davis.

....

"Well, what do you think?" Sally turned so Skitchy could see the split skirt she'd made from the back and sides as well as the front.

"I love it! Even more than the one Alma made for me. It's more close fitting. Just as graceful. I think a lot of women could wear it, no matter what size they are." Skitchy started to grin. "What would you think about calling it a sassy skirt?"

"That's perfect! It's sort of sassy for a woman to wear a skirt that's actually pants. And some people will recollect Sassy Quilters vests. That'd help us while we're getting started."

"Sally, are you sure you want to do this?"

"I am, Skitch. I've been trying to help John at the clinic and hospital. I'm not much good at it. Think he might even be glad to be rid of me," she laughed, "so he can hire a real nurse. Seriously, I love sewing and making things. That's what I'm good at. You're savvy about people and business.

We were great partners before. Why not again?" she said, with warm affection in her voice. "Mmm . . . Sassy Skirts!"

....

Skitchy was alone in Wilson's Store one afternoon three months later when Wade came in.

"Wade! What are you doing here?"

"Came in to buy some nails." He lowered his voice. "And to talk to you. Are you alone?"

"Uh-huh. But someone could come in any second." She stayed behind the counter and tried to speak as normally as she could. "You didn't need to come all the way to McAllister to buy nails. Why do you want to talk to me?"

"Well, you may have noticed that I like talking to you," he said grinning, "among other things."

Skitchy dropped her eyes, but when she was unable to suppress her smile anyway, looked at him. He was still grinning.

His voice became serious as the grin faded. "There's something in particular I want to talk to you about, Skitchy. Nettie has moved most of her things to her mother's house in Pecos. I'm staying at the ranch."

"Moved? Moved to live there all the time?"

"She says it's a trial move. But I don't think she'll come back. She hates the ranch. I've made it clear I won't move with her to Pecos. So really we're separated even if she doesn't want to call it that."

Skitchy was stunned. "I don't know what to say."

"You don't have to say anything." His face hardened. "I told Nettie that I'd only give her money to live on for the trial move for three months. After that, I'll only keep helping her if she agrees to a divorce."

"I thought she didn't believe in divorce."

"That's what she's always said. But I think in the end she'll agree to it. People will talk and that'll be hard for her. But she'll get through it somehow."

When Skitchy said nothing and Wade saw she was waiting, he went on, "Nettie said she'd think about it. That's more than she's ever said before. She said she'd pray about it. Talk to Brother Wright at the church. But whatever comes of that, I think she'll be able to see after three months that she can't afford to live by herself without my help.

"Guess that gives me a lot to think about, too."

"I surely don't intend to put you in the position of having to do anything you don't want to do. Put any pressure on you. It's very important to me not to do that. But I wanted you to know how it is with Nettie and me."

The tinkling bell on the store's door announced someone had come in to the store, startling them both. Skitchy turned toward the front door to see Martha Hoffman, the schoolteacher, moving toward them. Her voice calm in spite of the turmoil she felt inside, Skitchy said, "Good afternoon, Miss Hoffman. Be with you shortly." To Wade she said, "What size nails do you want?"

"Two inch," he said mechanically. "I'll need five pounds."

"Come with me," Skitchy said and walked to the hardware section of the store. She weighed the nails and put them in a sack.

As she handed the sack to him, he whispered, "Can you come to the ranch on Wednesday?"

"I think so. I'll do my best," she said in a whisper. In a normal voice, she asked, "Will there be anything else?"

251

"No, ma'am, that's all I need for today. Thank you."

....

When Wade left the store, Martha Hoffman smiled broadly. "*Eagle* is going to publish another one of Hutch's stories! And pay him the same as before. Will you tell him, please?"

"You bet! Law, Miss Hoffman, this is turning into something, isn't it? Just like you thought?"

"There's even more. And I think you should call me Martha. May I call you Skitchy? It seems to me conspirators ought to call each other by their first names," she said lightly. As Skitchy nodded, smiling, Martha went on, "The editor of the magazine thinks Hutch could write a whole book about his experiences growing up as a black boy and young man in this part of the country." Skitchy's eyes opened wide in surprise. "I know, it's amazing, isn't it? Our young Hutch! The editor writes he'll help Hutch submit a manuscript to a publisher he believes would be interested in Hutch's work. It would need to be typed and in the right format. Hutch will have to learn to type. But he's so bright I think he could learn in no time. I can get paper for him if there's some way he could get hold of a typewriter. Can you think of any way he could get one?"

"Not that I know of. But let me think about it. Maybe there's some way."

"If you come up with something, send Connie to school with something for me. Not a note but something she wouldn't usually bring to school. I'll understand. No one will pay it any mind if I come into the store again. I'll come anyway if I think of something. Let's plan to meet like this whenever we want to talk privately."

....

Skitchy knocked on the open door to the Tieger's living quarters. As Belle looked up from her crossword puzzle, Skitchy closed the door. "Belle, Wade came into the store today. Had something to tell me."

Jackson heard them talking and brought them a bourbon and soda to enjoy before supper. He quickly left their quarters and went to his office when he saw they weren't just chatting.

Skitchy sipped her drink and went on, her voice low. "He said he believes Nettie will agree to a divorce. He said he doesn't want that to put any pressure on me. But it surely gives me a lot to think about."

"You told me once you thought you loved Wade. Do you?"

Skitchy took a deep breath. "I do, Belle. More than I ever knew I could love anyone."

"Can't imagine you haven't thought about how it would be for Connie and Margaret if you divorce their father."

"That'll be the hardest part. I just can't see any way to make that not hard."

"And have you thought about Mama maybe being aggravated if you divorce Pink? And then maybe marry a divorced man? Not to mention a man you've been seeing for quite a while? And Law, people will talk, Skitch. Are you prepared for all that?"

"I'd hate aggravating Mama but I think she'd want me to be happy."

"It might help that it's Wade. She always thought the world of him. She'd probably have loved it if you'd married him in the first place. But still, he's not the same Wade as when he and Buddy were boys."

"And Minnie? What do you think about Minnie?"

"She may be pulled up short at first. But Minnie's for people living their own lives. Not letting other people live them for you. I think you can count on Minnie."

"Mama won't like people talking about me, will she?"

"No. But I think it'll be more important to her to see you happy. She'll take what comes. Just like you're going to have to take what comes. Can you?"

"I think so. I guess I'll find out, won't I? If that's the choice I make?" Skitchy's eyes dropped. Quietly, she said, "Thank you, Belle. I'm very lucky to have you for my sister."

....

"Sally," Skitchy said, "I think Sassy Skirts should hire someone to help with the cutting and sewing. I think we should take skirts to Wilson's in different sizes. So women can try them on. Place an order right then if they want one. If we can, I think it'd be good if we put some in O'Brien's Store in Pecos at the same time. If people see enough of them maybe they won't hold back ordering just because it's something so different from anything they've seen before. Might help sales if a customer can get one by Christmas. But we'll need help to do all that."

"Can we afford it?"

"I'll put up the money I make at Wilson's for a while. Until we have some money coming in from orders. Pink sends some money each month for the girls and me to live on at the hotel. So I'll be all right without my pay from the store."

"I wish I could put something in, too, Skitch. John's busy at the clinic but so often people can't afford to pay him. At least not much. Some months we struggle to make ends meet."

"I understand, Sally. I have another idea about something you could put in besides money." Skitchy saw Sally's face become curious. "Once we get orders we're going to need some women to do the cutting and sewing. We need to be able to fill orders before a buyer forgets she wanted a split skirt." She chuckled as she thought that sounded a lot like something her father might have said. She was tempted to think about how proud of her he would be, but shook that off to think about another time. After Sassy Skirts was as successful as she saw it in her vision of the future.

She went on explaining her idea to Sally. "At first, when we're just getting started, I think it'll be fine for someone we hire to do the work at home. But when we have enough orders it'd be best if all the work is done in one place. We'll need room to set up sewing machines and tables for cutting. We're also going to need space to store fabric and other supplies and finished skirts. I'll need a place to work. Keep track of orders and billing and all that."

"And I have an empty house that's just sitting there."

"How would you feel about having your house be Sassy Skirts' office and workshop?"

"It sounds perfect! The only thing is, no one's lived in the house for such a long time. It needs repairs and it's filthy."

"We could do the work a little at a time. By the time we need the house, we could have it ready. Ready enough anyway. What do you think?"

"You've got the know-how to make this happen, Skitch, and I think we make dadgum good partners. Just like we've been saying."

....

After Sally went home, Skitchy sat alone in her room, thinking about Sassy Skirts. Thinking about the future possibilities of the business. Thinking about how an independent businesswoman – yes, that's what she'd be – could, and, she resolved, would relate to a husband, if she had one. Thinking about how to balance all of that and the needs of her children. She felt a little wobbly thinking about what she was starting in the middle of a depression. Thinking about how there was no guarantee that Sassy Skirts would go as smoothly as she imagined. Thinking about how she'd tell Pink she wanted a divorce. Thinking about what might or might not be ahead for herself and Wade.

So, she asked herself, is this what you want? No ifs, ands, or buts? She stood up, went to the window and looked out. Looked out over Belle's garden, looked out over the chicken coop and the goat shed, looked out over what she could see of McAllister. She remembered how far she'd been able to see from the rocky point that day in the mountains. Wobble or no wobble, her voice was clear when she answered herself, softly but out loud, "You bet."

....

Everyone at the hotel gathered around the radio that hot September evening, the women fanning themselves as they listened to the news. Britain and France had declared war on

Germany after Hitler's forces invaded Poland. Last year's attempt to buy peace by giving Hitler part of Czechoslovakia hadn't worked. The President continued to reassure the country the United States wouldn't get involved in the war in Europe.

"But you know," Skitchy said, "Tom used to talk about how we're building airplanes for somebody. Got a letter from Alma yesterday saying Tom's factory is busier than ever. He's already lead man of a group working on bomber wings. Alma says he could get her a job if she wants one. She's thinking about it."

Jackson said, "If Tom could get Alma a job I imagine he could get one for Pink. Do you think Pink might want to go out to California when the work is finished on the mountain lodge? I recollect he used to talk with Tom about both of them going out there. How would you feel about that, Skitchy?"

Skitchy thought Pink probably would go to California. But go alone, when she told him she wanted a divorce. She surely didn't want to talk about that now. She wished she hadn't said anything about Alma's letter or Tom or bombers in California. "I don't know what Pink thinks about all that now. Haven't talked about it in a long time," she said, hoping there was no emotion in her voice. Hoping that would end that particular conversation.

....

Skitchy got out of bed quietly. Wade was sleeping soundly. She wanted to let him sleep even though she missed talking, lying close to him, and having a bourbon together after making love. He'd looked so worn out when she arrived at the ranch. He was working harder than ever but she thought he was worn out from more than that. He'd let another hand go. It had rained only once more since the day that had left everyone rejoicing and believing the long awful drought was finally over. Wade was not the only person in Reeves County feeling discouraged and exhausted. She knew it was becoming harder to keep believing in tomorrow.

She gathered up her clothes and put them on in the kitchen while the coffee was getting hot. She filled her cup and sat down at the kitchen table. Lying there on the table were some issues of *Eagle*, the magazine whose contest Hutch had won. She picked one up and looked through it while she sipped her coffee. She was startled when she saw the story on page twenty-one by Howard Roberts, the name Hutch and Martha Hoffman had chosen for his writing. Hutch had let her read the story as he'd written it in pencil on yellow lined paper. She hadn't yet seen it in print. Law, she thought as she started to read, isn't this something!

....

"Sorry to see you're reading that trash," Wade said grumpily as he came into the kitchen, dressed only in blue jeans, carrying his shirt.

Skitchy thought his voice carried more than just fatigue. "Why do you say trash?" she asked carefully. "*Eagle* thought this was the best story in the whole country by a young writer."

"Some colored boy thinks he can write trash about white people. If he works up enough of a lather, people will buy it. Wouldn't even read it if I were you."

"I already read it." She waited for him to say something but he didn't. He poured himself a cup of coffee, re-filled her cup, and sat down at the table. He rolled a cigarette and offered it to her but she shook her head. He lit it and took a deep drag.

Finally she said, "I'm really interested, Wade. What don't you like about this story?"

"Don't like it that coloreds learn to read and write. Then they write hogwash like that." His voice had a hard edge.

Skitchy searched for a way to say what she wanted to say that wouldn't make things head in a worse direction than they already seemed to be going. "I didn't think it was hogwash. It seemed to me a black youngster wrote about having a very tough time growing up somewhere unfriendly to black people."

"White people and coloreds have no business being friendly."

"Wade, maybe you don't know a black woman saved my life after my baby was born when a white doctor wasn't sure what to do. John MacLeod was the doctor. I know for a fact he respects that black woman very much. He'll tell you that if you ask him. The same woman may have saved my other little girl's life before there was a doctor in McAllister. Should she not have done those things because she was black and we were white? Was that too friendly?"

He scowled but said nothing. Drinking his coffee, he did not look at her.

Best to let this drop, she thought, and refilled their coffee cups. But then she thought, I can't pretend it doesn't matter to me. I can't pretend Reba and Hutch don't matter to me. She couldn't let it drop. "Have you ever known a black person you liked, or at least respected, Wade?"

"Can't say I have. Not too many of them around here. I've made it my business not to mess with them."

"I've known some sorry black people and some good black people. Just like I've known some sorry white people and some good. Maybe you don't know what it'd be like to know a good black person. If you've never known one."

"Daddy always said there was no such thing as a good colored." His voice wasn't quite as hard as it had been but still had a cold edge.

"When you used to come to our ranch, did Buddy ever talk about the old black man who lived by himself in the old bunkhouse? Did you ever talk to him?"

"I recollect seeing him around. We never talked."

"His name was Daniel. He was a slave on a farm near my grandfather's ranch in Falls County. When my grandfather came home from the army after the Civil War, there was nobody left on that farm except Daniel. He was starving. Too sick to work or go anywhere. He'd taught my grandfather and his friend to break horses and do lots of other things. Grandpa thought the world of him. He lived on Grandpa's ranch after that. When Grandpa was about to pass he asked my father to give Daniel a home as long as he lived. He came west with my folks. Daniel taught my brother how to break the toughest horses. There was no one Buddy respected more. I can't help wondering if Buddy never took you to meet him because he knew how you felt about black people. Didn't want you to be disrespectful to Daniel."

Stung, Wade dropped his eyes. When he looked up, he said, "I don't think Bud would think I'd be disrespectful to someone he introduced me to."

"Well, I wouldn't have thought you would either, before today."

Wade's eyes dropped again. He said nothing.

"I'm going home now. I think it'd be good if you read that *Eagle* story again. See if you can imagine how you'd feel and how you'd behave if you met the boy that wrote it. If you could see the world through his eyes, you might even be able to begin to see how some black people have good reason to hate white people. Or lie to protect themselves. Or whatever it is they do sometimes that you don't like."

Wade came out on to the porch and stood there, watching her as she drove away. Skitchy couldn't fight back the tears as she remembered the first time she'd seen him watching her as she drove away from his ranch. That seemed a long time gone.

....

Skitchy watched in the hot dry silence as Pink walked slow-footed down the street to the place where the bus would pick up men to take them back to Fort Davis. She could see his hands shaking. His head was down. As he moved into gathering afternoon shadows, the last thing she could see were his shoulders sagging, as they had from the moment he had turned from her. She took a deep breath and whispered, "Well, it's over."

Belle stepped out onto the porch. "Are you all right, honey?"

Skitchy only nodded, afraid she might be caught in a flash flood of tears if she spoke. Belle took her sister's hand and they walked together into the hotel lobby. No one else was there. Belle had made sure of that.

"Do you want company or would you rather be alone?"

"Alone for a little while. Not too long."

Belle came back a half hour later with a bourbon and soda for each of them. She offered Skitchy a cigarette, then put one into her holder.

Skitchy sipped the drink, its coolness welcome, took a long draw on the cigarette. "It wasn't as hard as I thought it'd be," she said, her voice low. "I think maybe he already knew."

"Want to talk about it?"

"He agreed to everything I asked. I'm grateful for that and I told him so. I'll need to send his things. He won't be coming back here."

"Do you think he'll go to California?"

"He didn't say, but I think so. He didn't ask any questions. It was enough that it was over for us." Strain came into her voice as she said, "He looked as if someone had passed away, Belle. The saddest thing was he said he'd failed again. That his life felt like a failure." A sob caught in her throat.

"Oh, honey," Belle said, moving to sit beside Skitchy on the settee, putting her arm around her sister's shoulders, wanting to comfort her. "That is sad."

"I think maybe divorce is like someone passing in a way," Skitchy went on. "A marriage has passed. Except you can't bury it and have nothing left to do but let the crying play out. In some ways maybe it's even harder." She took a deep breath. "But, Belle, I'm glad it's over. Never felt that way about someone's life."

Belle waited for a while. When Skitchy said nothing more, Belle said. "You must've thought about how you'll tell Connie. Margaret will be easier, she's so little. She seems to have already gotten used to him not being around."

"Connie's reading in our room. I'm going to go up now. Talk to her."

Belle squeezed her sister's hand once more and watched sadly as Skitchy slowly climbed the oak stairs.

....

That night Connie came to Skitchy's bed. "Can I please sleep with you, Mama?"

"You bet, sugar," and Skitchy held the covers so her daughter could climb in beside her. Skitchy drew her close and stroked her hair, as she had when Connie was little.

"I missed Daddy when he went to the mountains. I miss him different now. I feel sad."

"Of course you miss him, sugar, and feel sad. And I know for sure he misses you, too. He loves you very much. And so do I."

Connie snuggled closer to her mother.

Skitchy lay awake a long time after Connie's breathing told her the girl was sleeping soundly. She could hear the regular sound of Margaret's breathing as she slept across the room. She took slow deep breaths herself, hoping with all her heart that her daughters wouldn't have to pay too high a price for her happiness.

....

Skitchy was reading a magazine in bed a few nights later when she heard a light knock on the door. It was Rita Colquitt, her eyes bright and excited.

"Skitchy," Rita whispered, "come out in the hall for a minute."

"It's all right, Rita. Connie and Margaret are staying with Belle and Jackson tonight. What is it? You look so excited."

"There are three hotel guests registering downstairs!" Rita announced. "A couple and another man. I passed them on my way upstairs. We haven't had overnight guests for a while. Now here we have them two nights in a row! Isn't that good? I'm so glad for Jackson. I told Sister about it. And Josiah. Thought you'd want to know, too."

"I do, Rita. I'm glad, too, and I'm sure Jackson must be."

Jackson was glad. Years later, looking back, he'd say he could see the great depression began to come to its slow end in 1939. There were other signs scattered here and there, but after ten years of the hardest hard times anyone could remember, people in McAllister had given up thinking about those times ever coming to an end.

....

"Mr. Wilson," Skitchy said as she was getting ready to leave the store for the day, "I saw an old typewriter in the back storeroom the other day. I'm looking for one, if it wouldn't cost too much. Is it something I could trade some of my hours for?"

"You can have it, Skitchy. I took it in trade thinking I'd learn how to use it. That was ages ago. Never even touched it. Don't think I'm going to after all this time. No one's ever come in the store asking for one. Yes, yes, just go on and take it. What do you want it for?"

She gulped. She hadn't expected to just find a typewriter sitting around. She hadn't expected someone would just give it to her. Nor had she thought about what she'd say if someone wanted to know what she wanted it for. "Oh," she stammered, "I thought I might be able to use it for Sassy Skirts," hoping he wouldn't ask anything more.

"I'm glad to make a contribution to what you and Mrs. MacLeod are doing. Good luck with your venture."

"Thank you so much, Mr. Wilson. For the good wishes. And for the typewriter."

....

Skitchy put a little sack of raisins in Connie's lunch as she left for school the next day. "Please give the raisins to Miss Hoffman, sugar."

"Miss Hoffman doesn't like raisins," Connie said. "I heard her say that."

Oh, Connie, who sees and hears everything and never forgets anything, Skitchy thought. "She might like these, sugar. And if she doesn't she doesn't have to eat them," Skitchy said somewhat lamely. "Just give them to her, please."

"Yes, ma'am," Connie said with a sigh, and went off to school.

....

Martha Hoffman came into the store the next afternoon and milled around looking at things idly while she waited for customers to leave. As soon as she and Skitchy were alone, Martha burst out laughing. "You should've seen Connie. She was so worried I wasn't going to like the raisins, I felt I had to eat a few, and I hate raisins!" Quickly growing serious, she said, "Tell me what's happened."

Skitchy eagerly told Martha about the typewriter. "Now it's up to Hutch."

"This is a marvelous opportunity for him," Martha replied. "But I'm also a little worried that it could make it harder to protect him from unwanted attention."

"I've been worried about that, too, and pondering about it. At first I thought I'd keep the typewriter at Sally MacLeod's old house where I work and Hutch could come there to write. But somebody would pick up on that sooner or later. And he'd be missed at the hotel. He still does a lot of work there. He writes in his room after supper. I think maybe it'd be best for him to write at the hotel like he always has. But my sister and brother-in-law would have to know what he's doing and give him more time to write."

"Will they?"

"I think so. I could talk to them but I think it'd be best if Hutch talks to my brother-in-law himself. Jackson would like it if Hutch takes responsibility for himself as a man. For what he wants in the world, even if he's black and young. Jackson has never held with laws like the one in Alabama that says a black person can't play checkers or dominoes with a white person. Hutch plays them with Connie a lot. Belle and Jackson know that. And I like to sit at the kitchen table and have a cup of coffee with Hutch's mother. Jackson tried to keep Reba and Hutch separate from the rest of us when they came to live at the hotel. But in the end it didn't make any sense. I think Belle and Jackson will say what he wants to do is all right."

....

Two days later, Hutch came out of Jackson's office, beaming. He strode into the kitchen where Reba and Skitchy were waiting anxiously. "They said yes," he said calmly.

Reba became teary, went to her son and hugged him. "There's more, Mama. And I want Mrs. Campbell to hear it, too."

Reba poured coffee for all of them and they sat down together at the table.

"I showed Mr. and Mrs. Tieger the stories in *Eagle*, like we talked about," he began. "I told them I am Howard Roberts. Why I use a different name. Now this is the part that's different from what we talked about. The part I decided on myself. I told them I've earned money for my stories. I expect to earn more. I can pay rent and something for food for Mama and me. I'd like Mama to be paid for her work. I want to spend my time writing. I told them I have a typewriter," he grinned at Skitchy. "I can pay for paper. Miss Hoffman will buy it for me. I told them I plan to go to New York," he glanced at Reba but then quickly looked away from her stunned expression, "when I finish writing my book. For now I'd like to stay here. Not make any fuss about what I'm doing. Except the people who live here would know I'm doing something different than I was before."

Skitchy, as stunned as Reba but less tongue-tied, said, "And Mr. and Mrs. Tieger said yes to all of that?"

"They want me to be careful. Not make any noise typing when people we don't know are in the hotel. But yes, ma'am. They said yes."

"Hutch, that's wonderful. I'm so glad. And I'm so proud of you!" Skitchy beamed.

"Thank you," Hutch said warmly. "Mama, I hope you aren't upset about the New York part. I don't want to stay here in Jim Crow country where I can't risk having my book published under my own name. I'm going to write it as a novel. If it's fiction what I have to say may not upset so many people. But I want everybody to know my work is written by Hutchens Borden."

Reba's face became calm and she looked at him with those dark deep eyes that Skitchy sometimes thought could see into someone's soul. "Hutchens Borden." She seemed to taste his name on her lips, savoring something delicious. "Write your book, Hutchens Borden. Go to New York. Go where you can be what you want to be. Be how you want to be. Be who you are. And nobody to tell you any different."

....

"Four people want sassy skirts already!" an excited Skitchy called out as she hurried into the front room of Sally's old house where her partner was unpacking fabric.

"Sure enough? That's wonderful!"

"My friend Emily wants one for herself and one for her daughter. And Brin called from Pecos yesterday. I'm so glad we had the telephone put in right away even though I never dreamed we'd be getting calls so soon. Anyway, Brin tried on one of the samples I took to her store. She wants one even though she doesn't know how much we'll charge yet. One of her friends wants one, too. "We're off, Sally!" and she caught her friend's hands and both of them spun around.

....

Skitchy was alone in the house the next morning, trying to finish her work on Sassy Skirts' costs. Figure out a price for skirts. She was slow at this kind of work and found it taxing, so she liked to work when she was alone and everything was quiet. Deep in concentration, she was caught entirely by surprise when she heard Wade's voice at the open doorway. Her heart leapt in spite of her instructions about how to be when she saw him again.

"Skitchy, can I talk to you?" His voice was warm and familiar but she could hear nervousness underneath.

"Wade!" It had been more than a week since they parted on uncertain terms. She felt suddenly nervous herself. "Come in. Would you like some coffee?"

"I would, but mostly I want to talk to you. Do you have time?"

She saw no possibility of returning to the work she'd been doing. She'd pushed thoughts of him aside with increasing difficulty as the days had gone by. Gathering up papers spread out on the table that served as her desk, she said, "I'll get the coffee. Pull one of those boxes over here so you have some place to sit."

He looked around as he sat waiting. The house had once been one of the nicest in McAllister, large and well built. It still had traces of architectural adornment but most prominent now were peeling walls and cracked trim around the doors and windows. Some repair work was underway here and there but Wade thought they had a very long way to go. Skitchy was using an old table as a desk. Wooden boxes served several purposes.

Skitchy came back with the coffee, annoyed that her hands were trembling and coffee was spilling into the saucers. "Sorry," she said, handing him a cup. She sat down as matter-of-factly as she could.

"I'd be worried if you weren't jittery, too." He drained the coffee from the saucer into the cup, took a sip. Searching her face for some clue about what she might be thinking or feeling but seeing nothing, he decided the best thing was to just say what he wanted to say. "I've been thinking a lot about everything that happened when you were at the ranch the last time. And what you said. Been hard for me to figure how you could see things so differently from the way I grew up believing. I never thought colored people were like me in any way. That's what I was taught."

"I understand that," Skitchy said softly. She'd surprised herself by how strongly she'd reacted to Wade's feelings about black people. She supposed she must have been taught something about black people and Mexicans, the only people she knew who were considered different from herself in West Texas, but she couldn't remember anything in particular. She'd just always liked some and didn't like others. Like everybody she met. She knew something about the way Wade had spoken about black people seemed not right to her, even if she didn't know why. But not right enough to walk out of his house as she had that day? That was what had surprised her. Now she wanted very much to hear what he had to say. "We grew up with different ideas, Wade."

"It's worse than you know, though. And I want you to know everything." He could feel his throat tightening as he spoke. Trust her, he told himself.

"I do want to know everything, Wade. I always have. Please go on," she said, wanting to encourage him.

Throat still tight, voice strained, he began. "The Ku Klux Klan was very active around Georgetown when I was a student at Southwestern." His felt his face contorting and couldn't do anything about it. "I rode with them once, Skitchy. We burned a cross at a black school and another one at a shack where a colored family lived." He shuddered and grew quiet. When he looked at her and saw she was listening, no condemnation in her face, he went on.

"It made me feel sick to my stomach. I wanted no more part of it. I don't mean to excuse myself, but it's easy to get hot yourself when a fire's raging all around. Please try to understand. I know you hated hearing me talk the way I did."

"I'm afraid I have trouble understanding, Wade. You said you rode with them. You decided to do that in the first place."

"You're right. I did. I already thought that way. It seemed exciting. I thought my father would be proud of me. He'd been in the Klan before he came to West Texas. He was only sorry it wasn't organized around here. He was on the committee though, as they called it. The committee did things they thought were necessary to keep coloreds and Mexicans in their place. Everything was supposed to be secret. But he bragged to me about it." He felt relieved to have all of that out. He still felt the jitters about what her response would be.

Skitchy's stomach knotted when she thought about Wade's father maybe having something to do with the burning of the café down the street from Josiah Tieger's hotel. She knew Taylor Martin had passed away before Hutch's school was burned. But even if he hadn't actually done either of those things, she felt he was so bound up with those who did, it didn't make any difference to her. She struggled to keep hold of the reins of her feelings so she could speak. "What do you think about the things your father did? That he bragged about?"

"I'm going to risk telling you the real truth. The whole truth, Skitchy, because I love you and I want only honesty between us." His throat relaxed a little, speaking of the way he felt about her. "I see a colored man and as natural as it feels to take a breath, I don't like him. I want to keep him in his place and stay in mine. I don't think about it. It just happens. Kind of like a mule that kicks and bites even when no one's doing anything to him."

He paused to take a deep breath and see if she would say anything. When she didn't, he went on. "But I can think about things. Not just kick and bite like a stupid mule that doesn't know any better. I don't want to be the kind of person who treats another person some way before I even know anything about that person. I don't want to be treated that way. Can't imagine anybody does. My father was wrong. What I learned from him was wrong. What I did burning those crosses was wrong."

He dropped his head and grew quiet again. She waited. When he lifted his head his eyes met hers before he looked away again.

"I was never as good as Bud at breaking horses. But I can break most horses. I've even broken a stubborn mule or two. I believe I can break the stupid stubborn mule in me. I surely intend to try."

She wanted to put her arms around him and have all the ugliness go away. But he was talking about a change so wide and deep she still felt wary. "Wade, I don't doubt you mean everything you're saying. I'm actually very touched. But I'm afraid if you try to make a big change like this for me, because you think I want you to, it won't work."

His voice grew somber. "It's true. I'm afraid of losing your respect. It'd just about kill me to lose you, Skitchy, because of being a mule instead of a man who thinks for himself. Makes his own choices. But it's more than that. I want to do it for myself, too. I need to do it for myself. Maybe I can even make up somehow for the hurt and fear I'm sure I caused those people when I helped burn those crosses. For the hurt and fear I've caused people when I didn't even know that's what I was doing."

She noticed he said "people" and not "coloreds." It didn't sound to her like he'd thought about how to say that ahead of time. She allowed herself to think maybe he could change himself. It mattered to her that he wanted to. The wary feeling began to lessen and she felt her heart warming.

"How would you feel about getting to know Reba and her boy, Hutch? I don't mean just be around them like you were at Sally and John's wedding. Really talk with them. Find out what they're like. Sounds to me like you have feelings about black people like they were all the same but don't really know any particular black person. What a real person with a name and a life and feelings and who has a mind, too, is actually like. Take Hutch for instance. He's very good at taking care of Belle's garden. He plays checkers with my daughter. He's teaching her dominoes because playing those games is so much fun for her. He's very smart and reads anything he can get his hands on. He's blind in one eye because he was beaten badly when he was little. Tried to go to the white school after the black school was burned down."

"That shouldn't happen to any child," he said, his voice solemn.

"We surely agree about that."

"Sounds like I might even like him."

"Well, you never know. You might."

"I think I should go now. I want you to know that I don't expect anything, Skitchy, because of what I've said. I want you to see for yourself how things unfold." He stood there awkwardly, wanting desperately to kiss her, but not wanting to take anything for granted when he had just said he wouldn't. He turned and walked quickly toward the door.

....

Skitchy wished she'd gone into his arms and kissed him, as she'd wanted to. She'd felt his awkwardness and hadn't made it any easier for him as she just stood there. Annoyed with herself, she felt completely unable to go back to her work on costs and pricing. Feeling like she wanted to pound on something, she went to a back room where they were building a large cupboard out of scrap pieces of wooden crates. She was wrestling a large slab of wood into place when she heard footsteps. "Sally?" she called out. "I'm back here."

"It's not Sally. It's me. I needed to come back."

She was startled hearing Wade's voice again when she had expected Sally. The wood slab slipped from her grasp. A rough edge ripped her hand and left a large splinter embedded in her thumb. Both hurt badly and her hand was bleeding profusely when he came into the room.

"Sorry I startled you. Skitchy! You're hurt!" He hurried to where she stood, looking around for something to use to stop the bleeding.

When she heard the warmth and concern in his voice a tear moved down her cheek. She sat down abruptly on the floor. He took her hand to look at the wound and the ragged protruding splinter. She watched mutely as he took off his shirt and tore a piece from it.

"Hold this tight against the bleeding," he told her while he tore strips from the shirt to wrap her hand. It hurt him to see her hurt. You should've waited, he told himself. But he pushed that thought aside, focusing on attending to her.

"Skitchy," he said gently, "the splinter is a big one and in deep. I think John should remove it. He can give you something so there'll be less pain. Your hand should be cleaned up. I think it'll need stitches, too. I want to take you to the clinic. We may have to explain some things but I'll try to think of something. Is that all right with you?" She nodded and he lifted her from the floor, held her closely as he walked her to his truck.

....

Skitchy woke early in the afternoon. Her hand hurt and she grunted softly. Wade's face appeared above her. She noticed he was wearing one of John's shirts.

"Skitchy." He wanted his voice to be gentle for her and comforting. "John's taken care of your hand. Everything's going to be fine."

"I'm thirsty," she said. "Can I have some water?"

"You bet," and he held the glass for her. "Sally has some soup for you when you feel like it."

She started to try to sit up as she suddenly realized people might be worried about her. She hadn't come home for the noon meal and there would've been no answer if anyone called the house to check on her. "I need to get home."

"No you don't. Sally already called the hotel. She told them what happened and where you are. You don't need to do anything except just rest."

She let herself relax and lay back. Then she noticed he was not relaxed. "Is anything the matter, Wade?"

"Sally and John know about us, Skitchy." He saw a shadow cross her face. "I guess I couldn't hide very well how worried I was about you. And then of course, what was I doing at the house was a logical question. I didn't have a very logical explanation. Sally put everything together with other times she'd noticed something between us when we were together."

"It wasn't terribly difficult." Sally's voice from the doorway was warm and smiling. "How about some soup?

Reba brought it for you." She came to Skitchy's bed with the soup and bent to touch Skitchy's cheek affectionately. "Dear friend, you've nothing to worry about from me. Or John. We know what it's like to go a different way from most people. In particular when they think they know better than you how you should live your life. We're tickled to death for both of you." She smiled at them and closed the door as she left.

As Skitchy ate the soup hungrily, Wade said, "I talked to Reba for a bit when she brought the soup."

"And . . . ?"

"And it was all right. I thanked her for the soup. She wanted to know how you hurt your hand so I told her about that. Well, not everything . . ."

Skitchy chuckled softly. "Sorry. It just struck me funny. Imagining you telling Reba, but not everything." He dropped his eyes, but she saw he was laughing with her, almost in spite of himself.

"It wasn't as hard as I thought it'd be. I kept reminding myself she saved your life."

"It'll get easier, too. You'll see." That's enough for now, she thought, and changed the subject.

"I recollect you said you needed to come back to the house, Wade. What for?"

"I wanted to tell you Nettie's agreed to a divorce. She's going to stay in Pecos. Live in her mother's house. I was afraid it might seem like I was pushing you, telling you that. But after I left, it just didn't feel right not to tell you. That's why I came back. Or maybe I came back because I wanted so much to tell you." He dropped his eyes, raised them again. Looked at her with a look that brought her heart up into her throat. "I had to come back. I wanted you to know I'm going to be free."

She heard the catch in his voice and took a deep breath herself. "I'm glad you did, Wade. I've got something to tell you, too." She took another deep breath. "I told Pink I want a divorce. He's agreed to it. He won't be coming back to McAllister when the work on the lodge at Fort Davis is done." Her voice grew soft even though it was clear and firm. "I'm going to be free, too."

Neither of them spoke as they sat looking at each other.

1940

Will Conger, the red-faced sheriff, swaggering and carrying his paunch as if it were part of his badge, took off his hat and settled in the chair in front of Jackson's desk. Jabe Alexander, a dry thin rancher Jackson had known for years, took a chair against the wall. "Well, Jackson," the sheriff began, "we want to talk to you about this colored boy you have living here. Him and his mother."

Jackson had been tense and his mind racing ever since the two men came to the hotel unannounced, but he made a great effort to appear calm and stay calm. "You bet, Will. What about them?" He tried to make his voice open and friendly, to seem forthcoming even though intending to say as little as possible as vaguely as possible.

"How long they been living here?"

"Reba Borden's been my cook for many years. In the beginning she rented a house near town. Then with the stock market crash and the depression, I couldn't afford to pay her any more. She couldn't find other work and couldn't pay her rent. Like a lot of people in town who traded for things, I traded a room off the kitchen for her work. And her boy's."

Jabe Alexander had been sitting back, listening. His posture didn't change as he spoke with a slow twang, but he seemed eager to get into the conversation. "We hear they have the run of the place, Jackson."

"Well, I don't know what you've heard, Jabe, but I'd hardly put it that way. Reba does other things, too, besides cooking. When I had to let my Mexican girl go, Reba helped to take up the slack. You came in through the lobby. You saw that has to be kept picked up, cleaned. And the dining room. All the guest rooms are on the second floor. There's work to be done all over the hotel."

"And the boy? What does he do all over the hotel?"

Jackson wanted to be careful to say nothing about Hutch that wasn't true, even while avoiding the point of their questions. "Hutch's done a lot of different things around the place since he was a little boy. Tending my wife's garden. Gathering up dirty laundry. Taking clean laundry around. Emptying trash. Bringing things to people when they need something. Things like that."

"What does he do now? We hear he spends most of the time in his room. What does he do all day?"

"He's been paying rent the last few months. I've never asked people who pay rent what they do in their rooms."

"Where does he get money to pay rent?"

"I've also never asked people where they get money to pay me, Jabe."

"Colored folks shouldn't be renting a room in a hotel for white folks."

"Well, I'm sure I don't need to tell you times have been tough. I need all the rent money I can bring in to keep the place going. But I don't know what else I could do anyway. I don't know of any colored hotel in McAllister. And Reba Borden is a dadgum good cook. I need her."

"Mmm," the sheriff murmured, his tone relaxing. "We all know times have been tough."

But Jackson saw Jabe Alexander scowling and knew he wasn't going to be satisfied as easily as the sheriff. Chances are Jabe's really behind this, Jackson thought. He debated about asking what it was they'd heard but decided against it. "Well, if there's nothing else I can do for you, Will, Jabe, I'm pretty busy this morning."

"Best you be careful, Jackson," Jabe Alexander said. "Mark my words, these colored folks can be trouble."

"Oh, the last thing I want is any trouble," Jackson said carefully. He watched the two men swagger across the lobby, the taste in his mouth sour. Never wrestle with a pig, he remembered his grandfather saying. You both get muddy and the pig just likes it.

....

It rained that afternoon, a soft steady rain. Everyone in McAllister was glad. But no one ran out into the streets or did any of the other things that had hang dogged them when it had rained the last time and then relapsed into drought.

"I hope it keeps up but let's see what happens," Jackson said as he and Belle stood on the hotel porch with Connie and Margaret, watching the rain. "But I'm surely glad it's raining."

At his ranch, Wade was quietly grateful for the rain. Grass could replenish one more time. He'd figure one more time how many cattle he might be able to fatten and sell. There might be calves to brand one more time. He'd ride the fences one more time to make sure posts were secure and work with Marvin to make repairs. He'd check the cisterns for leaks one more time. He'd feel like a rancher one more time.

....

Belle asked Reba and Hutch to come in from the kitchen after supper. She announced to everyone gathered in the dining room, "My mother's going to come to live here for a while." The warmth of Belle's broad smile told everyone she was as pleased as Skitchy, who sat grinning at the end of the table, and Connie, who yelped with delight.

When Kate Chapman arrived, her things were taken up to a room across the hall from Rita Colquitt. She settled in and soon she was telling stories to Margaret at bedtime, tickling her back as she "drew" the stories she told. Brushing Connie's hair and braiding it almost every morning. Listening to Rita's soap opera stories with her. Visiting with her daughters and Jackson. Walking to church whenever there were services. In what seemed like no time it was as if she'd always been there.

Skitchy had been shocked when she saw how much older her mother looked. Kate's hair was now white smudged with yellow. Years of sun and wind had dried her face into deep furrows and jowls sagged even her lean cheeks. Her shoulders were rounded, her hands gnarled with rheumatism. Kate Chapman didn't like complaining from anyone, so when she spoke of the sadness of fading eyesight, which now made it impossible for her to sew or read for herself the letters she received and relished, Skitchy and Belle both knew it was a deep sorrow for her.

"Belle, are you surprised how much older Mama looks?"

"Oh, I think we all look older, honey."

And as Belle spoke, Skitchy noticed that her sister's hair was much more gray than brown and that she wore her glasses all the time now. Jackson's hair was almost gone.

When Skitchy looked in the mirror later that afternoon, she saw that at thirty-four there were fine and a few not so fine wrinkles around her eyes and mouth. And there was something more, something she couldn't quite put her finger on. She was used to thinking of herself as still a girl in so many ways. But it wasn't a girl who looked back at her.

....

When everyone gathered around the radio to listen to the news after a supper of scrambled eggs and bologna, beans, and cornbread, there were murmurs of surprise and some nervous comments when registration for the first peacetime military draft in the country's history was announced. The President still reassured the people the United States was not going to get into the growing war in Europe.

"Doesn't make much sense, if you ask me," Kate said quietly but firmly, "to say you need an army but you're not going to use it."

Skitchy said, "John MacLeod's been talking about trouble coming with Japan for ages. He's much more worried about that than what's happening in Europe. But I don't hear anybody else talking much about Japan. Maybe the President wants us to be ready just in case something happens, in Europe or Japan."

"I hope you're right," Belle sighed.

Skitchy heard a dark note in Belle's voice and remembering her sister's first love, killed in the Great War in Europe, a chill came over her. Jackson heard it, too, and wanted nothing more than to change the subject. "Well, if men get drafted, it'll mean lots of new jobs. And not just jobs for the troops. There's all the support the military needs, too. It could be a big help to get the country out of this dadgum depression!"

Later, as Skitchy and Kate climbed the stairs together, Kate asked, "Is Belle all right? Seemed like she was ruffled when we were listening to the news."

"I just think she hates the idea of another big war," Skitchy said, not wanting to worry Mama that Belle might still pine for Sam Mueller.

"Well, I do, too. And what about you, honey? Are you all right? I heard you coughing before and again just now when we came up the stairs."

"Oh, I don't think it's anything, Mama. I feel fine. I was just thinking the other day about how I'm not a girl anymore."

....

On a hot dry morning, the sky hazy with dust, Skitchy packed the Model-A she'd borrowed from John MacLeod with things she and the girls might need. They all waved to Kate and Belle standing on the hotel porch, then Skitchy turned her attention to the road ahead.

When Pink had written, asking her to bring the girls to San Saba Springs to say good-bye before he left for California, she'd been glad to say she would. But now she felt awkward about seeing him. It's for the girls, she reminded herself. Who knows when they'll see their father again?

....

Pink paced nervously in front of the post office in San Saba Springs where the Fort Davis bus had dropped him off for the day, impatiently kicking small stones with the toe of his work boot. He looked up when he heard a car coming, dropped his head once again when he saw it wasn't their old Model-T but a Model-A. He was surprised when he heard Connie's familiar voice, "Daddy! Daddy!" and the car pulled to a stop near him.

"Pink," Skitchy said as she got out of the car, nodded toward him. He's thinner, she thought. His hair is surely thinner. Getting pretty gray, too. He looks a lot older.

"Skitchy," he said, reaching for her outstretched hand. Connie hugged him. Four-year-old Margaret got out more slowly, hanging back, unsure. Pink scooped her up and kissed her on the cheek. "How's my girl?" but she responded by whimpering to get down. "It's all right, honey. You just take your time."

Skitchy saw a tear in his eye and felt a sadness she hadn't expected well up within her. Looking down the years she could see they weren't likely to be easy for father or daughters. She chose not to keep looking and shook off the sadness. "I'll pick them up at two o'clock, Pink."

Pink replied, "If you don't mind waiting a little bit, I'd like to give Margaret a chance to get more comfortable with me while you're still here. Is that all right with you?"

"All right," she said reluctantly, reminding herself again that this visit was for the girls as much as for Pink.

"Why don't all of us go get something cold to drink?" To Connie he said, "Would you like that?"

"Yes, sir."

They had lemonade in the hotel dining room. Skitchy pushed her feeling of awkwardness aside, suggesting to Connie, "I'm sure Daddy would love to hear about school. Maybe you could tell him about your dominoes games, too."

Soon the twelve-year-old girl and her father were talking easily and Margaret was beginning to relax and perk up.

"Girls, you and Daddy have a good time," Skitchy said, eager to excuse herself. "I'll see you this afternoon. So long, Pink."

She was aware that Pink was looking after her as she left the dining room but she kept looking straight ahead and walking straight ahead. It's harder being with Pink than I expected it to be, she thought. But you can do this for the girls, she told herself. You can do this.

....

It was cool at this elevation and the air was pleasant. Skitchy thought she might look around town for a while, then spend the rest of the time at the park on the edge of town. She planned to get something cold to drink to go with the biscuit and peanut butter and jam sandwiches she'd brought for lunch. She had a new issue of *Eagle* with another of Hutch's stories to read.

She parked the Model-A at the park, intending to walk back the three blocks to town. As she was pulling on a light jacket, she saw an animal grazing at the far edge of the small park. Even though her mind was on going into town, something made her look more closely.

It was a female Bighorn!

Skitchy stood perfectly still. Looking. Looking. Hardly able to believe what she was seeing. Finally the sheep sprang away. She walked closer to the place where the animal had been, her eyes following it up the side of the mountain. Suddenly she saw a Bighorn ram standing on a rocky ledge. The great horned creature was even more beautiful and more majestic than she'd imagined! She'd always thought she would whoop with joy if she saw a Bighorn, ewe or ram. Instead she stood calmly, filled with deep joy. Reverent joy.

She kept standing there, looking, long after both sheep had bounded up the mountain out of sight. They're doing just what they're meant to do, she thought. Just where they're meant to do it. I could learn something from that.

....

Connie and Margaret both fell asleep on the drive back to McAllister. Skitchy delighted in this time she had to herself, time to savor the images of the Bighorns forever stored now in her memory. She only reluctantly put away the wonder of them as she parked the car in front of the hotel.

She took Margaret out of the car gently, carried her upstairs, a sleepy Connie trailing behind. As she came downstairs, Jackson was waiting for her.

"I heard you coughing, Skitchy. That cough didn't sound good. I would've taken Margaret upstairs for you."

"Thanks, Jackson. I didn't think about it ahead of time. I'm all right, though. Please don't worry."

"All right. Whatever you say. I need to talk to you about something when you get home from taking the car back to

Sally and John. Be obliged if you'd come to my office when you get back."

She could hear some urgency in his voice. "I'll come as soon as I get back."

When she came into his office it was almost dark but Jackson hadn't turned on the light. Even in the dim light she could see he was frowning, sitting at his desk. "Come in, Skitch," he said, reaching for the lamp switch.

"What's on your mind, Jackson?" she asked as she sat down.

"Jabe Alexander's nephew came to the back door this afternoon. Said he wanted to talk to Reba. Hutch came and got me. When I went back there, the nephew -- he's named Jabe, too -- said he was doing some work for the sheriff. Said he wanted to find out the last time any hobos came around. I don't believe that story for a minute. I think they sent him to check on Reba and Hutch. Maybe see something. Scare them while they were at it."

"You sound worried."

"I am worried. I told him, and I told him to tell them, I won't have anyone on my property bothered. They talk to me if they want to talk about anything. I don't know if that'll take care of it. I surely hope so. I thought you should know."

....

"Here's your lunch, Mrs. Skitchy, Mr. Wade," Reba said as she put down the sack on the kitchen counter in Sassy Skirts' house. "I made some bologna sandwiches the way you like them and some ice tea."

"Thank you, Reba," Wade said. "You're the only person I know who can make a bologna sandwich taste really good."

"Thank you, Mr. Wade. I like making them in particular because you like them so much."

A little awkwardly, he said, "Will you have some ice tea with us?"

Skitchy, seeing that Reba wasn't yet quite that comfortable with Wade, said warmly, "Sit down for a minute, Reba. Take a rest. Have some tea if you'd like to." She coughed a little and saw Wade glance at her. She was glad he said nothing. It aggravated her that people seemed to be making so much of her cough.

"Well," Reba said, "I'll sit for a minute. Then I need to be getting back." She looked surprised when Wade brought a box for her to sit on. "Thank you, sir," she said, a little flustered but not too flustered to sit down.

....

When Reba had gone and Skitchy and Wade had finished their lunch, Wade stood and stretched. "Well, sugar, I'll need to be getting back pretty soon. Anything else I can do for you around here before I go?" He and John had spent most of the morning doing some of the heavier work that Skitchy and Sally had asked for help with. When John got a call from the clinic Wade had stayed to finish up. He figured Marvin, his best hand, could manage things at the ranch.

Skitchy looked up at him, almost shyly. She's incredibly appealing when she looks like that, he thought. Maybe I'll go ahead and ask her today, and he thought about staying a while longer.

"I want to tell you something, sugar," Skitchy began. "I don't know why I feel so shy about telling it." She paused, took a deep breath. "I saw Bighorns at San Saba Springs when I took the girls to say good-bye to Pink."

"Skitch, that's wonderful! I'm so glad for you. Was it like you thought it'd be?"

"Better," she said quietly. "The ewe was grazing near the park. When she went up into the mountains I saw a ram standing all by himself on a ledge. He was marvelous! They both jumped from place to place. Even where it was steep, just like I'd heard. Both of them were marvelous!"

"I think you're like a Bighorn, Skitchy. Able to jump sure-footed from place to place. Even where the going is steep. Marvelous."

"That's about the most wonderful thing anyone's ever said about me."

"Well then, I'm glad I'm the one that said it," he grinned. He paused and his face grew serious. "I have something else to say I hope you'll think is wonderful."

She thought she knew what he was going to say. She could feel her heart beating faster.

"I love you so, sugar. I want us to get married more than anything in the world. Will you? Marry me?"

Smiling broadly, she nodded with a slow deep nod that said more than words.

He gathered her in his arms. Joy rose up from deep within him as she returned his passionate kiss. "And is it all right with you for everybody to know about us? The girls in particular?"

She nodded again. "But I want to give the girls time to get used to the idea of you and me."

"You bet. Your girls are very important to me, too, Skitchy. I want you to tell me however you want it to be with them."

....

"Mama," Skitchy said to her mother in a quiet, serious voice, "I want to talk to you about something very important."

"You sound so serious, honey. What is it?"

"I've fallen in love with someone. I didn't ask Pink for a divorce because of this other man. It might look like that, though, to people who don't know the whole story. I imagine some of them will talk whether they know the whole story or not. I want you to know the whole story." Skitchy was grateful when she saw that her mother was listening with a look of curiosity on her face. "You know him, Mama. I'm in love with Wade Martin."

Kate's eyes flew open in surprise. "Wade?"

"He's shown me a way to be alive I'd only dreamed of. We're going to get married, Mama."

"Well, I can see why you might think people will talk."

"I can't help that, Mama. I just have to not pay it any mind. But I mind very much how it is for you."

"Skitchy, I've never wanted anything but what's good for you. What makes you happy. Is this good for you? Are you happy?"

"It is good for me, Mama. And I'm so happy!"

"And the girls? Is this good for the girls?"

"They're just getting to know him. You've known him a long time. What do you think about Wade and the girls?"

"Wade was a fine boy and I can't imagine he's anything but a fine man. Just give the girls a little time. I think it'll be fine."

"Wade and I've talked about doing just that. Oh, Mama, thank you. Thank you for understanding. I love you so much."

"Well, of all Buddy's friends, I was always partial to Wade. Law, I probably shouldn't say this. I'd have loved it if you'd married him in the first place."

Skitchy laughed and said to the puzzled Kate, "That's just what Belle said, that you'd have loved that!" Then Skitchy grew serious. "I'm so sorry, Mama, about everything with Pink. I was so crazy over him. I thought he'd make me happy. I surely did. You and Daddy were wonderful to us and I think we both disappointed you. I wish Daddy could know how sorry I am about the whole thing. I surely want you to know."

"That's all a long time gone, honey. Best you walk today's road as best you can. I hope you and Wade will be very happy."

....

"Mr. Wilson fired me today," Skitchy said as she marched into the lobby where Belle was behind the counter, smoking a cigarette and tapping her pencil on the crossword puzzle in front of her.

"What?"

Skitchy could hear the shock and dismay in her sister's voice and knew she didn't need to say it again. She plunked her purse down on a chair. Plunked herself down on another chair.

Jackson's office door was open and hearing them, he came out to the lobby, his concern apparent in his frown. "What the devil happened, Skitch?"

"He said people had complained to him that I'm not a good Christian woman, divorcing my husband and planning to marry a divorced man. He said they didn't like being waited on by someone like me. I think he's talking about Widow Quenk." She saw their surprise and added, "Oh, you bet. She and Mr. Wilson have been an item for quite a while. It was Widow Quenk who first started giving me nasty looks at church. My friend Emily told me she even complained that I was allowed in the church at all. Now that everybody knows about Wade and me, it's gotten even worse."

"That silly old busy-body," Belle said with disgust as she ground out her cigarette in the ashtray and popped the holder into her pocket. "All the silly old busy-bodies should mind their own business."

"Well, there's more. Mr. Wilson said he hadn't been willing to let me go just because of the divorce, even though he didn't think divorce was right. But then he heard Rita telling her sister yesterday about Hutch's story in the new issue of *Eagle* when she saw it on the magazine stand. Mr. Wilson asked her what she was talking about. I know Rita would never tell about Hutch on purpose. I'm guessing whatever she said made things worse, though, because Mr. Wilson asked me point blank about the typewriter. He said he gave it to me for Sassy Skirts, not for some colored boy up to no good. It was downright nasty the way he said that. Then he said I was fired. Just like that."

"Skitchy, I'm so sorry," Belle said.

"I surely need the money. Going to be hard not having it. And now I won't be able to sell skirts in Wilson's either." She looked at Jackson. "But I'm even more worried about Mr. Wilson's maybe being one of the people in town determined to keep black people in their place. What if he makes trouble about Hutch?"

"I think we just have to hold our cards," Jackson said evenly. "See how the hand plays out."

....

"You need to play inside, sugar," Skitchy told Margaret. "I'm sorry, but there's too much dust for you to play outside today." She watched as the little girl pursed her lips and sat down dejectedly, looking out the lobby window.

"Too much dust, Molly," Margaret told her doll, scowling. "We don't like dust, do we?"

"I don't like it either, sugar," Skitchy said, coughing. "But it's best you don't breathe that stuff. You don't want to start coughing." Dusters came much less often now and carried lighter dust and a smaller load, but Skitchy hated them as much as ever. She still worried about dust hurting her children. Sometimes she wondered if dust had anything to do with her own cough. "Would you like to come with Reba when she brings lunch? She can cover your face if the dust is still blowing. You can eat lunch with me."

Brightening, Margaret asked, "Can Molly come, too? She likes to have lunch with you. I'll cover her face. And after lunch, can we take our naps there?"

"You bet. Ask Reba to bring a quilt to make a little pallet for you to sleep on."

....

After Margaret and Molly were tucked in for naps in the back room, Skitchy went back to her work figuring out the latest costs and pricing for split skirts. She dropped her pencil with a gasp when she saw she finally had it! The costs work, she thought. The pricing works! I'm finally able to tell Sally for sure I'm satisfied we can sell skirts at a decent price and still make a profit! She felt calm deep joy, much like she had felt when she saw the Bighorns.

....

Skitchy and Wade sat on the porch of the ranch house enjoying a bourbon and soda before supper. Planning to spend the night there and go back to McAllister in the morning, Skitchy felt very relaxed and happy.

"I've an idea I want to talk to you about, sugar," she said. "I want to know what you think."

The serious yet excited tone of her voice made him curious.

"I've been thinking about how Sassy Skirts can sell skirts after what's happened with Wilson." They no longer called the mercantile store proprietor Mr. Wilson, both of them so disgusted with the man. "We still have O'Brien's in Pecos, of course. But I'm thinking maybe I could stretch farther."

Wade was listening intently now. "What does stretch farther mean?"

"Well, I went all over to buy quilts. Why not go all over to sell skirts? Any town with a mercantile store or even better, a bigger clothing store, might be interested in selling split skirts. If it's an area where women ride horses. Odessa and Lubbock maybe. I'd need to wait until we've sold enough skirts in Pecos to have enough money to make skirts to offer in other places. I'm thinking I could do it sort of a town at a time. What do you think?"

"That's a great idea! I think you can take the bit in your mouth, sugar, and do yourself proud! The skirts are great looking. You and Sally both talk about how comfortable they are for riding. I think when women get used to wearing something different from what they're used to, they might like wearing split skirts whether they're riding a horse or not. Sounds good enough to me to think maybe you could even get a loan from the bank in Pecos." He saw her surprised look. "If you present them with a solid enough business plan. Loans are awfully hard to come by but I hear not impossible."

"It means a lot to me to hear you say that, Wade." Her voice grew light then and she smiled at him. "I'm thinking very seriously of keeping you around." Just as quickly, she grew serious again. "No, I don't want to kid around about that. It's too wonderful that you care so much about what's important to me."

"I've always thought that was a pretty fair way to think about what loving someone means. Of course what's important to you is important to me."

Skitchy became very quiet and a shadow crossed her face. "What is it, sugar?" Wade asked.

Maybe it's time, she thought, to take the bit in my mouth about the rest of it, too. Have to, sooner or later. Gathering as much resolve as she could muster, she took a deep breath. Words came tumbling out.

"What's important to you is important to me, too. I know ranching is important to you. I recollect you saying you never wanted to live anywhere except on your ranch. I always thought of course we'd live here after we were married. Except that I didn't exactly think about it. But now I surely am thinking about it. When we talk about what Sally and I might be able to do with Sassy Skirts, I can see that where you and I are going to live isn't that simple. It'd be hard for Sally and me to do what we need to, if we live in different places. She has to be in McAllister because John's clinic and hospital are there. Just like your ranch is where it is."

She caught her breath, aggravated with herself for not speaking calmly as she had wanted to. But when she could see that he had been listening and now was just waiting for her to say everything she wanted to, she went on, trying to speak more slowly. "Then there are the girls. They've never lived anywhere except in town. I think living on the ranch would be a big adjustment for them. They'll need me more than they do now, when they have hotel family around all the time. But that's going to be hard for me if I'm working with Sassy Skirts the way I need to." She paused. "And want to."

She stopped. He was still listening, his expression serious but clearly open to what she was saying. That encouraged her to go on. She took another deep breath and was annoyed when she coughed. She decided to ignore the cough. "I just can't see how to fit everything together when some of the things most important to each of us are so different." She could feel herself frowning a little, even though she felt relieved by having given a voice to all she'd been thinking about but keeping to herself.

He stood up, came to her. Pulling her up, he took her in his arms. His voice low and calm, he said, "We have some things to figure out, sugar. I've been thinking about all those things, too."

She looked at him, surprised. "You have?"

"I have. We're smart people, Skitch. We can figure something out. We'll make it work somehow."

....

296

Reba folded the last of Hutch's clothes, packed them carefully into the worn suitcase that had been her father's and would now carry Borden possessions from one place to another for a third generation. Hutch tied up a small box containing a few books, the almost finished manuscript of his novel, and several stories he planned to sell to take care of himself in New York.

"You have your ticket?" Reba asked.

Hutch patted the pocket of his jacket. "Yes, Mama. And the money." Both of them were still astonished that Jackson had taken up a collection to help him get started in New York. Besides everyone at the hotel, Martha Hoffman, Sally and John MacLeod, and Wade Martin had pitched in. Even Margaret had put in two pennies, all the money she had. With the money collected by the black church, presented proudly to Hutch last Sunday morning, he had almost sixty-five dollars.

"Well, son," Reba began but her voice choked. Hutch had decided it was time for him to go after Jabe Alexander had come poking around. But Reba knew it was more than that. He was ready to go. He wanted to go. They hugged each other tightly, but she soon loosened her arms. She didn't want to make his leaving harder. They walked together from their room through the kitchen into the lobby.

Hutch started to shake hands with those gathered to say good-bye and wish him well. Skitchy couldn't help noticing the warmth with which Wade shook Hutch's hand. After getting to know the young man, she knew Wade had come to respect and admire him. She became teary watching them. When Wade's eyes met hers, he nodded a serious but smiling thank you to her.

When Hutch came to Connie, she reached up to give him a hug. Jackson, somewhat uncomfortable with the hug, decided it was time to wind things up.

"Hutch," he said, "I think I speak for everyone when I say we're all proud of you. And wish you the very best. I asked you to come to the lobby to say good-bye because I thought it only right for Hutchens Borden to leave here through the front door."

....

When Skitchy went to get coffee for herself and Belle later that day, even through the closed door to Reba's room off the kitchen, she heard a soft wailing. Skitchy had a heavy heart herself. She missed Hutch even though she'd known this day would come. Had wanted it for him. She thought of trying to comfort Reba but decided against it. Probably best to leave a proud strong woman who would very likely never see her son again to go through what she must in her own way.

Reba fixed supper that evening even though Belle had told her she didn't need to. "I do need to fix supper, Mrs. Belle, thank you anyway," Reba had said. When she brought the meal of chopped lettuce and tomatoes mixed with mayonnaise and a macaroni and cheese casserole to the table, no one would have been able to tell from her demeanor that anything in particular had happened that day that was out of the ordinary.

....

Sally put down the phone and laughed.

Skitchy looked up. "What is it?" she asked.

Catching her breath, Sally choked out. "Well, that was Brin, calling with orders from O'Brien's. You'll never guess who's ordered a sassy skirt!" She started to laugh again. "Nettie Martin!"

Skitchy started to laugh, too. Then grew serious. "It's kind of sad though, too, I think," she said. "Maybe it's just as well everybody doesn't always know who's really behind everything." She was thinking about Hutch and the white people in McAllister who'd helped him. Hutch, settled now in a room in New York, finishing his book. When *One Eye Blind* by Hutchens Borden hits Reeves County, she thought, some people will find it hard to stand.

It didn't cross her mind that Nettie Martin would find it impossible to stand finding out, a few days after Christmas, who'd made the split skirt she was wearing. So impossible to stand she would take down her father's shotgun from its holder in the cabinet in the hallway of her house. Put the barrel in her mouth. Pull the trigger.

1941

Wade had told Skitchy he'd go back to the ranch after Nettie Martin's funeral in Pecos, that he needed some time alone. So she was surprised when he came to Sassy Skirts' house much earlier than she'd expected him, still wearing a dark suit and dress hat. Seeing his head down and shoulders slumped, she tried to make her voice warm, not too light or too heavy. "Hi, sugar."

He only nodded, took off his coat and hat. He sank into the chair across from her, sat slouched and quiet for a long while. "It was hard, Skitch," he said finally, his voice low. "Really hard."

She wanted to comfort him but wasn't sure how to do that. "Is there anything I can do?"

"I just want to be with you, sugar. I've known most of those people all my life but I hated them today. I heard some of them saying Nettie shouldn't have a Christian funeral and burial because she killed herself. So why did the self-righteous hypocrites even come then?" He grew quiet. After a minute he said, "I know they talk about you, too. And about me. And about us. You stand it much better than I do. I'm so sorry you have to put up with it."

"I try not to pay them any mind, Wade. I wish they didn't talk because I think it aggravates Mama even though she says it doesn't. Maybe the girls hear it, I don't know. But I just ask myself, would you rather not be with Wade? You know the answer to that," and she came to put her arms around him, pull his head gently to rest against her. After a time she said, "Are you all right, sugar? Honestly all right, about Nettie?"

"There was nothing I could do for Nettie. I know that. She thought things in her mind. When what was real wasn't like that, she never could stand it. Some times were worse than others. The Wade Martin she wanted never did exist except in her mind." He pulled Skitchy closer. "I'm glad she's gone. Do you think it's awful to feel that way?"

"No," Skitchy said softly, "I don't. Daddy used to say some people bring out the best in you and some don't. Some even bring out the worst. Best you hold close to you just the ones that bring out the best."

"Well, I'm with someone right now who brings out the best in me," he said as he stood up, put his arms around her and kissed her softly. "Now I'm going to make us a bourbon. Shake off this mood. Then I'd like for us to go to the ranch. I'd surely like it if you would spend the night. Can you do that?"

"I was actually thinking the same thing right before you said it. Connie's already planning to stay with Belle and Jackson tonight. Margaret wants to do whatever Connie does, so she's sleeping with Mama. I don't even have to figure anything out," she said, laughing lightly.

....

Skitchy was wakened early the next morning by discomfort in her chest. It was already getting warm and she could hear the wind buffeting the window. She felt as restless as the wind and was lying there, trying to decide whether or not to get up, when she heard the telephone ring. Wade got up to answer it and quickly came back into the bedroom.

"It's Belle," he said, his voice concerned. "She needs to talk to you."

A stunned Belle told Skitchy their sister's husband had been in a terrible accident near Big Lake. Bob's car had gone off the road and turned over. He was already gone when someone found him.

"Do you want me to go to Big Lake with you?" Wade asked as she hastily got herself together.

"I think it's best you don't, as much as I'd like you to. This'll go very hard with Minnie. I think it'll be easier for her if there's just family for now. This doesn't feel like a time to have any attention on us."

"Whatever you think best." After a minute, he asked softly, "Are you all right, sugar?"

"I feel sad and worried for Minnie, but I'm all right."

....

"Sugar, let's take a walk," Kate said to Skitchy just after breakfast the day before Bob's funeral. "Belle will clean up the kitchen, won't you, Belle?"

"You bet."

Belle's voice sounded funny to Skitchy and her sister didn't look at her. Something's up, Skitchy thought. I wonder what Mama wants to talk about. But she didn't ask. She took one of Minnie's bonnets from a hook by the back door, put it on for protection from the Big Lake sun, already promising a blistering day.

The two women walked along the dusty dirt streets in silence for several minutes. When Kate spoke, her voice sounded a little strained, her daughter thought, but clear and firm.

"I wanted to talk to you before you go back to McAllister. You might not like what I have to say, honey. If you don't, just toss it up in the wind like a tumbleweed and let it blow away."

"I want to hear whatever you have to say, Mama." Skitchy found herself a little surprised to say that with such conviction. She'd often tried to avoid listening to her mother when she sounded like this but it felt different this morning. Something told her she needed to hear what was on her mother's mind.

"It's about you and Wade, honey. You're both free now. I don't understand why you haven't gotten married. It was one thing when you had to wait. But nothing's stopping you now. Have you changed your mind?"

Mama was asking the question Skitchy had been avoiding asking herself. "No, Mama, I haven't changed my mind. I love him. I want to spend the rest of my life with him."

"But . . . ?"

Mama had heard the but when Skitchy herself hadn't heard it. Her thoughts swirled and her heart felt twisted in a knot. They kept walking, Mama saying nothing more.

Finally, Skitchy said, almost in a whisper, "I love him, Mama. I feel so happy and alive with him. But if we get married and live at his ranch, I don't see how I can still do my work. Making Sassy Skirts happen makes me feel happy and alive, too. I feel like I'd just be torn to pieces if I had to give up either one. I don't want to give up either one. That's the but. I don't know what to do, Mama."

"Skitchy, when I was young, I felt a calling to be a midwife. I felt it first when I helped my mother deliver my last little brother. Then when she passed, it fell to me to take care of all of my younger brothers. So I put away wanting to be a midwife. I didn't forget, though. Then when I met Ephraim Chapman, I thought I couldn't just leave my family even though I wanted to marry him."

"But you did marry Daddy."

"My pa got married again. That was what set me free. His new wife was a strong, wonderful woman. Ada told me I should live my own life. Not someone else's life. Not only marry Eph but be a midwife, too, if that's what I wanted. So I told Eph I wanted that."

"And what did Daddy say?"

"He said we'd make that happen if that was what I wanted. And we did."

"But you and Daddy could make that happen and live together. Have your family, too. Wade says he thinks we can figure out some way to get married and I can still have Sassy Skirts. But his life is on his ranch. Mine is in McAllister. I just can't see how that can work out."

"I don't know if it can, sugar. You may have to make up your mind about what you want the most, if you can't have both."

As they turned and walked toward Minnie's house, Skitchy thought about all her mother had said. She was glad her mother had been able to have what she wanted for herself and also what she wanted with the man she loved. Skitchy strained to try to imagine that for herself. She could not. I think I'll have to choose, she thought. The idea of actually choosing, and all that would mean, tore at her. She felt like a small gray bird torn by buckshot she'd seen when she was a child, the memory vivid for her still. The bird lying there on the ground, terror in its eyes, breathing hard until the small torn body had stopped breathing and lay still.

"I'm surely not going to toss what you've said into the wind, Mama."

....

People were leaving the cemetery but Skitchy stood rooted by the grave of Ephraim Chapman. It was not far from the fresh grave of Bob Skinner and the old graves of Polly, Minnie and Bob's daughter, and the tiny graves of Polly's twins. Standing there amidst the grim evidence of the shortness and unpredictability of life and unable to erase the memory of the torn bird, Skitchy tried to think. How might it be if she was at the end of her own life? Which choice would she wish she'd made?

She'd been awake most of the night after her talk with Mama, going over and over things in her mind. Up to now, she'd imagined marrying Wade and living with him and her girls on the ranch. Still somehow having the fledgling business she was trying to build with Sally flourish into the successful Sassy Skirts she envisioned. Now she could see no way to have all of that, notwithstanding Wade's confident assurance they'd work it out somehow. She couldn't even be doing as much as she was now with Sassy Skirts without help with the girls from Belle and the others at the hotel. And Wade was a rancher. She'd always known that. If she wanted to make a life with him, she'd have to choose him and choose life on the ranch. Let Sassy Skirts go. Or choose Sassy Skirts. Let Wade go.

Which choice would she wish she'd made? The question kept repeating in her mind. No answer came. She took a couple of deep breaths and was annoyed when that triggered the coughing she was beginning to find more than a nuisance, and tears.

She brushed away the tears when she saw Belle and Jackson waiting for her at the gate to the cemetery. She was glad at least she wouldn't have to explain the tears. She was, after all, in a place of loss and sorrow.

....

The day after they got back from Big Lake, copies of *One Eye Blind* arrived at the post office in Pecos in the morning. A blue norther arrived in the county that afternoon. The storm the book would stir up was not yet apparent to many people, but Martha Hoffman knew it was coming when she picked up the large package, coming as surely as the storm that threatened with thunder and lightning. Rain had already begun to pour from the rapidly lowering roiling dark clouds as she hurried into the hotel in McAllister.

"Miss Hoffman!" Jackson exclaimed as he came out of his office. "What in the world brings you out in this weather?"

"Hutch's book came this morning. I picked up the copies at the post office in Pecos and I wanted to bring them right away. Be sure you all got them. I think there are people who may try to stop the book from getting around."

"Well, thank you. But I'm sure we could've waited until the storm passed."

"Actually I couldn't wait, Mr. Tieger. I'm leaving here tomorrow."

Skitchy came into the lobby in time to hear what Martha Hoffman had said. "Martha! What do you mean you're leaving?"

"Skitchy," Martha said breathlessly. "I'm so glad you're here. I was afraid I might not be able to see you. Say goodbye."

"What's happened?"

"I think someone at the post office in Pecos has been watching the mail I get from New York. And what I send. Here in McAllister, too, I'm pretty sure. James Alexander's father came to the school last week and practically said as much. Accused me of helping Hutch with his writing and helping him get what he's written published."

"Jabe Alexander is James' father," Jackson told Skitchy.

"That's right," Martha Hoffman said, surprised. "Do you know the family?"

"Well, I know Jabe Alexander the uncle. He's had a burr under his saddle about Hutch for a good while."

"I didn't know that," Martha said. "Well anyway, Mr. Alexander said people in this county won't stand for any white man or woman helping that black boy -- only he didn't say black boy -- to write trash about white people. White people around here in particular. He told me if their suspicions panned out, they'd see to it I lose my job. Maybe even something worse could happen. That if he were me, he'd get out of West Texas while he still could. I figured they'd surely know when the books got here. So I thought I'd best move on. Leave as soon as the books came. I'm going to my brother in Illinois. Try to find another job there. And maybe that way there won't be any trouble for any of the rest of you who've helped Hutch."

"Oh, Martha! That's awful. What can we do, Jackson?"

"I don't think we can do anything, Skitchy. If Miss Hoffman is willing to do what she says, that's about the best we can hope for. It's a sorry thing when someone has to be a scapegoat but maybe it's for the best. Since they already know about her involvement with Hutch."

"That's exactly what I think, Mr. Tieger. It's best for all of us. I knew something like this could happen when I started helping Hutch, but it was important to me so I did it anyway. I've no regrets. If these sorry bigots believe I was the only one, or anyway I'm the only one they can put a finger on, let them hang everything on me. I'm leaving here anyway. There's no point in you folks getting mixed up in it."

Skitchy scowled, hating the helplessness she felt. "Martha, I'm honored to be your friend. Will you write to me when you're settled?"

"I'd love to, Skitchy, but I think it's best if I don't. They may watch for any mail from me. See if they can figure out anyone else who might be involved. I don't know about phone calls but it's probably best if we don't take any chances. Calls have to go through the central switchboard. The operator knows who calls who. I'll hold you in my heart. I ask you to hold me in yours." She hugged Skitchy tightly, shook hands with Belle and Jackson. "I'd like to go out through the back, please. Hutch wrote something for his mother in a copy of the book. Asked me to be sure she got it. I want to give it to her myself. And say good-bye. Then go while the storm's still a good cover."

....

Skitchy felt out of sorts. She'd talked to Wade on the phone since she got back from Big Lake, but hadn't seen him for a week. He'd been busy rounding up and branding calves at the ranch. There'd been much she needed to do with Sassy Skirts after being away. She felt impatient to talk with him, but not on the phone. What she wanted to talk about had to be in person. She hoped he'd come soon.

On the drive back to McAllister from Big Lake, like a sudden flash of lightning heralding a change in the weather, she'd seen another possibility. A third possibility, different from the choices that had been tearing at her. Everyone expected them to marry. Even the two of them. But what if they didn't? What if they just kept on as they were? Wade living and working on his ranch, Skitchy living and working in McAllister. Spending as much time together as they could. People would talk. But they talked anyway. How much worse could it be?

She'd felt a pang when she thought it might be worse for Mama. And Mama might be less accepting of an unmarried daughter who lived like that. Still, that felt better to her than either of the awful choices she'd been struggling with. She'd decided to tell Wade that was what she wanted. She was determined to tell him today. Hoping he'd be able to see eye to eye with her, she felt very jittery.

She fixed a fresh pot of coffee. Did some work that didn't take too much concentration. She rested for a while. Still feeling tired but determined to talk to him, she started to cough just as she heard him come in the front door.

"Skitch, I heard you coughing again. Are you sure nothing's wrong? I wish you'd see John and be sure."

"I don't think it's anything. But anyway I don't want to talk about that now," she said, irritation in her voice that she didn't want to be there. She wanted to talk about what they were going to do even though she thought it might be best to wait until she felt calmer, more composed. She pressed on.

"Wade, I need to talk to you about something very important for both of us. I know you said you thought we could work something out about where we're going to live. But I don't see how I can do my work with Sassy Skirts living at the ranch. Sally is here in McAllister. The workshop and office are here. When I'm calling on stores in other places, who will look after Margaret? And Connie for a while yet, even if she doesn't think she needs looking after?" She paused to collect herself so she could say what she'd decided to say.

He could feel her consternation and hear it in the rush of words. "I've been thinking about all that, too, sugar. Before you say any more I'd like to tell you about an idea I have. See what you think. All right?"

"All right," she said, afraid he could hear the wary tone in her voice. She could hear it herself, but she was determined not to be pulled away from telling him what she'd decided.

"I'll get us some coffee." He kissed her on the cheek, took away her cold coffee, and poured hot coffee for them. He sat down across from her, his voice tingling with excitement.

"What if we had a little house here in McAllister? Spend some of our time here and some at the ranch, especially when the girls aren't in school. If I needed to be at the ranch I could always go there even if you were in McAllister. You could do the same if you needed to be in town, for the girls or for Sassy Skirts."

Stunned, Skitchy stared at him. As the whirlwind of thoughts and feelings began to settle, she said, "That sounds wonderful. I'm not sure how we could afford it, but it sounds absolutely wonderful."

He leaned forward toward her, allowing his excitement more rein. "I helped Nettie's folks buy the house in Pecos. I probably never told you that. Anyway, I talked to the lawyer while you were in Big Lake. He says I'm going to have the house now. I don't ever want to live there so I'm thinking to trade it for a house here in McAllister. Belle and Jackson would need to keep helping out with the girls but I think they would. I thought it was kind of crazy at first how life is at the hotel, but it seems to work for everybody." He grinned. "In fact, sometimes I've wondered if any of you could stand it if the girls lived someplace else all the time."

Skitchy's shoulders began to relax and her expression brightened a little. "And what about the ranch? There's a lot for you to do there. How would you make that work?"

"I think Marvin would jump at the chance to help manage the ranch if I give him a little land and some cattle to run as his own. He's a good man and he knows what to do. I wouldn't need to be there all the time. His wife could take care of the house. I think you'd like Frieda, but you and I wouldn't be living there all the time anyway."

She wanted desperately for it all to be as he was saying. He'd changed the way he felt about black people. Maybe he could change the way he felt about the ranch, too. But she needed to be sure. "You've always talked about how important the ranch is to you. How all you ever wanted was to be a rancher."

He looked deeply into her eyes. "Nothing is more important to me than you, Skitchy. I've been thinking that for a good while. But when Minnie's husband passed, I thought a lot about how things can just change in a wink. I don't want to miss a minute we could have together. I want you to keep on with Sassy Skirts. It's important to you and I don't want you to give it up. And I can have enough ranching to keep me happy if I'm there some of the time. Here in McAllister some of the time." He sat looking at her, wanting to grin but holding it back until he heard what she'd say. "Well, what do you think of my idea?"

"I think it's a perfectly fine idea," she said. "Fine." She felt tears of happiness coming up. She came to him.

He stood to meet her, gathered her into his arms and held her close. When he kissed her, she returned his kiss passionately.

She stood back a little to look at him. "Let's get married as soon as we can."

"Well," he grinned, "if I'd known all it was going to take for us to get married was figuring out how to live in two places at the same time, I wouldn't have fooled around so long."

....

Belle was brushing her hair, almost ready for bed, when Jackson came in, turning his head this way and that to ease a stiff neck and stiff shoulders.

"Sorry to be so late, honey. Pretty busy day. Lots of people came into the drug store today. We're almost full here again tonight. Surely do need to hire some more help. Been trying to figure how soon to do it."

"Well, I guess that's a better than average problem to have, isn't it?"

"You bet," he smiled. He unbuttoned his shirt and stretched his neck a little more. "There was something you wanted to talk to me about. Is now a good time? Are you too worn out?"

"Now is fine," she said as she climbed into bed, plumping the pillows behind her so she could see him. "Skitchy and Wade are going to get married next month. They want to live part of the time in McAllister and part of the time at Wade's ranch. She asked me if the girls could still stay with us some of the time. When she and Wade are at the ranch. Or when she's busy with Sassy Skirts. Or just when the girls want to, the way they do now. Connie could stay at the high school here and she really wants to do that. If they can find a new teacher, Margaret could go to school here, too. What do you think?"

"I know you love having them around. So do I. To tell you the truth, I feel like they're part ours. But please don't tell Skitchy I said that."

"I won't," she said, laughing lightly. "I feel the same way." Her voice grew more serious. "Thank you, honey."

"No need to thank me, Belle. I love our girls, too."

....

It was a clear cold day the Sunday before Thanksgiving, with no wind and no dust, relished by Skitchy as if that was a wedding gift. Sally had made a new dress for her, V-necked and short sleeved, with a full shorter skirt, in Skitchy's favorite shade of green, her first new dress in years. Belle rolled her sister's hair softly on each side in the new style. Walking down the stairs into the hotel lobby, Skitchy felt shining joy as she came to stand next to a grinning Wade, resplendent in a dark blue suit, white shirt, light blue tie, and new boots, his hair freshly cut for the occasion.

"I've never seen you look more wonderful," Wade murmured happily as he kissed her after they'd made their promises to each other.

She smiled and whispered back so only he could hear, "Well, you look wonderful, too, all dressed up and everything. But personally, I can hardly wait for us to get home and undress each other."

Wade spontaneously laughed out loud, startling everyone. But then his smiling ease with whatever it was Skitchy had said broke the seriousness of the gathering into instant festivity. Jackson turned on the radio to popular music he knew Skitchy liked. He was delighted when Bing Crosby crooned one of her favorite songs, and she and Wade began to dance. Sally and John MacLeod joined them. On an impulse which got a nod from Belle, Jackson asked Rita to dance.

Reba brought out the cake she'd made. Belle poured coffee, adding brandy for those who wanted it. Kate Chapman, just come from Big Lake to be in McAllister for the wedding, beamed at her daughter and new son-in-law from the rocking chair where she sat with Margaret. Connie sat trying to look as adult as possible as she drank her first cup of coffee. Rita Colquitt told her sister about everything in a low whisper, including, she said with her eyes closed, that she'd danced with Josiah.

Just the week before, Wade had finished work on the small house on Austin Street. The outside needed painting badly, but that was a luxury for better times, as it was for most of the houses in McAllister, weathered by years of blasting sand and baking sun. They did paint all the rooms inside, making great fun out of the choosing of colors. The front bedroom was Skitchy's favorite green. Connie and Margaret had settled on a soft shade of pink for the back bedroom they'd share. Belle made curtains for all the rooms as a wedding gift. Sally and John gave their friends an oak bed and dresser and a beautiful quilt Sally made. Wade brought a few things from the ranch. A bed and dresser for the girls' room, an old table and chairs for the small kitchen, each chair painted in a color chosen by the person who would sit in it. The front room was empty and all the furnishings spare, but everything was theirs and cherished.

The newlyweds went to the house after an hour of celebration at the hotel. Just as Skitchy and Wade had seen Sally and John home after their wedding, so now Sally and John went with Skitchy and Wade to their new McAllister home. Jackson sent a thermos of coffee and brandy. After the men took off their coats and ties and the women kicked off their shoes, they sat around the green kitchen table and drank it with laughter and the warm comfortable pleasure of sharing joy with good friends. Skitchy noticed John noticing her coughing once or twice but he said nothing and neither did she. She was unwilling to think about that this evening.

"Thank you both so much," Wade said to their friends warmly as they were leaving, "for everything."

"You bet," Sally said, just as warmly. "John and I wouldn't have wanted to miss this day for anything!"

Wade closed the door and turned to his new wife. "Well, sugar, here we are. I'm surely the happiest man in the world."

"Well, then, how come you still have your clothes on?" she demanded, laughing as she threw herself into his arms.

They held each other in a long embrace, then walked slowly, arm in arm, to their bedroom. After they'd made love for the first time as husband and wife, they'd tell each other of their joy at having bound themselves together at last.

....

Two weeks later there was much excitement around the hotel. Skitchy and Wade had gone to the ranch the day after the wedding and had been there ever since. They were coming to the hotel for Sunday dinner and to play cards before taking the girls home to their new house.

Belle was glad the hotel's overnight guests all left after breakfast. Just about everyone was busy after they got home from church. Upstairs Jackson cleaned up after the departed guests. Connie and Belle packed the last things Connie wanted to take with her, and chatted with Grandma. Downstairs Reba was getting chicken ready for frying and biscuits ready to put in the oven. Margaret watched intently by the window in the lobby where the light was good as Rita patched Molly, Margaret's rag doll, to get her ready for her three block journey.

....

At the ranch Skitchy said a warm good-bye to the mare she'd come to love, scratching the horse's neck and delighting in being nuzzled in return, while Wade closed up the house. Skitchy's attention quickly turned toward McAllister when she climbed into the truck. She was eager to see the girls. She and Wade had only had coffee this morning and imagining Reba home from church and preparing dinner by this time, Skitchy was looking forward to a delicious hot meal on this cold December day. She and Wade talked easily with each other as the miles disappeared into the dust behind them.

....

The meal was indeed just as delicious as Skitchy had imagined. Fried chicken, mashed potatoes and gravy, and green beans from Belle's garden canned in the spring, were topped off with a warm peach cobbler Wade enjoyed so much he had three helpings, much to Reba's delight. They were all cleaning up the dishes from the table and laughing as they got cards ready for a cut-throat game of Hearts, when the telephone rang.

"Law, who's calling on a Sunday?" Belle lamented as Jackson headed for the telephone. But then Belle heard something in the tone of Jackson's voice and even though she couldn't hear clearly what he was saying, it was enough to stop her light-hearted conversation. When he came back to the dining room, his stunned face blanched, she went to meet him. "Honey, what is it?"

He couldn't seem to get words out and went to the radio and turned it on, the volume high. Everyone hurried to gather around the rounded wooden box. All of them would remember for the rest of their lives the precise details of where they were, what they were doing, what they heard, the tension of immobilizing body sensations and frozen emotion, as they listened to the President telling the country the Japanese had bombed Pearl Harbor in Hawaii that morning. WAR! The country was suddenly embroiled in a second worldwide war only twenty-three years after the end of the first Great War.

Margaret heard the grown-ups talking about these things but she didn't understand. She knew only that something terrible had happened.

Skitchy saw her younger daughter huddled against the wall and went to her, knelt and put her arms around the little girl. Trying to ignore her own sinking stomach, Skitchy spoke in the most soothing voice she could find, trying to explain in words a five year old could grasp. She found it difficult since she was still struggling to grasp the jolt of it all herself. She was glad when Wade came to them. With a glance she invited him to join them. He picked Margaret up and held her close, telling her gently that the terrible thing that had happened out there in the world was far far away. Would not, could not, hurt them here. She was safe.

"Where's Molly?" Margaret called out, her arms still tight around Wade's neck as her eyes searched the space. Connie brought the doll to her sister and Margaret hugged it close to her. "It's all right, Molly. Wade says nothing's going to hurt us."

....

The hotel was quiet after Skitchy, Wade and the girls had gone. Kate and Rita had said good night and climbed the stairs slowly together. Reba had gone to bed early. Jackson left the door of their quarters open in case a hotel guest arrived even though he thought that unlikely this late. He and Belle sat in their front room, quietly sipping a brandy.

"Did you see how Wade was with Margaret this afternoon?" Jackson asked.

"I did. I could see how scared she was. I was trying to think if there was anything I could do when Wade just stepped up. He surely is a fine man. I'm so happy for Skitchy."

Jackson offered to refill her glass. Belle shook her head. "I'll have a cigarette, though. I've misplaced my holder but I'll try one without it."

"Maybe it's time you got that gold holder I promised you a long while ago," he said as he reached out to light her cigarette.

"Law, Jackson, I'd forgotten all about that."

"Well, I haven't. I'll see to it." He leaned back in the chair and took a couple of long draws on his cigarette. She saw a shadow cross his face and knew he'd changed the subject in his mind.

"This war is going to be a big one," he said solemnly. "And a long one, I'm afraid. It'll affect the whole country. Will reach us right here. Some of our boys from the county will go, I have no doubt." He immediately wished he hadn't said that, afraid it might remind her of her lost love, killed in the big war of their youth. He'd always taken such care to respect her feelings for the man, he could hardly believe he'd been so clumsy.

"Jackson, I need to tell you something," she said, and her voice was serious and light at the same time. "When I heard about this new war it brought back the memories I've carried for so long of the young man I loved before you and I were together. I did love Sam once. But it's way past time for me to let go of those old cobwebby memories. What I've been hanging on to has been just an illusion for a long time, I can see now. Please forgive me. You're real and always have been. When you talked about the cigarette holder before, I thought about how you've never forgotten anything you thought was important to me. You've always been strong and constant. The most wonderful husband I could've ever wanted. I love you with all my heart. Not all of it except for the part that once belonged to someone else. All my heart."

Tears sprang to Jackson's eyes in spite of the pride he'd always taken in maintaining coolheaded composure. Haunted by the specter of Sam Mueller, he'd believed he'd never measure up to Belle's long ago love. Never have her heart entirely, no matter how hard he tried. No matter how successful he was. No matter how well thought of he was by others. He could feel his heart pounding as the shadowy phantom dissolved. He and Belle were alone in their room.

When he calmed, he whispered from the depths of his love for her, "Belle. My darling Belle. There's nothing to forgive, my darling. I love you so." He reached for her and kissed her gently, a kiss she returned with the same quiet deep feeling.

Belle's voice was clear and strong when she said, "Maybe the war isn't all bad if it's helped me see what I should've seen long before now. I'll have another brandy after all, Jackson. I want to toast to us. And whatever the new year may bring."

1942

"I'm afraid this is terribly serious, Skitchy."

John's voice -- Dr. MacLeod's voice -- froze her to the chair across from his desk. She found herself looking out the window, noting the houses across the street that needed painting, a Mexican boy walking along the street clutching his worn coat around him, a Model-A adding to the dusty haze in the air. She made a great effort and pulled her eyes back to the man sitting on the other side of the desk who was making a great effort to keep his composure.

"Sorry, John. What does that mean?"

"I can help some with the pain in your chest and shortness of breath. Keep you as comfortable as possible. But I'm afraid I can't make you well."

What is he saying? she thought. What is he talking about? The possibility she grasped only dimly was not possible. She sat there, numb, no sense of time passing.

"Are you saying I'm going to die?"

West Texans seldom used direct words for anything having to do with death and he felt the impact of her words slam into him. "That is what I'm saying." His voice broke. "I'm so sorry, Skitchy."

Her body shuddered as if trying to wake from a nightmarish dream. "How long do I have?" Her voice sounded as mechanical as she felt.

"That's hard to say. My best guess is about six months. Maybe as long as a year."

"That just can't be!" she blurted, her voice almost shrill now. "I'm still a young woman. I have things to do. Children to take care of."

She'd only been back from her trip to Lubbock, Odessa, and Midland for a month. The excitement of selling split skirts to stores in those towns had fueled her determination to make another trip soon. To San Angelo, she'd decided. Excitement and determination had also helped her push away a growing feeling that something was not right in her body.

When that not-right feeling became intense enough, she'd finally resolved to see John for a check-up. But she'd gone over the new orders with Sally first and reviewed all the numbers, excited for what this was going to mean for Sassy Skirts. She had begun planning the San Angelo trip. She designed a sign and made arrangements for it to be installed over the door of what she now always called the office. Then she'd made the call to John's clinic.

She tried to shake all that off now. Put her attention where she wanted it to be. But she found that harder to do than she could ever remember. She heard John's voice speaking to her from what sounded like a long way away.

"Would you like me to tell Wade?"

"What?" She tried to gather her thoughts. "You mean tell Wade how sick I am? That I'm going to die?"

"I'll do that if you'd like me to. If it would make it easier for you."

"Thank you, John, but I want to tell him myself. I need to tell him myself. But thank you."

....

Color drained from Wade's contorted face, a mirror for Skitchy's own distress. She wanted to comfort him but desperately needed comforting herself. She felt unable to move. He stood up from the kitchen table, came to her. She gratefully went into his arms. No sooner had he touched her than the tears erupted despite her determination to stay strong. Sobbing, she was unaware at first that he was sobbing too. They clung together there in the kitchen for many minutes.

"Is John sure?" Wade asked finally. "Did he say he was sure?"

"He didn't say it like that. Those words. But you know John. He wouldn't have told me a thing like this unless he was sure."

She grew quiet again. "Please let's talk about things later. I just want you to hold me right now."

....

On a rainy afternoon a week later Skitchy and Wade sat in the kitchen in their house after Connie and Margaret had gone to the hotel where they were going to spend the night. Cups of coffee gone cold sat on the table. Skitchy had no idea how long she'd been sitting there, trying to think about what she wanted and needed to do to prepare her daughters for the changes that were coming. She was startled when Wade spoke.

"Why don't we go to Scott and White? It's not that far to Temple, and Scott and White's one of the best hospitals in the country. We can get enough money together to do that. I can borrow against the ranch if I need to. Let's find out what the doctors there say. I can't believe there's nothing that can be done."

"Oh, Wade, part of me wants to put up a fight, like you're talking about. But another part of me knows that's not going to do any good. I don't want to spend the time I have chasing all over the place, hoping and trying to make things different from the way they are. I don't want to just fritter away time and energy I could have for things that really matter to me. I don't know if I can do this thing the way I want to, Wade. But I want to try. Please help me?"

"I will. I promise. I'll do the best I can."

....

"I want to spend as much time with you as we can possibly manage to spend together," Skitchy told Wade two weeks later. "I want to be with the girls and leave them with as much of me as I can. I want to spend time with Belle. And there'll be things we need to talk about, about the girls. With Jackson, too. I want to have time with Mama. Maybe go see Minnie if I can. I want to leave Sassy Skirts in good shape for Sally."

"Whoa! Slow down, sugar, please. John told you to take it easy and that surely doesn't sound like taking it easy. I want you to take good care of yourself."

She smiled, chagrined. "It's hard to think I can't just do things the way I used to. But I think I can do more than John thinks I can. I recollect Daddy saying it's best to live, really live, while you can. Then you're not so likely to quibble at the end because you wasted so much life. I wonder if maybe that's what he wanted to tell me. Remind me about, when he was dying. When we were saying good-bye. He taught me so much about how to live. It'd be like him to want to teach me about how to die." She saw Wade pull back just a little. "Is it hard for you when I say 'die' and 'dying'?"

"Well, I'm surely not used to it. Those words sound hard."

"They are hard words. To me they're also strong words. They hold me up somehow. The spindly ones don't, even though they're the words I've heard all my life. In fact, the spindly words make me mad sometimes. It helps me to say the hard, strong words. I think it'll help me to hear them, too. I want to do the best I can to really live for however long I have.

"I never thought much about words mattering. But I can hear something in what you're saying. And anyway, it's for you to say, sugar, what helps you."

He grew very quiet and his eyes filled again with tears, looking at her as if he couldn't take in enough of her. "I don't know if I can stand living without you, Skitchy."

"I know, sugar. I feel the same way. I can hardly stand the thought of leaving you."

"But we don't have a choice. We must stand it somehow. I've not been much of a crier but it surely feels a little better to cry. Maybe I can stand it if I cry enough. If we cry for each other. If we cry together. Can we do that for each other?"

What he said suddenly struck her as sweetly funny and she said, smiling, "Well, if we could take off our clothes for each other, love each other better for having done that, we can surely cry for each other. Crying could take off something even deeper than clothes, I think maybe. Help us to see each other better. Love each other even better than we have."

....

When there were guests in the hotel, Kate Chapman was most comfortable in the kitchen. It felt a little like her kitchen at the ranch. And she liked visiting with Reba more than with Rita, who talked to her departed sister most of the time now. Or being alone in her room upstairs when Belle was busy and her granddaughters were at school or with Skitchy and Wade.

"Good morning, Mrs. Kate," Reba said warmly. 'Can I fix you a cup of coffee?"

"No thank you, Reba. Not this morning. I don't have much of an appetite for anything."

Reba saw at a glance the slump of the older woman's shoulders, the deep sadness in her eyes. "Please don't pay me any mind if I'm talking out of turn," Reba said, stopping her work at the sink and drying her hands, "but I think maybe it'd do you good to talk about Mrs. Skitchy. I worry when I know there's pain around and someone's not talking about it." She sat down at the kitchen table opposite Kate.

A shadow passed over Kate's face. Her voice thin and low, not much more than a raspy whisper, she said, "I don't know why the good Lord keeps taking my children and lets me live so long."

"Mmm." Reba wanted the older woman to know she was listening.

"I've lost my husband and four children already, Reba. I lived through that. But I seem to have forgotten how I was able to do it. Here Skitchy's still alive, but I feel like I'm walking around in a dust storm so thick I can't see my way. I'm blown this way and that. I feel like I'm just wandering around in circles."

Kate lifted her eyes from her lap and looked into Reba's dark eyes, filled with sorrow, just like her own. She saw a tear glisten against the black woman's dark cheek.

"Well, I guess maybe you stored all that old grief in your heart," Reba said. "Now your heart just can't hold any more."

The true words reached a place deep within Kate. She felt grief rising from that deep place, as she'd seen water rise from a well newly dug deep in the earth. Tears welled up from that deep full reservoir.

When Kate looked up she saw Reba's face also washed with tears. Reaching across the table, Reba gently took Kate's hand.

They were sitting like that when Jackson opened the door to the kitchen, saw them, and stepped back, quietly closing the door. He'd told Belle that morning that he thought her mother was keeping all the sad shocking news about Skitchy bottled up inside, and he thought that wasn't good for her.

"That's Mama's way, Jackson. Our family's never talked much about sad things."

"I understand, honey. It's not been my way either. But this is such a heavy thing. It has surely helped me to be able to talk about it with you. I would never try to tell Kate what to do or not do. I'm just a little worried about her, that's all."

It had lifted his heavy heart a little when he saw the two women together in the kitchen.

....

"Jackson?"

He got up quickly and helped Skitchy to a chair. She was weak now and he knew a visit to his office must be important if she'd come there. He sat down in the chair next to hers instead of going back to the chair behind his desk.

"Thank you," she said. "I need to talk to you. Is this an all right time?"

He could hear urgency through the tiredness in her voice. "You can talk to me any time, Skitch."

"Well, I'll get right to it then. Before my energy runs out." She took a deep breath without noticing that he did also. "Jackson, when your grandfather left you the hotel, how did he do that?"

"We found a note on his desk. The note said he wanted me to have the hotel if I wanted it."

"Looks like there'll be some money from Sassy Skirts. I need to know how to have my share go where I want it. Can I write a note like your grandfather did? Give it to someone? Is that how I should do it?"

"Nobody questioned my grandfather's note, Skitchy. They could have, though. Best if you make a will. The lawyer in Pecos could do that for you. Then there wouldn't be any question about what happens to the money."

"I don't think I can make it to Pecos. I hate to ask Wade. This is so hard on him." She struggled to keep distress from whirlwinding her resolve away like a tumbleweed. "Jackson, would you go see the lawyer for me? I know it's a lot to ask."

"Skitchy, I'll do anything I can to help you," Jackson said, his voice filled with warmth as well as concern for her. "I feel honored you'd ask me. I haven't known what to say or what to do, and I'd like so much to be able to do something. You surely are like a sister to me." He stopped, the tear in his voice finishing for him.

She looked at him for a long moment, a tear in her own eye. Then she opened her purse and took an envelope from it. Handing it to him, she said, "I've written down what I want. I figured to just give this to you, but now I think you should give it to the lawyer. He can use what I wrote? To know what to put in the will?"

"I'm sure he can. And I'll bring the will back here for you to sign. Make it easy for you. As much as I can make any of this any easier."

She heard the catch in his throat. "Thank you, Jackson. For this and for everything you've done all these years. You've been a true friend, and more. I've always felt I could trust you about anything. Our family was lucky when you came into it. I feel like I've had a brother after all." She reached out her arms to him and he rose to help her to her feet. They held each other for a moment. "Thank you," she said again, her voice firm and clear.

....

Three days later Belle walked over to Sassy Skirts' office from the hotel as soon as she opened the letter from California. The sisters had found comfort in the close wordless times they spent together since Skitchy had told Belle the dreadful news. They also found comfort talking together, in particular about the girls, and planning for them. But Belle didn't think what she had to talk to Skitchy about today would hold comfort. She walked briskly through the dusty heat of mid-day, resolved to keep her emotions under control as best she could.

"Honey, I got a letter from Pink," Belle began. "He wants Connie and Margaret to come to California and live with him.

329

He says he'll get a bigger place closer to where Alma and Tom live so she can help him with the girls."

Skitchy felt an intense flare of anger. "You told him I want them to live with you and Jackson? For you to raise them? That you want that, too? That the girls want that?"

"I wrote all of that to him when you asked me to. Connie has been talking with him on the phone and she has told him that, too. He talks a little with Margaret, but I don't think about California. I think you're going to have to talk with him yourself, honey."

"As if I don't have enough to think about and take care of already." She could hear the ill humor in her voice and felt badly. "Sorry to be so cranky, Belle. I'm grateful for everything you're doing to help. It just makes me so mad that Pink wouldn't respect my wishes. I want the girls to live with you and Jackson. Why would he object to them living with you? I want them to have times with Wade, too, but Pink doesn't have to know that."

Uncertain, Belle said softly, "They're Pink's children, too, honey. He does have a right to make his wishes known, under the circumstances."

"The circumstances . . ." Skitchy began, then her voice collapsed.

Belle put her arm around her sister's shoulders, not knowing what else to do or what else to say.

Skitchy searched Belle's face, as if she were desperately looking for something there. In an agonized voice, she whispered, "Oh, Belle, I don't know if I can stand the circumstances."

....

"Mama, I don't want to go to California," Connie began, "and I think it'd be awful for Margaret. She doesn't really know Daddy very well, even with talking to him on the phone. And Alma even less. It's going to be hard enough without you," her voice broke in a sob. "At least she should be here with people she knows. People she loves and who love her."

"I know, sugar," Skitchy said weakly, touched by Connie's concern for her little sister. Skitchy was thin now and tired easily. She knew she should probably not still be going to the office but she was determined to finish the contracts with all the stores. Leave the books in good order so Sally could carry on with cutting and sewing and shipping split skirts. She closed the books on the desk in front of her with a deep sigh and looked at her daughter. "Let me move over to the couch, sugar. Then we'll talk."

"I'm afraid we don't have a choice about this," Skitchy said, resignation in her voice, when Connie had helped her get settled, carefully putting pillows behind her mother's back and head. "Wade says the lawyer in Pecos told him you'll have to go if your daddy's insisting. He is insisting. I have an idea, though." She was interrupted by intense coughing and sagged back into the pillows.

While Skitchy rested, Connie tried to gather herself together. She didn't want to make things harder for her mother. She tried to stay as even and calm as she could.

"If your daddy promised to let you come back if you want to, after you've finished high school, would that make it easier?"

"He already told me he wants me to go to college. But I don't want to go to college."

"I know him, sugar. He wants you to go to college, but he won't make you if you don't want to. He couldn't anyway," and Skitchy chuckled a little. Connie also chuckled, almost in spite of herself. Her mother knew her also.

"You have to work things around sometimes. Ask him now to promise he'll let you come back without making a fuss after you finish high school, if that's what you want to do. Pay for your ticket. I think he'll agree to that. Then you'll know for sure you can come back if you want to."

"You know what I deep down want to do?" Skitchy waited, curious. Connie didn't talk often about herself or what she wanted for herself. "I want to work for Uncle Jackson and Auntabelle at the hotel. I've watched what they do. I'm sure I could do it. And maybe one day it'd even be my own business. Like Sassy Skirts is your own business. I know I would come back if things might work out like that."

"Have you told Auntabelle and Uncle Jackson any of that?"

"No, ma'am. I thought that would seem cheeky. And please don't you tell them."

"I won't. That's for you to tell if it gets told. But if I were in your place, I would risk cheeky if I wanted things to work out the way you say. Auntabelle and Uncle Jackson love you, Connie, as if you were their own. I think they'd be tickled to know how you feel about the hotel."

"You think so, Mama, sure enough? Well, then, I'll talk to them. And I'll talk to Daddy about that promise."

....

Skitchy felt impatient waiting for Wade to get back from the ranch. She wanted him to attend to what he needed to, yet wanted him with her all the time. And today hadn't been a very good day. She felt the edges of her world narrowing and found it increasingly difficult to think clearly about things happening beyond the shrinking scope of her attention.

When she heard him open the front door she felt a wave of hot impatient anger rising up within her. By the time he came into the bedroom it had spilled over. "Don't tippy toe," she said, making no effort to curb the nasty tone in her voice. "I've been awake for ages. Just waiting for you to get back so I could get to the bathroom. Have something to eat."

"Are you hungry?"

"I could eat something." The nasty tone was even nastier.

Steady now, he told himself. Fight a bucking horse, it's going to throw you every time. Ride it out. He took a deep breath. "I'm sorry it took so long, sugar," he said as evenly as he could. "There was more I needed to do at the ranch than I thought. Reba said she'd look in on you. Bring you lunch. I thought you'd be all right."

"Reba did come. I wasn't hungry then. She put the food in the refrigerator so you'd just need to heat it up."

"I'll do that now."

She could hear him in the kitchen and the swirl of sadness and anger began to dissolve. Skitchy, she told herself, you've got to get hold of yourself. The world doesn't revolve around you. You're acting like a kid who thinks she doesn't have to mind anybody.

"Reba brought one of your favorites, a macaroni and cheese casserole," he said as he came back into the room. "It's getting hot in the oven. Should be ready in a few minutes. Is there anything you need right now?"

"I need to say I'm sorry. Don't know what gets into me sometimes, sugar. You've just been wonderful. I feel like a varmint, sniping at you like that."

Wade felt the gristle in him become tender. He came to the bed and sat beside her carefully. "Kiss me, varmint," he said, keeping his voice light, "and you're forgiven. And get an early supper besides." He leaned toward her, kissed her softly. His face grew serious then. He stroked the hair back from her forehead, wishing he could do far more than he could to ease things for her.

"Wade, will you take me to McMinn Springs?" Skitchy asked as they ate the macaroni and cheese. "I'd like to see it one more time now that the springs are flowing again. See green things. Maybe we could even take a picnic. I'd like that so much. Can we do that?"

Wade felt uneasy about taking Skitchy any distance from home and medical care if she should need it. But he didn't want to say no to something she wanted, especially when he didn't know how much longer it would even be possible to do things like take a trip to McMinn Springs. His thoughts flashed rapidly. "I think the truck would be too rough but I think John would let me borrow his car. In fact, how about asking Sally and John to come with us?"

"Sounds like fun."

"Good. I'll talk to John and we'll figure something out around his schedule."

He took a couple of deep breaths and relaxed. Arranging to have the company of good friends who could also help him if he needed help with Skitchy, not to mention that one of the friends was Skitchy's doctor, put his mind at ease about making the trip.

....

"Pink?"

"Skitchy?" Pink's voice on the other end of the line sounded surprised.

"Uh-huh, it's Skitchy. It's hard for me to talk for very long so I'd like to get right to what I'm calling about. Is that all right with you?" She also didn't want to be on the phone with him any longer than was absolutely necessary, but didn't want to say that.

"Of course," Pink said, his voice with a trace of concern.

"I want to talk about Margaret. I'm worried about her." She waited to see if he'd say anything. When he didn't, she went on. "She's only five and she's having a hard time understanding what's happening. She's very quiet. She doesn't play very much like she used to. She's waked up at night crying a few times."

"I'm sorry to hear that."

"Besides all that's going on with me, she knows you want her and Connie to come there. Live with you after . . ." Her voice trailed off and she didn't finish her sentence.

She took a few deep breaths, wishing he'd say more. But she thought she could feel him stiffening and thought she'd best go on. "I think it'd be easier for her if she stayed here for a while, with Belle and Jackson. Mama's living at the hotel now and Reba is still there. Maybe you recollect how Margaret feels about both of them."

"Yes, I do."

"I think being with people she feels close to, in a familiar place, would help her a lot to make the adjustments she's going to have to make. Having to also get used to a new place to live would be asking a lot. And you'd be working all day. Alma will be almost like a stranger to her now. Please, Pink, let her stay here for a good while."

"How long do you have in mind?"

Skitchy was glad to hear his question. He'd really been listening, she thought. She started to cough. "Excuse me a minute, please." She felt more drained after the coughing but also thought maybe it gave him some time to be thinking things through. She knew he usually made better decisions that way. "Sorry," she said, "that just happens sometimes. I won't be able to keep talking much longer."

"I'm sorry it's hard for you, Skitchy. How long do you think Margaret needs to stay in McAllister?"

"Oh, yes, how long? Sorry, my mind wanders sometimes. Well, I think it'd be best if that could be flexible. Maybe six months. Maybe even a year. You and Belle can talk and work that out between you. When Belle can see how Margaret's doing."

"All right," Pink said, some resignation in his voice.

Skitchy had heard that in Pink's voice so many times and thought less of him because of it. She was glad for it this time. She thought it would be all right to ask for the rest of what she wanted. "Would you keep sending some money for Margaret? Belle and Jackson would never ask but I know it'd help a lot."

"All right," Pink said again.

"Thank you for giving this to our little girl, Pink."

"I'm giving it to you, too, Skitchy. I'm sorry about all that's happening. I hope this'll give you some peace of mind, at least about Margaret. And I want what's best for her, too. I've been praying for you and I'll keep doing that. And for both our daughters. I'm sure they're going to miss their mother terribly."

"Thank you, Pink," she said, glad for the softness in his voice and in his words.

....

The sound of the springs bubbling into the clear pool was soothing to her. Skitchy leaned her head back and closed her eyes, listening. She thought briefly of the cottonwood tree somewhere near which bore initials Pink had carved into its bark. That had been on a day at McMinn Springs much like this one. But a long time gone. She wouldn't have tried to find the tree and look at it, even if she could. But nevertheless she thought warmly for a moment of the man who'd told her, after all that had happened between them, that he was praying for her.

She opened her eyes to Wade's face, bending near her, when she heard his voice. She noticed lines etching into his tanned face and hair graying at the temples. She wondered when that had happened. She smiled at him, loving him and deeply grateful for his presence.

He smiled back at her, thinking she looked wonderful there under the great cottonwoods she loved so much. He didn't see the gaunt body, the drained complexion. "Can I get you anything, sugar? Some ice tea?"

Sally watched them from nearby, and caught John's arm so that he wouldn't intrude on an intimate moment. "They seem to be more in love than ever, John. That's the only thing that seems to really matter to either one of them now."

"Maybe when all is said and done, honey, it is the only thing that matters," and he squeezed her hand tightly.

....

After they finished the lunch of fried chicken, potato salad and watermelon Reba had made for them, Skitchy said to Sally, "I want to be buried in one of the new split skirts like we're sending to the store in Lubbock. And a Sassy Quilters' vest, if you can find one. Is that all right with you?"

A teary Sally replied, "Oh, Skitch, it's so much more than just all right. I'm honored to do that for you. I still have a vest and it just happens to go beautifully with the skirt you like so much from the new designs."

"Thank you, dear dear friend," Skitchy smiled. She was quiet for a moment, then looked around at all of them. "Reba asked me the other day if she could put a copy of *One Eye Blind* in the coffin. Sort of a remembrance and thank you from her and from Hutch. I told her I'd love that. That actually gave me the idea of asking Jackson to put in a little bottle of bourbon. He was the first person to offer me a drink and that felt to me like he was the first one to notice that I'd grown up. If anyone else wants to put anything in, I'd like that."

When John saw she was smiling as she spoke, he said lightly, "Skitchy, you're the first person I've ever known who's planning her own funeral. You almost seem to be enjoying it, from the look of it."

Her voice soft and clear, she said, "The grief I feel when I think about leaving all of you is actually the worst pain I've ever had in my life, John. Yet somehow I feel joy more, too. The joy of loving. Knowing I'm loved. It comforts me to think about having some of the things that connected me with people I love close to me when we say good-bye. And maybe it'll comfort all of you to say good-bye with more than just grieving for me. I'd like to think that anyway."

She looked at Wade, smiling, her eyes with an almost mischievous look. "I have something in mind I'd like very much to have from you. I'll tell you what it is later, when we're alone."

He saw it in a flash as real as if she'd shown it to him: the old blanket he carried in his saddlebag. The old blanket on which they'd lain the first time they made love that day out on the range. That day he'd asked her to ride with him and she'd said yes. That day that had changed their lives forever. He grinned at her and she grinned back.

1943

"I want you to do something for me, Wade."

"Anything, sugar."

"At the funeral, I want you to speak for me. The preacher will talk about me passing into eternal rest in the arms of my loving maker or something like that. That's what they always say at funerals. I don't believe that but I know lots of people do. It's all right for him to say it. Maybe it'll comfort Mama and some of the others. But even if you're all sad, I want everyone who can to be glad for me, too. So I need you to speak of that for me. Even if people can't hear it now, maybe they'll be able to recollect it later. The girls in particular, I hope. One day maybe they'll be glad for me. Maybe it'll even be a comfort for them."

She was very weak and when she closed her eyes he was afraid for a moment she wasn't going to be able to tell him what she wanted him to say. But he waited, holding her hand, stroking it softly.

After a few minutes she opened her eyes. "When I saw the Bighorns that day I saw something else, too. They live in hard places. It's the way they're made. To live the way they do. Where they do." Smiling, she seemed to be looking at something only she could see. Her voice grew stronger. "You told me once, sugar, you thought I was like a Bighorn. You could say, I guess, that I've lived my life in a hard place. But it feels to me like the life I was made for. I'm glad for my life. I want you to hold me in your heart that way." She looked deeply into his eyes. "I'm so sad to be leaving you, Wade. But I wouldn't trade a minute of what we've had for years and years more of living, without what we've had. I'm so grateful for what we've had."

She rested again but only for a moment. "I want you to say I thought once I was nobody. Nobody living in the middle of nowhere. But I learned that I am somebody. I loved and I was loved. And I found somewhere for myself. Right here where I always was. Where I was meant to be." She closed her eyes again but kept a tighter grip on his hand than he thought she could. "Do you understand, sugar?"

"You bet," he said softly, his throat too choked to say more even though he wanted to. This woman, he thought, has always had more grit than I could ever imagine having.

"Skitchy," he said, his voice filled with tears now. He wanted to tell her how much he loved her and to promise to remember all she'd said, but he couldn't make the words. He lifted her hand and kissed it gently, leaving his lips there for a long time. He put her hand down when he could see that she wanted to speak again.

"I'm almost finished," she said, her voice weak but clear. "Say for me, the last thing. What I want everyone to recollect about me who can: I am glad for my life. Grateful."

....

As the days passed into months and the months into years, Wade would go to Skitchy's grave often. He would tell her when old Rita Colquitt passed. He would tell her when Sally sold Sassy Skirts to a clothing company in Fort Worth for more money than the two women had ever dreamed of. He would tell her when Jackson did not wake up one morning. He would tell her that Belle kept the hotel and ran it with Connie's help. He would tell her when Hutchens Borden won a big prize he couldn't remember the name of, for one of his books. He would tell her when her mama and then Sally were laid in their graves. He would stay the whole morning the day he told her the grave being dug a few feet away was for Belle. He would tell her when his arthritis got too bad and he sold the ranch and came to live all the time in their house in McAllister. He would tell her he had coffee with John MacLeod at Connie's hotel most afternoons, and sometimes with Reba who still lived in the little room off the kitchen. He would tell her how Margaret was in California when there was a letter from her in her Christmas card. He would tell her that he lived knowing he was someone and had lived somewhere with another someone he loved beyond measure, and he would tell her that he was glad and grateful, too, for his life.

ACKNOWLEDGMENTS

I've done my best to present an accurate picture of a region and of the time during which *The Middle of Nowhere* takes place, but this is a novel, a work of fiction. I've told of events to make them seem as real as possible, but some events are imaginary in whole or in part and I've taken liberties with some dates and places. Except for the historical figures of President Franklin Roosevelt and Amelia Earhart, the characters are entirely imaginary. There are many imaginary places, most notably the town of McAllister.

Two museums and a number of publications were particularly helpful in developing cultural and historical background. The West of the Pecos Museum in Pecos, TX and the Annie Riggs Museum in Fort Stockton, TX are both housed in buildings which were once hotels and both still bear witness to what hotels in small West Texas towns looked like and felt like as they were in the past. In addition, both offer publications (some no longer in print) which were sources of information about the region and the historical period that I've come across nowhere else. For example, Alton Hughes' *Pecos: A History of the Pioneer West* was an invaluable resource for everything from plant life to high school football. Without Olan M. George's *Roundup of Memories* there would have been no split skirts in my novel and the characters wouldn't have eaten nearly as much bologna and scrambled eggs during the Great Depression.

What it was like to live through severe drought in West Texas came alive for me in Hallie Stillwell's *My Goose Is Cooked,* and this rancher's firsthand account of a flash flood in a dry creek bed made it possible for me to write about an event not unlike one that occurred in my own family years before I was born.

Many thanks also to the Visitors Center in Georgetown, TX and to the excellent Museum in that town. I originally went to Georgetown to learn more about my family genealogy but I found much more than the family connections I was looking for and some of what I found made it's way into *The Middle of Nowhere.* Of special note was *Georgetown's Yesteryears: The People Remember.* This vibrant collection of oral history contained many stories from the era of my novel, including accounts of such diverse activities as those of the Ku Klux Klan in the area and the Georgetown polo team (yes, really). I drew from many of the personal accounts for insight and background about what it was like to live through the Great Depression.

The Worst Hard Time, Timothy Egan's gripping account of the terrible decade during which the Dust Bowl took its toll on land and people, also deserves special mention. Reeves County, TX was not strictly speaking within the Dust Bowl but a vast phenomenon like that does not stop precisely at a boundary drawn on a map and West Texas did suffer on the dust laden fringe of things in the 1930's. Egan's work served as an extraordinary resource as I sought to imagine what that might have been like.

I suppose any novel is partly autobiographical whether the novelist intends it to be so or not. I was born in Wink, Texas, a few miles from Reeves County where my grandparents actually had a ranch from the late 1800's until the 1930's. Their ranch was the starting point that became this story. I

was steeped in the land during the early years of my life but most of all steeped in its lore as it was embodied in my family. I didn't make up dishes poker, for example, or "you bet" as a phrase always to be understood in context.

West Texans are nothing if not individualistic. Yet there are times the individual could not survive without the support of community. I intended to explore the relationship between individual and community in the interactions of the characters in the novel. I had not expected to experience a deepened sense of that relationship in my own life. That's what happened, however, as people gave graciously of their time to read drafts, ask questions, challenge, protest, suggest, identify something missing. The novel would not be what it is without their candid, patient, valuable input and encouragement. What will go out as "mine" is, in that sense, not entirely mine. "Thank you" feels inadequate to its task of acknowledging the contributions of Mary Alice Ambrose, Constance Welch, Jennifer Duke, and Steve Romey. Milania Austin Henley and Jim McDonald belong in a category all their own: How do you thank someone for giving so generously of their very competent and loving attention, over and over and over again?

Then there is the young hay farmer whose name I wish I knew who saw my husband and me walking along a remote road in Reeves County and stopped to make sure we were all right because as he said, "You sure don't want to get stuck out here in the middle of nowhere." His comment stayed with me and inspired the title of my novel.

Comments about **The Middle of Nowhere** *are welcome at*
www. PaulaDuncanMcDonald.com

CPSIA information can be obtained at www.ICGtesting.com
Printed in the USA
LVOW132353100912

298263LV00001B/101/P